JOHN KENEALY

TAOS

A Ben Adams Western Novel

Contents

1

Chapter 1

Maddie Ferguson pulled her long, honey blonde hair back in a ponytail, and gathered it up with a strip of rawhide as she stepped through the front door and out onto the porch of her cabin. She stood on the porch for a moment, and adjusted the belt on her oversized, canvas work pants. The baggy pants, and flannel blouse barely concealed her curves. She loved the ranch house that she, her husband Cam, and their young son, Tad shared until that fateful day last summer. The memory brought tears to her green eyes. She wiped them away before they reached her freckled cheeks. No time for self pity.

It was late April on the San Miguel, and the spring run off had not yet begun. Cam and Maddie had picked this spot ten years ago, right after the wedding and the trek west from Virginia. They fled the crowds, Cam's low-life family, and Maddie's overbearing parents. Cam, though not at all like the rest of his family, was looked down upon by Doctor and Misses Gallagher, Maddie's parents, and it was obvious that life in Virginia would mean a constant push-pull between the two sets of in-laws.

So, they sold their belongings, cashed in their wedding gifts, and bought a wagon, a team, and supplies, and headed for Colorado. They knew little about the brand new state, other than it had mountains, rivers, and space. Magical space. Even the name - Colorado, sounded magical. And Colorado, at least this part of it, surpassed their wildest dreams for beauty and bounty.

The San Miguel begins its course high up in the San Juan Mountains of Southwestern Colorado. It starts out as a cascading freshet, but levels as it bangs against the Uncompahgre Plateau, a Ute term for "rocks that make water red," before flowing into the high desert, and joining the Dolores River about fifteen miles east of the Utah Border.

Thunder Valley Ranch, they called it, because of the wild thunderstorm that blew through the San Miguel Valley, when Cam and Maddie first found the place in early summer ten years ago. It was perfect, still is, Maddie thought, as she reminisced about that first year. High peaks of the San Juans provided a spectacular view, and the Uncompahgre Plateau would provide plenty of grazing land for the cattle they planned to raise. They had a ready market for beef in the mining towns of Placerville, Telluride, Nucla, and others. Just upriver was a beautiful alpine environment, ideal for elk and deer hunting, while pronghorn inhabited the plateau. The San Miguel was full of fat, fast growing cutthroat trout, which pleased both Cam and Maddie to no end, for they had grown up in the shadows of the Blue Ridge, and loved fishing for speckled trout in the mountain streams of their youth.

As Maddie tended to the chickens, she thought about that first lean winter. She and Cam had built a strong, if small cabin, and had dried meat from the elk, and deer that Cam had shot. They also dried beans and corn, to supplement their diet. Maddie had managed to keep a small flock of chickens through the winter, which offered them a few eggs for variety. They made it though, and Cam added to their small cattle herd the next spring, by selling fresh fish and eggs in the nearby mining towns. Cam expanded the cabin that spring, which doubled it in size. He even built a beautiful front porch, and designed a shower!

Their family grew too. Tad was born in late October, though not without complications. Cam rode straight down to Durango to fetch Doc Gilbert, and though Tad was fine, Doc Gilbert informed Maddie that she would not likely bear any more children.

Tad was the apple of her eye. She saw Cam in him, more each year he grew. He would have been a tall, strapping man, just like his father, with the same steel-gray eyes, and sandy hair, if he had survived. The tears flowed freely at the memory of the loss of her husband and son.

"You gotta shake it Maddie, darlin'," she said to the breeze. "Nothin's gonna bring 'em back, least of all cryin' about it."

Maddie wiped her face with her apron.

She had survived, though, and this fine spring day was one of promise. She made it through a winter on her own, and the ranch had held up. Success. She felt the warmth of the sun on her face, as she planted seeds in the garden, which she had finished turning over yesterday. She would plant enough to feed herself, and some to sell. Beans, corn, squash; all would grow well in the ample sun of Southwest Colorado.

Although the warm spring day was a promise of things to come, this was the first year that Maddie would start all on her own, and the chores seemed overwhelming. The rancher down river, Doniphan McCarty, however, promised to have his cowboys round up, and brand her calves with her double lightning brand, at a cost of one for every ten calves they brand. Maddie didn't have much choice. He could have branded all the calves he found with his Circle M, and no one would be the wiser. Unfortunately, Maddie suspected Doniphan was interested in marrying off his ne'er-do-well son, Rance, to her, to consolidate ranches.

Maddie knew that the key to her land was the High Meadow. Cam, though not a rancher, had instincts. When they surveyed the land, he had noticed the path to the caldera. The High Meadow, Cam had explained, was the key to surviving in dry years. When the plateau got hot and dry, and hard on the cattle, they could be summered in the large caldera, which stayed cool and damp. The last few summers had been dry, and Doniphan McCarty had mentioned more than once that if he had settled in the San Miguel Valley before Cam and Maddie, he would have grabbed that land for himself.

"No way, he's gettin' this ranch!" Maddie shouted to the wind.

It was midday, and the sun overhead was getting hot.

"Time for a break," Maddie said, as she wiped her brow. She stood up from her planting, left the garden, and carefully closed the gate behind her. She surveyed her surroundings as she walked to the cabin. Maddie's chest swelled with pride at what she and Cam had built. The homestead was well planned out and tidy. A small feeder stream powered a sawmill that cut boards for the cabin, wood for the fire, and planks for other projects around the ranch. The hen house, and pig barn were close to the cabin with roofed paths to fend off winter snows. If nothing else, Cam was practical, and it had probably saved her life this past winter. Again, she felt a deep pride in her lost husband, and fought off tears.

Maddie stepped up onto the porch, grasped the ladle tethered to the rain barrel, dipped, and took a long drink. Her thirst satiated, Maddie grabbed a bamboo fly rod that they had taken out west from Virginia, off pegs on the cabin wall. Then, she tied a soft-hackled wet fly onto the catgut leader, and walked to the river bank.

From experience, Maddie knew that the river's cutthroat trout would put on the feed bag, as it were, with the first warm days of spring. She walked to the river with a lively spring in her step, the prospect of a large cutthroat overshadowing her loss, for the moment. A few minutes later, she was standing on her favorite rock, which allowed her to cast out, and drift her fly into a run that always seemed to hold sizable trout.

Maddie carefully checked her knots, then dipped her fly into the cold water to wet it thoroughly before casting. Careful not to tangle, she flipped her fly into the current, then, when the horse hair line was taught, she picked it off the water, back cast, and flicked the rod forward, which landed the fly out in the current, and slightly upstream. Maddie let the fly drift, and sink down in the flowing waters. She let the fly swing in the current, imitating an emerging insect.

Bam! She felt a hard tug on the fly, but, after a long Rocky Mountain winter, her reaction was slow, and she missed the strike.

"Darn!" Maddie exclaimed.

Excited, Maddie repeated the cast, this time letting out a few more feet. The fly hit the water and submerged. Maddie deftly handled the line, just how her father had taught her on the Rapidan River in Virginia. Again, the fly swung in the current, and she lifted the rod tip a bit.

Nothing.

Repeat. A Few more feet out, drift, raise the rod tip.

Bam! This hit was harder than the first, and nearly pulled the rod out of her grasp, but Maddie was ready this time. She reared back, nearly doubling the rod over, as she drove the hook deep into the fish's jaw.

Feeling the sting of the steel, the cutthroat trout leaped a full two feet above the water, and flashed pink, yellow, and crimson before it hit the surface, and charged upstream. Maddie let the fish run, knowing full well that swimming upriver would tire the trout out more quickly than a downstream run. After swimming upstream about forty feet, the trout turned, But Maddie was ready. She had leapt off the rock to shore, and was prepared for the trout to streak down the river. She sprinted downstream ahead of the large trout, which took the upstream pressure off of it, and caused the cutthroat to turn back upstream, and fight the heavy current. Maddie knew she had won the battle at this point, and after a few more minutes, she landed the foot and a half long cutthroat. After taking a moment to admire the beautiful fish, she dispatched it, with the butt of her knife, and cleaned the trout.

Preoccupied with cleaning the large trout, Maddie never heard the horse step up.

"Nice fish."

Maddie spun around and looked up into the bluest blue eyes she had ever seen in her life.

2

Chapter 2

The previous summer. . .

    There was a faint orange glow in the eastern sky, as Cam cinched down the saddle of his horse.

"Are you sure he'll be alright? Tad isn't even seven yet," Maddie said, wringing her hands in her apron.

"Oh, Mad, Tad rides with me every day, he'll be fine on his pony. He's as good on his pony, as many are on their horses. He was born to drive cattle," Cam replied.

"He's my baby, Cam. You and Tad are all I have out here," Maddie wimpered.

"It'll be easy, Mad," Cam said as he embraced her. "Just a short trip to Telluride with a small herd of cattle. We'll be three days getting there, and two back."

"I just wish that you had someone else going along," Maddie implored.

"Oh, not McCarty's offer, again," Cam complained. "He'd charge me an arm and a leg, and his cowboys are mostly drunks and ruffians."

Tad, who had been tending to his pony, joined his parents.

"It's okay, Mom. I'll stay close to Dad. I promise!"

Maddie took her son into her arms. Tears streamed from her eyes.

"I know you will, Tad," Maddie said through the tears. She held his face in her hands, and kissed his forehead. "I love you, my son."

The three shared a hug, before Cam and Tad mounted their beasts, and rode off.

Maddie watched them ride out to the small herd. Tears streamed down her cheeks.

* * *

After her husband and son left, Maddie tried to keep herself busy. Not difficult on a ranch, even a small one like the Ferguson's. She started by opening the door to the chicken coop, and collecting eggs. Next, the chickens got watered, and the pigs were fed the table scraps.

By this time, the sun was over the horizon, and the dew sparkled in the morning light. Maddie hugged herself as she felt the warmth of the sun rejuvenating her body.

Her blood ran cold, though, at the sight of a lone rider on the horizon. Maddie ran to the cabin, and entered. She grabbed her scattergun off its rack, and took a handful of shells from the space Cam had built into the wall next to the gun rack.

Cam had prepared her for this very moment. He had explained that a shotgun would be much more effective in these situations. Her aim didn't have to be exact, and at close range, a full-on hit from the twelve gauge would blow a man clear out of his saddle. Maddie loaded both barrels of the side by side, and headed for the door.

When Maddie stepped out on the porch, she recognized the rider, and a shiver ran down her spine. Riding a large bay mare was Doniphan McCarty.

Doniphan looked to be about sixty, though his weatherbeaten face could easily belie his age. He sat tall in the saddle, and his gray mustache framed his thin lips, and flowed down either side of his chin. Doniphan had beady black eyes that Maddie felt were undressing her whenever he gazed upon her.

Having noticed that McCarty did not dismount when he rode into the dooryard, Maddie stayed on the porch, so as not to be stuck looking up at him. This man was all about power, and she wasn't about to give him any advantage.

"What brings you out here on this fine, fresh morning, Mister McCarty?" Maddie asked, trying to cover her disdain.

"I was hoping to have a chat with Cam, if he's around."

"Well, you missed him," Maddie replied. "But, I'll be happy to let him know you stopped by."

"Any idea when he will be ridin' in?" McCarty asked, as he shifted in his saddle to make himself seem taller, and more imposing, which was not lost on Maddie.

"I can't rightly say, Mr. McCarty. Could be anytime, could be a while," Maddie replied.

"Like I said, I'll be happy to relay a message."

McCarty kicked his horse forward so that he was eye to eye with Maddie. She involuntarily stepped back in disgust of this man, and he smiled in response, with the knowledge that he had penetrated her shield.

"I'll be back another time," McCarty said before he rode off.

* * *

Cam and Tad had an uneventful cattle drive to Telluride. Cam enjoyed watching the pride on Tad's face as he rode down the main street of the silver mining town on his strawberry roan pony ahead of the small herd of cattle, to the cheers of the townsfolk.

"Now, there's a real cowboy!" one shouted.

"Yippee Ki Ae!" cried another. And so it went down the street until they reached the stock pen.

A teen-aged boy opened the pen gate as they rode up, and the small herd of some forty steers filed in. After the last steer ambled through the gate, the boy closed and locked it.

Bill Haney, the local stock buyer, stepped out of his office, and met Cam and Tad as they dismounted.

"Hey Cam, good to see you," Bill said, as he stuck out his hand to shake.

"Hello Bill," Cam replied, as he took Bill's hand. "This is my son, Tad."

"Put 'er there, Pardner," Bill said to Tad as he reached down with his open hand for Tad to grab.

"Hello, Sir," Tad said with a proud grin as he took the man's hand.

Bill stood up straight, and turned to Cam.

"What do we have?"

"I've got forty head of prime beeves, and I'm looking for twenty-five dollars a head."

Bill whistled.

"Pretty steep, Cam."

"Man's gotta make a livin', Bill."

"I understand, but I gotta get my share, too. I'll give you twenty."

"I take all the risk," Cam answered. "Breed 'em, birth 'em, brand 'em, grow 'em, drive 'em. You buy 'em, butcher 'em, and sell 'em."

"I can only sell 'em for what folks'll pay for 'em. You knowed that, Cam."

"Can you do any better than twenty?"

"Twenty-two is the best I can do."

Cam looked at Tad, who shrugged his shoulders.

"I guess it'll have ta do. I don't much feel like drivin' them steers back home," Cam said.

"Then it's a deal," Bill said, and the two men shook hands. "Let's go inta the office and settle up.

* * *

"I'm sorry we got took, Pa," Tad said as they rode back down the main street of Telluride.

Cam took a moment to gaze at the San Juan Mountains, which surrounded the town.

"Took? We didn't get took, Son. I wasn't expectin' any more than twenty dollars a head for them critters, and we got paid twenty-two! No, we didn't get took!"

"But I thought you said you wanted to get twenty five dollars a head," Tad said.

"That's called dickerin', Tad, my boy."

"Dickerin'?" Tad asked.

"Yup. You never tell a man what you really need to get, or you'll end up gettin' took. Always ask for more, within reason, and he'll pay you somewhere's in the middle. Then, you treat him like you're doin' him a favor. That's dickerin."

"You sure are smart, Pa."

Cam laughed, and reached over and patted Tad on the back.

"You hungry, Son?" Cam asked.

"You bet!" Tad exclaimed.

The two rode to Marissa's Cantina, dismounted, and tied up their mounts. Cam always picked Marissa's when he was in Telluride because it wasn't frequented by the local miners, a bunch that tended to be hard drinking, hard cursing, hard fighting, and all around ill-tempered.

Cam led Tad through the door, and they sat down at a table near a window in the brightly decorated cantina.

Presently, a petite woman with raven hair and eyes that danced, walked over to them with a pitcher of water and two glasses.

"Welcome señors," Marissa said as she placed the glasses on the table, and filled them from the pitcher. "You hungry, el niño?" she asked Tad.

"You bet, Ma'am!" he exclaimed. "My Pa and I been drivin' cattle for three days, and have been dickerin' on the price. I got a big appetite!"

Cam laughed heartily, and both Marissa and Tad laughed along with him.

"We'll have steak and eggs, fried taters, a big glass of milk for my boy, and I'll have a beer. Thanks, Marissa," Cam said.

"Coming right up, Señor Cam," she replied.

Cam noticed a group of three cowboys drinking and talking quietly at the bar. One of them looked vaguely familiar, so, when Marissa returned with the drinks, he asked her if she knew them.

"Oh, Señor Cam, they work for Señor McCarty, " she replied, disdain in her voice.

"Hmm, thank you, Marissa," Cam replied.

"De nada," Señor Cam.

Cam wondered why McCarty would have sent three of his men to Telluride this time of the year. Bill hadn't said a word about them bringing cattle into town. He wouldn't pass up a chance to share that news.

"Who are those guys, Pa?"

"Just some fellers who work for Mr. McCarty, Son."

"Oh, I don't like him, Pa," Tad replied.

"We don't have to like everybody, but we have to be. . ."

"Neighborly! I got it, Pa!"

"Good job, Tad."

Marissa returned with their meals.

"Here you go, Señor Cam, and my little vaquero," she said as she placed their plates on the table.

"Thank you, Marissa," Cam replied, and Tad beamed.

Cam noticed McCarty's men walk out, then ride off.

* * *

After their meal, Cam and Tad rode to the stables.

Jesse Anderson, who owned the stables greeted them. Jesse was an older man, in his sixties, Cam guessed. He had a short, grizzled beard, and his once black hair had turned white. Jesse walked with a limp, which Cam had heard he got from a wound suffered as a cavalryman at First Manassas.

After the war, so the story went, Jesse had bummed around for a few years before moving west. He had worked as a camp cook at some of the mines, before saving up enough money to open the stables. Jesse loved horses, and it showed in the way he cared for them.

"Hey, Cam, Tad."

"Hello, Jesse. Can we get some food and water for our rides?"

"Sure thing. That'll be four bits."

Cam pulled the money out of his bag, and handed the payment to Jesse, who nodded his thanks.

"Say, Jesse, did three of McCarty's men stop by?" Jim asked.

"They just rode out about half an hour ago."

"Did they say anything?"

"I didn't hear nothin', but I mind my business anyway. Much safer like that."

"Yup. Okay, thanks."

Jesse got two buckets of feed and handed one each to Cam and Tad, then fetched two pails of water for the horse and pony.

"Let's take a walk while the critters eat," Cam said to Tad.

"Yay!"

Cam led Tad out of the stables, and they walked down the boardwalk. They passed a noisy saloon, a gambling hall, and a bank before entering Eliza Small's General Store.

The proprietor, a fifty-something spinster, who had her hair pulled back in a tight bun, was sweeping up when Cam and Tad entered. She looked up, and smiled with recognition.

"Well hello, Cam, and look at you, Tad! My have you grown!" she exclaimed.

"Hello, Eliza, how are you?" Cam asked.

"I'm good, Cam. What brings you to town?"

"Tad and I drove a small herd of cattle in. Gotta keep those miners fed, I guess," Cam replied.

"Those damn miners, oh, I'm sorry, I shouldn't use that language in front of Tad."

Cam looked at Tad, who was preoccupied with exploring all the wonders of the shop.

"I don't think he heard a thing, Eliza," Cam laughed, as he nodded toward the boy.

"Anyway, those miners, sure, they bring in business, but they are such a hard lot, drinkin', gamblin', and the harlots they attract! It's shameless!"

"I understand, but without the silver mines, you and I wouldn't be standin' here talkin' to each other," Cam replied.

"I guess you're right, Cam. I just get frustrated with what they're doing to our town."

"I only come in once in a while to sell some cattle, and buy supplies. I don't see it every day," Cam replied. "I don't have much to complain about like you do."

"Well, I'm sorry for complainin'. What can I do for you?"

"I think my pardner there would like a bag of candy as payment for his hard work. Let him pick out a pound of whatever he wants."

Tad's ears had perked up. "A whole pound? Wow, thanks, Pa!" Tad exclaimed.

"You earned it, Tad."

Eliza grabbed a paper bag and drew a line on it about three quarters of the way up, and handed it to Tad.

"Here you go, young man. You fill it up to that line with whatever you want. That'll make a pound."

"Gee, thanks, Miss Eliza!" Tad beamed, and headed to the candy bins.

"He's a good boy, Cam," Eliza said.

"Thanks, we are proud of him. He's had to grow up quick out on the ranch."

"They all do out here," Eliza replied. "Things goin' good for you and Maddie at the ranch?"

"Yeah, growin' every year. Why you ask?"

"That damn McCarty was in last week talkin' about how afore long, he was gonna own the whole San Miguel Valley."

"Interesting. I saw three of his men today, but they hadn't brought any cattle inta' town," Cam said.

"That's strange. Be careful, Cam."

"Thanks, Eliza."

"My bag's full, Miss Eliza!" Tad yelled.

"Good for you, Tad. Let me package it up."

"Thanks, Eliza," Cam said, and put cash on the counter.

Eliza began to make change, but Cam stopped her.

"Keep the change, Eliza. I appreciate your kindness."

"Well, thanks, Cam. You be safe, and give my regards to Maddie."

"Will do. See you next time we're in town," he replied. To Tad he said, "C'mon pardner, let's get our critters."

"OK, and thanks for the candy, Pa."

"Thank you for all the hard work, son!"

* * *

Cam and Tad had ridden until early evening before they stopped to make camp for the night. Cam chose a spot next to the San Miguel, and while Tad collected wood for a fire, Cam assembled a fly rod in hopes of catching a few trout.

After the rod was assembled, Cam got the fire going. When there was a good flame, he said to Tad, "C'mon boy, let's go catch some dinner."

"You bet!"

The pair walked down to the San Miguel, and Cam set his son up with the fly rod on a gravel bar that pointed downstream at a forty-five degree angle.

"You remember how to cast?" Cam asked.

"I sure do, Pa!" Tad replied.

"Alright, take the rod, and cast your fly straight out into that current, there," Cam instructed.

Tad cast as told, and let the fly swing down through the glide.

The crack of two shots rang out, and echoed from mountain to mountain. Tad and Cam dropped, dead.

Three men mounted their horses, and rode off.

3

Chapter 3

Maddie wished she had packed the six shooter that Cam had implored her to carry with her at all times. For, though handsome, this man was a stranger to her. She stood up with the cutthroat trout still in her hand.

"Well, thank you, mister," she replied to his comment on her fish, as she eyed the cold steel Colts slung low on his hips.

"I've been riding all morning, and I'm sure hungry, if you're willing to share," the man's eyes flashed blue lightning, as he spoke.

"This fish is more than I can eat. Sure, you can join me," Maddie replied.

"Thank you, Misses Ferguson," the man replied.

"How did you know my name?" Maddie snapped.

"Bill Haney, in Telluride, said thet you may be lookin' for a hand or two," he replied.

"Gun hand, or cowhand?" Maddie snapped back, as she gazed at his twin revolvers.

The man climbed off his large bay stallion, and led it to the San Miguel to drink.

"I'm always one, sometimes, I'm t'other," he replied in a slow, western drawl.

"You have a name? Since you already know mine?"

Folks call me Taos," the man replied, as he took off his black, broad-brimmed sombrero and brought it across his body in a wide sweep, as he bowed simultaneously.

Maddie let a smile slip.

"You have a real name?"

"In another lifetime," the handsome young cowboy said as he pushed back his sandy hair, and replaced his sombrero.

"So, you've been searchin' for the elephant?

"You might say thet," Taos replied.

"Well, let's go get some lunch, Mister Taos."

* * *

Doniphan McCarty rode up to the crowd of cowboys who were branding calves.

His son, Rance, a smallish man in his mid-thirties, with brown hair, and watery gray eyes, walked over to greet him.

"Hey, Pa," he said.

"Rance," his father nodded as he spied his disappointment of a son, over his hawkish nose.

"We got the Double Thunderbolt calves corralled off from the rest, over yonder," he said as he pointed to a makeshift corral a hundred yards away.

"Good. Brand half of them with hers, and half with ours," McCarty replied.

"Half? I thought we were takin' one out of ten," Rance replied.

"Are you thet stupid?" McCarty snapped. "You understand we need thet ranch?"

"Sure, Pa, but. . ."

"But, nothin! We've gotta bleed that bitch dry! I made her a fair offer for that ranch last fall, and she told me to go stuff it. She's gonna pay for that."

* * *

Maddie wasn't sure what it was about this tall, handsome, stranger, Taos. So many people out here had tried to take advantage of her after Cam's death. The ranch turned out to be more valuable than she had imagined, and people wanted to get it by hook or crook, especially Doniphan McCarty. But there was something in his eyes. She was sure that he had done wrong, probably the worst kind of wrong, or he wouldn't be using a pseudonym. Somehow she knew, deep in her bones, that this man Taos was, in his heart, a good man from a good family. She decided she would trust him. She needed somebody to trust. She knew she couldn't survive much longer without someone to help her keep the ranch going.

She stoked the fire in the kitchen stove.

"Got any cornmeal? I'll get the fish ready for fryin'," Taos said.

"Yes, I do. It's in the cupboard right in front of you."

"Thanks," Taos said, and opened the cupboard. He grabbed the sack of cornmeal, and prepared the fish for frying.

Maddie put her big, black, cast iron pan on the hot stove, and added bacon drippings. While the pan heated, she took out two plates, and two forks, and placed them on the kitchen table. She also took some biscuits out of her bread box, and put them in a small dish.

When the grease began to sizzle, Taos put the trout in the pan.

"That's gonna be darn good. Thanks fer sharing," he said.

Maddie poured two glasses of water, and replied, "Like I said, it was more than I could eat on my own."

Taos shrugged his broad shoulders, and, after a few long moments, flipped the fish.

"So, I take it that you're lookin' for a job," Maddie said.

"Yes, I am, Misses Ferguson," Taos replied.

"I don't have money to pay you," Maddie said, as Taos took the trout off the pan, and placed it on the platter.

He deftly removed the bones from the fish, placed the platter on the kitchen table, then sat down..

"I'll work for my keep, an' a percentage of the profits, when we drive the cattle to market," if that's fair," he replied.

"I guess it depends on what kind of percentage you are thinkin' of," Maddie said, as she sat down.

Taos passed the platter to Maddie. She served herself then passed the platter back to Taos, who slid the rest of the trout onto his plate.

"How does twenty percent sound?" Taos asked, as he grabbed a biscuit.

"I have to ask you something before I make a decision," Maddie said.

"Okay."

"My guess is that you've done something pretty bad if you ain't using your real name. What I want to know, Mister Taos, is if you are an honest man," Maddie said.

"Misses Ferguson, I believe that I am a good man, that was put in a position in which I had to do bad things. Yes, I have killed men. Not as many as some have, but more than I am proud to say. I never killed anyone who didn't need killin', and I only killed for my family, and in self defense. I don't want to say more'n thet. If thet ain't enough, I understand, and I'll ride off as soon as I finish washin' the dishes," Taos replied.

4

Chapter 4

T he Red River has its birth high up on the north face of Wheeler Peak, New Mexico's highest mountain, and winds its way through the steep pine studded valleys of the Sangre de Cristo Mountains of Northern New Mexico, until it meets the Rio Grande near Questa. Colonel and Mrs. Adams settled on the Red River shortly after the Civil War ended.

Colonel Adams, who hailed from Wisconsin, had served with the famous Iron Brigade in some of the bloodiest battles of the Civil War. Adams had been on Brigadier General John Gibbon's staff, and had shown remarkable bravery on August 28, 1862, at Second Manassas. The Brigade stood fast through attack after attack under a superior force, under the command of Major General Thomas J. "Stonewall" Jackson on the Brawner Farm.

Adams also performed valiantly at Turner's Gap, where the Iron Brigade received its nickname, during the Battle of South Mountain, a lead up to the bloody Battle of Antietam. The Wisconsoners had advanced up the National

Road, forcing the Confederates all the way back to the Gap.

General McClellan asked General Hooker, "What troops are those fighting on the Pike?"

Hooker replied, "General Gibbon's Brigade of Wisconsin men."

McClellan replied, "They must be made of iron."

The name stuck.

Adams continued to fight bravely, and had risen to the rank of Colonel by the Battle of Gettysburg. Adams was a dervish on his steed, which had been shot out from under him on the first day of the battle. Early on the second day, an artillery shell removed his left leg below the knee, and he was left to watch his Brigade get destroyed as he sat in a hospital tent. The Iron Brigade lost 1,153 out of 1,885 men during the three day battle.

Adams was never the same after Gettysburg. He continued to serve, but his wound kept him off the battlefield. After the war, he returned to Wisconsin, but couldn't bear to face the families of the lost men of the Iron Brigade. Colonel Adams sold his home. He and his young wife, Lorena, and their young son, Ben, moved west.

They eventually settled on a beautiful spot not that far from Taos, New Mexico, on the lower Red River, less than one hundred miles from Santa Fe, which would prove to be a great market for their cattle. The property had quality water, and had ample sage lands for grazing. The plethora of piñon pine gave them the name of their ranch: Los Piñons.

After a year at the ranch, Lenora gave birth to a daughter, Sage.

The first twenty years at Los Piñons had been wonderful. The Colonel had built a profitable ranching business, became a respected citizen in the area, and slowly put the War behind him. Ben had grown up tall, handsome, and strong. He grew up a little wilder than the Colonel would have liked, but he was as good, or better a cow hand than any of the men they had hired. He was also good with a gun. Too damn good.

Sage's beauty was matched only by that of the valley that they had settled in. Her hair was the color of autumn aspens, and, like her brother, her eyes flashed like blue lightning. Sage was tall, and strong, but she had a feminine side too, and she was also nobody's fool. Ben managed the cowboys, and

Sage managed the books, as the Colonel, and Lenore stepped back into semi retirement.

Times were changing, though. The discovery of gold, silver, and copper in the Sangre de Cristos brought a different class of people to the valley. It wasn't just that, though. The Red River was changing, and deformities were showing up in the cattle raised in the Red River Valley.

* * *

Colonel Adams sat outside on the front porch of his adobe ranch house. The setting sun glowed orange in the western sky. The Colonel laconically tamped the ashes out of, then filled his ever present corn-cob pipe, struck a match, and touched it to the tobacco.

As he watched the tobacco spark, light, and send orange embers into the air in front of his face, the Colonel was reminded of the constantly burning copper smelter that had been built high in the mountains to the east.

While the Colonel puffed on his pipe, Ben stepped out through the front door and onto the porch with two glasses of whiskey. He handed one to the Colonel, and sat down next to his father.

"Beautiful evening," the Colonel said.

"Sure is, Colonel," Ben replied before taking a sip.

"I've been thinkin' about that smelter."

"What about it?" Ben asked.

"They are stripping all the ponderosas, boilin' that ore down, leaving slag everywhere. I bet it has somethin' to do with the defects in our cattle."

Ben took another sip from his glass, "And the trout have suffered. They are disappearing from the river above our springs. Something is definitely wrong."

As the sky darkened, a new orange glow appeared to the east.

"See, there it is," the Colonel said.

Ben nodded.

Sage and her mother stepped out onto the porch.

Lenore, who was an older version of her daughter, took a deep breath of the piñon and sage infused evening air.

"I so love it here," she whispered.

"What's that glow, Daddy," Sage, the only one who did not call the Colonel by his rank, asked.

"It's a copper smelter, my dear," he replied, as she sat in his lap, like she had done since she was a child.

"How come I haven't seen it before?" she asked.

"Because there were tall ponderosas in the way before, but they've cut 'em all down," Ben answered.

"Ben, maybe we should take a ride up there tomorrow. I'll pack a lunch, and we can make a day of it," Sage offered.

"Good idee," he replied.

* * *

Sage and Ben got an early start in the morning. Ben cooked a breakfast of steak and eggs, while Sage made lunch. They worked quietly, so as not to wake their parents.

After breakfast, Ben went to the barn to saddle the horses, while Sage cleaned up. They met out in front of the porch.

The first glow of a crisp, clear morning was showing as they rode off.

"I just love the smell of the mountain air," Sage said, when they were out of earshot of the ranch house.

"It sure is nice, makes a body feel alive," Ben replied, as they rode the trail upriver.

"I'm glad we have some alone time. I don't feel comfortable talking business with Mom and Dad around," Sage said.

"What's the matter, Sage? This sounds serious," Ben replied.

"Just trends, but it bears looking into."

"Alright, what are you seein'?"

"Well, first of all, Dad's spendin' is going through the roof."

"Really? What's he spendin' money on?" Ben asked.

"You know how he likes to ride into Questa every day? Well, he's buying lunch, and having drinks while he's in town."

"Are you sure?"

"Yup, I rode into town yesterday, and asked around. He isn't just buying for himself, he's buying for others, too," Sage answered.

"He isn't meetin' a woman, is he?" Ben asked.

"That's what I was wondering at first, but it seems he's reliving his wartime exploits."

"Odd, he hasn't talked aboot the war for yeahs. Somethinn' must be up."

"It wouldn't be such a big deal, financially, if it weren't for the deformed calves. They are putting a hurting on this operation. We will need to nearly double the number of cows we raise to account for the loss."

"I knew it was bad, and we are recoverin' some with the veal operation, but I didn't realize just how bad it is," Ben said.

"Do you think it has to do with the mining operation up river?" Sage asked.

"Makes sense. Thet is the only thing that has changed. Hold up a minute." Ben said.

Sage and Ben stopped their horses, dismounted, tied them to a piñon tree, and walked to the river bank.

Once at the water's edge, Ben squatted down, reached into the water, grasped a large stone, pulled it out, and turned it over.

"Look, see? Remember when we was kids, we used to turn over the rocks to see all the crawly bugs on the bottom. Now, nothin'."

Ben threw the rock back in the river, and grabbed another one. He turned it over. Nothing.

"There is something wrong!" Sage exclaimed.

"They's more. Look into the river. What do yu see?"

"The water is crystal clear," Sage answered.

"Right. No weeds, no fish, no insects. This river is dead" Ben growled.

They walked back to their horses, untied them, and re-mounted. They continued up the trail in silence for some time. Each was lost in their own thoughts and concerns about their father, the river, and the mine.

"Ugh! What's that smell?" Sage gasped.

"I think it's the smeltinn' operation," Ben replied.

"It stinks! If whatever is making that smell is getting into the river, that's probably what is killing it, and causing deformities in our cattle," Sage said.

"Thet's my guess, but we'll have ta find out fer sure," Ben answered.

5

Chapter 5

Having agreed to take Taos on as a ranch hand, Maddie offered him a tour of the grounds.

"You and Mister Ferguson, sure built a nice place here, Misses Ferguson," Taos said after the tour of the house and surrounding buildings was complete.

"Please, just call me Maddie, Okay?"

"Alright, Miss. . . uh, I mean, Maddie," Taos replied. "Ken I get a look at the rest of the ranch?"

"Absolutely. Let's start with the High Meadow."

"High Meadow?" Taos asked.

"It's the reason Cam picked this spot for our ranch. The plateau has great grazing, but it can get awfully hot and dry out there. When the weather gets rough in the summer, we move our cattle up to the High Meadow in the mountains behind the ranch house. It stays cool, and there's always plenty of water up there. It's also why Doniphan McCarty wants my ranch. He's limited, as am I, to how many beef the land will carry down here, but there is virtually unlimited grazing in the High Meadow."

"It sounds wonderful," Taos replied. "Let's go take a look."

They saddled their horses, and headed up a trail that followed along a large tributary to the San Miguel.

"This sure is beautiful," Taos said as they rode together up the trail.

"This is nothin'," Maddie laughed.

They continued up, and the air turned cool. The foliage grew thicker and greener, as they climbed. Eventually, they rode through a narrow pass in the wall of the mountain. A stream cascaded along to the left of them as the rock walls closed in tight.

Maddie led them up over a rock lip, and the world opened to them. It was the greenest caldera that Taos had ever seen, and was rimmed by a snow-covered ridge.

Taos let out a long whistle, then said, "My lawd, this is the most beautiful place I have evah laid eyes on!"

They let their horses run, and they galloped down into the huge meadow. They splashed through the stream, then stopped to graze on the emerald green grass..

"Amazing, isn't it?" Maddie asked, and caught the bright blue flash of Taos' eyes. Those beautiful eyes! *My heart could melt looking into those eyes,* she thought.

"Unbelievable," Taos replied. "I ken see why McCarty wants it!"

* * *

After exploring the vastness of this caldera, the High Meadow, they began the ride back down the trail to the ranch. As the pair left the tall pines, the country opened up into mixed piñon pine, and sage. Taos spotted a sage grouse, and, fast as lightning, drew one of his Colts, and blew the bird's head off.

"Nice shooting!" Maddie exclaimed, amazed at not only his accuracy, but the quickness with which he handled the Colt.

"Thought this would feed us for supper," Taos replied, as he jumped from his horse. Taos trotted over to the game bird, picked it up, and brought it back to his horse. He lashed it to the saddle, and re-mounted.

The ride the rest of the way down to Thunder Valley Ranch was uneventful. The pair made small talk about the beauty of the area, and promise of the ranch's future.

For the first time since Cam and Tad were murdered, Maddie had a positive feeling in her heart. *What is it about this handsome stranger?* She wondered.

* * *

It was late afternoon when they arrived back at the ranch. After getting the horses settled in the pen, and checking on the pigs, lambs, and chickens, they began preparing dinner. Taos cleaned the grouse, while Maddie stoked the oven fire, then scrubbed and chopped potatoes. She also filled a big pot from the well that Cam had put in the kitchen, and placed it on the stove.

"Heah's your bird," Taos said, as he entered the cabin.

Maddie took the cleaned sage grouse from Taos, put it in a baking dish, and added the potatoes. She seasoned the bird and potatoes while Taos washed his hands in a washbasin. Maddie put the dish in the oven.

"I've got water heating in that pot. When it's warm, I'm going to take a shower. There should be enough water for you too," Maddie said.

"Shower? Yu have a shower?" Taos asked.

"Yup, Cam was quite the handyman, and rigged a pump to get hot water into a tank above the bathroom so it can shower down."

"Well, I'll be!" Taos replied.

While dinner baked, they each took showers. Refreshed, and in fresh clothes, they sat down to enjoy the game bird.

* * *

After the dinner dishes were done, Maddie took two small glasses out of a cupboard, then removed a bottle of whiskey. She turned to Taos, and nodded.

"I'd be most obliged," Taos drawled.

Maddie poured whiskey into the two glasses, and walked over to Taos, who was cleaning the revolver that he had shot earlier. As she handed him the glass, their eyes met. Her heart melted, and she froze for just a moment.

"Thanks, Maddie," Taos said, and broke the spell.

Maddie took a jump back, and spilled some of her whiskey.

"I uh, I'll get that," she stammered.

"Relax, I've got it," he said, and took two strides to the sink and picked up a dish rag. He stepped back to the table, and wiped up the spilled spirits.

After Taos sat back down, Maddie said, "Thank you. I just don't know what has gotten into me."

"Nothing to worry about," Taos said. "Now, how about tomorrow?"

"After morning chores, we should head out on the range. I want to stop at the branding station, to see how that's going," Maddie replied.

"Branding station?" Taos asked.

"Yup, McCarty's men are branding my calves for me. We made a deal," Maddie replied.

"Oh," Taos' eyebrows raised. "What kind a' deal?" he asked.

"I didn't have anyone to help me brand. McCarty offered to brand my calves at a cost of one for every ten."

"Seems a little steep, but, given the circumstances, yu didn't have much choice in the matter," Taos said. "You think he'll be honest about the numbers, considerin' he wants you out'a business?" Taos asked.

"I'm sure worried about that, Taos. I don't trust him at all, but, like you said, I was stuck in a corner, and didn't have any choice. He could have just taken them all, and I wouldn't have any way to prove it."

"We'll see what we can figure out tomorra'. Hopefully, they ain't cheatin' you, but we'll have to figure out how to deal with it if they is."

"Thank you," she replied.

They sat quietly, sipping their whiskey for a while, as Taos finished cleaning his Colt.

"Well, I should take my gear and head out to the barn," Taos said.

"Barn? Why?"

"Um. Uh, I just figgered that's where I should sleep," Taos stammered.

"Of course not! I won't have you sleepin' in a barn! Not while I've got a perfectly good empty bedroom in the house," Maddie insisted.

"Well, thank you," Taos said.

Maddie stood up, and waved to Taos to follow, which he did. She walked him to Tad's room.

"Look, this room has been empty for almost a year. I packed away all of Tad's things months ago. I couldn't bear to look at them any longer. I want you to use it. Besides, I'll feel safer with you in the house. To be honest, I haven't had a good night's sleep since I lost Cam and Tad. You'll be doing me a favor," Maddie argued.

"Well, I sure am obliged." Taos replied.

* * *

Taos was washed and dressed, and had the coffee brewed, when Maddie emerged from her bedroom in her nightgown. He tried not to stare, as her body swayed freely under the garment. Quickly, he turned and poured her a cup of coffee.

"Good mornin'," he said with a smile, as he handed her the mug, and did his best to keep his eyes on hers.

"Good mornin' to you, and thanks for the coffee," Maddie replied.

"I collected eggs fer breakfast, if you like," Taos drawled. "I can cook 'em while you get dressed."

"Thank you, Taos," Maddie said.

Taos watched her as she walked to the bathroom, then he began cooking breakfast. He scrambled a half a dozen eggs, and heated up a few slices of bread on the stove, while Maddie got washed and dressed.

Maddie came out of the bathroom just as Taos was serving breakfast. She had her hair tied up in a bun, wore blue jeans, and a red and black checked flannel shirt.

"Smells darn good!" Maddie said, flashing her bright green eyes at Taos.

"Have a seat," Taos replied, and pulled out a chair.

"Why, thank you, sir," Maddie replied with a smile.

"I got all the mornin' chores done. We jus have ta saddle our hosses, and we'll be ready ta ride," Taos said.

"You sure have been busy this mornin'," Maddie said as she dug into her eggs.

"Jus' tryin' to earn my keep," Taos said.

After breakfast, they saddled the horses and rode out onto the range.

6

Chapter 6

Ben and Sage rode up to the mining area. It was a wasteland. The trees were gone. Mud and stumps took their place. The air had a distinct metallic odor, and burned their eyes and throats as they neared the huge smelter.

There was an enormous pit in the side of the mountain, and slag was spread everywhere. Next to the pit was a building, which looked like it housed offices. Next to that was a larger building, the size of a cow barn from back east, from which protruded two large stacks that spat out fire and smoke.

Presently, a man exited the smaller building, mounted a horse, and rode down in the siblings' direction.

"Looks like we got company," Ben drawled.

As the man approached, he raised his hand up for them to stop.

Ben and Sage reined up their horses and waited.

The man was in his late-thirties, by the looks of him, big-built, had red hair, and carried two large pistols, meant for effect, but were not carried the way someone handy with a gun would carry them, Ben noticed.

"Ken I help yu with sumpin'?" the man said, in an overly loud voice.

"I'm Ben Adams, and this heah is my sister, Sage," Ben drawled.

"Well, yur tresspassin' on Copper Mountain Mining land."

"We sure don't mean any harm, mistah," Ben replied. "We have a ranch down by Questa, and had an easy day, so we packed a picnic, and went fer a ride."

"I see. Well, my name's Trent Culpepper, an' I'm the foreman hereabouts."

"Mister Culpepper, would you mind showing us around your operation?" Sage asked as sweetly as she could muster. "We've never seen a copper mine before."

"Well, I guess it wouldn't do no harm, missy," Culpepper replied. "C'mon, follow me."

Culpepper turned his steed and rode to the office building. Ben and Sage followed.

As they approached the building, a man appeared in the window. He looked tall, had gray hair, and a jawline that looked like etched stone. This was not a happy man.

When they reached the railing in front of the building, Culpepper dismounted, tied his horse to the rail, and said, "Wait heah."

He entered the building, and shut the door behind him. Neither Ben nor Sage could make out what was being said, but it was obvious by the yelling, and tone of voice, that Culpepper's boss wasn't happy that he had let them on the property.

When Culpepper returned, his face was bright red.

"I'm sure sorry we caused yu trouble, Mistah Culpepper," Ben drawled.

"Ah, don't worry about it," Culpepper said. He looked over his shoulder, and then continued in a lower tone, "Mistah Van der Veer can be a little short tempered, doesn't want me kept from my work, but he agreed ta let me give yu a show around the place."

"Thank you, Mister Culpepper, we are much obliged," Sage replied.

"Why don't you two tie up your hosses, and we can walk over ta the mine and the smeltin' operation," Culpepper suggested.

Ben noticed that Van der Veer was staring through the window, his jaw still set tightly. It was obvious from his expression that, though he had exploded at Culpepper, he hadn't gotten his way. Ben decided to file that information for future use.

Ben and Sage followed the direction, and tied up their horses. They followed Culpepper to the large, open pit mine, where about fifty men were breaking up chunks of ore, and tossing them into wheeled bins that were on railroad tracks. The tracks went into the large building with the smoke stacks. There were large stacks of tree length logs outside the smokestack building, and men were cutting the logs up into four foot lengths. Other men were leading teams of horses that were skidding tree length logs across the barren wasteland.

"This heah is the mine. Those men down there are diggin' the ore. Then it goes into the smelter in that buildin' theah," Culpepper explained, and pointed at the big building with the smokestacks. "They's two smelters in theah, that melt down the ore. The copper, gold, and silver get split away from the junk metals, and other stuff."

"Purty big operation," Ben remarked.

"And all the junk metals is what we see spread all over the place?" Sage asked.

"Yes, miss. It's called slag," Culpepper answered.

"And it just lays on the ground like that. Hmm, any idea what's in it? Sage pressed.

"Yu sure are nosey for a purty little thang," Culpepper growled.

"I'm sorry Mister Culpepper," Sage replied. "I'm just tryin' to understand yur operation."

"Not a lot of trees left here. What happens when yu run out of wood to keep the smelter hot?" Ben asked.

"We're already buildin' wagon roads ta haul the trees we need. They's enough timber in this area ta supply the smelter for a hunnert yeahs," Culpepper responded, red faced.

He took them to the smelting operation. They were slammed back by a hot wall of air, when he opened the door.

"It sure is hot in here," Sage yelled over the noise of the bellows, and fire, which caused an overpowering wheezing and roaring sound.

Barebacked men worked the equipment, as sweat streamed off their bodies.

"This is where the copper is split from the ore. Fust, it gets washed to get dirt off'n it. Next, it gets crushed, in that thingamabob over theah, an' then' it gets melted down in the smelter. At the end, the copper gets split from any gold, and silver, and they get poured inta' molds ta make ingots. Now, let's get outta' heah!"

They three rushed out of the rancid, sweltering air of the building, and gulped the cool mountain air outside of the building.

"Well, other than the bunkhouses fer the men, and the mess hall, that's aboot it," Culpepper puffed.

"Thank you for yur time, Mistah Culpepper," Ben said.

"Yes, I learned a lot," Sage added.

They walked back over to the office, and, when they got there, Van der Veer stood, menacingly, on the porch, hands at his hips.

"So, you got your tour, then," He snapped.

"Yes, Thank you, Mistah Van der Veer. I'm Ben Adams, and this is my sistah, Sage." Ben reached his hand out to shake, but Van der Veer kept his hands on his hips.

"I know who you are," he snapped. "You're a couple of busybodies from down in the valley who are tresspassin' on my land."

Ben's eyes flashed, and his hands hovered over his Colts. "I'll tell you who we are. We're ranchers from down in Questa on the Red River, and we've been heah a lot longer than yu an' yur mine have. You show up, now we got deformed cattle, and the trout are disappearin' from the river. I've got every right to find out what's causin' it."

"You ranchers think you own everything. I employ over a hundred men full time here. Good payin' jobs. The kind that'll bring prosperity and civilization to this country. How many men do you employ, Mister Adams?"

Ben stood quietly steaming, too angry to respond.

"I thought so. You've had your tour, now get off my land before I have you thrown off," Van der Veer said.

"We'll leave, but this ain't ovah," Ben growled.

"You got a hundred men, Adams? 'Cause I do."

Van der Veer stepped in front of Ben, and got very close. He spoke in a low growl. "And I'll tell you somethin' else, Mister Adams, the money this mine produces is booming the economy from here to Santa Fe. If yer lookin' for a fight, you're gonna have one hell of a fight on yer hands. Good day, sir."

Ben and Sage mounted their horses, and rode off.

7

Chapter 7

After an hour's ride, Maddie and Taos reached the branding operation. The area was wild with activity. At least a dozen cowboys were hustling about, two were funneling calves into a makeshift corral, others were separating calves from their mothers, two were flipping the calves, and holding them down, while another branded them. Another held a book, and counted the calves as they were released into a larger makeshift pen. Another appeared to be the foreman, since he rode back and forth between areas, and gave orders.

"Looks like we should talk ta that feller there," Taos said, as he pointed toward the foreman,"

"That's Rance McCarty. His father is Doniphan, the one who owns the outfit," Maddie replied.

"What can yu tell me aboot him?" Taos asked.

"Well, he ain't that smart, an' he's kinda a weasel, tries to act tough, but he ain't," Maddie replied.

"Well, I guess it's aboot time Mister Rance McCarty an' I get acquainted," Taos drawled.

They spurred their horses, and rode directly toward Rance McCarty.

When Rance heard the horses riding toward him, he looked in their direction, and his expression relaxed when he saw that his father was not one of the riders.

"Hey-ya, Miss Maddie," Rance called, as she and Taos approached.

"Hello, Rance," Maddie said.

"Who's yur frien'?" Rance asked.

"Rance, this is Taos, he's my new foreman," Maddie replied.

"Foreman? Don' yu need a crew to have a foreman?" Rance snickered, the set of his shoulders dripped with the arrogance of a small man with too much power.

Taos spoke up, "You also need a brain, but that don't seem to be stoppin' yu."

Rance's watery gray eyes flashed with anger as he reached for his six-gun.

Taos' twin Colts were leveled on Rance's chest before Rance could break leather.

"I'd think twice aboot that, if I was yu," Taos drawled.

Rance reluctantly, but wisely, let his revolver drop back into its holster.

"Rance," Maddie started, her voice quivering, "we're here to see how the brandin's goin'."

"Oh," he replied, gathering his composure, now that Taos had holstered his Colts. "We finished brandin' yur calves yestiday."

"We'd like ta see the numbers," Maddie said.

"Yup, we'll have ta ride over ta Brumley, theah," he pointed to the man who was tallying the branded calves.

"Well, let's go talk ta' him," Taos said.

The three rode over to where the calves were being branded. The smell of scorched fur and flesh hung over the area.

When they arrived, Rance yelled, "Less hole up a bit boys, take a break."

The crew of cowboys stopped what they were doing, and to a man, began rolling smokes.

"Brumley, yu got the calf numbers for Misses Ferguson?"

Brumley, who looked like he would be more at ease in a bank than out on the open range, looked up from his tally book. "Just a minute, boss. I'll dig 'em out."

"Nice operation yu got heah, Rance," Taos offered.

"Yu got much experience with ranchin'?" Rance enquired, regaining his air of arrogance.

"Grew up on a ranch in New Mexico. Guess, I been thru this once or thrice," Taos drawled.

"I see," Rance replied, rubbing the day-old stubble on his chin, in an effort to portray nonchalance.

"Got it here," the bespectacled bookkeeper said.

"What's the tally?" Maddie asked.

"Well the book shows a total of ninety-three, minus the agreed upon ten percent, gives a total of eighty-four branded with the double thunderbolts," Brumley replied.

"What?!" Maddie exclaimed. "I had well over two hundred pregnant cows!"

She spun in her saddle, and snapped at Rance, "What's goin' on here?"

"The numbers don't lie, Maddie," Rance spat back, a new confidence in his voice.

"So what happened to the rest of her calves?" Taos said, a strange coolness in his voice.

"Could a' been wolves, coyotes, the winter. Who knows?" Rance mocked.

In a flash, Taos' guns were leveled on Rance once again. "I think you know," he said in a near whisper.

"Look, suh, the numbers is what they is. She could have nothin'. My men rounded up what they could find, we split off ten percent of 'em, and branded the rest with the double thunderbolt," Rance replied sarcastically.

Maddie turned to Taos, "We figured somethin' like this would happen. We know what we're dealin' with. C'mon Taos, let's go."

"I'll be watchin' yu, McCarty," Taos said, as he backed his horse away, both guns leveled at Rance's chest.

* * *

"I'm gonna end up killin' him," Taos drawled as they trotted their horses back toward the ranch.

Maddie looked at Taos. His calm demeanor didn't match his words.

"Oh, Taos, those words are so dreadful," Maddie cried.

"It's the way of the West, Maddie. There ain't much law out heah. A man's gotta stand up fer hisself."

"And what about a woman?" Maddie demanded. "What's a woman to do?"

"Miss Maddie, it's tougher yet on a woman than 'tis on a man, especially if she's alone."

"Like me?"

"I'm sorry Maddie, but it's just the way 'tis. They's a lot of men out heah wantin' ta take advantage of a woman in one way or another. The McCarty's is that kinda men."

"Are there other kinda men?" Maddie asked.

"They ain't no saints out heah, Maddie. Most scores out heah are settled with a gun, but not everybody's bad."

"And what kind of man are you, Taos?" Maddie asked. She reined in her horse at the gate to the ranch. Her bright green eyes took him in as he formed an answer to her question. She saw the struggle in his deep blue eyes, and felt for him, because she knew what he must say.

"Maddie, I told you I done some bad things. I done them for good, though. I never killed nobody that didn't deserve it." He looked her straight in the eyes, and continued, "Maddie, I believe that I am a good man. I'm the kind a' man that a woman like you can trust. I have a sister back in New Mexico, and my father is a gentleman, my mother a lady, and I know how to respect a woman. But I'm a ruthless killer, when someone I care aboot is threatened."

"And does that include me?" Maddie asked.

"I told you I'm gonna end up killin' Rance McCarty."

* * *

After his incident with Taos and Maddie, Rance got his men back to work, and rode back to his father's ranch house.

Doniphan McCarty was enjoying a cigar and a glass of whiskey on the porch when he saw a rider in the distance. He gulped the last swallow, and poured another glass. He sipped the amber liquid while he watched the rider approach. Before long, it was evident that the rider was Rance.

"He should be overseein' the brandin'," McCarty said aloud. "Somethin' must be wrong."

He stepped down off the porch, and met his son at the railing. Rance dismounted his horse while his father tied it to the rail.

Rance, who, at five foot seven, was a full four inches shorter than his father, looked up at the older man, as he caught his breath from the hard ride.

"What is it, Rance?" the older man asked.

"We got trouble, Pa," Rance panted.

"What is it?" Doniphan demanded.

"That Ferguson woman has hired a gun!"

"What'dya mean?"

"She says he's her foreman, but he's sure quick with a six shooter. He had two guns leveled on my chest afore I could even clear leather."

"Dammit!" Doniphan exclaimed.

"They's onta us, but they got no evidence," Rance said.

"A man like that don't need no evidence. I've got another plan. We'll get that ranch one way or t'other."

8

Chapter 8

The Colonel sat on the porch smoking his ever present pipe when Ben and Sage returned from the mine.

"Well, you two sure left early this mornin'," the Colonel said as they approached. "A little brother and sister alone time?"

Ben and Sage dismounted, and stepped up onto the porch.

"We got problems, Colonel," Ben said as he dusted himself off with his sombrero.

Lorena stepped out with a tray holding a pitcher of water and glasses.

"Thought you might like a drink after your ride," she said.

"Thanks, Ma, but I'll probably need something stronger than that," Ben replied. He filled a glass for himself and his sister. He gulped down the water, and said to the Colonel, "Have a seat."

The Colonel poured three glasses of whiskey. Lenore didn't drink spirits.

"Alright, son, what is it?" he asked.

Ben took a long sip from his glass, swirled the glass for a moment, and watched the amber liquid intently before answering his father. "Sage and I rode up yonder to the copper mines," he said, his arm pointed in the general direction. "The river up that way's got nothin' in it. No bugs, an' no fish."

"Nothin'! I saw it for myself," Sage interjected.

Ben continued, "We got up ta the mining area, and it is a wasteland, worse than the driest desert. Trees are all gone, an' slag is strewn all over the place."

The Colonel gulped his whiskey, and poured another glass. He rubbed his chin, "You think this is connected to our cattle?"

"I could see where the rain has washed the slag into the river. I think it's poisoning the river, and causin' the problems with our cattle," Sage said.

"We got a tour from the foreman, a guy named Culpepper. He ain't bad, mostly just a blow hard. Got in trouble with his boss, Van der Veer, who threatened us pretty bad," Ben added.

"I thought Ben was gonna shoot him, Dad!" Sage exclaimed.

"I sure wanted ta, after the things he said, and I may have ta yet," Ben drawled. "He said some other things that worried me, Colonel."

"Like what?" his father asked.

"He said that he's got a hundred men ready to fight, an' he also said public opinion is against us, on account that the mines are bringin' in so much money."

"So, he's threatenin' us with another Lincoln County War, is he," the Colonel answered.

"Even if we got all the ranchers together, I don't think we could mount a hundred men," Ben replied.

The older man stood up, and looked out over his ranch, and the surrounding mountains. He seemed to grow in stature as his family watched. When he turned to them, he was no longer the retired old man, he was Colonel Adams again.

"Ben, in the mornin', I want you to ride over to the Parker's ranch. Talk to Jack, an' fill him in. Have him send men to the ranches to the north and east. Sage an' I'll ride south to see Frank Lynch, an' Travis Clark. We'll set a meetin' up here for a week from tomorrow. That'll give everyone time to get their affairs in order.

Sage pulled a chair up next to the Colonel, and sat down.

"There's something else, Daddy," she said softly

"What is it, my dear?" he replied.

"I've been doing the books. You sure are spendin' a lot of money down in town these past few weeks."

"I've earned it. Can't a man spend his money as he pleases?"

"Sure, I guess so, Daddy, but folks tell me you've been buyin' drinks for everybody in the bar," she replied.

"So, like I said, I earned it."

"But Daddy, we're losin' money. We can't continue like this with what's happenin' to the cattle. We'll end up losin' the ranch."

The Colonel was struck. He looked Sage straight in the eye. "I had no idea it was that bad, Sage. It ends today. I promise."

* * *

Ben rode up along Cobresto Creek, a major tributary of the Red River. He noticed the river was alive, aquatic insects were hatching out of the water, and trout were feeding on them. The Cobresto began in the mountains to the north-east of Questa.

There ain't no mines on the Cobresto, and look at it, Ben thought. This was just more evidence that the mining operation up river from Questa was the cause of their woes.

Ben was happy to take the ride, it was nice to be with his own thoughts, and, more importantly, he would hopefully, get a chance to see Ida Parker, the only girl in Northern New Mexico that he cared for.

It was mid-morning when Ben reached Cobresto Creek Ranch. He rode through the arch leading to the sprawling adobe ranch house. Ben spied a number of men watching a cowboy breaking a bronco. Ben noticed Jack Parker cheering among them.

Jack Parker had settled in the area about the same time as the Colonel had. He was a few years younger than the Colonel, and had fought in the war as well, as a cavalryman. He served under Custer at Gettysburg, and was one of the lucky ones to survive the many charges on the East Cavalry Field, and hold the line against the Rebels. Jack and the Colonel often traded war stories when they got into the amber. Jack was short of stature, which had landed him in the cavalry. He learned horses during the war, and brought this knowledge west from Michigan afterward. Jack's wife, Sofia, came from a proud Spanish family, the Corderos, who had been in the territory for over two hundred years.

"Hey Jack," Ben shouted over the din, as he dismounted.

Jack turned when he heard the voice, and, when he recognized Ben, his dark eyes sparkled, and he flashed a big, toothy smile.

"Haloo, Ben Adams!" he shouted, and slapped the younger man on the back. "What brings you up on the Cobresto?"

"Ken we talk in private?" Ben asked as they clasped hands.

"Sure, sure, my boy. Let's go over to the house. I'll see if Sofia ken boil us a pot of coffee."

They stepped up on the front porch, and dusted themselves off with their sombreros before entering the house.

The house was beautiful inside. There were exposed beams in the ceiling, and the walls were whitewashed. Trim was a turquoise blue.

"Kick the dust and mud off'n yur boots afore you come in my house!" Sofia shouted from somewhere in the building.

"She rules with an iron fist," Jack whispered.

"Yur the boss outside, she's the boss inside. Same with the Colonel and my mother," Ben laughed.

"Hey Sofia, Ben Adams is heah, we got any fresh coffee?" Jack yelled.

"Dammit, Jack! Why didn't you say we had company?" Sofia said as she stomped toward the front of the house.

"I just did!" he shouted back.

"You drive me crazy!" Sofia said when she entered the room. "Hello, Ben! How's your mother?" She asked.

"She's good, Misses Parker. Thanks fer askin'," he replied.

"Good. I'll get coffee on. Can yu stay for dinna?"

"Yes'm, thanks," he replied.

"Oh, good! The boys will be eating with the cowboys, but Ida should be in shortly," Sofia said, with a knowing smile, as she started the coffee.

Jack opened a jar and grabbed a couple of pieces of beef jerky, and handed one to Ben.

"Thanks, Jack," Ben said.

"It'll keep body and soul togethah 'till dinna's ready," Jack said. "Have a seat, my boy, and tell me what brings you to Cobresto Creek Ranch."

"Thanks, Jack," Ben said as he took a chair. "We got problems, Jack," he said at length.

Jack sat down across from Ben. He was no longer smiling, and the seriousness of his expression showed his age. "Alright, shoot," he replied.

"Wal, I'm sure you heared aboot the copper mines up on the Red," Ben replied.

"Sure, but they don't bother us none heah," Jack said.

"Not yet," Ben countered. "I gotta tell yu what it's doin' ta us, Jack."

"Whatdya' mean?"

"Since the mine went in, the Red is dyin', an we've been seein' deformities in our calves," Ben said.

"Jesus, I'm sorry ta' heah that, Ben, but what does that have to do with me?"

"Sage an' I rode out ta' the Copper Mountain Mining company yestidy. It's a friggin' mess. They've cut down all the trees around it, and they's got slag spread everywhere. We got a look see from their foreman, a man called Culpepper, but his boss, Van der Veer chewed him out, an' chewed us out. When I mentioned what the mine was doin' ta our operation, he threatened ta go to war with all the ranchers around heah. Said he had a hundred men, and asked me how many the ranchers could muster."

"So, what's he doin'? Threatenin' another Lincoln County War?" Jack demanded.

"That's exactly how the Colonel responded. Van der Veer said that minin' is gonna civilize the area, an' nobody will support the Ranchers," Ben replied.

"So, what does he want? To replace us with a bunch of alfalfa desperados?" Jack slammed his fist on the table just as Sofia placed a mug of coffee in front of Ben, which made it jump.

"An' don't yu think he won't place a mine up on the headwaters of the Cobresto in a twinklin' of a bed-post, ifn' he finds copper up theah," Ben argued, as he grabbed his mug. "Thanks, Misses Parker."

"My pleasure, Ben," she replied.

"Lands sakes!" Jack exclaimed. "I'm wit' yu an' the Colonel. What can I do ta' help?"

"The Colonel wants to have a confab at the ranch a week from today. Also, could you spread the word around heah?" Ben drawled.

"Sure, I'll send Cabe and Jack Junior out in the mornin'," Jack replied.

Just then, the front door opened, and Ida entered.

Upon seeing her, Ben stood and nodded, "Hello, Ida," he said.

Ida, who was a couple of years younger than Ben, and nearly as tall, with long, jet black hair and almond-shaped eyes that flashed like obsidian in the sun, stopped dead in her tracks at the sight of him. This was the effect that he had on every single woman in the territory. Ben, in fact, was the most eligible bachelor in Northern New Mexico, and young women swooned just at the mention of his name.

"Well, lookie loo if it ain't Ben Adams," Ida replied in her best "butter wouldn't melt in my mouth" voice, while batting her long, black eyelashes at him. "What brings yu up heah to the Cobresto, on this fine day?"

"I'm heah to do some business with yur Pa, but is a delightful surprise to see yur smilin' face," Ben replied in a slow drawl.

"Surprise? Yu ride out ta' my ranch, an' say yu are surprised to see me? Ha! I ain't buyin' what yur sellin', Mistah Adams!" her warm, golden brown skin seemed to glow as she laughed.

Ida stepped to the sideboard and put her basket of fresh vegetables down, the slit in her skirt showed a flash of well formed legs as she walked. Something that Ben did not miss.

"Well, it's just that I wasn't expectin' ta' be heah that long, but yur mother was kind enough ta' invite me for dinnah," Ben replied.

"Ida, you wash up an' help me with dinnah' and leave the menfolk to their conversation," Sofia said.

"Oh, Mother!" Ida exclaimed. 'Ah was just chattin' with my dear friend, Ben Adams."

"I knowed exactly what yu was doin'," Sofia said. "Now, wash up."

"Yes'm," Ida replied, her playful mood ended.

9

Chapter 9

"Yu mind if I ride with yu a bit?" Ida's voice carried from behind Ben as he mounted his horse. "Why, not at all, Miss Ida," Ben replied as his eyes leveled on hers. "As long as yur Ma and Pa are good with it."

"I don' need theah permission," she snapped back. "I'll go saddle my hoss."

"I knowed better'n ta' ask yu if yu need help," Ben said.

"Ha, so yu can learn a thing or two," Ida said over her shoulder as she headed for the stable.

A few minutes later Ida rode out on a palamino horse, her skirt split, and her bare legs showing. Ben sized her up, and thought that she was the prettiest woman in the territory. They rode together silently as they left the ranch.

After a few minutes on the trail, Ida spoke up, "Yur really worried aboot the mine, ain't ya?"

"Yup, the Colonel, my Ma, Sage, an I have worked awful hard to make a go of it, jes like yur family. An jes when we are seein' some real progress, this miner feller shows up, and evethin' we worked for is shot ta' Hell.

"Yu think the local ranchers will be of any help? Cause I don't," Ida said. "Sure, my Pa will, but the rest just can't see inta' the future. This meetin' next week will feature a lot a' hot air, an' no results. Mark my words."

"I don' think we have a choice. Van der Veer said he has a hundred men to put to bear on us," Ben countered.

"I don't think they's a good solution, Ben, but violence isn't the way," Ida said lowly, and softly.

"But we may not have a choice."

"They's always a choice," Ida said, her cheeks reddening.

They rode silently for a while until the trail paralleled a waterfall and large pool.

"Why don't we stop heah, an' rest for a bit, then I'll ride back home?" Ida asked.

"Sure. The hosses could use some water anyway," Ben replied.

They stopped, and dismounted. Ben took the saddles off their horses, and sent them to the stream to drink while he placed the saddles in a shady spot under a piñon pine.

Ida untied her kerchief and dipped it in the cool water, then wiped her face and neck with it.

"Whew, that's much better," she said. "A body sure does get hot ridin' the trail, don't it?"

"A body sure do," Ben agreed after he splashed water on his face. He walked to the falls and filled his canteen with cold mountain water. He walked back to Ida and said, "Drink?"

"Sure, an' thanks, Ben," Ida replied as she took the container from him.

Ben watched as she drank, and noticed the way her breast heaved as she breathed between gulps.

After Ida finished, Ben took a long swallow from the canteen, then walked to the shade, and sat sideways on his saddle. Ida followed him and sat down. They leaned against the tree, and watched the waterfall.

"Sure is pleasant heah, Ben," she whispered.

"Yes it is," he replied, feeling her closeness.

She inched a little closer to Ben until their bodies were touching. He didn't move away.

"Ben, can I ask yu somethin?"

"Sure, Ida, shoot," he replied.

"Do yu like me, even just a little?" Ida asked.

"Well, of course I do," he said.

"Then, why don't yu ever show it? All the cowboys can't keep their eyes offin' me, an' I don't want nothin' to do with them, but you, Ben Adams, act like I'm not even here!" she pouted.

"Look, Ida, yur the purtiest woman in the territory, no doubt about it. I guess I'm just not good at this kinda thing. Of course I like yu, but. . ."

"But nothin'! If yu like me, even just a little, kiss me now, or, or don't ever talk to me again!"

Overcome by emotion, Ben reached over, wrapped his muscular arms around Ida, and pulled her close. Their lips met, and he felt the hot fire of his passion stream through him. She gave as good as she got in their kisses.

Then, she pulled back.

"Yu mean it, don't ya'?" Ida asked.

"Mean what?" Ben replied, his brows furrowed.

"These kisses, silly!" I don't want ta' just give away my kisses for fun. Yu gotta mean it, or I ain't kissin' you no more!"

"Of course I mean it," Ben said.

"Then why don't yu come visit me anymore? You only came out to talk to my Pa," Ida snapped back. Her cheeks blazed red.

Ben slowly arose. He walked over to the river bank, picked up a rock, and skipped it on the pool. He slowly turned, his face was crimson, and Ida leaned back, having never seen him so angry before.

But she had mistaken passion for rage. Ben crossed the distance between them in a flash, grabbed her arms, lifted her up, and pulled her to him. He enveloped her in his sinewy arms, and kissed her full and hard on the mouth.

He let her go.

"Do yu still think I don't care?" he hissed.

Taken aback, cheeks flushed, Ida replied, "Wal, I'm beginnin' ta' think you may at that, Ben Adams."

* * *

The memory of their kisses replayed over and over again in Ben's mind as he rode home.

We live in tumultuous times, he thought. He truly cared for Ida, but how could he make a go of it with her with what was going on? *We is in for a war, I knowed it. Thet Van der Veer is gonna push us hard, an' we's gonna have ta' push jess as hard back at him.*

The early evening sun cast long shadows as he approached the ranch. In the amber light, he noticed a cloud of dust from the Colonel's buckboard, and he rode out to greet him and Sage.

"Halloo," Ben said as he approached the buckboard.

"Halloo, yerself," Sage replied.

"How did it go?" Ben asked.

"I think we're gonna have a good meetin' next week, the Colonel replied, but I don't think we kin muster anywheres neah a hundred men," the Colonel replied as they rode toward the ranch. "And how about you?"

"Jack Parker is in fer sure, and his boys are ridin' out tomorrow to talk to the ranchers to the north."

"And how about Ida? Did yu see her?" Sage asked, eyes sparkling at the chance to tease her older brother.

"Yup," Ben answered laconically, knowing full well that his sister wouldn't let it go.

10

Chapter 10

Doniphan McCarty entered the Telluride savings and loan. Mason Fillmore, the Bank Manager, looked up over his reading glasses, and pushed back the combover that had fallen along the side of his face while he was working. He stood up and knocked over his chair, and fumbled to right it.

"Mister McCarty, what brings you to Telluride?" Fillmore enquired in a shaky voice.

"Is there someplace, uh, private we can talk, Mistah Fillmore?" Doniphan asked directly, skipping pleasantries.

"Of course, right this way, Mister McCarty," Filllmore said, and led McCarty to an office. They entered, and Fillmore offered McCarty a seat.

After they sat down in the tiny, drab office, Fillmore spoke. "What can I do for you, Mister McCarty?"

"I have a proposition for yu, Mister Filmore," McCarty said.

Interested, Fillmore leaned forward. "Yes?"

"I want ta' pick up the note on Maddie Ferguson's ranch," he said.

"This is highly irregular, Mister McCarty," Fillmore objected.

"There will be a handy profit in it for the bank, and for you, personally," McCarty replied.

"Uh, are you trying to bribe me, Mr. McCarty, because if. . ."

McCarty cut him off. "Bribe is such a nasty word, Mistah Fillmore. I'm offering yu a business proposition. I would merely be paying yu for your services."

Fillmore slid back in his seat. "What kind of profit are we talkin' about, Mister McCarty?"

"I'm prepared ta' pay the bank two percentages over what she's payin' an' I'll pay you a ten percent closing fee for yur service, above and beyond the bank's fees."

"Well, then, I think we have a deal, Mister McCarty."

* * *

After finishing the morning chores, Taos sat down on the porch, and wrote a letter to his sister; the second since he had left their ranch along the Red River. Though less than a year, it seemed ages ago. He had lost so much, done so much. At least he knew Sage and his mother were safe, and the ranch was safe. That sometimes made it worth the shame of all the killings. They got what they deserved.

Writing to Sage was always difficult, but he owed it to her, to let her know that he was alright. That he was doing good, or at least trying to. The first few months after he left, he had been out of control. Didn't care whether he lived or died, but he had a new purpose in life, and he owed it to Sage to let her know. He also wanted news on Ida. Had she changed her mind? Would she see him?

When he finished the letter, with instructions to use the name "Taos" on any return mail, he folded it up and prepared it for the post office. He stuffed the letter into the breast pocket of his hickory shirt, then stepped into the cabin, where Maddie was working on some sewing.

"I'm ready ta' ride inta' Telluride. Yu got yur list of things yu want'?" Taos asked, when Maddie had looked up.

She took a moment to process what he was saying. "Sure do, thanks. Let me get it."

"No rush," Taos replied. "I'll be back tomorra' afternoon. Yu sure yur alright?"

"I'll be fine, I promise. Not like I ain't been heah alone before," Maddie replied.

* * *

Maddie watched from the porch as Taos rode off. He stopped and waved his sombrero before riding over a knoll and out of site. She gave a big wave back, then wiped away the tears that were streaming down her cheeks. What was it about this quiet man that affected her so? She had spent many a night alone in the cabin after losing Cam and Tad, and she had cried on many of them at first. She had cried for their loss, but this was different. Taos would be back in a day. Maddie would be alone just one night. But dammit, she missed him already.

Maddie lingered on the porch for a few minutes before heading back to her sewing. She locked the door behind her, and checked to make sure that her shotgun was loaded. It was. Then she sat back down in her sewing chair.

* * *

Days like these were toughest on Taos. The ride to Telluride gave him too much time to think. Life was easier when he was working hard. As he rode the trail, he thought of home, family, and the wake of violence that he left in New Mexico. Breaking Ida's heart is what shook him the most. The vision of hatred on Ida's face, as she held her dying father in her arms, haunted him. Her last words drilled into his psyche: "This is on you, Ben Adams, my father's death is on you. It's a black mark on your soul. I hope you rot in Hell!"

He had known then that there was no sense in trying to talk to her, explain that he had been fighting for not only his future, but his family's future, and the future of ranching in northern New Mexico. He did the only thing that he could do. He had mounted his horse, and rode off. Not into the sunset, but into a year of perdition.

11

Chapter 11

Taos entered Telluride, and rode directly to the Post Office, in hopes to mail his letter to Sage before it closed.

The postmaster, Red Timmins, was locking up, as Taos dismounted.

"Ken I get this heah letter mailed, afore you close up for the day?' Taos asked, holding up the letter.

"Well, the mail's already gone out today. I can take it, but it won't go out until tomorrow," the Postmaster said, as he looked over his spectacles at Taos.

"It's been almost a year, another day won't matter much," Taos said, as he handed the Postmaster the letter.

"Follow me," the man said, and they stepped inside the Post Office.

After getting his letter in the mail, Taos mounted his horse, and rode to the stockyard.

Bill Haney saw him as he rode up, and gave Taos a big wave.

"Halloo, Taos," he said, offering his hand in greeting.

Taos took Bill's hand, and shook it hard.

"How goes it?" Bill asked.

"I came ta' thank yu, Bill," Taos replied. "I've been workin' for Maddie Ferguson."

"That's great to hear!" Bill exclaimed. "She's a sweet woman. Such a shame about her husband and kid."

"Yup," Taos replied. "She told me aboot that. Say, Bill, do you know anythin' about Doniphan McCarty?"

Taos noticed Bill's face flush for just a second, before he answered. "Let's walk into my office."

Taos followed Bill into the sales office, a drab affair with a desk, some charts on the wall, a map of the area, and a couple of old chairs.

"This sure is a fancy outfit, Bill," Taos drawled.

Bill pointed to a chair, and Taos sat down. "No sense in spendin' money on extras," Bill replied. "I got what I need here."

"So, why the hush hush about McCarty?" Taos asked.

"Sorry ta be so spooky, but McCarty seems to have eyes and ears all over," Bill replied. "Most people believe that he had sumthin' ta do with Cam and Tad Ferguson's killin'."

"Maddie hasn't said that, but I got thet feelin'," Taos replied. "I'm pretty sure they's out ta steal her ranch."

"Wouldn't surprise me. Everybody knows that she's got the best ranch in the territory, with the alpine meadows above the ranch house."

"She showed that spot to me t'other day. Best grazing land I've seen in a long time."

"I seen McCarty in town jes a few days ago. He stepped inta the bank," Bill offered.

Taos rubbed his chin in thought for a moment. "Hmm, maybe I'll stop at the bank in the mornin' afore I ride out."

Bill stood up. "Be careful. The Banker's name is Mason Fillmore, an' I don't trust him. If he's in cahoots with McCarty, you'll end up with a target on yur back."

"I've dealt with more dangerous men than McCarty," Taos replied.

"Don't underestimate him, Taos."

"Thanks for the advice. I should get my hoss taken care of, and get a room fer the night. If'n I have time, I'll stop by after the bank," Taos said, as he offered his hand to Bill.

"Take care, my friend," Bill said, as Taos exited the office.

* * *

Maddie had kept herself busy all day. She knew this routine well. For months after Cam and Tad had been murdered, she would work herself to exhaustion, then eat dinner, shower, and collapse into bed. She didn't know why, but she felt a deep sense of loss when Taos rode out earlier in the day. Why? She had known him only a short time. Why did she feel so attached to him? Sure, he was handsome, damn handsome, she admitted to herself. He also had a gentle way about him, even though she knew he had killed before, perhaps many times over. She had seen how fast he drew his pistols. That doesn't happen by accident, she told herself.

As she went through the motions of frying steak and potatoes, her mind kept returning to the short time she had spent with Taos, and how his quiet strength, and kindness, had provided her comfort. She kept picturing his eyes. Those eyes that seemed to look deep into her soul when they were upon her.

Maddie plated her dinner, and sat down to eat. She was a good cook, but the food tasted bland this evening, like it had for so many months. After she finished pushing the food around her plate, Maddie put the scraps in her bin for the pigs, washed the dishes, dried them, and put them away in the cupboard. Next, she began heating water for her evening shower. Then, she took the shotgun off the rack, made sure it was loaded, and went outside to do a last inspection of the evening. She checked the chicken coup, barns, and other outbuildings, then scanned the horizon. No riders. Good.

Maddie strode back inside the ranch house and locked the door behind her. She put the shotgun back on the rack, and went around the house, closing and locking windows. As the sun lowered, her feeling of aloneness grew.

She pumped hot water up to the shower, stripped naked, and took a moment to admire her body in the full length mirror that hung from the bathroom door. Almost thirty, and I'm still looking pretty firm, she thought. She imagined herself with Taos as she stepped into the shower. Goosebumps raised on her flesh, as she soaped up her body, and she felt tingles as her soapy hand hovered over her privates.

Maddie had never imagined herself with another man after Cam was killed. She had just shut down that part of herself. Not that men weren't interested. They sure were. She was considered an attractive woman, and of course, there was great value in her land. But, this man, Taos, had reawakened something inside her, and now it wanted to be fed.

* * *

Taos had spent the night at the Silvermine Hotel. It was not the kind of place he would have picked if he had a choice. It was loud, rowdy, full of miners, gamblers, and whores. There wasn't much choice in a mining town, though. He had seen how his home had changed with the copper mines. Sure, cowboys could be rough and rowdy, but mining, maybe because of the money involved, brought a different sort.

He was happy to check out, and walked over to Marissa's Cantina, entered, and sat down.

"Coffee, Señior?" Marissa said as she approached Taos' table.

"Yes'm," Taos replied.

"I no see you in here before," Marissa said as she filled his mug. "New in town?"

"Just heah on business," Taos replied.

"Welcome to Marissa's Cantina. I'm Marissa," she said.

59

"Thanks. Folks call me Taos."

"Nice to meet ju, Señor Taos. What can I get ju for breakfast?"

"I'll have half a dozen eggs, fried, bacon, and four slices of toast, thanks," Taos said.

"Ju mucho hungry this morning, Señor Taos!" Marissa exclaimed.

"I have some business, then a long ride. I'll need the fuel," Taos smiled.

"I get that right in for ju, den, Señor," Marissa said, with a big smile, before she turned away.

Taos sipped his coffee, and looked around the place. He was glad that he didn't have breakfast at the hotel. Too loud, too many busybodies, and it smelled like stale beer. Marissa's by contrast, was clean, and quiet. Everyone in the cantina was minding their own business.

While waiting for his breakfast, Taos thought about where his life had taken him over the last year. He had spent many months hanging out in places like the Silvermine, he was one of those rowdies. His life had changed in the past few weeks. He owed it to Maddie for trusting in him, and he would repay her with his loyalty. Doniphan McCarty crossed his mind. This was one bad hombre, who was bent on taking Maddie's ranch. Taos was not going to let that happen. His first step would be to talk with Mason Fillmore at the bank. If Fillmore was like all the other bankers that Taos had known, getting him to squeal wouldn't be too hard.

Taos jumped out of his deep thoughts when Marissa arrived with his breakfast.

"Theese is one heavy plate, Señor Taos!" Marissa exclaimed as she placed his food on the table. "More coffee, Señor?"

"Thanks, Marissa. Sure, I'll take another cup," Taos replied.

"I be right back."

After breakfast, Taos walked toward the bank, which had just opened. The bank president, Mason Fillmore, took a quick step back, when he saw the double pistols hanging low on Taos' hips.

"M-may I help you, sir?" Fillmore said. His voice cracked.

"I'm lookin' for Mason Fillmore," Taos replied.

"That'd be me. How can I help you, Mister ah," Fillmore said.

"Folks call me Taos, Mistah Fillmore. I'd like to speak to yu in private."

"Of course, come this way," Fillmore said, and turned.

Once inside his office, Fillmore offered a seat to Taos, and sat down at his desk. "How can I help you?" he asked.

"Well, I work for Maddie Ferguson over at the Thunder Valley Ranch," Taos replied. He noticed Filmore's face tighten, which confirmed his suspicion that Fillmore was in deep with McCarty.

Fillmore shifted uncomfortably in his chair. "And how does this concern the bank?" he asked.

Taos arose to his full height, and towered over the mealy mouthed banker. "I know thet Doniphan McCarty is out ta git Maddie's ranch. I also know thet he was seen goin' inta yur bank t'other day. If'n I put two an' two together, it add's up ta' some purty bad sess," he seethed.

Fillmore tried to stand, but Taos' hand shot out, and drove him back into his seat. The banker's head snapped back.

"See here, my man'" Fillmore said after he had gathered himself. "What you are saying is purely coincidence," Fillmore stammered.

"It may be, or it may'nt," Taos replied, but any funny business, and I'm takin' it outta yur hide," Taos spat out, before making his exit.

12

Chapter 12

The day of the big meeting of the area ranchers had arrived. Ben had worked with a number of the cowboys to clean out one of the storage barns, and set it up with chairs, while Sage, her mother, and the camp cooks worked to ready the noontime meal. Everything was ready. Now, it was time to wait and see who actually showed up.

The Colonel was fidgety all morning. "Any sign of 'em?" he demanded of Ben when he entered the house.

"Not yet, Colonel," he replied. "It's still early yet."

"Our future is on the line, Ben. We can't fight this one alone," The Colonel said.

"I know," Ben replied. "They'll come through. We jus' gotta get 'em ta understand thet this is a threat ta our way of life, not jus' one ranch."

The Colonel looked out a window, and noticed a cloud of dust in the distance. "Looks like someone's comin'!"

Ben rushed to the window. "See, I told ya! Looks like three carriages."

The Colonel went to the front door, followed by Ben. They stood on the porch and watched the carriages drive through the gate and down their lane. As the carriages approached, the Colonel and Ben stepped down to greet the visitors. Riding on the first Carriage were Jack and Ida Parker.

"Halloo, Jack! Thanks for comin'" the Colonel said, as he offered his hand.

Jack took the Colonel's hand as he stepped out of the carriage. "Been too long, Colonel. Jus wish we were meetin' over better circumstances."

"Good mornin' miss Ida," Ben said, as he helped her out of the carriage.

"Well, good mornin' to you too, Mister Ben Adams," Ida snapped back, her eyes flashing.

One of the Colonel's cowboys took the horse and carriage into one of the stables.

"Where's yur boys?" the Colonel asked.

"Sumbuddy's gotta keep the place goin'," Jack replied.

'If you don't mind headin' over yonder to the large shed, we got refreshments ready, and we'll join ya as soon as we get everybody here," the Colonel instructed, as the next carriage approached.

Don Ramon Padilla was from one of the very earliest Spanish families to settle during the first Spanish colonial period, which dated from 1598 to 1693. His family had ranched in Costilla, near the Colorado border for over two centuries, and his son, Antonio, was considered the best vaquero in all of northern New Mexico Territory. Antonio also had an eye for Sage Adams, though Sage did not return the interest.

"Don Ramon, welcome to my humble ranch!" the Colonel exclaimed, as he bowed to the patrician rancher.

"Thank you, Señor Adams. You know my son, Antonio?"

"Yes, yes, of course," the Colonel replied, and nodded to the younger Padilla.

"Ranching has been a way of life for my family, and my people, for many generations, Señor Adams. When I heard that mining was threatening our way of life, I knew that I must attend this meeting," Don Ramon said.

"I sure am obliged to you for makin' the trip, Don Ramon," the Colonel replied. "Ben, please show Don Ramon, and Antonio to where we'll be meetin'."

"Yes sir, Colonel," Ben replied, and took the Padillas toward the large outbuilding where the Parkers were waiting.

Like clockwork, as Ben and the Padilla's left, the third carriage pulled up. In the carriage was Clinton MacNeill, and his son, Clint Junior. Clinton, like Jack Parker and the Colonel, was a veteran of the Civil War, however, having hailed from the Shenandoah Valley, he served under Stonewall Jackson at First Manassas, the Valley Campaign, the Peninsula Campaign, Second Manassas, Fredericksburg, and at Chancellorsville. After Jackson's Death, MacNeill served on Lee's staff until Appomattox. He retired as a major. He left for the west shortly after the war to start a new life. Old Clint MacNeill, though a Confederate veteran, was good natured around his Yankee counterparts.

"Clint MacNeill, you old war horse," the Colonel boomed as he approached.

"Howdy, Colonel," MacNeill replied.

"Thanks for comin'," the Colonel said.

"Hell, I wouldn't miss this shindig for the world! We can fight on the same side, for once."

"I like your way of thinkin'," the Colonel replied. "C'mon with me, I'll show you to where we're meetin'."

After the Colonel got the MacNeill's to the meeting site, he and Ben walked back to the porch, where they sighted more carriages headed for the ranch.

"Looks like we're gonna have a good crowd," Ben said.

* * *

After everyone had arrived, the Colonel and Ben entered the building. The room had more of a party atmosphere than a meeting called for such a serious purpose as the future of ranching in northern New Mexico Territory.

Sage and her mother had laid out a beautiful spread, and the ranchers were taking full advantage of it, and the opportunity to catch up on each other's daily lives.

Antonio Padilla had cornered Sage, and, as Ben tried to help her escape from the pompous bore, he was waylaid by Ida Parker.

Ida's eyes flashed, and her raven hair flew as she grabbed Ben's arm. "You gonna ignore me all day, Ben Adams?" She demanded.

"Why, Miss Parker, I'm doin' nothin' of the sort," Ben replied, his blue eyes flashing back at Ida's.

"You'd better kiss me quick," she demanded.

"I will, I promise, Ida," Ben whispered. "But I gotta get my sister away from thet chucklehead, Antonio, first."

"I'll help you! It'll be fun! Watch this!" Ida exclaimed, and marched over to where Antonio had Sage cornered.

"Antonio Padilla! How dare you! And after the things you said and promised the other night!" Ida yelled, then slapped the unsuspecting man across the face.

Startled, and red faced, Antonio stammered, "What are you talkin' about?"

"You know exactly what I'm talkin' about, you filthy two timer," Ida was relentless. "Now get out of my sight!"

Still in shock, and red with embarrassment, Antonio rushed to the door, and ran out.

"That was amazin', Ida!" Ben exclaimed.

"You mean that weren't real?" Sage asked.

"Just actin', my darlin'," Ida replied. "Ben said he had to get that scallywag away from you."

"Thank you! Just bein' near him makes me feel all overish," Sage replied.

Ida turned to Ben, and grabbed his arms. "So, how about that kiss?"

"I guess I owe you, at thet," Ben laughed, then leaned down, and planted a kiss on her full lips.

13

Chapter 13

I t had been a long two days, and as the sun went down, Maddie started to worry. Had something happened to Taos? Cam and Tad were murdered on the way back from Telluride. Or had he simply rode off never to be seen again? *Let's face it, I really don't know Taos. Sure he has been helpful, kind, and pleasant to be around, but he could have just had enough, and wandered off. Or, McCarty's men may have ambushed him.* It was that last thought that haunted Maggie. *I couldn't live with myself, knowin' he was murdered for takin' my side,* she thought.

It was with this heaviness in her heart, that Maggie began her evening routine. For the first time in many months, she felt lonely. Sure, she had spent a lot of time alone, but now, she felt empty. When she had finished her evening chores, she stepped into the ranch house, and locked the door. Again, as she did the night before, she locked all the windows, then prepared for her nightly shower.

* * *

Taos didn't want to bake the big bay, but his meeting at the bank put him well behind schedule. He also had to pick up the supplies on Maddie's list before riding out of town. It was a long ride, and he reckoned that he would reach the ranch well after dark. He was sure that would worry Maddie, but he just couldn't push the bay any harder than he was.

He stopped along a creek to water his horse, who he had named Grant, after the General and President. Grant was a gift from his father, and turned out to be a magnificent animal. Grant was strong, able, well built, with plenty of stamina.

Taos took the saddle off of Grant, and led him to the creek. The horse drank well, while he took out some grain from one of the saddle bags, and placed it on a flat, streamside rock. He reached into another saddle bag, and pulled out some hardtack and jerky, then sat down for a quick meal. After his drink, Grant found the pile of grain, and devoured it.

Watered, fed, and rested, Taos and Grant got back on the trail. As he rode along, Taos thought about Maddie, and Ida. The two women were polar opposites. Yes, both were attractive, even beautiful, but in very different ways. Maddie had that wholesome beauty, fair skin, green eyes, and a few freckles. Ida on the other hand, had a devilish beauty, with her raven hair, mocha skin, and dark, flashing eyes. Maddie seemed level, true, and strong, while Ida was flighty at times, and explosive with passion, or rage, at others.

As he rode, Taos wondered if he would ever see Ida again, and if he did, what would he say? Would time heal her hurt at the loss of her father? Would she hold on to the hatred? He guessed that she would. Could he ever go back to being Ben Adams? Could he make a new life here in Colorado, near, yet so far from northern New Mexico? He certainly felt something for Maddie. He hadn't fully identified it yet, but it was there. Thoughts of Ida clogged his senses. One thing he knew for sure, he'd have to figure out what to do about Ida before he could move on with his life.

* * *

After showering, drying off, and putting on her nightgown, Maddie did one last walk through the house. It was after dark, but she ventured out onto the porch for one more look in hopes to see Taos riding in. Her heart sank, as the moonlight showed nothing.

Maddie stepped back inside, and locked and barred the door. She had the ranch house buttoned up tight. Next, she took the shotgun off the rack, and as was her habit, taught to her long ago by Cam, she checked to see if it was loaded. Then she put it on the bed, and climbed in next to it, so it would be at the ready.

She took a long time to doze off, and then, she slept fitfully. Every little noise had her sitting upright, shotgun in hand. Then she would doze again. Having decided it was just the noises of the night on the range.

After what seemed an eternity of restless sleep, Maddie heard a different noise. She slipped out of bed, put on a robe, picked up the shotgun, and stepped out of her bedroom.

She heard it again, a tapping sound. But, where did it come from? She cocked her head slightly, and heard it again. Her brain was foggy, and she had trouble waking up.

The tap was louder this time, and she could finally identify the tapping as knocking at the front door.

She walked up to the door, leveled the shotgun, and asked, "Who's out there?" In her bravest voice.

"Maddie, it's me, Taos," came the muffled reply.

"Oh, thank the Lord!" she exclaimed, as she threw the shotgun down on the kitchen table, then rushed to unbar, and unlock the door.

When the door swung open, Maddie was ecstatic to see Taos' tall, solid frame crowding the doorway. He stepped in, and she fell into his arms.

"Oh, Taos, you're home!" she whispered into his chest. Thank God you're home! I was so worried about you, thought something happened, or maybe," She stopped herself. She must not speak of her insecurities.

"I'm just glad you are here safe and sound," she whispered.

"I'm glad to be home," Taos whispered in Maddie's ear, as he felt her body lean into his. Home, that sounded good. It had been a long time since Taos had felt at home anywhere.

Maddie caught herself, and stepped back. "You must be hungry," she stammered, as she felt her blood surge, and warm her all over.

"It's late, and yu must be tired," I can wait 'till mornin'," Taos replied.

"I'll hear none of that," Maddie said. "You get washed up, and I'll fix you somethin'."

"Yu sure?" Taos asked.

"I'm sure I'm sure," she replied. "Besides, I couldn't sleep now if I wanted to. You go wash up."

Taos did as he was told, while Maddie started a fire in the stove.

* * *

Taos sat down to a full breakfast consisting of fried eggs, bacon, biscuits, and beans, plus a mug of hot, black coffee.

"You tryin' ta' fatten me up fer Thanksgivin'?" Taos asked, his blue eyes twinkled.

"I can't have you wasting' away to nothin', now can I," Maddie replied. Her eyes smiled back at his.

"Thanks, just the same. This is darn good."

"What kept you so long?" Maddie asked, after taking a sip of her coffee.

Taos finished chewing a mouthful of food, swallowed, and spoke. "I had to make a stop at the bank, so I had to wait for it to open before I could ride out."

"I didn't realize you was goin' to the bank," Maddie replied.

"I wasn't plannin' to, but I had a talk with Bill Haney. I went to thank him for sendin' me yur way, an' he mentioned thet he had seen McCarty at the bank t'other day, an' he looked like he was upta no good," Taos replied.

Maddie bit her lip. "What happened at the bank?"

Taos paused to swallow. "I let the banker know thet any underhanded deals with McCarty would be detrimental ta his health."

"What do ya' think McCarty could do to me through the bank?"

"Does the bank hold a note on yur ranch?" Taos enquired.

"Yes, not a lot of money, but the ranch is collateral on the loan," Maddie said. Her eyes widened. "You don't think?"

Taos slammed his fist on the table, and his plate jumped. "That son of a . . . I bet thet's what he was plannin'! Probably wanted ta buy the note, then call it in!"

Maddie's hands went to her forehead. She stood and paced, then turned back to face Taos, who was standing by this time. "You don't think the scoundrel went through with it?" she asked.

"I'm sure McCarty had a tidy sum in it for Fillmore in the deal," Taos said. "Fillmore knows I'm on ta them, though. I doubt he'd go through with it. Poor bastard, uh excuse my language, the poor fellow is stuck between McCarty an' me."

14

Chapter 14

T he Colonel stood at the front of the crowded building. He beamed with pride over the turnout, which was much better than he had expected. Ranchers that he had invited, had invited other ranchers, and they had shown up.

The Colonel held an ax handle, and he rapped it on the table in front of him. The room quieted, and the ranchers turned toward him.

"Let's get this thing started," he said. "I'm sure you all have an idea why we're all meetin', but let me give you all the story, so we all know exactly what we're talkin' about."

The Colonel walked around to the front of the table, and half sat on it. "As you all know, I've been ranchin' here in Questa for some time now, and my family and I have built a reputation for producin' prime livestock, and we have. But times have changed. We're havin' lots of cripples borned, many die right after they're calved. The river is dead. This all happened after the

Copper Mountain Minin' Company opened." He stopped to fill his pipe, light it and take a puff. "Ben and Sage took a ride up the Red River. No bugs, no fish. Sterile as a mule. They rode upta the Copper Mountain Minin' Company, and got a first hand look at the operation, which is owned by a Mr. Van der Veer. Quite the nasty sort, as Ben an' Sage tell it. They got a good look at the devastation, slag all over the place, cuttin' down trees to beat the band. It's pretty obvious that they's poisonin' the river. When Ben said somethin' about it, this Mr. Van der Veer threatened him with all out war. Said times were a changin'. The country was gettin' civilized, there ain't no room for cow punchers, and ranchers, and ranchin'. Said he had a hundred men willin' and ready to fight. Said us ranchers couldn't raise near that many." The Colonel took a long suck on his pipe before letting the smoke out slowly. He scanned the room before he spoke again.

"Now, I know you all are thinkin' it's only the Colonel's ranch. The mine ain't hurttin' us. And, that may be true, for now. But, sure as I'm standin' heah before you, it will come to you. All the mountains around this territory is full of minerals, and when they suck 'em outa one mountain, they're gonna go on to the next. And thet may be the one that poisons your water."

Jack Parker stood up, and looked over the crowd.

"I've seen this happen first hand back east. In Pennsylvania, the trees are black with coal dust, and the rivers is choked with it. Kids all have a cough. There's no good in it," Parker said.

Ramon Padilla stood up next. "It was a matter of time. There have been problems in Colorado, not far from my ranch."

"And how did they handle it up there?" the Colonel asked.

"They found ways to compromise," Ramon replied. "The mining companies were willing to limit their impact on the surrounding areas. They left certain valleys alone, so ranches would have clean water."

"We could do that here. I looked over the map. There's another stream that runs away from our ranch, and dries up in the desert to the east. It wouldn't bother nobody if he used that. We'd just have to get him to move his smelting operation a half a mile," Sage said.

"All due respect, little lady, but it sounds like this Van der Veer ain't the compromisin' type," Clinton MacNeill spoke up.

"I can't imagine he wants a war," another rancher shouted from the back.

"I don't think he cares much one way or t'other," Ben said. "Besides, he's got all the power. I don't think we could put together much more than fifty good men to go toe to toe with him."

"I think it's worth a try," the Colonel said. "We can put together a proposal. We can offer manpower to help move his operation. Ramon, Jack, Clinton, and I'll pay Mr. Van der Veer a visit."

"What ifn' he don't go fer it?" a rancher yelled.

"Well, we'll have to cross that bridge when we come to it, I suppose," The Colonel said.

"I'm pretty sure he's gonna laugh in our faces," Clinton MacNeill said. "We better have a plan for thet."

"I agree with Clint," Ramon spoke up. "If Van der Veer says no, we'll need to have a response ready."

"He ain't afraid ta go to war. He made thet clear," Ben said. "Is theah somethin' else thet ken be done?"

"What about the territorial governor?" Ida asked.

"We can write him a letter, but what good it'll do, I don't know. Far as I can tell, there ain't no laws that've been broken," the Colonel replied.

"Maybe in the interest of keepin' the peace, he'd get involved," Ida Parker said.

"Sage, you got good handwritin', write up a letter, an' we'll all sign it," the Colonel said.

"Yes, sir," she replied, and left the building.

"I think that we should be ready ta go to war," Ben said.

"I agree with Ben," Clinton MacNeill said.

"Same here," Frank Lynch said.

"Let's take a minute," Travis Clark said. "Do we want ta' get inta' a war with a man who has twice our number?"

"I know it seems a lot ta' ask. After all, it isn't your ranches on the line, for now. But it will be soon enough," the Colonel said. "I can't make any of you go to war, but I've talked it over with my family, and my hands, and we're gonna do what we have ta' do."

"Same here," Clinton MacNeill said.

* * *

Sage rushed in with the letter, and handed it to her father.

"Thank you, my dear," he said. "Listen up, listen up," he shouted over the din.

"I'm gonna read the letter that my daughter, Sage, was kind enough to pen for us. Then, if so inclined, please come up and sign it, or make yur mark."

The Colonel began reading. *"Dear Governor Ross, We, the undersigned, members of the Northern New Mexico Territory Cattlemen's Association, are writing to make you aware of a situation that threatens, not only us, and our way of life, but has the potential to threaten ranchers in all of New Mexico Territory. Recently, a mining company, The Copper Mountain Mining Company, owned by a Mr. Van der Veer, began operations on the headwaters of the Red River. Since then, the Red River has been impacted by the operations. Whole mountainsides are being stripped of trees, and slag wash is running into the Red River. This has directly affected the Los Piñons Ranch, based on the lower Red River, in Questa, owned by retired Colonel Adams and his family. A well-known, and profitable, ranch has been experiencing extremely high calf mortality rates, and deformity rates since the Copper Mountain Mines opened.*

The Association is concerned that a once thriving business will be destroyed by this mining operation. We are also concerned that this kind of operation could open up anywhere in mineral rich, northern New Mexico, and threaten a traditional way of life for all ranchers in the area.

In addition, when Colonel Adams' son and daughter visited the mining site, they were accosted by the owner, a Mr. Van der Veer, and threatened with an all out war.

We, as an association, understand that there are different interest groups vying for use of the land, but, when one mine threatens a ranch, and harms the area's woods and waters, that is something else. We implore you, your honor, to step in, on our behalf, and the behalf of the future of the Territory of New Mexico.

Sincerely, The Northern New Mexico Territory Cattlemen's Association."

The Colonel took a breath, and charged his pipe before speaking again. "Well, there you have it. I think it is a fine letter, and I'm gonna sign it. How about all of you?"

A resounding cheer filled the room.

"Next order of business. Who should deliver it?" The Colonel asked.

"I think it should be your son, Ben, Colonel," Jack Parker said. "He's been there, seen the operation, and met Van der Veer."

"I agree," said Frank Lynch.

"All in favor of Ben Adams ridin' down to Santa Fe to deliver the letter to the Governor, say aye."

They shouted "aye!" in unison.

"Alright then. It's settled. Don't forget to sign on your way out," the Colonel said.

15

Chapter 15

Mason Fillmore fidgeted on the rented horse. Boston was not the kind of place that allowed for a lot of interaction with large animals. The only thing that worried the banker more than falling off his horse was how McCarty was going to react to him backing out on the deal to cheat Maggie Ferguson out of her ranch. Making a little extra money was not worth looking down the business end of that wild-eyed cowboy's Colts. Though, he wasn't sure he would fare much better with McCarty.

After the long, dusty ride, on which he fell off the horse twice, Fillmore rode through the gate, and up to the sprawling ranch house. As it happened, Doniphan McCarty had just stepped out on the porch for a smoke, and his face reddened when he saw the tenderfoot banker ride up.

He threw his cigar into the dust, and stormed over to Fillmore.

"What the hell are you doin' here?" he demanded. "We can't be seen together."

Fillmore dismounted, rather clumsily, and tied his ride to a post. "That's what I am here to talk to you about, Mister McCarty."

"Oh, it is?" McCarty sneered.

"I just can't go through with it," Fillmore stuttered.

"Let's take a walk, Mason. I can call you Mason, can't I, uh, Mason?"

"Um, sure, Mister McCarty," Fillmore replied.

McCarty steered Fillmore around the back of the house.

"You see, Mason, we had a deal, and nobody breaks a deal with me."

"I understand that, Mister McCarty, but I just can't go through with it," Fillmore pleaded.

"And you must have a reason for your change of heart. Need more money? Greedy, is that it?" McCarty snapped back.

No. Not at all, Mister McCarty," Fillmore answered.

McCarty turned and faced Fillmore. "What is it, then, Mason? What could have made you turn on such a sweet deal? Not your conscience. Lord knows a man like you ain't got no conscience. You screw people all the time. Don't you, Mason?"

"Mister McCarty, now that just isn't fair."

"Then, enlighten me." McCarty said.

"I just can't do it," Fillmore snapped back.

McCarty rubbed the stubble on his chin for a moment. "Somebody got to you, didn't they?" he asked in a quiet voice.

"Mmm, yes, sir," Fillmore replied.

"And he scared you, did he?" still quiet, and soothing.

"He was the scariest man I've ever seen."

"And does this scary man have a name, Mason?" McCarty cajoled.

"Um, yes, kind of," Fillmore replied.

"Kind of?" McCarty asked.

"He said folks called him Taos," Fillmore replied.

McCarty's face reddened, and his dark eyes narrowed for just an instant.

Then, he composed himself. "Well, why didn't you just tell me in the first place? I certainly can't fault you for that, Mason, now can I?" McCarty said, as he put his left arm around Fillmore's shoulder.

"Thank you for understanding, Mr. McCarty," he said, visibly relieved.

"Not at all," McCarty said, as he pulled the Derringer from his vest pocket, jammed it into Fillmore's ribs, and pulled the trigger. "Not at all," he repeated, as Fillmore's limp body hit the dust.

* * *

On his father's orders, Rance McCarty tossed Fillmore's corpse into a wagon.

"You know what to tell the Marshall, right?" McCarty asked.

"Yes, sir," Rance replied before climbing up and settling into the bench seat. "I was lookin' for some cattle thet wandered off in the direction of the Ferguson ranch, and I found him layin' on the ground, jess a moanin' an' a groanin'. I kneeled down ta check on him, and seen he was hurt bad. Had a bullet hole in his side. I seen he was tryin' ta say sumpin' an' I leaned over. He whispered, 'Taos', then he died. I loaded him in the wagon, an brung him in," Rance recited.

"Good. Now, get goin'," McCarty said.

Rance snapped the reins, and yelled, "Yee ha!" and the horses started.

McCarty stood and watched as his son drove out. He took out a cigar, bit the end off, stuck a match off the sole of his boot, and lit the cigar with a big puff of gray smoke.

"That'll fix him."

16

Chapter 16

The Governor's door opened, and Ben, who had been waiting not so patiently, stood up to greet him.

"Mister Adams? Sorry to keep you waiting," Governor Ross said, as he stretched out his hand for Ben to shake.

"Ben, please, and not at all, sir. Thank yu for yur time," Ben drawled, trying not to let his annoyance show. He knew the Governor had a reputation of letting people stew, in order to feed his air of self importance, and, also, to put them off their game. Still, it was tough to not let it bother him.

Ross held the door for Ben, and said, "Come in, and make yourself comfortable."

Ben walked in, and took a seat in front of the Governor's desk. Ross walked around the desk, lifted up a cigar box, and offered Ben a cigar.

"Smoke?"

"No thank yu, sir."

"Suit yourself," Ross said, as he took a cigar for himself, clipped the end, with ivory handled scissors, and struck a match. He lit the cigar, and puffed out clouds of blue-gray smoke. After a pause, he said, "I read your letter. You're here to represent The Northern New Mexico Territory Cattlemen's Association?"

"Yes, sir," Ben replied.

Ross took another long puff, then blew it out in Ben's direction, and looked for a reaction.

Ben sat cool as a cucumber. He was ready for this.

Seeing no reaction from Ben, Ross stood up, and gazed out the window at the native people selling their wares in the plaza. He turned to Ben. "Come here. Take a look out this window, and tell me what you see, Ben."

Ben stood, and stepped to the window. He took a look out at the Santa Fe Plaza, in front of the Palace of the Governors. "Well, I see the Plaza, lots of people, folks ridin', folks sellin', and folks buyin'." Ben drawled.

"Who do you see selling their wares, Ben."

"Well, it looks mostly like Navajo ta me, sir."

"That's what most people call them. They were once a very proud people, called themselves the Diné People. Means Children of the Holy People. Had a civilization going back a thousand years in these parts. Now look at 'em. Out there peddling trinkets, hoping for a few extra cents, here and there. Practically beggars."

"I'm sorry fer that, sir, but I don't understand what that has ta do with us," Ben replied.

Ross took a long drag from his cigar, turned toward Ben, and let the smoke go.

Ben flashed red, but kept his composure. After all, this was the Territorial Governor that he was speaking to.

Ross took a moment before speaking. "Times change, Ben. That's my point. Times changed for the Diné, times are changin' for you cattlemen. The Diné didn't, or couldn't, change with the times. Now, you see them, the greatest tribe of the southwest, sellin' junk to people who don't need it.

Cattle are being grown all over the west, Ben. Doesn't matter whether it is in New Mexico, Texas, Oklahoma, or wherever. New Mexico, though, is full of minerals. Not every place is full of minerals, Ben. The future for New Mexico is in mining, not ranching. Now, take another look out that window, Ben. Is that how you want to see yourself? Times are changing. Change with them, or get left behind."

* * *

The Colonel, Jack, Ramone, and Clinton made the long trek up to the Copper Mountain Mines. The men shuddered as they passed the devastation caused by the mining operation.

"I never dreamed it would be this bad," Jack Parker said.

"Yup, this is somethin' y'all have to look forward to, if we don't make a stand now.," the Colonel answered.

"Let us hope that this Van der Veer is as reasonable as the mine owners to the north," Ramone offered.

"I doubt it, from what I've heard, but we don't have much choice, now do we," Clinton replied.

As they approached the main building, a stocky fellow stepped out, and approached riders.

"Thet must be Culpepper. He fits the description Ben gave me," the Colonel said, before he spurred his horse, and rode toward Culpepper.

The others did likewise.

When the four ranchers had met up with Culpepper, he spoke up, "You men must be lost, so I'll give yu directions ta where you need ta go."

"We ain't lost, mister," the Colonel replied.

"Didn't yu see the No Tresspassin' signs?" Culpepper asked.

"We did," the Colonel replied.

"Then, whatcha doin' on minin' company land?"

"We came to talk to Mister Van der Veer," the Colonel said.

"An' who should I say is callin'?"

"Representatives of the Northern New Mexico Cattlemen's Association," the Colonel said.

"Well, Mister Van der Veer is a busy man. I'll tell him, but I ain't makin' no promises," Culpepper replied, before he turned around and sauntered back into the main building.

A few moments later, he reappeared.

"It must be yur lucky day. Mister Van der Veer says he will see you. Follow me."

The ranchers dismounted, tied up their horses to the hitching posts, and followed Culpepper inside. Then, he directed them to a door, and ushered them into a large room with a long table surrounded by chairs. Van der Veer was sitting in the largest of the chairs at the head of the table.

Van der Veer stood up. "Welcome, gentleman. I'm Hendrik Van der Veer, I own and operate the Copper Mountain Mining Company." He offered his hand.

"I am Colonel Adams."

"Jack Parker."

"Ramon Padilla."

"Clinton MacNeill."

Each man shook Van der Veer's hand.

"Have a seat, gentlemen," Van der Veer said.

Each man sat down.

"My understanding is that you represent some sort of cattleman's group," Van der Veer said.

"The Northern New Mexico Cattlemen's Association," the Colonel corrected.

"Ah, yes, whatever," Van der Veer dismissed. "Now, what is it that you want from me? I'm sure you all didn't ride up here just to say hello."

"That's true," the Colonel replied. "My son and daughter rode up here a while ago."

"Oh, yes, I remember them quite well. Impertinent pair, I must say."

"I've raised them to speak up," the Colonel replied. "Anyway, this mine is destroying my ranching operation."

"Your ranching operation is your responsibility, not mine," Van der Veer said.

The Colonel's face reddened, and he stiffened in his chair. Ramone put his hand on the Colonel's shoulder, and spoke up, "You see, Mister Van der Veer, the Red River, which runs through Colonel Adams' ranch has been poisoned by the runoff from your mining operation. We are all in favor of different interests being successful, but one shouldn't impair another. We have a proposal for you that we believe will satisfy all sides."

"Why should I listen to any proposal of yours? I'm doing fine right now. I employ over a hundred men on better wages than your cowboys make. Why should I change anything?"

"In the spirit of being good neighbors, sir," Ramone replied. "In southern Colorado, the ranchers and miners have worked it out, so both prosper. I don't see why we can't work something out here, too?"

"Because this ain't Colorado, and I don't care if you succeed, or not," Van der Veer snapped.

"Let's be reasonable," Clinton said. "Hear our proposal."

"Sure, I'll listen, but, unless you can convince me otherwise, I ain't changin' a thing."

"Fair enough," Ramone replied. He unrolled a map that he had been carrying, and spread it out on the table in front of Van der Veer. He pointed to a spot on the map. "This is your mining operation here, Señor." He moved his finger. "And this is the Red River. And this is the Colonel's ranch. You can see how waste from your operation is going directly into the Red, and to the ranch."

He moved his hand again to point out a small brook. "You see this brook, Señor? This brook dries out into the desert, over here. If we help you move your operation just over the ridge, here, the wash will go into the dry desert, and not hurt anyone," Ramone said.

"I've heard your proposal. Now, get out," Van der Veer snapped.

"My son is, right now, on his way to meet with the Governor. We will see about that," the Colonel said.

"A waste of time, I assure you. I said get out, or do I have to have you thrown out?"

"We'll leave, but you ain't heard the last of this," Jack Parker said.

* * *

Ben figured The Colonel wouldn't be happy with the outcome of his meeting with Governor Ross, but was not prepared for the outburst.

"Confound that sonofabitch! He's the one that acquitted Johnson, you know! Disgraced himself to the flag he fought under!" He went on for some time, before Ben cut in.

"Listen, Colonel. Swearin' ain't gonna' change anythin'," Ben interjected.

"Pour me a bourbon, boy. Make it a double. And, pour one for yourself. We gotta figure this out," the Colonel ordered.

Ben did as he was told, and the two walked out to the porch, the place where they did their best thinking, and drinking. The Colonel took a long, slow swallow from his glass before sitting down. Ben took a sip, and leaned on the rail. He took in the expanse of prairie in front of him.

"Whatcha' thinkin', Ben?" the Colonel asked.

"I'm just thinkin' about how hard yu, Mother, Sage, and I have worked to make this ranch what it is, and how quickly we may lose it all," Ben replied, eyes still on the prairie.

"Between that sonofabitch, Van der Veer, and the no good Governor, looks like we may have a fight on our hands," the Colonel said. He took another hard swallow of the Kentucky straight, and continued, "I'll be goddamned if I let that bastard steal what we have built here!"

"Looks like we'll have ta set up another meetin'. Only this one'll be fer keeps," Ben replied.

17

Chapter 17

Maddie and Taos were mending a fence by the chicken coop when Sheriff Jim Nolan rode up.

Startled, Maddie said, "Good mornin' Sheriff, what brings you out here?"

"Mornin', Maddie. Ah need to have a conversation with you, and your man, heah."

"Sure. Coffee?"

"No thank yu," he said as he dismounted, which better revealed his imposing figure. At Six foot-three inches, with broad shoulders, Jim Nolan was a big man. The little bit of gray hair at his temples was the only thing that belied his true age of forty-five. "This'll only take a few minutes."

Taos had stopped working, and sized up the Sheriff while he and Maddie spoke.

"Well, at least come out of the sun onto the porch," Maddie said.

"Sure," he acquiesced.

The three walked toward the ranch house, the Sheriff led his horse, and tied it to a hitching post, as they got to the porch. Once on the porch, the three sat down.

"I'll get right ta it," the Sheriff said. "It seems the local banker, Mason Fillmore, was found shot on yur land, sometime yestiday.

"Oh, that is just awful!" Maddie said.

"The person who brought him in reported that the last word he spoke was, 'Taos', and I assume that would be you," the Sheriff said, turning his gaze toward Taos.

"Thet's what folks call me," Taos drawled.

"I'm Sheriff Jim Nolan, and, I believe that you'll find that I am fair,"

"Who brought him in?" Maddie asked.

"It was Rance McCarty. He said he was out roundin' up strays, when he saw Fillmore, near dead," Nolan replied.

"Well, everybody knows that the McCarty's are out to get my ranch," Maddie replied, her hands fidgeting with her skirt.

"True, Maddie, but your man, Taos, heah, paid a visit to the bank a few days ago, and the bank tellers say that Mistah Fillmore was visibly shaken when he left."

"Sure, I stopped in," Taos offered. "I had it on good confidence that Doniphan McCarty had paid him a visit a short time ago. I expected that McCarty was going to buy the note on Maddie's ranch, and then call it in. So, I went ta speak to Fillmore. Sure, I threatened him. Told him if he was up ta any funny business, he'd have ta deal with me. That was it."

Nolan eyed Taos' guns. "Forty-fives?"

"Yes, Taos said, and unbuckled his gun belt, then handed it to Nolan.

"Nice looking firearms. You got any others?"

"Just my Winchester," Taos replied.

"44-40?" Nolan asked.

"Yessir," Taos said.

Nolan turned to Maddie. "Ken you show me his room?"

"Uhm, I guess so," she replied.

"Taos, stay right here," Nolan said to the tall, lanky, cowboy.

"I ain't movin'."

Maddie entered the house, followed by the Sheriff, who had Taos' gun belt slung over his shoulder.

She walked him to Taos' room. "Here it is, Sheriff."

Maddie stood outside the room with her arms crossed, as Nolan searched the room.

"What are you expectin' to find, Sheriff?" she asked.

"I'm not expectin' anythin'. But, I'm just makin' sure Taos was tellin' the truth aboot his guns."

"What he told you is all I've ever seen," Maddie offered.

Having finished searching the room, Nolan said, "I expected as much. How about you? Any firearms?"

"Just that old scattergun over yonder," she said, pointing at the shotgun on its rack. "And a big old six shooter, that I never learned how to use, as much as Cam tried to get me to practice."

Nolan nodded and walked out of the house, followed by Maddie. Once on the porch, he handed Taos his gunbelt.

"Satisfied?" Taos asked.

"Yup. Fillmore was shot with a slow moving .41 caliber bullet at close range. In fact, theah was burn marks on his clothing, and his flesh. Plus, the angle of entrance was probably made by a man much shorter than yu."

"Yup, my forty-fives would have blown right through him at close range like thet. I bet Doniphan McCarty has a pocket pistol. I also bet thet Fillmore rode out there to back out of a deal, and got killed fer it," Taos opined.

"You shoulda' been a lawman, Taos," Nolan said. "I guess I'll ride out and pay Mistah McCarty a visit. Not that it'll do much good. I'm sure he's ditched the Derringer by now. Have a good day, and sorry to bother you."

"Not likely anyone 'll be pinning a tin star ta my chest anytime soon. No bother at all, Sheriff, just get that bastard, McCarty," Taos said.

"Good luck, Jim," Maddie said.

Nolan untied his horse, jumped in the saddle and rode off, with a wave of his Stetson.

"Do you think McCarty did it?" Maddie asked, after Nolan rode out of sight.

"No doubt in my mind," Taos replied.

"What an awful man. He'll stop at nothing to get this ranch," Maddie said.

"I'll stop him."

18

Chapter 18

J im Nolan had spent many years on the range, and had dealt with some pretty rough characters, but men like McCarty were the worst. He had stared down some of the fastest guns in the west. Men like Doniphan were different. They'd plug you in the back, and think nothing of it. Jim knew to be on guard, as he rode onto McCarty's ranch.

Doniphan McCarty, along with his son, Rance, and a few of his cowboys were watching a bronc being busted, when Nolan rode up.

McCarty turned his head at the sound of hooves, his eyes widened, and face reddened, for just an instant. Something that was not lost on Jim Nolan.

McCarty nodded at Nolan. "Well, hello, Sheriff. Haven't seen you out heah in quite some time."

"That's so. You got someplace we can talk quietly? Tough to hear somebody with all this hootin' and hollerin'."

Why, sure, Sheriff. Why don't we head over ta the house. It'll be cooler on the porch, out of the sun, anyway," McCarty replied.

Nolan dismounted.

"Rance, water the Sheriff's hoss," McCarty yelled over the din the cowboys were making.

"Yessir," Rance replied, and took the reins from Nolan.

"I'm sure obliged," Nolan said.

"Yup," Rance replied, averting his eyes.

"Well, let's get to it," McCarty demanded when they stepped up onto the porch.

Nolan took his time sitting down, fetched a cigar from inside his vest, bit the end off, put the cigar in his mouth, struck a match, and lit the cigar. He took a long, slow drag, then expelled the smoke in a drawn out woosh.

"I'm sure Rance told you aboot findin' that banker, Fillmore out on the Ferguson ranch," Nolan replied.

"He mentioned it."

"Did he mention that he tried ta pin the blame on Fergusson's man, Taos?"

"All's I can recall is thet he told me Fillmore's last word was Taos. I don't see how thet's pinnin' the blame on anybody," McCarty sneered.

"No, I guess not. Not directly, anyway."

"So, why is yu here, Sheriff?"

"I had Doc Evans take a look at Fillmore's body. He found the bullet, lodged against a rib. Fillmore was shot at close range."

"That's too bad, but why are you tellin' me?" McCarty demanded, his face reddening.

"It's just that Taos has two Colts, which, at that range, would have gone right through Fillmore. The entrance wound was made by someone much shorter than Taos."

"Maybe by that Fergusson woman? Lots of women carry a pocket pistol."

"Who said anything about a pocket pistol?" Nolan asked.

"Well, it'd have to be, wouldn't it? Close range and all?" McCarty stammered.

"That's what I think, but didn't say it. Do you have such a pistol, Mr. McCarty?"

"Why would I want one of those things?"

"People do all kinds of things for all kinds of reasons, Mistah McCarty," Nolan replied.

McCarty gathered himself up. "I don't like what yur insinuatin' Nolan."

"I'm not insinuatin' nothin', Mistah McCarty. I'm merely investigatn' a murder. So, I ask again. Do you have a pocket pistol, Mistah McCarty?" Nolan replied.

"You ken search me, and my whole goddam ranch, for all I care," McCarty snapped.

"There'll be no need for that," Nolan replied. He knew that McCarty had long since disposed of the weapon. He was sure that McCarty had killed Fillmore, but there was no way that he was going to be able to pin the murder on him. "Thank you for your time."

* * *

It was dusk when Taos noticed the rider approach. He checked his Colts, just to be sure, then called to Maddie.

"What is it?" Maddie answered.

"Rider commin'. Get that scattergun," Taos yelled.

Maddie ran into the house, took the shotgun off the rack, grabbed a handful of shells, loaded the weapon, and ran back out onto the porch. In the meantime, Taos had picked up his Winchester, which he always kept near at hand.

Maddie and Taos watched anxiously, as the rider continued his approach. After a few long moments, the rider was recognized as Sheriff Nolan.

Both Maggie and Taos relaxed with the recognition.

"Don't shoot!" Nolan shouted, with a laugh.

"I'm sure glad it's you, Sheriff" Maddie replied.

"News?" Taos asked

Nolan dismounted before answering. "McCarty is guilty as hell, but I can't prove it."

"That figures," Maddie replied, as she clenched her fists for a moment.

"Mind if I cool down, feed, and water my hoss before ridin' out?" Nolan asked.

"I'll have none of that!" Maddie snapped. "You'll stay here the night."

"Oh, Miss Maddie, I can't put you out like that," Nolan replied.

"You'll stay here. It's just another potato in the pot, and we'll make room inside for you to sleep."

"I'm much obliged," Nolan said.

After Nolan's horse was taken care of, the three went into the ranch house. The smell of beef stew filled their senses as they passed through the door. Taos struck a match, lit the gas lamps, and a soft yellow glow filled the room.

"My, thet smells good!" Nolan exclaimed.

Maddie scrubbed and chopped up a large potato, and, as promised, put it in the pot. "There! As soon as that softens up, we can eat."

"I can't thank yu enough," Nolan said.

"Ridin' all night, after ridin' all day, an't good for yu or your hoss," Taos drawled.

"You must be parched, Marshall. Let me get you a big glass of water," Maddie said.

"Much obliged," Nolan said.

Taos and Nolan sat at the kitchen table, while Maddie fetched the water.

"Outside, yu said thet you knowed McCarty is guilty," Taos opened the conversation.

"Yup, but I got no evidence. I could tell by the way he reacted ta' things I asked, and said. He also let a couple a' things slip."

"He's one slippery snake," Taos replied.

"He sure enough is," Nolan said as Maddie placed two glasses of water on the table.

"Thanks, Maddie," Taos said.

"Thank yu," Nolan offered.

"So, he murders the Banker, and just gets away with it?" Maddie demanded. Her eyes flashed, and her cheeks burned red.

"McCarty is the worst kind of bad,' Nolan replied. "I'd much rather face a lightnin' fast gunslinger than his type."

"What do we do now? He's out to get my ranch by hook or crook," Maddie complained.

"We keep an eye on him, Maddie. Not much else I can say," Nolan answered.

"Don't yu worry aboot thet," Taos replied. "I'll keep on the lookout for him, an' his tricks.

Maddie stirred the stew, then took out eating utensils, and placed them on the table. Taos set three places, while Maddie took out bowls., and placed them next to the pot. Next, she took a fresh-baked loaf of bread out of the warmer, sliced it, put it on a board, and brought it to the table.

"Thet smells jus' wonderful," Taos said. He grabbed the butter off the countertop, and brought it to the table.

Maddie ladled out the stew, and Taos took the bowls, and set them on the table.

"This looks delicious!" Nolan exclaimed.

"We got plenty, so eat up, Sheriff," Maddie said as she sat down.

After dinner, while Maddie took her evening shower, Taos and Nolan sat in front of the fire, each had a glass of whiskey.

"Thet Maddie Ferguson is one heck of a woman," Nolan said. "Good-lookin', hard-working, and a good cook, ta' boot!"

"Yes. I'm lucky ta be workin' for her. She's a good boss, too."

"If I was ten years younger, an' single," Nolan sighed.

Taos finished his glass, and put it down. "Well, we should get yu settled for the night. Yu got a long ride tomorrow," he said, not wanting to engage in that line of conversation. After all, he had his own feelings for Maddie.

19

Chapter 19

The next morning brought promise of real heat. It was already warm by the time Nolan had ridden out.

After the morning chores were finished, Maddie and Taos walked to the rain barrel, which was getting low, for there had been little rain this spring. Taos dipped the ladle into the barrel, and then handed it to Maddie, who took a long drink, and handed it back. He did the same.

Taos wiped the droplets of sweat off his brow with his shirt sleeve.

"It sure is gonna' be hot today, Maddie," he drawled.

"And tomorrow too, I fear," she replied. "It sure is gettin' to be dry."

"Yup," Taos agreed. "I've been thinkin'."

"About what?" Maddie asked.

"Aboot, mebbe we should drive the herd up to the High Meadow."

"Do you really think it's necessary?" she asked.

"I'm not sure, but since McCarty's latest trick didn't work, I'd be expectin' him ta come up with somethin' else," Taos drawled.

Maddie's face flushed. "Oh, you are right! There's no tellin' what he might do."

"Yup, an' if the herd is up in the High Meadow, it would be safer. Plus, if it is gonna be as dry as it looks, better ta make the drive while the cattle is in good health."

"I agree," Maddie said. "When do you want to get started?"

"I think we should take a ride out this afternoon and' start roundin' 'em up. Then, get an early start in the mornin'," Taos offered.

"That makes sense," Maddie said. "Let's go eat some lunch."

* * *

After lunch, they saddled up, crossed the San Miguel, and rode together, out to the prairie. Away from the rushing river, the air was much hotter. They found their cattle feeding near feeder streams, and resting under patches of cottonwoods.

"Looks like it won't be too big a job roundin' 'em up," Taos said.

"I think we should start movin' them to the ranch. What do you think?" Maddie asked.

"Yup, we can move 'em to this side of the San Miguel to spend the night, then cross 'em over, and drive 'em up the canyon to the High Meadow tomorrow," Taos replied.

"If you ride around the other side, I'll work 'em from here," Maddie said.

"Yes, ma'am," Taos said before spurring his horse.

Maddie watched in amazement as Taos worked the herd. Together, they had the dogies rounded up and heading toward the San Miguel in short order. This was the first time in a year that she felt a real sense of purpose. She was proud of her abilities, and she loved the teamwork. She felt like she and Taos had been riding together for years. He seemed to always guess what her next move was going to be, and complemented it on his side of the herd.

They stopped pushing the herd a hundred yards from the river. The cattle settled, and began grazing. Some wandered to the water to drink.

Taos rode up to where Maddie was sitting on her horse, in the shade of a cottonwood tree.

"You ain't bad in the saddle, Maddie," Taos drawled.

Maddie beamed knowing that this was a big compliment coming from Taos. "You ain't so bad yerself," she answered, in imitation of Taos' drawl.

Taos laughed, and rode closer. "We make a good team," he said, his eyes fixed on hers.

When she stopped melting, she said, "Yes, I think we do," with a smile on her face, and a twinkle in her eye.

Taos noticed her chest heaving, and felt a warm rush through his body.

"I don't know about you, but I could use a cool drink of water," Maddie said.

Shaken from his spell, Taos replied, "Sure, thet sounds good."

They rode down the river bank, and crossed the San Miguel. Then, up to the stables, where they dismounted, unsaddled, and watered their horses.

When they got to the rain barrel, Taos dipped the ladle, and handed it to Maddie. Their eyes met as she grasped the ladle. Neither one looked away for a long moment. Her green eyes were riveted to his blue eyes. Finally, Taos let go of the ladle, and the spell was broken. Maddie fumbled with it, and spilled water on her chest as she tried to drink. Her face reddened. She dropped the ladle in the barrel, and sprinted to the door.

Taos fetched the ladle from the barrel, filled it, and slowly drank the cool water. He pulled the red bandana from around his neck, and poured some of the water on it. Taos wiped his neck and face, before putting the bandana on the porch railing. With a sigh, he headed to the cabin door.

Maddie was sitting at the kitchen table, sobbing, when Taos entered the cabin. He hesitated for a moment, before walking to the table. He grabbed a chair and sat down next to her.

"Maddie, what is it?" he asked.

"You must think me a silly school girl," she stuttered through her tears.

"Not at all," Taos whispered. He put his arm around her shoulder, and she turned and collapsed into his arms.

"Oh Taos, I'm so sorry, I don't know what's come over me. I feel so stupid.

Look at me!" Maddie pulled away from Taos, and showed him the water spill on her blouse.

"Maddie, that ain't nothin' to worry about," he replied in a soothing voice. "Look, sooner or later, we're gonna have to face it." He got up and grabbed a hand towel from the sink, and wiped her eyes, then sat down.

Maddie sniffed, and took the towel from Taos' hand. "Face what?"

"Don't you see? We have feelin's fer each other," he said.

"Each other?" she whispered. "All along, I thought it was just me likin' you, and, when I spilled the ladle on myself, I just felt, well, stupid," she replied.

Taos took her in his arms, and they kissed, a soft, gentle, but powerful kiss.

Maddie felt his warmth envelop her. Emotions swirled through her being. She felt safe in Taos' arms, felt his strength: not just his muscles, but his inner strength, which energized her. She felt other things, too. She loved the scent of him. That smell of healthy sweat that comes from hard work. She hugged him hard, as if to squeeze his soul inside her.

Her breasts heaved against Taos' chest, as she held him, kissed him. What started out slowly, became frantic. It was as if she had to get the past year's loneliness out all at once.

Taos' head spun. He had this beautiful, sensual, strong woman in his arms, yet his thoughts drifted to Ida. He had to figure this out.

Suddenly, he pulled away, and stood up.

Startled by the suddenness of Taos' movement, Maddie said, "What's wrong? I'm so sorry! I thought you liked me. You just said you did?"

"It ain't yu, Maddie. Sure I like yu. I really do," he replied, as he fidgeted with his hat, which he had removed.

Maddie stood and faced him, she tried to be brave. "Then what is it?"

20

Chapter 20

This meeting between the regional ranchers was much more solemn than the first one. The men knew what they were up against, and a decision had to be made, and argued over what the best strategy was.

The Colonel slammed the butt of his pistol on the table in front of him. "Order! Order!

Order!" he shouted over the din.

The room quieted.

"We all know why we are here," the Colonel announced. "We sent a letter to the Governor. My son, Ben, spoke with him. Me, and some others, you know who you are, rode up to the mines, and spoke with the owner, Van der Veer. We offered a compromise. We got nothin' but threats for our trouble.

Now, I have my ideas of what should be done next, but not all of you are faced with goin' outa' business like me and my family is."

Tasker Patchet, who owned a ranch outside of Abiquiu, stood up. He rubbed his hand over the gray stubble on his chin. Then, he stepped up to the front, and turned to the crowd. "Look, Colonel. I was all fer writin' the letter to the Gov'nor, and I was all fer your son, Ben to state the case. I was all fer talkin' to Van der Veer. But, it looks like our race is run. Are we really gonna sacrifice lives fer just one ranch? We all heared Van der Veer can put up a hunnert men agin' us. We can't match thet, an' keep our cattle cared fer. I'm sorry Colonel, I jest ain't ready ta' make a sacrifice like thet." Patchet walked back to his seat with his head down.

Jack Parker raised his hand.

"Jack," the Colonel said.

Jack stepped up to the table, and faced the crowd. "Look, what the Colonel says is true. We ain't threatened directly like he is. But, they ain't no mines on the headwaters of the Cobresto, like they is on the Red. We is all dependent on water to survive. There ain't one of you in this here room thet can survive without clean water. If some minin' operation opens in the headwaters of the Cobresto, I'll be facin' the same thing as Colonel Adams is. And I'd be lookin' to all of you to help me out. It's time ta' make a stand. If we roll over now, we ain't gonna stop rollin' 'till every one of us is outa business."

There was a mix of cheers and boos, as Jack took his seat.

The colonel hammered his pistol butt on the table. "Order!" he shouted, and the room quieted.

Clint MacNeill spoke up next. "Some of us heah have seen the ravages of war. It sure ain't pretty. I can tell yu thet. But, sometimes a man's gotta fight, if he's a man. I agree with Jack. Sure, the rest of us ain't bein' threatened now, but we could be, and we'd want the support of the rest of yu. What's the sense in havin' an association if we don't stand up for one another?"

Ramon Padilla stood up and walked to the front. The room quieted, as Padilla, whose family had ranched in northern New Mexico for centuries, commanded special respect.

When he reached the table, Ramon took a moment to gather himself.

"We have acted in good faith. We have made a plan, and presented it to Mister Van der Veer. He scoffed at us. Ben Adams brought our concerns to the Governor. He scoffed at Ben. You all know me, and my family. I am a man of peace. We have tried the road of peace, but we have been turned away. It is time to try a new road. The road of force. Thus far, we have heard nothing but threats from Van der Veer. He says he has a hundred men. I say good for him. But, how many of these men are experienced riflemen? My vaqueros, and your cowboys have been huntin', and practicing with firearms since they were children. Also, as Clint MacNeill has said, many here in this room have experience with war. They have held positions of command. This is vital experience. If we are going to vote today, I vote for war."

The room exploded.

Colonel Adams pounded on the table until order was restored.

"Anybody else have somethin' to say?"

The room remained quiet.

"So, we'll put it to a vote. All in favor of takin' the fight to Van der Veer say aye."

There was a resounding "Aye" from the crowd.

"All agin' goin' after Van der Veer, say nay."

The room remained silent.

"Well, there ya' have it. I'd like ta' meet with Clint, Jack, and Ramon in the house. The rest of you, grab somethin' to eat."

* * *

Lorena and Sage had put out a pot of coffee, and a large plate of biscuits, along with butter, and a few kinds of jam, on the kitchen table.

The men entered the house, and sat at the kitchen table. Lorena poured them coffee, and Sage passed around the biscuits.

"Let's get right to business," the Colonel said. "I think the best plan is a surprise attack."

"I agree," Jack Parker said. "Thet is a good way ta' make up fer our lack of numbers."

"Speakin' of thet, we need ta' figure out exactly how many men we have available," Clint said.

"We'll get that before everyone leaves, but let's use a figure of fifty good men, fer now," the Colonel answered.

"I think we should march up there in the evening, and attack early in the mornin' when they ain't ready," Jack offered.

"I agree," Ramon said.

"I think we should go in two groups, and form a hammer and anvil," Clint said.

Ben, who had already been in the house, and listening from the living room, walked in.

"A few sticks of dynamite would go a long way to stirrin' up confusion," Ben drawled.

21

Chapter 21

Taos sat back down beside Maddie, and looked into her green eyes.

"Maddie, yu know I had a life before this'n," he drawled.

"Yes, of course," she sniffled.

"When I left, I left a lot a' things undone. Theah was a woman. Ida Parker. She's the daughter of a rancher close ta my parent's ranch."

"You are a remarkably handsome man, Taos. I'm sure you had many women interested in you," she replied, trying to be brave.

"Well, we was in love, and the last time I seen her, she had her dyin' father in her arms, and she blamed me fer it. Said she never wanted ta see me agin', so I rode off. It's been a long year."

"And you still love this woman?" Maddie asked, as she fidgeted with her skirt.

"Maddie, I don't rightly know. But, afore I can move ahead, and make a commitment ta yu, I gotta know."

* * *

Maddie was in limbo. Her hands shook as she buttoned her blouse. *What am I going to say to him?* She thought. He was right, they had developed feelings for each other. She knew that she was falling for this man called Taos. But, what about this Ida Parker? Where did she fit in? Was he still in love with her? Just as important, was she still in love with him? What if she was? Had too much time gone by? Could she put her feelings on hold? The smell of hot coffee broke her spell.

Maddie finished dressing, and left her bedroom. Taos, looking as wonderful as ever, had just poured two coffees, and was frying eggs.

"Good mornin', Taos," Maddie squeaked, and immediately felt ashamed that she hadn't composed herself better.

Taos turned toward her. His blue eyes flashed, and she melted. "Aboot last night," Taos started.

"Please, Taos. I don't think I'm ready to talk about it," Maddie said. "We have a lot of work to do today, and I need to concentrate on that." Her lips trembled as she spoke.

"I understand," Taos replied.

* * *

Hard work was the best medicine. Working together was a pleasure for Maddie and Taos. The tension between them faded away as they drove the herd across the San Miguel. They quickly moved the beeves past the ranch house, and to the trail leading to the High Meadow.

Maddie felt the cooling air on her cheeks as they gained elevation. The cattle must have felt it too, because they livenned their pace. She took a glance toward Taos, who was working on the other side of the trail. She was in awe. He seemed so comfortable in the saddle., with little muscular moves, he guided Grant, who responded magnificently. Horse and rider were as one.

While Maddie had to work hard and spend a lot of energy for results, Taos and Grant wasted none.

Taos noticed her looking at him. He flashed a smile, and gave her a quick wave. Maddie blushed, having been caught, but mustered a smile, and a little wave back. She knew that she loved this man, though she really didn't know anything about his past, other than the little bit that he had shared. And, what about this Ida? Where did she fit in? Maddie knew that if she had a chance, she and Taos could have a wonderful life together.

It was mid afternoon by the time they reached the gap heading to the high meadow. When they got through the opening, the herd spread out among the bright, green grass. They actually seemed to frolic with joy.

Taos rode over to Maddie, who was admiring the herd.

"Beautiful, ain't they," Taos said, over the din.

"They sure are!" Maddie exclaimed.

The two dismounted and let their horses graze. They walked over to the brook, and drank. When refreshed, Maddie said, "Oh, I do love it here."

"It's one of the most beautiful places thet I evah seen," Taos agreed, as he gazed out at the high peaks that surrounded the deep green meadow.

"Taos, I have an idea," Maddie said.

"What is it?" he enquired.

"You know that I love you, but we can't be together until you figure out what you're gonna do about Ida. Now that the cattle are safe up here, why don't you ride home to see Ida, and your family?"

"Are you sure? What about McCarty?"

"The cattle are safe here, and I've managed to hold McCarty off for a year. I imagine another month or so won't matter," she replied. "I can't go on not knowing where I stand with you."

22

Chapter 22

The Colonel's eyes lit up. "Dynamite, you say? Please elaborate, Ben."

"I think if we get theah early, and have everyone in position. Someone could ride through the row of bunkhouses and toss a stick of dynamite inta each one," Ben replied. "This would keep them from gettin' setup ta defend themselves."

"Splendid idea, my boy," the Colonel agreed.

"I agree," said Frank Lynch.

"Since it was yur idee, I think yu should carry it out," Travis Clark said.

"I think that's settled, then," the Colonel announced. "You okay with that, my boy?"

"Sure. I wouldn't suggest something that I wasn't willin' to do myself," Ben replied.

"Ramon, why don't you spread your map out on the table heah, so we can make our plans," the Colonel said.

Ramon took the map out of its tube, and spread it out. The ranchers gathered around, and got to work.

* * *

It was well past midnight when Jack Parker entered his ranch house. He was hoping to sneak in quietly, but had no such luck. Ida was waiting for him. She was vehemently opposed to going to war with the miners, and had let him know it in no uncertain terms on more than one occasion. He had a feeling that this was going to be another go around.

"Yur up late," Jack said, meekly, as he entered the house. He knew how Ida's temper could flare. She was like her mother in that regard. Sweet on the outside, but always this simmering fire that could explode at any time. Jack was afraid that this was going to be one of those times.

"I'm just waitin' up for you Daddy," Ida replied, in a "butter wouldn't melt in my mouth" tone.

"There's no need fer that, Ida, I'm a big boy. I can take care a' myself," he replied.

"I ain't so sure of that," Ida snapped back. Her voice hardened..

"Ida, honey, we've been through this before," Jack pleaded.

"Don't you patronize me, Dad," she snapped back. "Those Adams' are gonna get a lotta' people killed. I don't want you to be one of them."

"Ida, ain't you bein' a little melodramatic? It's only right that I support the Adams' and their ranch. The same thing could happen to us."

"But it ain't, and I don't think their ranch is worth you dyin' over!" Ida's voice hit a crescendo.

Jack's voice boomed, "Now, you listen heah, daughter of mine. I don't need to ask your opinion, or your permission about anything. You remember that!."

Ida took a step back. That was the first time her father had ever raised his voice to her.

"Daddy, it's just that I know how pushy, and persuasive the Colonel and Ben can be," she said in a near whisper, calming herself. "There must be some other way."

Jack had actually startled himself. "I'm sorry for yellin' Ida, dear." He wrapped his arms around his daughter, and held her. "Everythin's gonna be alright. We've tried everything they is ta get that Van der Veer to compromise, but no luck. He ain't budgin'. He practically threatened war."

* * *

Despite being up so late, Ida was out of bed, washed, dressed, had breakfast, and was on her way out through the ranch gate before sunrise. She had packed food, and water. This was going to be a long day.

She stopped to rest at the waterfall where she and Ben had their tryst. Her face heated and burned red, as she recalled their kisses. She loved Ben, but this thing about going to war with the mining company was just crazy, she thought, as her horse cooled in the plunge pool below the falls.

The Colonel was behind it, Ida thought. Ben Adams was a bit wild, but not reckless. His father was always talking about his days in the war, and she believed that he wanted to relive past glory. And, he could be very persuasive. After all, he got almost all the major ranchers in northern New Mexico Territory to follow him.

She ate some jerky, had a drink, and topped off her canteen, and gave it a good soak in the stream to help keep the water cool for the day. She let her horse graze for a few minutes, and her thoughts returned to Ben, and their kisses. Then, back to what to do about convincing Ben to put a stop to this madness. People were going to get killed. She just knew it.

After a while, she saddled up and hit the trail. Eventually, she saw the gate to Los Piñons Ranch. Ida rode in through the gate, and made sure to latch it after her. She could see the ranch house up ahead, and girded herself for the conversation that she had to have with Ben.

* * *

The Adams' had just finished eating lunch, and the Colonel and Ben sat out on the porch, while Lorena and Sage finished up the dishes.

The Colonel lit his pipe. "I think we came up with a good plan last night," he said, after taking a long puff on his pipe.

"Probably the best we could have. Bein' outnumbered, it makes sense to take 'em by surprise," Ben drawled. "I'll pick up the dynamite tomorrow mornin'."

Lorena stepped out on the porch carrying a tray of iced tea, followed by Sage who carried a tray of apple pie.

"Who wants dessert?" Sage asked.

"That sure looks good," the Colonel said.

Sage served pie, while her mother poured iced tea.

Ben took a fork-full of his pie. "You've outdone yerself, sis," he exclaimed, after he had swallowed.

They ate their pie in silence, until Sage looked up and said, "Rider comin'."

Ben stood up, went inside, and grabbed the eyepiece. He opened it up as he stepped back onto the porch, then put it to his eye.

"Well, I'll be," he said as he looked through the telescope.

"Who is it?" Sage demanded.

"Why, it's Ida Parker. I wonder what she wants," Ben replied.

"You, of course," Sage said. Her eyes twinkled.

"Yur funny," Ben replied.

As Ida rode closer, Ben stepped off the porch to greet her.

"Wal, halloo," he said in his best western drawl, as he grabbed the reins of her horse.

"Wal, halloo, back at you, Ben Adams," Ida drawled back, as she dismounted.

Ben walked with her and the horse to the pen, where he took the saddle off, and put it on a rail. Then, he gave the palomino a slap on its haunch to send it in, where it could feed and drink. Ida shared the experience of her ride with Ben on the way back to the porch.

When they reached the porch, Lorena said, "You must be parched, young lady. How about a glass of iced tea?"

"That sure would be wonderful," Misses Adams," Ida replied.

"You're sure a long way from home," Sage commented.

"Well, I have to talk to Ben about somethin'," Ida replied.

"I bet," Sage answered, sarcastically.

Lorena returned with a glass of iced tea, and handed it to Ida.

"Thank you," Ida said, happy for the distraction from Sage.

The Colonel pulled over a chair. "Have a seat, my dear," he offered.

"Thanks, all the same, Colonel, but my rear is sore from riding. I'll stand, if you don't mind.

"Makes no nevermind to me," the Colonel replied, and put the chair back.

There was an uncomfortable silence, while Ida gulped her iced tea. When she finished she said, "Thank you, Misses Adams, that was very refreshing." Then she turned to Ben, and said, "We need to talk."

"Sure, let's take a walk," Ben replied.

23

Chapter 23

It had been a difficult goodbye, but a necessary one. Once again, Taos was in the saddle. He had to go to New Mexico. He had to find out how things were going at the ranch. He had to see Ida; if she would see him at all. He rode toward Telluride, hoping that there would be a letter from Sage. It was odd that he hadn't heard from her in so long.

As he rode, his mind's eye kept replaying the image of the tears streaming down Maddie's cheeks. He had promised her that he would come back, no matter what. He was committed to his job, and helping her save her ranch from McCarty's clutches. He wasn't sure that she believed him.

He rode toward Telluride to check the mail one last time before heading home. The thought of home felt odd to him. It had been over a year now since he left Los Piñons. So much had changed. He had changed. He had done things that he wasn't proud of, but he survived. He had grown.

A life with Maddie could, would be wonderful. Taos knew that. But he couldn't move on until things were settled at home, and with Ida.

He stopped off at the Post Office first. The Postmaster, Sam Dunker, was in the back room when Taos entered. Taos rang the bell on the counter.

"I'll be right out," Sam yelled from the back room.

Taos whistled *Red River Valley* while he waited.

Sam walked out to the front, and Taos stopped whistling.

When he recognized Taos, Sam said, "I ain't got nothin' yet, son. I'm sorry."

Taos' shoulders shrugged, as his mood deflated. "Well, thank yu, anyway," he replied.

"Have a good day," Sam said, as Taos turned to the exit.

Taos' next stop was at the Sheriff's office.

Jim Nolan was at his desk when Taos entered. His eyes lit up, and he stood, when he recognized his visitor. "Taos," he said as he extended his hand.

Taos took the sheriff's hand, and replied, "Hello, Sheriff."

"Have a seat," Jim said.

"Thanks." Taos sat down.

"What brings you to Telluride?" Jim asked.

"Well, Sheriff, I need to ask a favor," Taos said.

"Favor?" The Sheriff's eyebrows raised.

"I'm headin' out to New Mexico for a month or so, an' I'm askin' if you don't mind checkin' in on Maddie from time ta time," Taos said.

"New Mexico? Unfinished business?" Jim asked.

"Somethin' like thet," Taos answered.

"Sure, I'll be happy ta do thet fer yu. I'll take a ride out in a couple of days."

"I sure do appreciate it. I'll check in on my way back," Taos drawled, as he stood up and extended his hand.

Jim took Taos' hand. "Take care of yurself, Taos. Maddie needs you. I hope that yu have a successful trip."

* * *

Maddie sobbed as Taos rode out of sight. Taos leaving was always tough, but this was different. He could be gone for weeks, months, or forever. It was the forever, and not knowing the outcome of his trip that made it so difficult to watch him ride away.

Maddie worked on the daily chores to keep her mind off of Taos. It didn't work. His clear blue eyes kept creeping into her consciousness, and her heart ached all over again. After her chores were done, she grabbed her fly rod, and walked down to the San Miguel.

Fly fishing had been a passion of hers since she was a kid in Virginia, and often served to settle her mind. This was one of those times. She needed to think things through, and the constant gurgle of the San Miguel, always had a soothing effect on her. For weeks after the loss of Cam and Tad, it was the only thing that gave her solace. She already had the rod rigged up, so she walked to her favorite spot, and began false casting. When she had enough line out, she cast the brace of wet flies out to a deep run, and just upstream from where she stood. She allowed the flies to sink, and followed them downstream with the rod tip. Just as the flies began to swing, she felt a hard tug on the line. She lifted the rod tip, and was hooked to a large cutthroat trout.

She deftly subdued the large fish, and admired the crimson slash under its jaw before she dispatched it. Nothing like fresh trout. She cleaned the fish, and put it in her creel with some wet grass. Maddie cast again, and was fast into another trout; this one not so big. She spent the late afternoon catching and releasing trout. As the sun dropped in the west, she packed up her gear and walked to the cabin.

After putting her gear away, Maddie started preparing dinner. While rice was boiling, she seasoned the trout and heated up a cast iron skillet, which she oiled with a prodigious dollop of bacon grease. When the grease was hot, she laid the trout in the pan. She fried the fish and placed it on a platter, then dished out the rice.

As she sat down to eat, thoughts of Taos entered her mind. When Cam and Tad were murdered, she had closed her heart. She never thought that she could love again, and now she had feelings for this wild cowboy who rode into her life, and just like that, he was gone, maybe never to return.

After a diner that she barely tasted, Maddie cleaned up and began her evening routine.

"Alone again," she said to the walls. She felt the ache of loneliness in her heart, but knew that she had to let Taos go if she was ever truly going to have him.

* * *

Ben put his hand out, but Ida didn't take it. He knew what this must be about, and it wasn't going to be pretty.

He led her to a stand of cottonwoods, and once standing in the shade he turned to her.

"What is it, Ida?" he asked.

"You gotta stop this, Ben! This attack is fruitless. People are gonna get killed, for what? A few cows?"

Ben stood quiet for a moment, he wanted to gather his thoughts before making his rebuttal. Ida could be very volatile, so he was careful how he replied to her. Arguing was never going to work with her.

"Ida, I just don't think that we are evah gonna see eye ta eye on this. I see it as more than 'just a few cows.' I see it as protecting a way a' life. Us ranchers live on and in the land. We depend on healthy streams and open, abundant prairie ta not only flourish, but for our survival. These miners are rapin' the land and water that we need. They take, but they nevah give back. When the minerals are gone, or too expensive ta extract, they'll move on and destroy another place. It's just the way they is. They aint like a few small time gold panners. This is big industry that is set ta destroy the west and any industry that depends on the land and water, not just our industry."

"You can talk all high an' mighty all you like, Ben, but it comes down to people gettin' killed, and killed to save your ranch," she seethed. "Mark my words, Ben. If you don't pull the plug on this, and my father is wounded, or worse, I'll never forgive you."

Before Ben could answer, Ida stormed back toward the corral.

He walked back to the house while Ida saddled her horse. *I love her, but she can be so headstrong and rigid,* he thought, as he walked.

"You an' Ida have a spat?" Sage asked when Ben returned to the porch.

"That's one word fer it," Ben replied.

"What happened?" the Colonel asked.

"She wants me ta call off the attack on the miners. She thinks it's just aboot a bunch of cattle. She just don't get the bigger picture," Ben replied.

* * *

After a fitful sleep, Maddie got up, got dressed, and made her breakfast. While eating, she decided that, after her morning chores, she would practice with the old six shooter that Cam had given her.

Her chores finished, she took the pistol out of her drawer, cleaned it, and grabbed a box of cartridges. Cam had bought the model 1851 Navy Colt for her because it was a dependable weapon, and the .36 caliber was easier for her to handle than a larger handgun, while still packing enough power to drop a man.

Maddie loaded six cartridges, and added caps. She walked out to the corral where Cam had placed a heavy board for just this purpose. She took a piece of charred wood, and drew a black circle on the board. Next, Maddie marked off twenty feet, the distance that Cam had recommended, and turned to face the board. She stood square, and held the six shooter with two hands, just like her lost husband had shown her. She squeezed the trigger and the gun made a boom. The kickback wasn't as bad as the shotgun, but still was a shock. When the smoke cleared, Maddie saw a hole near the middle of the circle. She fired off five more shots, and each one landed inside the circle. She was happy with her results, but could she use the Colt when it really mattered?

24

Chapter 24

Tonight was the night. The ranchers and cowboys gathered at Los Piñons before heading to the mines. They totalled sixty-three men, a larger number than they expected. The fighting force was split into three units: the "hammer" under the Colonel's command, the "anvil," led by Jack Parker, and a reserve unit of about ten men to be used to fill gaps as directed by Clint MacNeill. Each man had solid experience in the Civil War, and had commanded men on the field of battle, an advantage over their adversary.

The men loaded up with extra ammunition and plenty of water and jerky, for there would be no campfires for cooking, and mounted and rode off in three columns. Ben, whose saddlebags were full of dynamite, brought up the rear.

As the makeshift army rode off into the soft evening light, Sage and her mother stood on the front porch watching.

"It sure brings me back," Lenore said. "I always felt so helpless when the Colonel rode off to battle, though it's more personal this time."

"I'm beginning to understand, Momma," Sage replied. "How did you stand it all those years?"

"I prayed."

* * *

Ida was beside herself. She had argued with Ben, argued with her father, argued with her mother, all to no avail. Now, she was stuck at the ranch fuming. Her raven hair and black eyes glistened in the late afternoon sun.

"Ida, come inside," her mother called. Sofia knew that Ida had the same hot blood as her, but she had learned to keep it reined in, and Ida must too.

Ida reluctantly came inside.

"What is it mother," she demanded.

"Stomping around the dooryard isn't going to help anything," Sofia replied.

"How can you stand there so calmly when your husband's, my father's life is on the line, as is our ranch?" Ida asked.

"I have learned to accept the things that I can't change in life," Sophia replied.

"But, couldn't you have reasoned with my father? Tell him what is at stake?" Ida pleaded.

"And rob his dignity? Your father is a war hero. He believes in what he is doing. I believe in what he is doing. I believe in the cause," Sofia said.

"Don't talk to me about causes!" Ida shouted.

Sofia slapped Ida across the face. "Don't you ever raise your voice to me!"

Stunned, Ida ran to her room.

Sofia put her face in her hands and wept. Neither she nor Jack had ever struck Ida before.

But she can be so headstrong and disrespectful, she thought. *Just like me, when I was her age.*

Ida slammed the door to her bedroom and collapsed on her bed. The sting on her face hurt only half as much as the sting to her pride. *Why doesn't anyone else see the potential disaster?* She thought. "Honor. What good is honor if you are dead?" she asked herself.

* * *

The makeshift army made it to their planned staging area just before dark, and without incident. After the horses were taken care of, the Colonel gathered the men.

"Men, I've made many pre-battle speeches in my lifetime, but none of them as important as this one," the Colonel began. "In the mornin', we ain't just fightin' for ourselves and our ranches, we're fightin' for our way of life. Let that sink in," the Colonel urged. "These miners are gonna ruin the west. As you know, they's already destroyin' my ranch, an' there's no stoppin' them if we don't do it tomorrow.. This ain't just for me an' t'other ranch owners, this is fo' all of us. All yu cowboys who cherish ridin' the open range, they ain't gonna be no open range anymore if the miners get their way. We is all in this together. In the mornin' we have our time to shine! It's up ta us to save New Mexico, and the west! Now, you all know your parts, so get together in your places for the night, have somethin' to eat, and try to get some shut eye."

After the Colonel's speech, the men gathered in their respective units, dug into their jerky, and prepared for a cold mountain night.

* * *

Ida, who had cried herself to sleep with tears of rage, woke up well before dawn. She was still livid, and determined to put a stop to the attack. She washed up, got dressed, scrambled a few eggs, and ate them with sourdough bread. Next, Ida filled a couple of canteens and packed some jerky. Then, she carried her supplies out to the horse corral, roped her horse, saddled it, and rode off.

* * *

Ben was the first one up. There was a heavy frost at this altitude, and, without fires, the men were going to be slow moving. He had a simple breakfast of jerky and water before packing up. He rode to the first camp to check with the Colonel.

When Ben arrived at the Colonel's camp, he saw that the men were in various stages of readiness. The Colonel was a blur, going from man to man whispering orders. To Ben, he looked ten years younger. He was in his element doing what he loved best, planning a battle and commanding men.

"Good mornin' Colonel," Ben said when he caught up with his father.

"Mornin' boy," the Colonel answered.

"Nearly ready?" Ben asked.

"I had MacNeill send a runner to Parker to have his men ready at 05:30. We will be ready in 10 minutes. That will give us 15 minutes to get in position."

"Alright, I'll ride over ta the launch area and take a look around, while I wait fer yu and yur men.

* * *

Ida found it slow going in the dark, on a trail that she was not familiar with. She hit the ground with a thump, after riding into a low lying branch. This did not help her mood. Frustrated, Ida brushed herself off, and climbed back on her horse.

I'm never going to make it there in time, she thought to herself. *I just can't go any faster in the dark.*

* * *

Ben readied the dynamite as he waited for the Colonel and the other men. He could see the bunkhouses in the clearing ahead, as morning approached. The plan was easy; he would ride out and throw a stick of dynamite through each of the two front windows, then ride on to the next bunkhouse, do the same thing, and on to the owner's office and quarters. After that, he would ride on to Jack Parker's lines, and join them. If all went well, the Colonel and his men would charge and pick off the men that emerged from the bunkhouses. The ones that they didn't get would be chased straight into Parker's line.

Seems simple enough, Ben thought.

Presently, the colonel appeared with his men. Ben lit a cigar in order to light the dynamite quickly. The men got into place.

"Check your Winchesters," the Colonel ordered.

After the men complied, the Colonel looked at his watch, then nodded to Ben, who rode out to the clearing.

Ben lit a stick as he approached the first window, let it burn for a couple of seconds, then tossed it through before riding on to the next one. He repeated the process, and the first stick went off just as the second one flew through its window.

There was a loud flash, boom, then smoke billowed out of the windows. Just then, the second stick exploded with the same effect.

As Ben rode toward the second bunkhouse, men began piling out of the first. The Colonel and his men galloped onto the scene with guns blazing.

Miners dropped like rain, but some returned fire before turning and running. Just then, the second set of explosives went off, causing bedlam. Miners who were running, stopped and turned around, but ran back to the Colonel's men. Miners began to spill out of the second bunkhouse, firing wildly.

As Ben approached the office residence, miners, Culpepper, and Van de Veer, obviously awakened by the explosions, exited the house and set up a skirmish line on the porch. They began firing at Ben, who was in the middle of lighting another stick of dynamite. A bullet ripped through his left shoulder, which knocked him off his horse. While falling, he was able to toss the stick in the direction of the house, but it exploded with no damage.

Van de Veer saw his opportunity, and charged off the porch toward Ben, who struggled to pick himself up with the use of only one arm. Ben scrambled to get to his feet while Van de Veer approached with his pistol aimed at him.

Unable to get up, Ben kicked Van de Veer's legs out from under him. He landed with a thud. Ben took the opportunity to gather himself and get to his feet, while Van de Veer picked himself up. They stood face to face, Ben's left arm hung limp at his side, the pain screwed up his face.

"I have you now, you impertinent bastard," Van de Veer said as he raised his sidearm.

"Not so fast," Ben replied as his Colt forty-five cleared leather, and a bullet quickly ripped, planting a nickel-sized hole in the middle of Van de Veer's forehead.

The Colonel and his men continued to sweep past the bunkhouses toward the anvil set up by Parker and his men, but Culpepper and a few miners, still on the porch, put up a fight. Others began to rally around them, and, together, they laid down a deadly fire, which stalled the charge.

At this point, MacNeil noticed the stalemate and charged into the fray, which turned the tide of the battle.

The miners all began running toward Parker and his men, and were chased by the Colonel and his men. As they approached the tree line, Parker gave the order to fire, and a maelstrom of bullets flew out of the woods at the miners, and left many dead.

Culpepper rallied a charge, and they advanced toward the woodline again, firing as they went.

Parker and his men laid down a blistering return fire as the miners, who were now trapped, charged.

* * *

Ida rode to the sounds of the gunshots. Knowing that she was too late to stop the madness, she wanted to get on the scene to find her father. As she reached the edge of the battlefield, she could discern what was happening. Not seeing her father on the field, she knew that he must be at the woodline. She circled around to stay out of the line of fire and rode up behind the line of skirmishers.

As she approached, Ida spotted her father with his men, offering encouragement and directing their fire. Suddenly, one of the miners broke into the treeline and fired at Jack Parker. A red spot appeared in the middle of his chest, as he fell back. The miner was riddled with bullets.

Ida screamed as she leapt off her horse and ran to catch her father.

* * *

Ben had struggled to mount his horse. He had lost a lot of blood, and was having trouble staying in his saddle. He rode up behind the action, and watched the last of the miners surrender to the ranchers.

The men were cheering their victory, but Ben could see Ida holding her father, tending to his wound.

He approached, dismounted, and walked to them, his bloody arm dangling at his side.

Ida looked up at him, and ignoring Ben's wound, said, "Just look at him! He's dyin' Ben, and it's all on you."

Ben knelt down next to Jack and Ida. "I'm so sorry, Jack."

Jack spoke in a whisper, "We whupped 'em good, Ben. Don't apologize. If I die, I die proud and happy for this. We saved New Mexico."

"Save your breath, Dad," Ida pleaded, tears streaming down her cheeks. She tore part of her dress off and used it to plug the hole in Jack's chest. "We'll get you to the doctor, you'll be fine. You're a tough old war horse."

Jack looked at Ida and said, "I love you honey. Tell your mother that I was brave today, and that I love her." Then, with a woosh of air, he expired.

Ida turned to Ben, and she was in a rage. She stood up and punched Ben in the chest and face over and over again, until she was exhausted. Then, she stopped and said, in a very quiet and stern voice, "This is on you, Ben Adams, my father's death is on you. It's a black mark on your soul. I hope you rot in Hell!"

25

Chapter 25

Ben woke up in his bed. He could hear voices, but his vision was blurry. He blinked his eyes a few times and could now make out the figures of the Colonel, his mother, and old Doc Bailey.

"Where am I?" Ben asked, in a feeble voice. He cleared his throat.

His mother ran to his bedside. "Oh Ben, you're awake!"

"Am I gonna' make it?" Ben asked.

Doc Bailey sauntered over to Ben and said, "Well, I don't think that you're gonna be sayin' the big adios anytime soon, Ben, but you have lost a lot of blood."

"Is my arm gonna be OK?"

Doc Bailey took a moment to polish his spectacles. "You got lucky on that account, Ben. The bullet went right through you and never touched no bones. It'll heal. May take some time, but you'll be fit as a fiddle afore you know it," Doc Bailey replied. "Lenore, he's gonna have to eat a lot of red meat and liver to rebuild his blood supply. Also, get him out in the sun for a few hours a day."

* * *

The Parkers held a funeral for Jack, and let it be known that none of the Adams' were welcome. Every other ranch in Northern New Mexico was represented except Los Piñons. Sofia Parker had sent a letter of apology to the Colonel, and explained that Ida was still beside herself and blamed the Adams', and specifically, Ben for her father's death. Sofia had said that Jack understood the risks, and the rewards, and that there is no one to blame, but she had to consider Ida's state of mind.

* * *

Ben sat out on the porch, covered with a blanket. The sun felt good, but he chilled easily. He took walks around the ranch house, and traveled a little farther each day. He could feel his strength increasing, but Ida's words kept haunting him. Every time he thought about Ida, he sunk into a depression.

Ben was in one of these funks when the Colonel stepped out onto the porch with a bottle of Bourbon and two glasses. "You look a bit low, son," the Colonel said.

"I'm sure in a sore way, Colonel," Ben replied.

"You wanna talk about it?"

"It's Ida, and what she said to me that day."

"I heard her. I wasn't that far away. She had no right to say that, Ben."

"But, somehow I do feel guilty."

"Let me tell yu somethin' about Ida. Yu may not want ta heah it, but I'm gonna say it anyway. Sure she's beautiful, most beautiful girl in this part of the territory, next ta yur sister, but she's spoiled, Ben. Jack could never say no to her. She was too much like Sofia when she was young, an' I think he spent all his energy tamin' her. Headstrong, high spirited, and spoiled is a bad combination," the Colonel said.

"She asked me, even begged me to put a stop to the attack. I ignored her," Ben said.

"Ben, she had no right to do that," the Colonel said as he poured two glasses of Bourbon.

He handed one to Ben and said, "Now, take it easy with that, you're still healin'."

Ben took a sip of the amber liquid. His face flushed as he felt the warmth surge through his body. He took a moment to gather his thoughts before he spoke again. "Did we have any right ta ask others ta risk their lives fer us?"

The Colonel took a long drink from his glass and savored the taste before swallowing. "You know," he began, "I ordered nearly every poor Wisconsin mother's son into battle not knowin' who was gonna return on two feet, on a stretcher, or in a box, durin' the late war between the states. It wasn't easy, and I'd be lyin' if I said I didn't lay awake nights worryin' about those poor boys, but we had a greater purpose in fightin' the war. Hell, I even gave my own leg. We had to preserve the Union."

"And Ida would ask, why? Was it worth six hundred thousand of those poor mothers' sons to preserve the Union?" Ben replied.

The Colonel took another drink from his glass, and looked out at the Sangre de Cristo Mountains. He took a few moments to formulate his answer. It was important that he get this right.

The Colonel turned back to Ben, and said, "I guess, at some point, yu gotta' stand for somethin', Ben. Was it worth the sacrifices made durin' the Revolution to form this great country of ours? Was it worth fightin' the War of Eighteen-Twelve to keep the British from conscriptin' American sailors, and robbin' our cargo? If not, when is it ever proper to stand for anythin'? Is slavery preferable to freedom?"

Ben took a sip from his glass, and could feel the liquor acting on him.

"You're right, Colonel. But what do I do aboot Ida? She only sees it through the lens of her dead father. She hates me," Ben replied.

"You can't control that, Ben. She's gonna' think what she's gonna' think. Nothin' but time, if even that's gonna heal her, she's that headstrong," the

Colonel replied.

26

Chapter 26

I t was a few days after Taos had left for New Mexico, and Maddie was hanging her wash on the clothesline when she noticed a rider in the distance. She tried not to panic, but she had gotten so used to Taos being around in such a short period of time, that she felt unsafe without him.

She had started wearing the Colt in a gun belt around her waist, and kept the shot gun within arm's reach at all times. She tried to act nonchalant, and kept hanging clothes while keeping an eye on the rider.

Presently, she saw that it was Sheriff Jim Nolan, and she relaxed. After a few minutes, he crossed the San Miguel and she walked out to greet him.

"Hey, Sheriff, what brings you all the way out here?" Maddie asked.

"Halloo, Maddie, it's good to see yu," Nolan said as he dismounted. "Taos stopped by t'other day, and said that he was gonna' be away for awhile. Asked me to check in on you every now and again."

"Well, that was very kind of him," Maddie replied. "Can I interest you in a cup of coffee?"

"Sounds good. Thanks."

"Just give me a minute to finish hangin' these clothes,"

"Sure thing. I'll just fetch some water for my hoss," Nolan replied.

They finished their respective chores at the same time, and walked to the front door together. Nolan held the door for Maddie, and they walked inside.

"Have a seat, Sheriff," Maddie said.

"Call me Jim," he replied, as he took a seat at the kitchen table.

"Okay, Jim," Maddie said as she prepared the pot to make coffee, then stoked the fire in the stove. Next she went to the bread box and took out a plate of muffins. "I made these yesterday," she said as she placed the muffins on the table.

"They sure look good! I sure wish I could get my wife to bake muffins for me."

"Maybe do somethin' special for her, and see what happens," Maddie replied.

"Hmmm, I'll do thet. Maybe a dinner out. Thanks."

"You take milk and sugar in your coffee, Jim?" Maddie asked.

"Ha! What do yu take me fer, some kinda tin horn? I take my Arbuckle black, thanks," Nolan laughed.

Maddie poured two mugs of coffee and put them on the table, then sat down across from Nolan.

"So, how're you holdin' up?" he asked.

"I'm gettin' by. I have to admit that I sure got used to havin' Taos around," Maddie said.

"He was pretty vague with me aboot where and why he was goin'. Any idees?"

Maddie blushed, and felt a warmth run through her breast. "Well, Taos and I have become pretty close."

"I knowed it! I could tell by the way that he looked at yu!"

Maddie blushed even redder. "Well, he has some uh, unfinished business back home in New Mexico, that he has to take care of."

"Would that unfinished business have to do with a gurl?" Nolan asked.

"A lot of it does. He and this girl had a hard breakup. She said that she never wanted to see him again. Seems he may still have some feelings for her, but he has to figure it out. It's been well over a year since he's seen her."

"Whew! An' you're stuck heah fendin' off the wolves waitin' for him to get back," Nolan replied. "That's tough."

"Yup, but I understand that he has to have a clear head if he wants to move on with me or anybody else," Maddie said.

"For what it's worth, I think that he's an honest man, and a good man. I knowed he's been through a rough patch, but I can tell thet he's from good blood. If I wasn't a good judge of character, I wouldn't be sittin' here with you now."

"I really appreciate that, Jim," Maddie said before taking a sip of her coffee.

"This muffin sure is good, Maddie."

"Thanks, Jim."

"So, I was thinkin'. After I leave here, I'll take a ride over to the McCarty place, just to let 'em know thet I'm keepin an eye on 'em."

"Thanks, Jim. That means a lot to me," Maddie replied. "It'll make for a long day for you. Do you want to stay the night here after?"

"Thanks, Maddie, but I promised Didi that I'd be home sometime tonight. I may stop by for a little supper, if you don't mind," he replied.

"Not at all. I appreciate all that you are doin' for me."

* * *

The first couple of days on the trail were rough. Having a lot of time to think had not been good for Taos over the last year or more. He used to love to have time in the saddle, fishing, or hunting, alone with his own thoughts, but since the fateful day at the mining camp, that had all changed. Ida's last words continued to haunt him all these months. Now, thoughts of Maddie, and leaving her tortured him.

Taos tried to focus on the trail, the scenery, and the wildlife, but his mind kept returning to his predicament. He had no idea how Ida would react to seeing him again after all these months. Had she come to her senses? Had she cooled down? Had she moved on? And, how would he react to seeing her? Would he still feel the same attraction? What about Maddie? Taos knew that he could be very happy with her; probably happier with her than Ida, though Ida added that bit of spice and excitement, but that also meant intrigue.

* * *

Jim Nolan hated dealing with men like Doniphan McCarty. In his eyes, McCarty had no conscience. Everything he did was for his benefit, and his benefit alone. He cheated everyone around him, including his cowboys. He ruled his empire through intimidation and coercion, and killing a man meant no more to him than stepping on a bug. You couldn't ever let down your guard with him, or let him get the upper hand.

I wish he would give me an excuse to plug him, Nolan thought as he approached McCarty's ranch. As he rode through the ranch gate, Nolan checked his guns.

* * *

Taos was on his third day into the journey, and his mind kept going over the possible

scenarios of what may happen when he returned home. How would Ida react when she saw him? Would she even see him? And what about Maddie? She was an amazing woman. Was it fair to her? Was it fair if he didn't go home, and always wondered about Ida? Could he make a life with Maddie without seeing Ida first? These questions ran through his mind over and over again. He tried to concentrate on the beautiful scenery as he rode, but his mind kept wandering back to his predicament. He rode as if in a trance, and before he knew it, he was at the outskirts of Durango.

* * *

As Nolan approached the McCarty ranch house, he saw that runt, Rance McCarty, step out onto the porch.

"Gettin' bored in town, Sheriff?" Rance asked, in a sarcastic tone.

"Somethin' like that," Nolan replied, as he dismounted. "Yur father around?"

"Yu can talk to me," Rance replied.

"All the same, I'd rather talk to Doniphan," Nolan said.

"Suit yerself," Rance said, and turned and went back inside.

Nolan was left to wonder if Doniphan McCarty was even inside. While he waited, he checked his saddle, and adjusted a couple straps.

"What are yu doin' here?" Doniphan McCarty demanded, as he stepped onto the porch.

"Just payin' a neighborly visit to one of my constituents," Nolan drawled.

"Well, yur uninvited, and that means that yur trespassin'. We shoot trespassers around heah," McCarty said.

"Sounds like yur threatenin' an officer a' the law," Nolan seethed. He knew that he mustn't let McCarty get under his skin, but it was difficult.

"No such thing, Sheriff. I'm just statin' how it is out heah on the range."

"I know what yur aboot, McCarty, and I'm keepin' my eye on yu," Nolan spat back.

Nolan mounted his horse and backed away until he was out of pistol range, then turned and galloped off. *No sense in givin' McCarty the chance to shoot me in the back,* Nolan thought.

27

Chapter 27

Durango was a railroad town that was developed by the Denver and Rio Grande Railroad, as a way to service Silverton and the San Juan mining district. Railroad towns tended to be wild and wooly, as they attracted all kinds of people.

Taos found a hotel and checked in. He gave Grant to a stable boy, and paid him well to take good care of the horse.

After a bath, he sure missed the shower at Maddie's, a shave, and a change of clothes, Taos went out to get a bite to eat.

He found a cantina that seemed quieter than the other, more raucous places. The last thing that Taos wanted was trouble. A quiet dinner, early bed, and early on the trail was what he had planned.

Taos walked into the darkish cantina, and was greeted by a pleasant waitress.

"Good evening, Señor. Do ju want a table or a seat at the bar?" she asked.

"I'll take a table, thanks, and I'll start with a beer, please," he answered.

"Very good. Right this way, Señor," the waitress answered, as she guided him to a small table. She handed Taos a hand-written menu. "I'll be right back with your beer, Señor."

"Thanks, Ma'am."

Taos sat down and looked over the menu.

A few minutes later, the waitress returned with his beer.

"Thank yu," Taos said.

"Ju welcome, Señor. You know what you want?"

"Sure, I'll take the sirloin, rare, and mashed potatoes, please," he replied.

The waitress took his menu. "Very good. I put that right in for ju."

After the waitress left, Taos took a long sip of his beer, and got lost in thought.

Suddenly, he heard a loud voice. "Well, if it ain't Ben Adams."

Not having heard his name spoken aloud in about a year and a half, Taos was startled, and looked up to see a complete stranger standing on the other side of the dining room, looking at him.

"Don't know me, Ben Adams? Well, I sure as hell know yu," said the stranger, who was nearly as tall as Taos, and very muscular. He wore a gun belt, but it was obvious to Taos that he was not a fair hand by the way he had it hitched up high on his hip.

Taos stood up to face the man, who was crossing the room. "I'm sorry, you have me at a disadvantage," Taos said.

"Well, ain't that funny. I have yu at a disadvantage? Like when you rode through the mining camp throwin' sticks of dynamite in our bunkhouses?"

That morning came crashing back to Taos, the miners had certainly taken it hard. Only a few had survived, and this man must have been one of them. Taos had to answer the man, but he didn't want to inflame the situation.

"Fair enough," Taos said.

"Yu and yer cowboys ride in and start slaughterin' us, an' thet's all yu got ta say fer yerself?" The man was clearly incensed.

"We didn't have much of a choice," Taos said. "Our cattle was dyin' and bein' born deformed. We spoke to yer boss, Van der Veer, and he laughed in our faces, threatened that he had a hundred men who would kill us all if we interfered in his operation. I personally brought a letter to the Territorial Governor, and spoke to him aboot it. He said it's the price of progress. We were fightin' fer our way a life."

"Well, a lot a' good miners lost their lives that day. What aboot thet?"

"If yur boss had compromised even one inch, nothin' would a' happened. Thet's on him," Taos drawled.

It wern't him lightin' and tossin' the dynamite. Thet were yu!" The miner shouted.

The room began to clear.

The miner's hand hovered over the six gun at his side.

"Don't do it," Taos said, calmly.

The miner grabbed at his gun. It never left leather before Taos' iron boomed and blew a hole in the man's chest. The miner crumpled to the floor. Taos went over to him and checked for a heartbeat. Nothing.

Someone had run for the sheriff, and he had entered while Taos knelt over the dead miner.

* * *

Nolan was happy when Maddie's ranch house came into view. It had been a long day, and a nice meal would be a great respite before riding back to Telluride.

Maddie met him as he rode up to the porch.

"You look beat," Maddie said, as he dismounted.

"Long day in the saddle," Nolan replied, as he took his horse's saddle off.

"After you water your horse, just come on in. I have supper on the stove," Maddie said.

"Thanks, Maddie," Nolan replied.

Maddie went back inside and tended to dinner while Nolan took care of his horse, and washed up.

When Nolan opened the door, the aroma of roasting chicken wafted through his senses.

"That sure do smell good, Maddie," he exclaimed.

"It'll be done in about twenty minutes," she replied. "A glass of whiskey?"

"I could sure use one!" Nolan exclaimed.

Maddie took two glasses out of the cupboard, and the jug off the counter. She put the glasses on the kitchen table, and poured a couple fingers worth in each. She handed one to Nolan.

He touched his glass to hers and said, "To yur health."

"And yours," she replied.

They sat down at the table, and each sipped from their glasses.

"Tell me what happened with McCarty," Maddie asked.

"Wall, first off, I insulted Rance, and his father accused me of trespassin' on his land, and said they shoot trespassers," Nolan related.

"How did you handle that?" Maddie asked.

"I reminded him that he was threatenin' an officer a' the law, and he backed down a bit," Nolan said. "He knows I'm keepin' an eye on him. I made sure that I backed away. I didn't want ta take a slug in the back."

"I don't blame you for that,"Maddie answered. "Thank you for going over there."

"I hate men like thet. If I can make his life hell, it's worth it," Nolan laughed.

Maddie got up and took the chicken out of the oven to rest, she set the table, took wild rice out of a pot, and biscuits out of the warmer section of the oven. She put a plate of butter on the table.

"You mind carvin' the chicken, Jim?" Maddie asked.

"My pleasure, Maddie," he replied.

They made short work of supper and the clean up so Nolan could get on his way home.

Nolan mounted his horse. "Thanks for a great supper, Maddie."

"Thank you for all you've done, Jim." Maddie replied.

"My pleasure. I'll be out in two or three days to check on yu. Please be careful."

"Thank you, and I'll do my best."

* * *

The Durango Sheriff was a tall, lean man with silver hair, silver star on his chest, and a silver handlebar mustache. He wore his guns low, and walked like he had spent more than a few miles in the saddle.

"What's goin' on heah?" he drawled.

Taos stood up and looked straight into the lawman's steele-gray eyes, pointed at the dead miner, and said, "I just killed this man." He handed the Sheriff his guns.

"Honesty, I like thet. Mind tellin' me what happened?" the Sheriff said.

"Sure, he called me out about somethin' that happened over a year ago. He got worked up. I saw him hover over his gun and asked him not to do it. He went for his gun, I drew and shot him afore he could clear leather," Taos answered.

The sheriff, whose name was McCallister, turned to the waitress, and said, "Carmalita, is thet how it happened?"

"I didn't see the beginning, Señor, but that's how it ended," she replied.

McCallister looked Taos up and down. "I ain't never seen yu in these heah parts, son. Yu heah lookin' for trouble?"

"I've been workin' on a ranch up near Telluride, but I'm on my way to New Mexico to see family and to tend to some business," Taos replied.

"Yu got a name, son?" McCallister asked.

"Well, for the last year or more, folks have called me Taos, but my true name is Ben Adams," Taos replied.

"Yu got anybody thet can vouch for yu?" McCallister asked.

"Well, I guess Sheriff Jim Nolan in Telluride is as good as any," Taos said.

The Deputy walked in. He was a much younger man than McCallister, nearly as tall, and every bit as lean.

"Montgomery, glad yur heah," McCallister said. "Can yu take statements, and have somebody go get the undertaker?"

"Sure thing, Boss," Montgomery replied.

"Taos, I'll need yu to come with me," McCallister said, and turned for the door.

"Yes sir," Taos replied, and followed McCallister out.

They headed to the telegraph office, and McCallister held the door for Taos as they entered.

The clerk, who looked every bit the part right down to his ink-stained white shirt, bald spot, and wire rimmed spectacles, looked up from his work, and said, "Good evening Sheriff, how can I help you?"

"Hey, Smith. I need yu to send a wire to Sheriff Jim Nolan over in Telluride," McCallister said.

Smith grabbed a pencil and telegraph paper. "What do you want me to write?"

"Can you vouch for the character of a man known as Taos, name is Ben Adams. STOP He shot a man here in Durango. STOP Says it was in self defense. STOP Signed Sheriff Jake McCallister, Durango. STOP"

"I'll send it right now," Smith replied.

"Good. Let me know as soon as yu hea' back," McCallister said.

McCallister turned to Taos, and said, "Yu come with me."

They walked out of the telegraph office and walked down the street to the Sheriff's office. When they entered, McCallister put Taos' 45s in the safe. "I gotta ask yu to have a seat in the cell 'till Montgomery comes back with the reports an' we heah back from Nolan."

"I completely understand, Sheriff. It's what I expected," Taos said as he stepped into the cell.

McCallister closed and locked the door. "Did yu ever get to eat yur supper?"

"No, Sheriff," Taos replied.

"Call me McCallister. I'll go get you a steak and potatoes. Where were yu stayin?"

"Thanks. I'm stayin' at the Hotel," Taos replied.

"I'll have Montgomery get yur stuff an' bring it over. Hoss at the Livery?"

"Thank you, and, yes. I paid for one night," Taos said.

"Okay, we'll deal with that when the time comes. I expect thet yu'll be at least spendin' the night heah," McCallister said.

"I thought as much," Taos replied.

28

Chapter 28

Nolan felt pretty relaxed when he left Maddie's ranch, he had a full belly, a little buzz from the whiskey, and a full heart for doing a good deed. That's probably why he didn't notice the gunman off to the side of the trail.

A shot rang out. Nolan felt a burn in his side as he was knocked off his horse. He hit the ground hard, and rolled while pulling his 45. He laid down as if dead, and waited for the gunman to approach.

After what seemed an eternity, Nolan heard footsteps, and, as the gunman started to kick him over, Nolan grabbed his boot and lifted as hard as he could. The gunman fell backward and hit the ground. While the gunman was falling, Nolan got up on his knees, and aimed his 45 at the man's face.

"Drop it or die," Nolan commanded.

Ignoring the warning, the gunman lifted his pistol.

Nolan fired, and the top of the gunman's head blew off.

Exhausted from the exertion and loss of blood, Nolan collapsed.

* * *

After Nolan rode out, Maddie closed everything up for the night, then took her shower. It was a beautiful evening, so she poured herself another glass of whiskey and stepped out onto the front porch and sat down.

She took a sip from her glass, and took in the scenery. It was unusually calm, and the sky was turning crimson which reflected on the mountains to the east. Oh, how she wished that Taos was sitting with her to share the beauty.

Taos was gone only three days, and she missed him dearly. She prayed for his safe return to her, and the possibility of a life together.

Maddie was getting comfortable in her chair with her whiskey when she heard a shot ring out in the distance to the east. Less than a minute later, another shot.

Maddie jumped from her chair. That was the direction that Nolan had ridden.

"Oh, God, I hope he's okay!" she said out loud.

She ran inside and got changed into dungarees, a flannel shirt, and pulled on her boots. She quickly buckled on her gun belt, and grabbed the shotgun and extra shells. She ran out of the house and saddled her horse, mounted, and rode to the sound of the gunfire.

* * *

Maddie had crossed the prairie, and entered into a stand of aspens, as the ground closed in. It was getting dark, so Maddie knew she couldn't search much longer.

She rode over a knoll, and saw two horses standing and grazing in the near dark. As she approached, she saw two bodies on the ground. She spurred her horse to get there quickly. She jumped off her horse, turned the first body over, and gasped at the ghastly face of the dead gunman. She went to the next body, rolled it over, and saw that it was Nolan. She put her ear to his chest, and felt his heartbeat.

"Thank God he's alive," she said. Maddie quickly searched Nolan's body, and found the blood soaked tear in his shirt. She ripped it open, took water from her canteen, and washed the wound. It was a bloody mess, but looked like it only grazed through muscle, and did no real damage. She grabbed a handkerchief and put pressure on the wound to stop the bleeding.

Nolan began to stir. "Hey, what's goin' on?" he asked, in a gravelly voice.

"You've been shot, and lost a lot of blood," Maddie said. "Do you think you can get up?"

"I'll give it a try."

With Maddie's help, Nolan was able to gain his feet.

"Do you think that you can ride, Jim?"

"I'll have to, but we gotta get thet corpse onta his hoss."

"We'll ride back to my ranch, it's about half the distance than to town," Maddie said. "When you don't show up, Didi will send your Deputy out to look for you in the mornin'."

"I guess thet I'm in no shape ta argue," Nolan replied. "Let's see if we can wrastle thet body up on his hoss."

Maddie took the gunman's horse's reins, and led him to the corpse. Together, the two hoisted the body over the saddle.

Maddie got another look at the death gray face, and took a step back.

"I've seen him before!" she exclaimed. "He was in the McCarty branding camp when Taos and I rode over."

"Well, don't thet beat all," Nolan answered. "Maybe we can build a case agin' him."

Nolan tied the body to the man's horse. Then, with Maddie's help, climbed into his own saddle. She tied him to the pommel to make sure that he didn't fall off in case he passed out again.

They rode back toward Thunder Valley Ranch.

* * *

When they arrived at the ranch, Nolan was barely conscious. Maddie dismounted, and tied up her horse. She untied Nolan and eased him out of his saddle. She put his arm over her shoulder and walked him into the house. She sat him on a chair at the kitchen table. Then she lit lamps, grabbed a pair of scissors out of a cabinet, and cut off Nolan's shirt. Next, Maddie stoked the fire in the oven and put a pot of water on the stove. She took a look at his wound. The bleeding had mostly stopped, but it needed to be cleaned and bandaged.

"How does it look, Maddie?"

"I think you'll live, but I got to clean it real good, so you don't get an infection," she replied. Maddie had put away cloth rags for just this purpose. *There was no sense in panicking when you have to clean a wound,* she had thought at the time. She got the basket filled with rags out, and then put the hot pot of water on the table.

"This is gonna hurt a bit," she said, as she dipped a cloth into the pot of hot water.

"Do yur worst," Nolan replied.

He grimaced as she took the hot cloth and dapped the blood from the wound. She went through a half a dozen cloths before she was satisfied that the wound was clean. Next, Maddie bandaged the wound. "All set," she said.

"I sure am obliged, Maddie," Nolan said.

"I'm just glad that I found you," Maddie replied. "Now, what do we do with that body out in the dooryard?"

"Oh, him," Nolan replied. "Can we put him in yur shed for the night?"

"I suppose. I'll do it. I don't want your wound opening up," Maddie said.

"No, I'll help yu," he insisted.

They went outside, walked the horse to the shed, and Maddie opened the door. They flipped the corpse off the horse, and Maddie dragged him inside the shed. Next, she took the saddle off the horse and put it next to the body, then closed the door. She walked the horse to the barn and put it in a stall with water and grain.

Nolan had gone back inside, and took out a couple glasses and the jug of whiskey. He poured some in each, and brought them to the table.

Maddie came inside and barred the front door. She turned, and when she saw the whiskey, she said, "You read my mind."

Exhausted, they sipped their whiskey in silence, with Nolan making a groan now and again when he moved.

After they finished, Maddie rinsed the glasses in the sink, and put them up to dry.

"You can sleep in Taos' room. You know the way."

"Thanks, Maddie."

* * *

Didi barely slept. It was first light, and Jim still hadn't returned. She knew that he would be late, but this was not like him. In the twenty years that they were married, this had never happened before. *Maddie Ferguson is young and attractive, but Jim would never. . .* she thought.

She got dressed, and decided to go to the Sheriff's office. She knew that Jim's Deputy, Slade McDonald was spending the night there.

The morning was cool, and Didi was glad for the jacket that she had put on before leaving the house. She hurried to the office, knocked, and walked in.

Slade, a lanky man in his late twenties with carrot red hair and a freckled face, was having a cup of coffee when Didi rushed in.

"Mornin', Didi. Coffee?"

"Slade, Jim never came home last night," she blurted out. Tears erupted from her eyes.

Slade stood up. "Jesus, Didi, I'm sorry. Thet sure ain't like him. He had a lot of ridin' to do yestidee. Mebbe he got tired and camped out."

"He's never done that before," Didi said.

Slade put on his hat and gun belt. "I'll ride up ta the Ferguson Ranch. He was headed there and the McCarty place yestidee."

"I'm going with you," Didi said.

"Yu best not, Didi. I ken travel a lot quicker alone. No offense."

"None taken. I'll hold down the fort here," Didi said. "Thank you, Slade."

* * *

Taos had a fitful night in jail. The cot left a lot to be desired, but it was better than sleeping on the ground. He was already up when Sheriff McCallister entered the building.

"Mornin' Sheriff," Taos said.

"Mornin' son," He replied. "I ordered yur breakfast, and Carmalita should be by with it shortly."

"Thank yu," Taos said.

McCallister started a pot of coffee on the office stove. "I ain't heard nothin' from Telluride yet, but it's early," he said.

"I didn't expect to hear anythin' yet. I sure hope you heah back by this afternoon," Taos replied.

"I don't wanna hold yu any longer than I have to. Your story holds out, so I jus wanna make sure you ain't heah lookin' for no trouble."

"I understand, Sheriff. I sure would like ta get out on the road again, though."

"Just as soon as I heah back that yu can be trusted," I'll be happy to unlock thet door."

"Coffee?" McCallister asked.

"Please," Taos replied.

McCallister poured two cups of coffee, and handed one to Taos, through the bars.

"Thank yu, Sheriff," Taos said.

Carmalita entered the office with a tray of food, and put it down on McCallister's desk.

"Thank yu, honey," McCallister said. "Jess put it on the office bill."

"Ju mean de bill dat jur office don' pay," she replied.

"Uh, thet would be the one," McCallister replied.

"I am happy to pay fer my breakfast. I would have anyway," Taos interjected.

"No worries," McCallister replied. "This is jess a dance that me an' Carmalita do."

Carmalita walked over to the cell. "Thank ju Señor Taos, but Señor McCallister will pay, believe ju me."

Taos had a laugh at that. "Thank yu, Carmalita."

"I wish ju luck Señor Taos. Ju seem like a good man," she said.

"Thank yu."

Carmalita turned toward the door. "Señor Sheriff, I come back for de dishes later."

"Thanks," McCallister replied.

After she left, McCallister picked up a plate and walked to the cell door. "Sit on the cot, please, whilst I open the door."

Taos complied, and McCallister entered with a plate of bacon, eggs, beans, and bread.

* * *

Slade had packed jerky and water for the day. He rode out of town, as Didi watched, arms wrapped around herself, tears streaming down her cheeks. She tried to remain positive, but she had a bad feeling that something bad had happened to her husband, Jim.

Slade had tried to put on a positive face for Didi, but he, too, was worried. It was not like Nolan to not come home. He knew that Nolan had been checking in on Maddie Ferguson, and keeping an eye on McCarty. *Doniphan McCarty is one bad hombre*, he thought. *I wouldn't put anythin' past him.*

He kept an eye on the trail, looking for fresh tracks as he rode along. For many miles, he saw nothing. Then, as he got nearer to the open prairie, he saw a whole jumble of tracks, and what looked like blood in the sand.

Slade dismounted to get a better look. His suspicions were confirmed. It was obviously blood in two spots, and he recognized three sets of horse shoes.

"Sompin' sure happened heah," Slade said out loud. As he walked around the scene, he noticed two sets of male bootprints, and one set of female tracks. He noticed three sets of horse tracks heading back toward the prairie.

It looks like the answers may be at the Ferguson Place, Slade thought.

* * *

Maddie was up early, made coffee, and checked in on Nolan.

"How're you doing, Jim?" she asked as she peeked in on him.

Nolan looked up from his bed. She could see by his face that he had had a rough night.

"I been better, Maddie," he replied.

"You get any sleep?" she asked as he sat up. She handed him a coffee.

"Some, thanks. An' thanks fer the coffee," Nolan replied.

"I'll make breakfast, and then, we'll take a look at that wound," she said.

"I sure am obliged, Maddie," he said before taking a gulp of his coffee.

* * *

After Slade left, Didi poured herself a cup of coffee and tried to relax. She had too much nervous energy, so as soon as she finished her coffee, she began cleaning the office.

Men are real pigs! she thought as she began sweeping the floor. After what was probably an hour, there was a knock at the door.

"It's open. Come on in," Didi responded.

The door opened and Sam Hall, the telegraph operator, walked in. Hall was a middle aged, balding man.

"Hi Sam, what brings you here?" Didi asked.

"I've got a telegraph here for the Sheriff," he said as he held up an envelope.

"He isn't here right now, but if you leave it on his desk, I'll make sure that he gets it," Didi said.

"Thank you. I should get back to the office."

"Have a good day," Didi answered.

* * *

After breakfast was made, eaten, and cleaned up, Maddie prepared cloth strips again, and had water heating.

When the water was hot, she cut off the bandage and looked at the wound. It looked red and sore, but so far, there was no evidence of infection. "It's lookin' pretty good, Jim, but let me clean it up for you, and put on a new bandage."

"Thanks, Maddie," Jim said.

"I also have one of Cam's old shirts for you to put on after," She said.

"I sure am obliged," Nolan replied.

After Maddie finished applying the new bandage, she got right to the point. "What are we going to do about that dead body in my shed?"

Do yu have a buckboard?" he replied.

"Sure, out yonder," Maddie replied.

"We can load him in it, cover him up with somethin', an' I'll drive him inta town in a bit," Nolan said.

"You ain't going anywhere today. If that wound opens up, you'll bleed out," Maddie said.

"But we gotta do somethin' with him afore he gets ta stinkin'," Nolan said.

"I'll take him," Maddie replied..

"Thet won't work. I don't want you ridin' out on the prairie alone. Not with McCarty's men on the prowl."

"We don't have a lot of choice."

29

Chapter 29

T hunder Valley Ranch came into view. It had been a long ride knowing that at least one person had been shot, and maybe killed, but seeing the ranch energized Slade McDonald. Even his horse seemed to pick up the pace.

What a beautiful ranch, Slade thought as he gazed at the ranch house on the other side of the San Miguel, with mountains behind. Everyone knew that this was the best ranch in the region, and McCarty coveted it, and especially, the High Meadow in the caldera above the ranch.

As Slade rode through the gate, he saw a couple people standing near a wagon. He pushed his horse harder. As he approached, he could tell it was the Sheriff, and Maddie Ferguson loading something heavy into her buckboard.

He could see that Nolan's chest was bandaged.

"Hey, wait up!" he yelled.

Maddie and Nolan stopped and looked up when they heard the yell.

"Yu sure are a sight for sore eyes!" Nolan shouted.

"What's goin' on?" Slade asked as he dismounted.

"Whew, now thet's a question for the ages," Nolan answered. "Help us get this heah body in the buckboard, then we can fill yu in. I imagine yu an' yur hoss could use a break," Nolan answered.

Slade handled the brunt of the corpse's weight as they loaded it onto the buckboard, and covered it with a canvas tarpaulin. Maddie nearly got sick at the sight of it.

Next, Slade unsaddled his horse, gave it water and put it in the corral with a feed bag, while Maddie and Nolan went inside. Maddie put a pot of coffee on.

The coffee was finished just about the time that Slade entered the cabin.

Maddie filled three cups and put them on the kitchen table. Next, she took out a half a dozen biscuits and jam, and put a plate and a knife in each spot.

"Thanky kindly, Miss Maddie," Slade said, as he grabbed a biscuit. "So, whose gonna' spill the beans?"

Nolan filled Slade in on what happened.

"So, because my nurse says I can't ride back ta town, even on the buckboard, until my wound closes up, I'll need yu ta take the corpse back. Leave yur horse heah, an' I'll ride it back ta town in a couple a days," Nolan finished.

* * *

It was late afternoon, and Sheriff McCallister entered his office.

Taos sat up immediately, and asked, "Any news?"

McCallister took a moment, and stroked his thick mustache. "I jess was in the Telegraph Office. Smith says he ain't seen nothin' yet. Yu got anybody else thet can vouch fer yu?" McCallister answered.

"Well, the only other one in town that I can think of is Bill Haney. He's the stock buyer in Telluride," Taos answered.

The office is closed now, but I'll have Smith send a telegraph first thing in the mornin'," McCallister said.

Taos visibly slumped, but said, "Thank yu, Sheriff."

"I'm sorry, kid. I knowed yu want ta get on the road," McCallister said.

"I'm also concerned that Sheriff Nolan didn't get back to yu. Somethin' big must be goin' on," Taos said.

"Tell me more about what happened t'other night. Who was this guy?" McCallister asked.

McCallister listened intently as Taos related his story.

"The West sure is changin' fast, an' not always fer the better," McCallister drawled, after Taos finished. "They's a lot a' differnt interests, an' they sometimes come inta conflict. We've been pretty good in this area, but experiences like yurs are far too common. Look what happened when ranges began gettin' fenced off with the homesteaders movin' west. Yur too young to remember, but they was a lot o' people killed, on both sides."

"Yur right, Sheriff, I guess thet theys always been fightin' over territory an' resources," Taos said.

The door opened, and Carmalita entered carrying a tray with two plates full of food.

"Ju should have dinner at the cantina, Señor Sheriff instead of this place," she said as she put the tray down.

"I have a prisoner, Carmalita," McCallister replied.

"Ju should take him with ju."

"Everytime he walks into the cantina, he shoots somebody," McCallister drawled, with a twinkle in his eye.

"Ju are incorrigible," Carmalita replied as she exited the office.

After Carmalita left, McCallister picked up Taos' plate and brought it to the cell door.

"Yu know the routine, son," he said.

Taos stepped away from the cell door and sat on the bunk while McCallister brought in the plate of food.

"That Carmalita is sure somethin'," Taos offered.

"She sure is," McCallister agreed. "If I was twenty years younger, I'd sure be interested."

"Have yu evah been married, Sheriff?" Taos asked.

McCallister closed and locked the cell, then grabbed his dish and a chair. He brought them in front of the cell, and sat down to face Taos as he ate.

"Well, I was, a long time ago, son. I was a lot differnt back then. I was a young buck, sewin' my wild oats, as it were. I was ridin' for a rancher up in Wyomin', and fell in love with his daughter. She had eyes the color of robin's eggs and straw colored hair. Sweeter'n honey, she was. She fell hard fer me too."

McCallister paused to eat some of his dinner.

"I nevah deserved her," he continued. "She was everythin' thet was good an' wholesome. I was like a wild mustang thet couldn't be tamed. I couldn't stop carousin' and gamblin'. Eventually, her daddy ran me outa Wyomin'. He said if I eva came back, he'd shoot me. Neva have been back ta Wyomin'."

"That's quite the story, Sheriff. I'm sorry for that," Taos said.

"Don't be, son. I done it ta myself," McCallister said, between bites. "Life is a journey with problems to solve, lessons to learn, but most of all, experiences thet help one grow as a man."

"Powerful words, Sheriff," Taos said.

* * *

It was well into the evening when Slade arrived back in Telluride. He stopped at the undertaker's first, and had him take photos of the gruesome corpse, search for identification, and start the embalming process.

After meeting with the undertaker and offloading the corpse, Slade rode the buckboard to the Sheriff's office. He got out and tied the horse to the rail. He saw that light was on, so Didi must still be at the office.

Slade opened the door and stepped into the office. He didn't notice Didi right away, then as he walked in, he saw her head down on Nolan's desk, sound asleep. He walked over to her and gently jostled her shoulder.

Didi woke with a start. When her eyes focused and she recognized Slade, she asked, "Did you find Jim? Is he okay?"

"I did, and he will be fine," Slade said.

"Where is he? Why isn't he here?"

Slade pulled up a chair and sat down. "He's gonna be okay," he said.

"'Gonna be?' What does that mean?" Didi demanded.

"I'll give it ta yu straight. The Sheriff was ambushed on his way back ta town. He was shot at, an' had a bullet crease his side. It made a powerful bad wound, but didn't hit nothin' vital. Maddie Ferguson bandaged him up, but he can't be moved until it heals some. He lost a lot a' blood. I seen it in the sand," Slade said.

"Oh, my," Didi answered. "I'll go see him in the mornin'."

"I'll ride out with yu. I don't trust them McCarty's for nothin'."

* * *

Doniphan McCarty was in his office working on the ranch accounts, when Rance burst in.

"What is it, boy? Don't yu know thet when I'm workin' in heah, I don't want ta be disturbed?" Doniphan spat out, seething with contempt for his only son. Doniphan's wife, Jeannie had died giving birth to Rance. Doniphan had turned mean after that, and blamed Rance for her death.

Doniphan and Jeannie had settled in the Dakota Territory, and had a tough time making it because of the dry weather and poor soil until Doniphan traded his plow for cattle. After Jeannie died, Doniphan had pulled up stakes and moved, along with young Rance, to Colorado. They had tried a few different areas over the years before finally settling in the San Miguel Valley about seven years earlier.

"Chet Morgan ain't come back," Rance replied.

Doniphan's face flushed. He stood up, wringing his hands. "This ain't good. It ain't good at all. I could give a shit about Morgan, but we needed the Sheriff dead, dammit!"

"I jess hope they can't trace him back ta us," Rance replied.

"Deny, deny, deny," Doniphan said. "They got no written proof he ever worked for us. I never use names in my books, an' we allus pay in cash."

* * *

Didi had another fretful night, but she did manage to get more sleep than the night before. Knowing that Jim, the love of her life, was alive, and going to be okay, made all the difference.

Didi had moved west to Colorado with her family. Her father had planned on making it big in the silver mines. He made enough to feed his family, but not much more. Her mother, a talented singer, worked in various dance halls over the years, and Didi expected that she made money on the side providing men pleasure. Didi worked odd jobs growing up, and never expected to have much luck in life, until she met Jim. Jim Nolan was Didi's world. Didi knew that she wasn't a good looking woman, and men rarely noticed her at a party or a dance. Jim, however, was smitten with her as soon as he laid eyes on her. He was nearly ten years older than her, but he was tall with rugged good looks. He had a tough exterior, but a gentle heart. She had fallen for him too. They married after just six months of dating. The only disappointment in their marriage was her inability to give Jim a son. He never said anything, but, at times, she could sense his disappointment. She knew that they had a good relationship, but lately, she had been taking him for granted. Maybe they had just gotten comfortable together. Maybe she had just gotten lazy. He was a good man, and was always steadfast, and dependable. Things were sure going to change. This scare woke her up, woke up the fire in her heart for her husband, Sheriff Jim Nolan.

She got out of bed, did her toilette, got dressed, packed an overnight bag, and had her coffee, and fried a couple of eggs and made toast for breakfast. Next, she packed a basket with sandwiches, a canteen, and snacks. Didi hurried, in the early morning chill, to the Sheriff's office.

Deputy Slade McDonald was waiting, with the buckboard and an extra horse.

"Did you even sleep?" Didi asked.

"Jess a little, I suppose," Slade drawled. He took Didi's overnight bag and put it in the back of the buckboard, just behind the bench.

He helped Didi into the buckboard, and she put the basket in front of her feet. Then, Slade climbed up and took the reins.

Slade made a clicking noise, and the horse stepped forward. The buckboard lurched ahead with a start. They rode out of town in the pre-dawn light. The sun's first rays were touching the mountain peaks, which provided an ethereal glow to the atmosphere.

* * *

McCallister was up early and stopped off at the cantina to order breakfast for Taos and himself. He planned to be at the Telegraph Office as soon as it opened.

He was waiting in the chill morning air, when Smith, the Telegraph Operator, showed up.

Good mornin' Sheriff," Smith said. "You sure are here early. You must have an important cable to send out."

"Mornin' Smith. Yeah, I need to send another up ta' Telluride, pronto," McCallister answered.

Smith unlocked the door and said, "Follow me."

They stepped into the office, which was still dark, so Smith lit a couple oil lamps to brighten it up. He then started the oil stove to take the chill off before sitting down at his desk.

"Okay, Sheriff, I'm ready."

McCallister gave him the information and the message, as before. When he was done, he said, "Again, please let me know as soon as you hear back from Telluride. Thanks."

"You got it, Sheriff," Smith said.

McCallister exited the Telegraph Office, and walked toward his office. As luck would have it, he and Carmalita arrived at his door at the same time. He opened and held the door as Carmalita entered with a tray of food.

"Good timin', Carmalita," McCallister said. "Just gettin' back from the Telegraph."

Taos stood up when they entered. "Good mornin' Sheriff, Carmalita," he said, with a nod to each.

"I got ju breakfast here, Señor Taos," Carmalita said. "I hope ju got a good appetite."

"He's allus got a good appetite, Carmalita," McCallister answered. "Keepin' him heah is costin' me a fortune."

"Den why don' ju let him go, Señor Sheriff?"

"I will as soon as I get somebody to vouch for him," McCallister replied.

"He not a bad hombre, Señor, let him go," Carmalita pleaded.

"Thank you, Carmalita. I appreciate it, but the Sheriff has a job to do," Taos said. "Hopefully, we will hear somethin' back later this mornin'."

"Well, whenever ju are let out, Señor Taos, stop at the cantina for a meal on me," Camalita said as she headed for the door.

"Thank you, ma'am. I will," Taos replied.

After Carmalita left, McCallister brought Taos' breakfast to the cell door. "You know the routine, son,' he said.

Taos nodded and walked to the bunk and sat down.

McCallister brought in the dish, set it on the small table in the cell, then left the cell and re-locked the door.

"Thank yu, Sheriff," Taos said as he sat down to eat his breakfast.

McCallister sat down outside the cell and began eating. "I sent the telegraph earlier," he said.

"Thank yu, Sheriff," Taos said between bites.

* * *

Bill Haney had just settled down to his books after opening the office and lighting the small oil stove, when his door burst open.

Bill looked up from his books and saw a tow-headed, teenage boy standing in front of him.

"Can I help you?" Bill asked.

"Good mornin' mistah. I'm Zack Bannon. I have a message from the telegraph for yu," he replied. Zack put out his hand, which held some papers.

154

"Thanks," Bill said as he took the papers, which he proceeded to read. "Oh, my, he said. I best get to the telegraph office straight away." Bill reached into his pocket and pulled out a silver coin and tossed it to the boy. "Here ya' go, kid."

Bill got up from his chair and followed the boy out of his office.

* * *

McCallister was making the rounds of the downtown area of Durango. He gazed in wonderment at how much the town had grown in just a few years. This was a tribute to the railroad. Durango had become a railroad hub which served to gather and move goods, and people, around southern Colorado and northern New Mexico Territories. Growth had brought more prosperity, but it brought with it more problems too. Gambling was always a draw for bad men and loose women, each trying to make a quick score. It brought jobs, too, though, and families, a school, and churches. Sure, there was a rough element, but there was progress too.

"McCallister!" someone had shouted his name. He looked around to see Smith running toward him with a paper in his hand.

McCallister met Smith in the street.

"I have the telegraph that you've been waiting for," Smith shouted over the din of horses and wagons in the street.

McCallister ran to meet him. "Thanks, Smith," he said when they met.

The telegraph operator handed McCallister the message.

McCallister reached into his pocket and pulled out a pair of reading glasses, and took a look at the message.

"Good news," Smith said.

"The best." McCallister replied. "Thank yu for gettin' this to me, Smith. I am much obliged."

McCallister hurried back to his office.

Taos was stretched out on the bunk when the Sheriff entered. He looked up to see a wide grin on McCallister's face.

"Wall, it's yur lucky day, Son," McCallister said.

"You got the telegram?" Taos asked.

"Sho enough did. Yur friend, Haney came through, and corroborated yur story," McCallister said. The Sheriff wrote on a piece of paper, and handed it to Taos after he unlocked the cell door. "Give this ta ole Bob Tanner at the livery. It's a voucher for boardin' yur horse."

"I can't thank you enough, Sheriff," Taos said.

"I jess wish I coulda had yu outa heah sooner. Yu take good care a' yurself, Son. If yu ever come back to Durango, an' I hope yu do, I'd like ta have dinner with yu in the cantina. I wish you a safe and fruitful journey."

The big man stuck out his hand, which Taos grasped. "Thank yu, Sheriff."

30

Chapter 30

After Taos gathered his belongings and saddled Grant, he decided to take up Carmalita's offer for a meal.

Taos tied Grant to the rail and stepped in through the door. A picture of the last fateful time he had been in the cantina shot through his mind.

"Señor Taos, it is good to see dat ju are a free man," Carmalita said, which jostled Taos out of his trance.

Startled, Taos said, "Oh, Carmalita, thank you. I hope that it's okay that I take you up on yur offer fer a meal."

"I am a woman of my word. I am very happy that ju are free," she said. "Let me get you a table. Follow me."

Carmalita was wise to take Taos to a different table than last time, and gave him a seat that faced the door. "How is dis, Señor Taos?" she asked.

"Perfect, Carmalita," he replied.

"A beer, Señor?" she asked as she placed a menu on his table.

"Please," he replied, as he sat down.

Carmalita left to get his beer as Taos perused the menu.

"Ju ready to order, Señor Taos?" Carmalita asked as she placed his glass on the table.

"Sure, Carmalita. I'll have the T-bone, cooked rare, mashed potatoes, and green beans," he replied. "Thank yu."

"I be back right away."

Taos took a sip of his beer and contemplated the time lost over the last few days. He hated to lose the time on his quest to get home to New Mexico and settle things with Ida. He missed Maddie, though. His feelings for her were strong, but different from his feelings for Ida. How were things at the ranch? He hadn't heard back from Sage recently. Was there a reason for that? But there were positives too. He believed that he made a friend in Sheriff McCallister, who had treated him fairly. McCallister also gave him some perspective on life.

Carmalita approached the table with Taos' lunch. "Here ju go, Señor," she said, as she put the dish on the table.

Startled, Taos looked up from his thoughts. "Oh, thank you, Carmalita," he replied.

"Ju were deep in thought, Señor Taos. I'm sorry to startle ju," she said. "May I sit down?" Carmalita asked.

"Yes, of course," Taos answered. "I'm sorry. I was distracted."

"May I ask why?"

"I'm just thinking about things that I have to do, Carmalita," Taos said.

"I'm sure spending a few nights in jail was not in jur plan," she said.

"No, and it put me way behind my schedule, but it gave me some perspective, too."

"Well, Señor Taos, I hope that ju come back to Durango again, and if ju do, you stop to say hello. I wish ju the best in jur travels, and that ju figure out whatever it is that is bothering ju."

Carmalita got up from the table. "Now enjoy the meal."

"Thank you for everything, Carmalita," Taos said.

* * *

Slade drove the buckboard through the ranch gate. Didi could hardly hold her composure. Between her excitement to see Jim, and her concern for his health, she could barely sit still on the buckboard.

As they approached the cabin, Didi recognized Jim sitting on the front porch. She wished that Slade would hurry, but he was already going at a fast pace. He had already pushed the horses hard to get back to the ranch early in the day.

Jim noticed the buckboard coming through the gate, and his heart leaped when he saw two people sitting up front. He knew that Didi must have come with Slade.

Maddie was working in the garden when she heard the buckboard approach. She took out a kerchief and wiped her brow, then walked to the cabin. She arrived just as Slade stopped.

Didi jumped off the buckboard as Slade was tying it up and ran onto the porch and wrapped herself around Nolan, who had just stood up.

"Oh, Jim," Didi moaned. "I was so worried about you!"

"Ah, Didi, it'll take more than a measly bullet to knock this ol' hoss down." Nolan replied.

* * *

It was mid afternoon when Taos rode out of Durango. He knew that he wouldn't get too far before he had to set up camp for the night, but he wanted to get out of town. He wanted, no, needed to be alone. He thought best when he was alone. The trail went south along the Animas River for a few miles before heading east toward Pagosa Springs. The Animas is big water compared to the streams of New Mexico, other than the Rio Grande. Taos wished that he had time to explore it for trout, but that would have to wait.

He had been delayed enough.

He bid adieu to the rock strewn stream and followed the trail east. The country opened up to a plateau, and Taos could see the San Juan Mountains in the distance. After riding about four hours, he stopped to make camp by a small stream.

Taos unsaddled Grant, and led him to the stream to drink, then hobbled him where he could graze. Next, Taos found a sapling and cut off a branch and stripped it of sprouts and leaves. He opened up one of his saddle bags and dug out a hook and a piece of line. He tied it to the end of the branch, then found and caught a grasshopper. He baited the hook with the grasshopper, then found a deep pool in the stream. Taos flipped the grasshopper up to the head of the pool and watched it float down into the heart of the pool. The insect disappeared in a swirl, and the line went taught. About two minutes later, Taos landed and dispatched a beautiful cutthroat trout. He found another pool and repeated the process. After cleaning the fish, Taos gathered wood and started a fire.

There's nothin' like fresh trout cooked over a fire, Taos thought as he ate the succulent meat.

After his dinner, Taos cleaned up, brought Grant for another drink from the stream, and hobbled him for the night.

Taos knew that sleep wouldn't come easy, it never did since that fateful day. So, he sat up by the fire and watched the piñon burn, it crackled as it sent embers into the sky to burn out in the night air. After the fire burned down to coals, he spread out his bed roll, and added to the fire, then stretched out for the night. As he tried to sleep, the same memories flooded into his brain. The fight with the miners, Ida's harsh words, The Colonel's hurt expression as he rode away.

* * *

Maddie had made a big stew expecting that Slade and Didi would show up, and the aroma was wonderful when everyone entered the cabin.

"Maddie, I can't thank you enough for takin' care of Jim, and feedin' all of us," Didi said.

"It's the least that I could do. He got shot on account of protecting me," Maddie replied.

"We'll be outa your hair after lunch," Didi said.

"The heck you will," Maddie replied. "You won't leave until tomorrow after breakfast, at the earliest."

"That is mighty kind of you, Maddie," Nolan said.

Didi helped Maddie set the table, while Nolan and Slade stepped out onto the porch.

"How're you feelin', boss?" Slade asked, as he rolled a cigarette.

"I've sure been better, but the wound's healin'," he replied.

Slade lit his cigarette. "What are we gonna' do about McCarty?"

"I want ta' be pretty well healed before I pay him a visit," Nolan said.

"I oughta' go with yu," Slade replied.

"Yep. After this," Nolan pointed to his bandaged side, "I ain't takin' no chances. Yu ken head back ta town after lunch, an' I'll be back tomorrow afternoon."

"Alright, Boss," Slade replied.

Maddie stepped out onto the porch. "Lunch is ready."

* * *

Taos got up before the sun. It was better to be busy than to try to sleep. He kindled the coals from his fire, and prepared a pot to make coffee. Next, he brought Grant to the stream to drink, then let him graze.

He stood by the fire for a few minutes to take off the morning chill. After he was sufficiently warmed, Taos turned over a few rocks and grabbed a couple sowbugs, and attached them to the fish hook. He hiked upstream until he found a likely looking pool, and tossed the baited hook into the swirl of current at the head. The bait had barely hit the water when there was a giant swirl. Taos set the hook, and felt the throbbing tug of a large fish, much larger than the fish of the night before. The enraged cutthroat trout circled the pool and headed toward the tail end. Taos ran, splashing the water to scare the trout back into the pool. It worked! Just before the lip of the pool, the fish turned back up stream.

"I got you now!" Taos yelled as the fish wore itself out. He beached the seventeen inch hen cutthroat, admired its beauty then let it go. "I'll catch a couple smaller ones. You must be a prime spawner."

After releasing the large trout, Taos gathered up more bait and went to the next pool upstream. Again, he tossed his baited hook into the head of the pool. Again, a trout grabbed it. This time, it was pan-sized, at about thirteen inches. He quickly dispatched and cleaned the fish.

Taos took the fish back to the fire and roasted it on a stick. It only took a few minutes for the fish to cook on the hot fire.

After breakfast, Taos packed up and hit the trail. It was going to be a hot day. That would limit his miles for the day. As much as he wanted to hurry back to his parents' ranch, he wasn't going to kill Grant to get there.

* * *

After breakfast, Didi helped Maddie clean the dishes while Nolan, who's wound was healing well, packed up the buckboard. Slade had already rode out.

While working in the kitchen, Maddie had some time to chat.

"I've sure had an eye openin' in all this," Didi said.

"In what way?" Maddie asked.

"Jim and I have been married for a long time. I think that we got comfortable with each other. Not that we don't love each other, but after a while, the spark seems to go. Nearly losing Jim gave me a real scare. I realized how important he is to me. I'll never take him for granted again." Didi said.

"You mean the world to him," Maddie answered. "He said as much the other night."

"Thank you for letting me know. That means so much to me," Didi blushed.

"Let's pack a nice picnic lunch for the two of you," Maddie suggested.

"What a wonderful idea," Didi said.

Nolan looked up when the women stepped out onto the porch. "Didi, yu ready for a long day's ride?" he said.

"I sure am. We packed lunch in my basket," Didi said with a knowing smile towards Maddie.

"Thet sure sounds great," Nolan replied, as he took the basket from Didi and placed it in the buckboard. Next, he winced a little as he helped her up into the buckboard. Then, Nolan untied the horse and backed the small wagon around before climbing in and taking the reins.

"Thanks agin' for everythin', Maddie," he shouted as he got the horse started.

Maddie watched as the buckboard rolled out of sight. She hugged herself. She felt lonely for the first time in a few days.

31

Chapter 31

After days of hard riding, Taos was on his home turf, Los Piñons Ranch. He spotted the adobe ranch house in the distance, and his spirit lifted. Grant, too, seemed to sense that he was home, and picked up his gait. A rush fell over Taos. He suddenly realized how much he had missed his family. How would they receive him? Sage hadn't replied to his last two letters, or at best, they hadn't found him. Had he taken the coward's way out by riding off? Would they welcome him back? Was Los Piñons going to survive? These questions had haunted him from the day that he left the ranch.

* * *

"Rider comin', Daddy," Sage reported when she spotted the lone horseman approaching the ranch.

The Colonel, who had not fared well since the day that Ben had rode off, struggled to get out of his chair. "Go get me the binoculars," he said to Sage.

After returning with the binoculars, she handed them to the Colonel.

The Colonel steadied himself against the porch railing as he put the piece to his eyes. He took a long look.

"Well, I'll be darned!" the Colonel said. "If it ain't Ben!"

"Let me see!" Sage exclaimed. Is it really him?"

The Colonel handed Sage the binoculars. She put the field glasses up to her eyes. "Oh, Daddy, it is him!" she exclaimed.

Sage handed the binoculars to the Colonel and ran out through the ranch gate, no time to saddle a horse!

When Taos saw Sage running to greet him, he spurred Grant on, and the big bay covered the distance with amazing speed. When Taos reached Sage, he tightened the reins, and fairly leapt out of the saddle. Sage wrapped her arms around him.

"Oh, Ben! We've missed you so," she exclaimed. "It's been such a long time. I was worried that you were nevah comin' home."

Taos took her hand and they walked toward the ranch house.

"I've sure missed you too," Taos answered. "Did you get my letters?"

"I haven't gotten a letter from you in almost a year, Ben," Sage answered.

"Strange, I sent two in the last four months," Taos replied.

"Things have changed around heah since you left, Ben."

"How so, Sage?" Taos asked.

"Oh, Ben, there has been so much tumult. With the mine closin' there has been a lot of anger around town. Shopkeepers and bar owners have lost a lot of money. They blame the ranchers, in general, and us, in particular," Sage said. "They see you and Daddy as the cause of it all."

"They don't care that the mine was killin' the Red River?" Taos asked.

"No, and Mom doesn't dare go to town anymore. Daddy and I have to go to pick up supplies, and bear the sideways looks, and nasty comments. It's taken a lot outa' him. He always loved to go to town and hold court. Not anymore. It's sad, Ben," Sage said.

"I never would have guessed. Maybe that scoundrel, Van der Veer was right: people care more aboot money than anythin' else."

"No such thing as loyalty anymore," Sage replied.

Sage stopped and turned to Taos. "Ben, what brings you back after all this time?" she asked.

* * *

Nolan and Slade rode through the gate of the Circle M Ranch.

The ranch was certainly impressive, though less than ten years old, McCarty had built a large house, ample corrals, barns, bunk house, and other amenities. Word had it that he had a decent pile of cash when he came to the area. It was also said that McCary had stolen or swindled most of his money.

"How do yu want ta' handle this, Boss," Slade asked Nolan.

"Wal, McCarty's sure slick, an' he's gonna deny everythin'" Nolan answered. "I'll ask ta' see the books. I got the warrant from Judge Greene, so he has ta' show me 'em. But, if I had ta' guess, I bet we won't find Morgan's name anywhere."

"I'll keep my eyes peeled fer any funny business," Slade said as they approached the ranch house.

The lawmen dismounted and stepped up onto the porch. Nolan knocked on the door, and then took a step back, and to the side, while Slade stayed off a few feet and surveyed the area, hands hovering over his guns.

Nolan heard footsteps inside the house, and readied to draw iron.

The door opened, revealing Doniphan McCarty, a menacing expression on his face, wielding a double barrelled twelve gauge.

"Nolan, I told yu thet if you evah came back heah, yu better have a warrant, or I'd shoot yu as a trespasser," McCarty announced.

"Hold yer hosses, McCarty. I got a warrant from Judge Greene, an' I'm gonna take it outa my shirt pocket, so jus' relax," Nolan replied.

McCarty relaxed a little. "Leme see it," he demanded.

Nolan slowly took the warrant from his shirt pocket while Slade covered him, ready to draw.

"Heah it is, McCarty," Nolan said, as he handed the warrant to the rancher.

McCarty looked the warrant over and began to laugh. "Yu kin search all yu want, Sheriff, but yu ain't gonna find nothin'."

"Thet may be, but we gotta look. This is aboot a man named Morgan who took a shot at me an' creased my side. I heared thet he worked for yu." Nolan drawled.

"I never heard of him, but too bad he wasn't a better shot," McCarty snapped.

"Yu gonna let us in, or are we gonna have ta shoot our way in?" Nolan shot back.

McCarty stepped back from the door and waved the two lawmen in.

As he stepped through the doorway, Nolan spied Rance standing in the corner of the room holding a Winchester.

"I'd put thet down if I were yu, sonny," Nolan said.

McCarty nodded at his son, and Rance lowered the rifle.

Once the two lawmen were in the room, Nolan said, "Now, let us see yur payout books."

"I'll be jus a minute, Sheriff," McCarty said with a sneer.

Nolan and Slade looked around the room, which was nicely appointed. It looked like it had a woman's touch, though Nolan knew that his wife had died many years ago. Rance seemed to fidget about uncomfortably.

"Did this feller, Chet Morgan evah work heah?" Nolan demanded.

"Like my Pa said, I nevah heared a' him," Rance replied.

By the way Rance's eyes shifted back and forth as he answered, Nolan knew that he was lying, but to prove it was another thing.

Presently, McCarty walked into the room carrying a few large books. He slammed them down on a table. "Have at it," he said. "Yu can look all yu want, but, like I said afore, yu ain't gonna find nothin' that connects me to Chet Morgan."

"I nevah said I was lookin' for Chet Morgan. I only said Morgan," Nolan drawled.

McCarty rushed to backpedal. "Well, everybody around heah knows that Chet Morgan was a bad hombre, just lookin' fer trouble wherever he went. I jus assumed tet's who yu was lookin' fer."

"Is that so? I must not be doin' sech a good job of sheriffin', since I nevah heard of him before he tried to do me in," Nolan replied.

"Well, thet's between yu and yer constituents next election day, Sheriff," McCarty snapped back.

"I suppose it is," Nolan drawled. "Slade, let's yu an' I take a look see at these books."

"Yu got it, Boss," Slade replied.

"Yu can go aboot yer day, McCarty, I'll let yu know if'n we find sumpin'," Nolan said.

"I'll hang around, jus' the same," McCarty said. "Rance, I'm good heah, why don't yu go check on the men."

"Will do, Pa," Rance replied, as Nolan and Slade dug into the books.

* * *

Taos took a minute to formulate his answer. He had thought about this moment over and over on his trip back home to New Mexico, but now he was stuck on the words. How could he summarize the many months and experiences into a few short sentences? How could he explain his predicament between his old love for Ida, and this new, wonderful woman, Maddie that had come into his life? How could he make amends for abandoning his family when they needed him? He had to come face to face with that act of selfishness.

Taos started slowly, "Sage, I feel so bad aboot the way I rode off on you and the Colonel, and Ma. I jus' had to get out. I couldn't bear the way Ida spoke to me, I began to believe that Jack Parker's death was on my hands. . ."

"But, you know it wasn't," Sage interrupted. "That was Ida Parker poisoning your mind, and poisoning everyone else's minds about you. Ben, she ain't the woman you think she is."

"Sage, I know thet you've never liked her much," Taos replied.

"That's got nothin' to do with it. Losin' her father changed her. Yeah, she was always headstrong and ill tempered, but she's changed Ben. She's full of hate now."

"Do you think she'd see me?" Taos asked.

"I haven't an idea, Ben," Sage answered.

"It's been many months that I've been gone. I killed men; more than I care to admit, Sage. But, I never murdered nobody. For the last few months, I've been workin' on a ranch over west of Telluride. The ranch owner is a young widow. Her husband an' son was murdered by a local rancher who wants her ranch. I think that I love her, and she told me that she loves me. But, I still got feelin's for Ida, and I gotta see where I stand with her, and I can't be of help to anybody until I get myself figured out."

Sage's eyes flashed fire. "Forget Ida, Ben! She ain't no good for you!"

"I gotta see thet for myself, Sage."

Sage let go of Taos' hand and started marching toward the ranch. "Suit yerself," she said over her shoulder.

Taos took off his sombrero and whacked it against his leg, then pushed his hair back and replaced the sombrero. "Women!" He exclaimed, then began walking toward Los Piñons with Grant in tow.

* * *

"What's all the hub bub about, Colonel," Lorena asked as she stepped out onto the porch.

The Colonel, who had been watching Taos and Sage through the field glasses, turned to face his wife. "Ben's home," he said.

"Let me see," she demanded, as she grabbed for the binoculars. The Colonel handed them to her and she quickly put them up to her eyes. "Oh, my lawd! It is him! But why ain't they walkin' together?'

"They was. Must've had an argument, like they always do," the Colonel replied.

"Well, I best be gettin' to cookin' somethin'," Lorena said, then handed the binoculars back to her husband, and ran into the house.

The Colonel could tell that Sage was angry-very angry about something. She and Ben always had their spats, and they always made up, but from her body language, the Colonel could tell that this was something bigger.

As she approached the house, the Colonel could see that Sage's face was red with rage.

"Whowee, somebody's got your pot boilin' over," the Colonel said as Sage stepped up onto the porch.

"Not now, Daddy," Sage said as she dashed past him and into the house.

* * *

Nolan and Slade finished going through McCarty's books, and found nothing. McCarty had numbered his employees, and had not used names. There was no way for the lawman to distinguish one cowboy from another, and they were all paid in cash, according to the books.

"Satisfied?" McCarty sniped.

"Hardly," Nolan replied. "Show us yur office."

"But, yu already seen my books," McCarty replied.

"We seen the books thet yu showed us," Nolan said. "Now, let's see yur office."

McCarty turned, and over his shoulder, said, "This way."

Nolan and Slade followed McCarty down a hallway to a room off to the right. McCarty stopped, took out a set of keys, and unlocked the door, before waving the lawmen in.

Nolan surveyed the room, and noticed a black safe. He pointed to it and said, "Open it."

McCarty cursed under his breath, then walked to the safe, turned the combination, and opened the door.

"Empty it, an' put everythin' on the desk here," Nolan ordered.

"McCarty, obviously in a rage, emptied the safe as ordered.

Besides a pile of papers, there was a good amount of cash.

"Yu take the cash, McCarty. I don't want ta' be accused of stealin' nothin',"

170

Nolan said.

McCarty took the cash and left the office.

"Thet's a big pile a' cash," Slade said, after McCarty had left.

"Yup," Nolan replied. "Honest ranchers ain't nevah got thet much money on hand."

Nolan sat down at the desk. "I'll go thru these heah papers. You go through the drawers. Jus dump 'em out on the floor when yur done with 'em. Even if we don't find nothin' I want McCarty to feel some pain."

"My pleasure, boss," Slade replied.

* * *

The Colonel watched as Taos walked to the ranch house with Grant. Taos brought the large bay to one of the corrals, took off the saddle, and let Grant free to drink and eat.

"Not much of a sisterly welcome for the prodigal son, I reckon," the Colonel said as Taos approached the front porch.

"Hello Colonel," was all that Taos could muster.

The Colonel poured two glasses of Kentucky Bourbon and handed one to Taos. "Well, I for one am glad to have you back, Ben."

"Thank you, Colonel," Taos said as he took the glass from his father.

"Here's to my son's return," the Colonel said, and touched his glass to Taos' before taking a sip. "You know, I may be the only one who understands why you left."

Taos took a long draught from his glass. "How's that?" he asked.

"That's how we got out here. I packed us up and left Wisconsin because I couldn't bear to face all the mothers and widows of my men who were slaughtered in the war. Ida Parker was ridin' you like a rented mule. I could see how you needed to get away. Being here was gonna be a constant reminder of the fight with the miners and Jack Parker's death," the Colonel said.

"But, I abandoned you, Mother, and Sage at a time when you needed me," Taos replied.

"Son, the damage that mine did to the river is going to take years to repair, if it ever can be. You can't do anything about that," the Colonel said.

"I guess that I was naive about that. I thought that once the minin' stopped, things would get better," Taos replied.

"I'm guessin' that what you and Sage were fightin' about was why you came home. It wasn't really about the ranch, was it? Am I right?"

"It's complicated, Colonel, and Sage wasn't willin' to listen to the whole story," Taos replied.

The Colonel refilled their glasses, then sat down. "I'm listenin'. Take a seat," the Colonel said.

Taos sat down in the chair next to his father. He took a sip from his glass before he began.

"I know that I was gone a long time. I spent the first year or more runnin' from place to place, gamblin', drinkin', and carousin', just to put Ida and that day out a' my mind. I did things that I ain't proud of. I got into fights, and I gunned men down, but I never murdered nobody. I only shot in self defense." Taos stopped and took another drink.

The Colonel, who had been listening intently, mirrored Taos by taking a drink from his own glass before saying, "Go on."

"Well, I happened into Telluride, thinkin' about settlin' down a bit. I went to the cattle buyer, a man named Bill Haney, and chatted with him for a bit, and asked him if he knew of any ranches who was hirin' cow hands. He seemed to take a likin' to me, and trusted in me, because he mentioned a ranch out on the San Miguel, Thunder Valley Ranch, it's called. It's owned by a young widow, who's husband and son were murdered."

"Say no more! I know how this ends. You and this woman have fallen in love, but you still got feelin's for Ida. Right?" the Colonel said.

"Yes, sir, but that ain't all a' it. I couldn't even think of comin' home, Ida or not, if I hadn't gotten things right in my head. That's the part that Sage wouldn't give me a chance to say."

"She'll come around, Ben. Just give her time. Ida is another story altogether. She's full of hate, that one," the Colonel said.

"That's what Sage said about Ida," Taos replied.

Lorena burst out of the front door. "Colonel, why didn't you call me?" she demanded. "I heard voices out here, and saw Ben!"

Taos stood up and hugged his mother. "It's so good to see you, Mother," he said.

Tears of joy streamed down Lorena's cheeks, as she buried her face in Taos' shoulder.

"Oh, Ben, I'm so happy to see you, I've prayed for you every day," she whispered.

"I'm alright," Taos replied. "I'm sorry that I've been gone so long."

"I'm so glad that you're safe."

Sage stepped out onto the porch. Taos let go of their mother, stood still, and looked at his sister.

"I'm sorry, Ben. I shoulda' given you a chance to talk instead of stormin' off," she said.

'It's alright, Sage. I've been gone a long time, and left everyone in the lurch. I'm sure sorry for doin' that," Taos replied.

Sage stepped to him and Taos took her in his arms.

32

Chapter 32

Nolan and Slade had made a disaster of Donaphin McCarty's office. "Well, we didn't find nothin', but we did accomplish a lot," Nolan said.

"How's thet, Boss?" Slade asked.

"This is gonna' take him down a notch. He's gonna' be real pissed, but there ain't nothin' he can do aboot it," Nolan replied. "Now, let's go talk to his cowboys."

The two lawmen left the room, and walked out of the house without such as a nod to either of the McCarty's.

Nolan and Slade mounted their horses and rode over to a corral where cowboys were breaking a horse.

"Any of y'all knowed Chet Morgan?" Nolan asked as the cowboys turned to look at him and Slade.

"Who's askin'," a cowboy asked.

"Sheriff Jim Nolan and Deputy Slade McDonald," Nolan answered.

"Alright. Everybody knowed who thet bad hombre was," the cowboy replied.

"Did he evah work heah, for the McCarty's?" Nolan pressed.

"Hmmmm, I couldn't rightly say. How aboot you boys? Did Chet Morgan evah work heah?" the cowboy asked.

"I ain't nevah seen him workin' heah," a cowboy answered, with a grin.

"Me neither," answered another, with a laugh.

"Alright, let me ask this way, was Chet Morgan evah employed by the McCarty's," Nolan asked.

"Yu ought ta' ask Mistah McCarty thet question," the first cowboy responded coyly.

"I asked him and he said Morgan never worked for him," Nolan replied.

"Well, there's yur answer," he replied.

"Thanks for nothin'," Nolan replied. "C'mon, Slade. We's wastin' our time heah."

"Right, Boss," Slade replied.

The two lawmen turned their horses and rode off to the laughter of the cowboys.

"Well, thet didn't go as planned," Slade said as they rode off.

"Let them have their fun. We'll get McCarty in the end," Nolan asked.

"I sure hope so, Boss," Slade answered.

"Hey, what d'ya say we ride over ta' the Ferguson Place? We should check on Maddie anyway, an' I'm sure we could talk her inta' a home cooked meal," Nolan said.

I'm all fer thet, Boss," Slade replied.

* * *

Maddie had been working hard all morning. She was glad that she and Taos drove the cattle up to the High Meadow. She knew that they were much safer there, so she could concentrate on the crops, chickens, and pigs, along with other projects around the ranch. It was exhausting, though, and sometimes she thought it was just more than she could bear. Her current chore was cutting wood to split for the stove. It was backbreaking work, and her least favorite job around the ranch.

I'd much rather muck out the horse stalls, she thought as she lifted another log onto the sawhorse.

Getting wood was a huge process. She had to ride up to the High Meadow to cut down trees, then drag them down to the ranch. Unable to get the tree length logs onto the sawmill, Maddie had to do everything by hand. Next, she cut the logs into four-foot lengths. After that, she hoisted the logs into the sawhorse, and cut them into three sixteen inch pieces. After she had a sufficient amount cut, the splitting process began. It took all summer, a little every day, to put away enough wood to last through the winter.

As she sawed the current log on the saw horse, she looked out to the prairie, and saw two riders in the distance. She finished sawing the log, then checked her holster. She had made it a habit to carry her sidearm every day since Taos had left, over two weeks ago, now. She also kept her side by side within arm's reach, and she took a drink of water, and watched the riders. They were getting closer, so she picked up the shotgun, walked to the front porch, and waited for them to arrive.

* * *

After Nolan and Slade left, McCarty took the cash and walked back to his office to put it in his safe. When he entered the room, he saw the mess that Nolan and Slade had left.

"By Jesus! I'll get thet somabitch lawman!" McCarty yelled.

Rance heard his father yell, and ran to the office. He stopped in his tracks when he saw his father standing amongst the mess on the floor.

"He's dead!" Rance exclaimed.

"On our time, Rance. We ain't gonna get stupid. If Morgan had been a better shot, we wouldn't be in this mess," McCarty replied. "At least Nolan couldn't make a connection to us, or he would have been back in here after talkin' to the men." McCarty counted out $160. "Give $10 to each one of the men as a thank yu," McCarty instructed as he handed the cash to Rance.

"Good idee," Rance replied, and turned to go as his father cleaned up the mess.

* * *

Maddie relaxed when the riders came close enough for her to recognize Jim Nolan and Slade McDonald. She put the shotgun down, and set the sidearm tighter in it's holster as she watched the two lawmen ride toward the ranch.

"Haloo, Maddie," Nolan yelled as they got within hearing range.

"Haloo yourself, Jim Nolan," Maddie yelled back.

Maddie couldn't help but smile, and Nolan noticed the twinkle in her eye as the men rode up.

"What'er yu so happy aboot?" Nolan asked as he approached the front porch.

"Just good to see friendly faces, I guess," she replied. "It's been a lonely existence here lately."

"No word from Taos?" Nolan enquired.

"Not yet, but I don't expect to hear from him, at least not for a couple of weeks. It takes at least a dozen days to get there, so mail won't get here for a while, even if he has time to write," Maddie said.

"I guess yur right," Nolan replied as he and Slade dismounted.

"Hi there, Slade," Maddie said.

"Uh, hello, Miss Maddie," Slade replied, shyly.

"We jus' paid a visit to yur old friend, McCarty," Nolan said, then dipped water out of the barrel, while the horses drank from the trough, one of Maddie's new additions.

"Tell me more," Maddie replied, and waved the men up onto the porch.

Nolan sat down and said, "We couldn't tie him ta' Morgan, but made sure he wouldn't forget our visit."

"Do you think that there will be repercussions?" Maddie asked.

"There may be, but we gotta get him out in the open," Nolan replied. "How have yu been holdin' up?"

"I'm keepin' busy. I keep the holster on all the time, and the scatter gun within arm's reach at all times, but it is pretty spooky here all alone. It's odd, but I didn't feel so scared before Taos showed up, but I didn't realize how desperate McCarty was to get my ranch. The fact that he would have someone take a shot at you is unsettling to say the least."

"Yes, he seems to be more desperate," Nolan agreed.

"Hey, I bet you two are pretty hungry. How about I cook somethin' up?" Maddie said.

The lawmen shared a smile.

"I sure wouldn't say no to thet," Nolan replied.

"Me neither," Slade echoed.

"Could you two do me a favor while I'm makin' a meal"

"Anythin', Maggie," Nolan replied.

"I was workin' on sawin' firewood when you two rode up. Would you mind cuttin' some up for me while I cook?"

"It'd be our pleasure," Nolan said.

Pointing, Maddie said, "The saw horse is over yonder."

The men got up and headed to the sawhorse, while Maddie headed inside.

* * *

Nolan and Slade began sawing logs..

"Thet Maddie sure is one heck of a woman," Slade said.

"Hold yur hosses, cowboy! Maddie Ferguson is outa' yur league, plus, she's in luve with Taos."

"I was jus' sayin' Boss," Slade replied, as he sawed.

"Ha! We gotta find yu a woman!" Nolan laughed.

"They sure ain't a lot a' single women my age around Telluride," Slade replied, as he sawed another log. "Well, thet I'd want ta marry anyway."

Nolan loaded another log on the sawhorse, and tossed the cut pieces on the pile as Slade continued sawing. "Well, we'll jes' have ta' broaden yur horizons, Slade," Nolan said, with a laugh.

The men continued working in silence, and had added about half a cord of wood to the pile when Maddie called them to eat.

The men washed up before going inside the house.

* * *

Maddie had made a sumptuous meal of ham steaks, red-eye gravy, and biscuits.

"Oh, Maddie, you done outdid yourself!" Nolan exclaimed, when he saw the table of food.

"I appreciate all the work that you two did for me! It'd take me a week to cut and pile that many logs," Maddie said.

"I sure thank yu," Slade said. "I rarely get good home cookin'."

"You have to find yourself a nice woman," Maddie said.

"We was jus' talkin' aboot thet, wasn't we, Slade?" Nolan joked.

"Yes, Boss, I guess we was," Slade replied, shyly.

"Young Slade heah says they ain't no wimin' fer him in Telluride,"

"Well, we'll just have to start lookin' in Placerville and Durango," Maddie said.

"See, son? Jus' like I was tellin' yu. All ain't lost," Nolan joked.

Seeing that Slade was not enjoying the joke, Maddie changed the subject. "Tell me about your visit to McCarty's ranch."

Nolan took a bite of his red-eye gravy smothered steak. "Darn this is good! Uh, well, McCarty is too smart to leave a paper trail on any of his cowboys. We couldn't find nothin', but the cowboys was bein' pretty coy, so I know thet Morgan worked fer McCarty, but I can't prove it, an' I'm sure the cowhands'll lie in a court a' law if it means savin' their jobs. It's well known thet McCarty pays top dollar."

"So, what do you do now? What do I do now?" Maddie asked.

"We keep an eye on him an' hope he makes a slip. Yu gotta keep doin' what yur doin'. Keep yur pistol on yur hip, an' thet scatter gun by yur side. Keep yur doors and winders locked at night, an' pray that Taos comes back sooner rather than later."

Maddie was shocked by Nolan's words, and shot up from the table and ran to her bedroom and closed the door.

"I sure put my foot in it," Nolan said to Slade. "I was jus' tryin' to be truthful."

"Sometimes the truth ain't the best answer, Boss," Slade replied.

"I ken see thet now," Nolan said.

* * *

It was more than Maddie could take. She had been hanging on by a thread, but putting up a strong front. She was doing it, not just for Nolan and Slade, but for herself. She hadn't dared let go. When Nolan had told her that she was basically on her own, and had to hope for Taos to come back before it was too late, it was the last straw, and the flood gates opened. Maddie cried. She hadn't cried like this since Cam and Tad had been murdered. Her body was wracked by her uncontrollable sobs.

After a few more minutes, Maddie's sobbing slowed down. Embarrassed, she wondered how she could face Jim and Slade, but she couldn't spend the rest of the day in her bedroom. She dried her eyes, and straightened herself out, and decided to face the men.

When she opened the door, Jim and Slade had finished eating, and had washed and dried the dishes. She found them out on the porch.

Jim stood up when Maddie stepped out onto the porch.

"I'm so sorry, Jim. I don't know what's got into me," Maddie said.

"I'm the one who should apologize, Maddie," Nolan replied. "I shoulda' been more careful with my words. I'm jus' a big blatherskite, sometimes. I knowed yur all boxed up heah, and been through so much. I shoulda' been more considerate of yur feelin's."

"Thank you, Jim, I appreciate that. Thank you, and you too, Slade for cleanin' up after the meal."

"It weren't nothin', Miss Maddie," Slade replied. "Thank yu for the eats."

"Maddie, I have an idee," Nolan said.

"Oh?" she replied, her interest piqued.

"How aboot Didi an' I take a ride out heah the day afta' tomorra? We'll bring a picnic, so's yu ain't gotta worry aboot cookin'?"

"Really? You'd do that for me?" Maddie asked.

"Of course. What are friends fer, if we can't help each other oot?"

* * *

Maddie watched Nolan and Slade ride off. She could make it a couple of more days until Jim and Didi returned. *It was awful kind of Jim to offer,* she thought. *I do have good friends. Jim and Didi were the best, and Slade, that dear, shy young man. I'll have to find somebody for him! Bill Haney was a good man - he sent Taos to me. And then, there's Taos.*

Maddie snapped out of it and began suring up the ranch for the night. She felt good about all the wood that Jim and Slade had cut. She finished her evening chores, and got water heating for her evening shower.

After her shower, Maddie poured herself a glass of whiskey and stepped out on the porch. It was going to be a beautiful sunset. There were wispy clouds on the western horizon, which would produce great colors, and that light would reflect off the San Juans. *It would be so wonderful to share this evening, and all my evenings with Taos.*

33

Chapter 33

I t had been over a year and a half since Taos and his family sat down to dinner together. Lorena had made a family favorite, jack rabbit stew. Lorena had asked Taos to shoot one of the many on the ranch, and he went out and shot two, for good measure, in about fifteen minutes, the critters were that plentiful around the ranch house.

Taos had quickly cleaned and butchered the animals, and Lorena put them in the big cast iron pot that she used for her stews. Sage helped her peel and chop potatoes, carrots, and onions. Lorena also added some suet, since jack rabbit was such a lean meat.

The Colonel had gone down into the root cellar, and chose two bottles of Spanish Rioja to have with dinner. He opened the bottles to let them breathe, as Sage set the table.

While the stew was simmering, Lorena baked a loaf of sourdough bread.

The combination of aromas was enough to whet the most stingy appetite.

When everything was ready, the family sat down at the table, and the Colonel led the family in Grace. Then, they made a toast. Although Lorena rarely had a drink, she made an exception, now that her son was home.

The Colonel offered the toast, "To our wayward son and brother, may we never part for so long again."

"Cheers," the family replied, and everyone clinked their glasses.

After the toast, Lorena dished out the stew while Sage passed around the bread and butter.

It got quiet as everyone dug into the stew, then Taos broke the silence, "This is sure amazing, Mother. I can't tell you how much I've missed your cookin'."

"It's my pleasure, Ben. I'm just happy to have you home again."

"What's your plan goin' forward?" the Colonel asked Taos.

"Well, Colonel, I need to talk to Ida and figure out what I'm gonna do next. I have an idee aboot the ranch, but I can't share it until after I figger things out with Ida," Taos replied.

"Forget Ida," Sage said.

"Sage, please," Lorena implored. "Ben needs to figure this out on his own."

"Okay, but it ain't gonna end well," Sage replied.

"Sage, I appreciate your concern. Honestly, I do, but I gotta find out for myself. I know thet Ida is difficult, but I can't move ahead with my life until I talk ta her," Taos answered.

"I'm tryin' to understand, Ben, but you haven't seen the hate that I have. She doesn't only hate you. She hates all of us," Sage replied.

"Sage, we all know that, but sometimes a man just has to figure things out for himself," the Colonel said.

"Let's just enjoy our dinner, and rejoice that Ben is home," Lorena implored.

* * *

Taos woke up well before dawn. He hadn't slept well. Thoughts of Ida and Maddie kept invading his sleep. This was the day. His future, maybe his family's future, came down to how this day played out.

Taos cooked up a half a dozen eggs, and made toast. He ate in a hurry, then cleaned up his dishes before going outside and saddling Grant. He had packed grain, water and some jerky before riding out toward the Parker ranch.

The culmination of Taos' trek was now at hand. In just a few short hours, he would have his answer. Just seeing Ida after his long absence, would give him his answer. Would he still have the same feelings for her? Was she as full of hate as Sage said she was? Sage had never liked Ida to begin with, so she was certainly biased.

The ride went quicker than he thought it would, and he was surprised when the Parker Ranch came into view.

* * *

Ida had taken charge of the ranch after her father was killed in the battle with the miners. For her, nothing had been gained, even though the mine was closed. Folks in the local towns resented the ranchers because they weren't bringing in the money that they did when the mine was active. Some townsfolk were openly hostile to ranchers, while others were more discrete.

Like every other day, Ida was up before the sun to start the chores. No more lazing about, or being treated like a princess. When Jack Parker was killed, life hit Ida squarely in the jaw. Although she resented his death, she had a purpose in life now that she hadn't had before. She had spent her time with trifles, and flirting with cowboys, especially Ben Adams. But that was over now, she had been forced to grow up, and pronto.

Ida was meeting with a few of her cowboys when she noticed a lone rider heading toward the gate. The silhouette of the rider looked vaguely familiar, but she couldn't make an identification at this distance.

* * *

Taos rode through the Ranch arch, and saw Ida speaking to a number of cowboys.

"Well, here goes," Taos said to Grant as he approached the group. Ida was talking, and had her back to him.

When Taos was about thirty feet away, he said, "Good mornin', Ida."

* * *

Didi was happy to take the ride out to Thunder Valley Ranch with Jim. Since he had been shot, Didi had been doting over him. There was a new-found romance in their relationship. Didi had packed a basket with fried chicken, biscuits, and a mixture of dried fruits and nuts, she had also filled a jug with fresh made wild-berry lemonade.

The trip out in the buckboard was uneventful, though rough. It was nice to get to spend time with Jim, and she was looking forward to getting to know Maddie better. Women in town weren't always nice, and having a new friend like Maddie was something that Didi was looking forward to.

* * *

Maddie had a spring in her step all morning. She breezed through her morning chores in anticipation of Jim and Didi Nolan's visit.

It had been a difficult couple of weeks for Maddie. She missed Taos immensely. She had gotten used to not only his company, but his abilities and hard work around the ranch.

"Let's face it, Maddie, you are lonely, and scared," she said to the wind.

Maddie had done well to keep the ranch going in Taos' absence, and Jim and Slade had done a good job keeping Doniphan and Rance McCarty on their heels, but she knew that the Sheriff had overplayed his hand with no results. Doniphan McCarty would be emboldened by that. Maddie was glad to have company coming. Each day that she was not alone was a day that she was safe from the McCarty's.

* * *

Nolan and Didi rode out of the forest, and the Ferguson place came into sight.

"Won't be long now," Nolan said to his wife.

"Good thing, my bottom's gettin' sore," Didi replied, with a laugh.

Nolan chuckled. "Yup, these buckboards ain't known fer theah comfort," he laughed.

"I suppose it's better than riding a horse all this way," Didi said.

"It is if you ain't used ta ridin' a hoss every day," Nolan opined.

"I guess that's so," Didi replied. "I never thought of it that way. I'm just glad that we're almost there."

Nolan drove the buckboard through the gate and across the bridge that spanned the San Miguel.

Maddie, who had been sitting on the front porch in anticipation, got up and ran to meet them.

"Hello, y'all," Maddie yelled as she approached the buckboard.

"Halloo, Maddie!" Nolan hollered back.

"Hi, Maddie," Didi said, as Nolan stopped the buckboard.

They exchanged hugs, and the women headed inside while Nolan tended to his horse.

"Thank you for comin'," Maddie said. "It gets pretty lonely out here."

"It's my pleasure, Maddie. It can be pretty lonely in town too," Didi replied.

"Really?" Maddie asked.

"Folks aren't that friendly in town. They accept Jim 'cause he's the Sheriff, but I've sure had trouble makin' friends. To be honest, that's one of the reason's I was happy to come out here today. I think I could use womanly company as much as you, and I'm sure happy to have you as a friend," Didi explained.

"Well, I sure appreciate your friendship," Maddie replied. "And I can't tell you how much I appreciate you an' Jim takin' the trip out heah.

* * *

When she heard the familiar voice, Ida spun on a dime.

"Wal, look what the cat dragged in," she said. "Yu sure have a nerve comin' heah."

"I was hopin' we could have a talk," Taos replied.

"It took yu a year and a half to figger thet out?" Ida said.

"Somethin' like thet," Taos replied.

Ida turned to the cowboys. "I'll catch up with yu later." They nodded and got on with their work.

Ida turned and looked right at Taos. Her black eyes flashed fire. "Why did yu come heah?" she demanded.

"Wal, I see it was a mistake," Taos replied, and turned to walk away toward Grant, who was grazing nearby.

"Don't yu turn yur back on me," she seethed at Taos.

Taos turned on a dime, his blue eyes flashed, and his face turned crimson. He walked up to Ida, and, towering over her, said, "Sure, I been gone a long time. I've been mostly in the saddle this yeah and a half, an' I killed men, slept under the stars, an' nearly starved a time or three. . ."

"Yeah, and I mourned my dead father," Ida spit out as she slapped his face.

Stung, Taos took a step back, turned, mounted Grant, and said, "Adios," and rode away.

Ida stood and watched him ride off as tears welled up in her eyes.

* * *

Taos' cheek burned as he rode off. Oddly, he thought, his heart soared. He realized that he was now free of Ida. Seeing her, and feeling her strike him, made Taos realize that he was now free to love Maddie. She was true, strong, and steady, where Ida was flighty, always angry about something or at someone, and traveled in a whirl of drama.

Taos spurred Grant into a trot. His mind turned to Maddie, and the trip back to Colorado. Now that he had made up his mind, Taos wanted to get back to her as soon as he could. He worried about what the McCarty's were up to, and was sure it wasn't anything good. Before he headed back to Colorado, and Maddie, he had to figure out something to save the ranch. He'd take Sage, and ride up to the site of the mine. It had been a year and a half, and the river was still devoid of life, and most of the calves were either stillborn, or deformed. If it continued like this much longer, his parents would go bankrupt.

* * *

Ida watched Taos ride out of sight as tears streamed down her cheeks. *What have you done, Ida? Ben was the only man yu evah loved, an' yu just slapped him across the face.* She said to herself.

By one quick and thoughtless action, Ida's world came crashing down. Ben was the only man whom she had ever truly loved. All the other cowboys had just been flirtations. Ida realized that she would never see Ben again. She spent a year and a half drenching herself in her own misery, and blaming Ben Adams for a decision that her father made. It was easy to blame Ben, but she knew that something bad would happen, and it did. A lot of blood was spilled that day, and it didn't change anything. The Los Piñons was still failing because of contaminated water. Her ranch, she had to admit, was flourishing under her direction, even without her father. Yes, there was animosity in town, but, ultimately, they would come around because the ranches supplied steady income, and cowboys weren't as rowdy as miners.

* * *

It was dusk when Taos returned to Los Piñons. As he approached, he saw the glow of his father's ubiquitous pipe. Taos rode to the horse barn, dismounted, and unsaddled Grant, brushed him down, and put him in a stall with food and water.

Next, Taos walked to the ranch house, stepped up on the porch, and joined his father, who was enjoying a smoke and a glass of whiskey.

"You hungry?" the Colonel asked.

"I could eat," Taos drawled.

"Your mother saved a dish for you. Why don't you go get it, and eat out here?"

"Thanks, Colonel. I'll be right back," Taos replied.

A few minutes later, Taos returned with a bowl full of chili and a big slice of homemade sourdough bread. He sat down next to his father, and began eating.

"I'm guessing that it didn't go so well with Ida?" the Colonel enquired.

"Well, actually, it couldn't have gone better," Taos replied, between bites.

"Is that so?" the Colonel asked.

"Yep, I got theah, dismounted, said hello, an' she slapped me across the face," Taos replied.

"If that was good, I sure would hate to see bad!' the Colonel replied.

"Wal, it was good because it made me see Ida for who she really is. She's full of hate an' blame. It allowed me to move on from her," Taos said before taking a spoonful of his chili.

The Colonel took a sip from his glass. "I'm glad, Ben. I mean I'm glad that you can now move forward with your life."

"Thanks," Taos said, as he finished his dinner.

"So, what's next?" the Colonel asked.

"I want ta ride up ta the mine. Hopefully, Sage will come with me. I want to see if theah is anything that we can do ta fix things," Taos replied.

The Colonel poured a glass of whiskey and handed it to Taos. "I appreciate that, Ben," he said.

"It's my duty, Colonel," Taos replied.

"Is it? You've been gone for a year and a half. We've managed," the Colonel replied.

"But things ain't gettin' better, Sage told me as much. You and Mother can't last much longer if things don't turn around."

"We'll manage. We always have."

"This is different, Colonel. You've got a poisoned river thet ain't gettin' any better. Heck, you don't even know if yur well is any good," Taos replied.

Lorena stepped out onto the porch to collect the dishes.

"Thank you, Mother. That was wonderful," Taos said, then kissed her forehead.

"You are most welcome, Ben," Lorena replied, then went back inside.

Taos took a sip of his whiskey.

"You really think our well could be contaminated?" the Colonel asked.

"I don't know if the groundwater is affected, but it could be," Taos answered.

"But none of us is sick," the Colonel replied.

"Not now, but it's the kinda thing that could take years. What if Sage were to get married and pregnant?"

"Who said anything about me gettin' pregnant?" Sage demanded as she stepped out on the porch, and overheard the last of Taos' sentence.

"We was just talkin' about the well," Taos answered.

"What about the well?" Sage asked.

"Ben thinks that it may be contaminated, just like the river," the Colonel answered.

"I thought that the two of us could take a ride up ta the mine tomorrow mornin'," Taos said.

"I'd like that, Ben," Sage answered.

34

Chapter 34

"Yu think Taos is on his way back yet?" Nolan asked after they finished eating.

"If he isn't, he should be very soon," Maddie replied.

"So, It'll be a couple more weeks?" he asked.

"I think so, but I have no idea how long he will stay in New Mexico, or if he'll even come back at all," Maddie replied.

"Oh, he'll be back. I see the way he looks at you. He's head over heels in love with you," Didi said.

"He'll come back one way or t'other," Nolan said. "He's an honest man. He won't leave yu hangin'."

"Thanks, both of you. I really needed that," Maddie replied. "It's just that it seems so long that he's been gone. I get worried here all alone."

"Why don't you stay with us in town for a while? Didi asked.

"Oh, I'd love to, but I can't do that. If they see the place empty, there's no tellin' what the McCarty's would do," Maddie said.

"How will they know?" Ida asked.

"Every day, I see a rider out theah on the prairie. Not always the same one. I used my binoculars and thought I recognized one as one of McCarty's hands," Maddie replied.

"Oh, dear!" Didi exclaimed.

"That ain't good," Nolan said. Maddie, yu always keep yur guns loaded and at the ready?

"Yes, Jim. And I practice every day."

"Good. If you don't mind, I think it best thet we stay the night," Nolan said.

"I wouldn't have it any other way."

* * *

Taos got the horses ready while Sage made breakfast, and packed lunch.

Sage had just put the dishes on the table when Taos came in.

"That sure enough smells amazin'," he said.

"Thanks," she replied, as she sat down at the table.

Taos sat down and dug into his breakfast of sausage, eggs, and toast.

"I'm lookin' forward to today," Sage said. "It'll be good to get caught up."

Taos took a bite of his food. After swallowing, he said, "It sure will, and it'll give us some time to figger out a plan for our parents and the ranch."

"Do you really think it is that serious?" Sage asked.

"If we can't figger out a way ta clean up the river, yes, it is," Taos replied, between bites.

They finished their breakfast in silence.

After breakfast, Taos grabbed the packed lunch and brought it outside while Sage washed the dishes.

They saddled up and rode out of the ranch gate.

"I love this time of the mornin'," Sage said.

"Yup, I love the fresh mornin' air," Taos agreed.

"Do you think that there is anything that we can do about the water?" Sage asked.

"I don't know, but I think we need to take a look at the site, at least. Maybe we'll get an idee or two," Taos answered, as they rode along the river.

They rode for a while in silence, as the trail followed the river upstream. After an hour, they came to a clearing..

"Let's take a break," Taos said.

"I like that idea," Sage replied.

They dismounted, and hobbled their horses so they could graze, while they walked to the river. Taos squatted down at the water's edge and picked up a rock from the stream bed, turned it over, and looked at it. The rock was devoid of the usual insect life.

"Nothin'," Taos said.

"Same as last time we checked," Sage said.

"I was hopin' we would see some bugs, but they ain't nothin'," Taos replied.

"So it ain't any better after all this time?" Sage asked.

Just to be sure, Taos checked a few more rocks. "Nothin'," he announced. "I sure thought that the river would'a started comin' back by now."

"That can't be good for the future," Sage said.

Taos stood up, with a frown.

"What is it?" Sage asked.

"Wal, maybe that whole fight to close the mine was a waste of time an' energy," he replied.

"What do you mean?" Sage asked.

"We-I thought thet closin' the mine would end our problems, but it hasn't made a difference at all," Taos said.

"Maybe there is somethin' we can do. We won't know until we get there," Sage said.

* * *

Nolan and Didi said their goodbyes to Maddie, and rode the buckboard over the bridge and onto the trail.

"Do you think that she'll be okay?" Didi asked, when they had gotten outside of earshot.

"I don't rightly know. Normally, I'd say thet she's fine, but thet Doniphan McCarty is an evil, twisted man," Nolan replied.

"I sure hope that Taos gets back soon," Didi said.

"Yeah. I can check in on her every few days, but I can't be here all the time," Nolan replied.

He looked ahead and spotted a rider on the horizon.

"Let's go see who thet could be," Nolan said, and turned the buckboard in the direction of the rider.

Worried, Didi asked, "Is it safe?"

Sure. Ain't nobody gonna mess with the local sheriff and his wife in broad daylight," Nolan said.

"If you say so," Didi replied, unconvinced.

The rider turned away, so Nolan had the horse speed up.

After a few minutes, the rider stopped, he didn't want to seem suspicious.

Nolan and Didi caught up to the waiting rider.

Nolan took a minute to size the man up. He looked to be in his mid twenties, was lean, had a scrub of beard, and dark blue eyes. He wore a pair of Colts on his hips as well as a Winchester in a scabbard.

"What's yur name?" Nolan demanded.

"Who's askin'," the cowboy replied.

"Sheriff Jim Nolan. Thet's who," Nolan replied.

"I'm Johnson, Zeke Johnson," the cowboy replied.

"What yu doin' ridin' out heah in front of the Thunder Valley Ranch?" Nolan asked.

"It's a free country, ain't it," Johnson replied.

"Sure it is, but I knowed thet there have been some threats made, and I'm watchin' out fer the owner," Nolan replied, annoyed.

"I'm jus' ridin' lookin' fer strays, thet's all, Sheriff," Johnson replied.

"Yu ride for McCarty?" Nolan asked.

"Yeah, what of it?" Johnson replied.

"How long you been ridin' fer him?" Nolan asked.

"A few weeks, I guess," he answered.

"Where you from?" Nolan enquired.

"Oh, like most cowboys, I been heah and theah. Most recently from Wyomin', though," Johnson replied.

"Jus so yu know, that Doniphan McCarty is bad sess," Nolan said.

"He pays more than a fair wage," Johnson countered.

"I ain't sayin' he don't, but there'll be more to the job than cowboyin', if you get my drift," Nolan countered. "Fer instance, do yu really expect to find strays out heah?"

"Wal, I guess not. I was jus told ta ride out this way an' keep an eye out fer strays. I figgered it'd be an easy day," Johnson said.

"Anythin' else yu was asked ta do?" Nolan asked.

"Wal, Mister McCarty said fer me ta report any comin's or goin's at thet ranch over yonder," Johnson said, as he nodded toward Maddie's ranch.

"Any idee, why he'd ask yu thet?" Nolan enquired.

"He said thet they was likely stealin' his cattle," Johnson replied.

Nolan let out a loud guffaw. "Well, aint' that jus beat all!" he exclaimed. "McCarty's been tryin' to swindle Maddie Ferguson outta her ranch since her husband an' son was killed last year."

Johnson let out a deep sigh, and his attitude changed. "I sure had no idee, Sheriff," he said.

Nolan climbed down off the buckboard and signaled for Johnson to dismount.

When Johnson had dismounted, Nolan offered his hand, and Johnson took it.

"I have an idee," Nolan said. "Let's yu and I take a walk." He turned to Didi and said, "I'll jus be a minute."

Nolan put an arm on the tall, lanky cowboy's shoulder as they walked.

"I have a proposition fer yu," Nolan said. "Yu seem like a good egg, an' I'm sure yu don't wanna do nothin' ta hurt thet poor widow. Am I right?"

"I sure don't want no part in anythin' like thet. I've lived a rough life, Sheriff, but I an't done nothin' to hurt nobody intentionally," Johnson answered.

"An' I suspect Doniphan fer the murder of a banker outa Telluride, but can't pin it on him," Nolan added.

"I had no idee, Sheriff," Johnson said.

"What if I offer yu thirty dollars a month to keep an eye on the McCarty's?" Nolan asked.

"Jees, thet's five dollars more than I'm makin' now," Johnson replied.

"All you gotta do is keep yur ears and eyes open an' report ta me once a week."

"I can do thet," Johnson said.

* * *

Taos and Sage crested the hill to the site of the Copper Mountain Mine.

"Jesus," Taos said. "It looks just the same as last I was heah."

He and Sage looked out on the expanse that was once the Copper Mountain Mine. It was a scene of desolation. The buildings were nothing more than burned out hulks, and the slag was strewn everywhere. There was no life: no birds, no flowers, no other flora or fauna.

"Oh, Ben, this is horrible!" Sage exclaimed.

They dismounted and surveyed the area. It was every bit as desolate as it was on the day that the ranchers took down the mining company.

"Do you think there is anything that we can do to fix this?" Sage asked.

"I sure don't know. I was thinkin' about a couple a' things," Taos replied "It'd be a lot of work, though, an' I don't know if'n they would work."

"What do you have in mind?" Sage asked.

"Wal, I was thinkin' of makin' a bunch of charcoal to spread around it, to help filter, and also coverin' the whole mess with sand," Taos answered.

"That sounds like a huge job," Sage said.

"Yeah, and it may not even work," Taos said.

"Let's head home. It's spooky up here," Sage said with a shiver.

"A lot a' ghosts, I bet," Taos answered as he helped Sage mount her horse.

Taos mounted Grant, and they started back down the trail.

* * *

Zeke Johnson was like many young men who plied their trade in the American West. Born in Georgia during the Civil War, there wasn't much opportunity in the Reconstruction South, so Zeke headed west. Having grown up on a farm, he was used to hard work and livestock; important traits for a cowboy. He was also a fair hand with a gun.

Zeke had drifted throughout much of the west. He tried his hand at mining for a while, until he realized that the only people who didn't make money were the miners. He cowboyed for a few outfits, throughout Montana, and lately, Wyoming.

"Wyomin'," Zeke sighed. He would have liked to have stayed in Wyoming, but that was not possible, not after what had happened. He pushed it from his mind, and wondered about McCarty. He hadn't had a good feeling about the man, but he was offering more money than the other ranches in the area.

Could McCarty be the killer that Sheriff Nolan said he was? Zeke wondered. He took Nolan's offer, so he would have to find out.

He rode directly to the ranch house to see McCarty, when he had returned.

"What've yu got fer me?" McCarty said as Zeke rode up.

Zeek dismounted, tied his horse to the porch railing, and stepped up onto the porch before answering.

"I rode out theah like yu said, Mistah McCarty. I ain't seen nothin'," Zeke answered. "No cattle, no people, no nothin' out on the range. I did see a buckboard with a man an' a woman ridin' toward Telluride, but they was at least a couple people left at the ranch, near as I could tell," Zeke lied.

"Probably thet Sheriff Nolan and his wife," McCarty said. "They musta moved the cattle up ta the High Meadow. Yu didn't see any of our cattle out there, Johnson?"

"Not one dogie," Zeke replied.

"Alright, tomorrow, I want yu to ride up ta the High Meadow, an' see if'n they got any of our cattle theah. Rance'll show yu how ta get there," McCarty said.

"Yes, suh," Zeke answered.

* * *

Taos and Sage rode quietly back down the trail. Taos was in deep thought, when Sage broke the silence.

"Ben you haven't said a word about Ida," Sage blurted out.

Taos was startled from his thoughts. "No, I haven't," he replied.

Never one to let go, Sage pushed. "You gonna spill the beans, or what?"

Taos shrugged. He knew that Sage could be like a dog with a bone, so it was easier to just fill her in.

"Wal, yu were right. Ida's mind is poisoned by hate. She wouldn't talk to me, slapped me across the face," Taos shared.

"Oh, Ben, I'm sorry," Sage replied.

"Why? Yu was right," Taos said.

"But I didn't want to be," Sage said. "So, what now?"

"I have an idee, but I can't share it yet," Taos said.

35

Chapter 35

Taos had risen well before first light to begin his trek back to Colorado, and Maddie. He had said his goodbyes the night before. His mother had cried. After a year and a half away, he had been home for only a few days, but he had to get back to Maddie. He knew that McCarty would stop at nothing to get her ranch, and the longer he was away, the more likely McCarty would make a move.

The Colonel had offered Taos a pack mule to load with supplies, and Taos took him up on the offer. He was packing up the mule when Sage approached.

"What're yu doin' up?" Taos said.

"Oh, Ben, I couldn't let you go without seein' you off," Sage replied. "I ain't seen you in a year an' a half, and now you're leavin' so soon."

"We went through this last night, Sage," Taos said.

"I know, Ben, but I just had to see you off," she replied, as she put her arms around him.

Taos hugged his sister back. "I have a plan that will get us all together again soon, Sage, but I have to see if I can work it out, first. I gotta get back to Maddie, before her ranch is stolen from her, if it ain't already."

Sage let him go, and tears streamed down her cheeks as he mounted Grant and rode off.

After about twenty yards, Taos turned, took off his sombrero, and waved to his sister. Tears were running down his cheeks.

* * *

The sun hadn't risen yet when Zeke Johnson rode out from the McCarty ranch. Rance had given him directions to Maddie's High Meadow, and the story that he was looking for strays. In fact, he was ordered to get an estimate of the size of Maddie's herd, and keep an eye out for the man called "Taos."

After meeting Sheriff Nolan, Zeek had kept a closer eye on both Doniphan and Rance McCarty. There definitely was something about them that he didn't trust. If they were out to steal the Ferguson place, he'd have to figure out how to stop it.

Zeke followed the San Miguel up river until he reached the ford that Rance had told him about. He stopped and let his horse drink before making the crossing.

After he crossed the river, Zeke continued his trek up stream. Rance had told him that after the crossing, he'd be on Thunder Valley Ranch property, so he'd have to keep a low profile.

After another mile, he saw the ranch house in the morning light. He knew that the trail up to the caldera would be close on his right. He had to cross a brook that emptied out of it first. A few minutes later, he saw the brook up ahead. Unfortunately, he also saw a rider coming from the direction of the ranch house.

Zeke knew that if he turned around, he would only raise suspicion, and probably get fired by McCarty when he returned. So, he kept riding.

* * *

Maddie was up early, as usual. There was a lot to be done just to keep up. The chickens and pigs needed to be fed. The horses needed to be put out to graze. Wood needed splitting. And on it went. She had been spoiled when Taos was at the ranch. He was so big and strong, and efficient. That was the big difference. There was no waste in his movements. She loved watching him work, and not just because he was nice to look at.

Breakfast was finished and cleaned up, and she decided to finish her coffee out on the porch. She wanted to savor a few more moments before getting to work. Maddie sat down and surveyed the area. She loved the quiet, and the coolness of the early morning. The sun's rays were casting huge shadows in some areas, and illuminating others. As she gazed around, looking down river, she noticed a movement in the distance.

Maddie went inside and grabbed her binoculars. She stepped back out onto the porch and put the glasses to her eyes. She scanned the prairie, then west, looking downriver, and searched for whatever she had seen move. After a few minutes, she saw a rider come up out of a hollow.

Maddie went back inside and grabbed the shotgun and extra shells. She was already wearing her holster. She stepped back onto the porch and took another look. The rider was still there, and moving up river.

Maddie went to the horse barn and saddled her horse. She walked the beast out of the barn, mounted, and took another look through the binoculars. The rider was still approaching.

This was the moment that she had been preparing for, but hoped would never come. Someone was trespassing on her land. And she had to confront them, or people would be swarming all over her ranch .

As she rode out, Maddie said, "Probably one of McCarty's men."

* * *

Finally out of sight of Los Piñons, Taos stopped to gather his thoughts. It had been an emotional few days, and he was glad for the solitude. He was convinced that there was no way of cleaning up the river in time to save the future of the ranch. He'd have to talk them into moving up to Colorado, and hoped that Maddie would be good with his plan.

Leaving Los Piñons was difficult. Taos had truly missed his parents, and still felt guilty about leaving so abruptly after the battle with the miners, and now, he was leaving yet again. He had missed Sage sorely. The siblings, although they teased each other, were very close, and it broke his heart to leave her again.

Taos spurred Grant on, and the mule, which had been tethered to the horse, followed. He was glad for the mule. The beast of burden was a huge time saver. Having supplies for the trek back to Colorado would save him from detouring off the trail into towns for supplies, and he wanted to get back to Maddie as soon as he could.

* * *

Maddie kept her shotgun straddled across her lap as she rode out. She was happy to have the sun at her back. She'd take any advantage that she could get. The rider stopped for a few moments, then continued riding toward her.

Maddie approached the stream that drained the High Meadow, and stopped at the water's edge. The rider stopped on the far bank.

Maddie levelled the shotgun on the stranger, a lanky cowboy, who seemed to be in his twenties.

"Mind tellin' me what you're doin' on my land?" she asked, trying her best to put up a tough front.

"I'm lookin' for strays," Zeke replied.

"Who's strays are you lookin' for?" Maddie demanded, pointing the shotgun at the stranger's chest.

"I ain't gonna lie, Mrs. Ferguson, I work for Doniphan McCarty," he answered.

"I thought as much. You got a name?" Maddie enquired.

"My name's Zeke. Zeke Johnson, Ma'am," he replied.

"Well, Zeke Johnson, how come I've never seen you before?"

"I only been working fer McCarty a few weeks," Zeke replied.

"Why does he think that his strays are on my land?"

"He said that yu been stealin' his cattle," Zeke replied.

"Ha! Now don't that beat all!" Maddie said. "He's been stealin' my cattle, and tryin' to steal my ranch for the last year and a half. And he says he thinks I'm stealin' his cattle? Ain't that rich?"

"I just do what I'm told," Zeke said. "I'm supposed to go up to the High Meadow and look fer McCarty cattle, and keep an eye out fer a man called Taos."

"I appreciate your honesty, Zeke, but it doesn't change the fact that you're trespassin' on my land," Maddie said.

Zeke started to cross the creek.

"Hold it right there," Maddie shouted as she raised the shotgun at Zeke's chest.

Zeke reigned in his horse. "Whoa there! No need to shoot," Zeke said.

"Then don't give me a reason to," Maddie snapped.

"Sheriff Nolan sure was right about yu, Miss Ferguson," Zeke said.

"Sheriff Nolan? How do you know him?"

"I met him a few days ago. McCarty had me out on the prairie keepin' an eye on things, an' The Sheriff an' his wife was out on a buckboard an' rode up on me."

"And what did he say about me?" Maddie asked.

"Wal, he told me aboot yur husband and son, for starters, an' I'm real sorry aboot thet. He also filled me in aboot the McCarty's. I knowed thet that Doniphan was a mean cus, but I never figgered he was evil," Zeke said.

"So, why do you stay?" Maddie asked.

"Wal, Sherrif Nolan an' I had a talk aboot thet. He tol' me aboot the banker, thet McCarty killed, and how he's been tryin' ta swindle yu. He offered me a job spyin' on the McCarty's, an reportin' ifn' they do anythin' untoward."

"You got any proof of that?" Maddie asked.

"I'm gonna reach inta my saddle bag, so don't shoot," Zeke replied.

"Just move slow," Maddie ordered.

Zeke dismounted and opened up the saddle bag, and reached into it.

"Go slow!" Maddie ordered.

Zeke eased out a folded piece of paper, and walked to the water's edge.

Maddie rode across the creek and took the paper from Zeke's hand, and said, "Don't mount your horse until I say so," then she rode back across the creek to read it.

When Maddie reached the other side, she turned around to face Zeke. Maddie kept an eye on Zeek as she unfolded the paper.

Maddie looked at the paper. It was indeed, a writ, bearing Jim Nolan's signature, stating that Zeke Johnson was, indeed, in the Sheriff's employment. She folded the paper back up, and rode back across the creek, then handed it back to Zeke.

"You could have just told me about this from the get go," Maddie said.

"I don't think that you would have looked at it," Zeke replied.

"Probably right," Maddie said. She extended her hand. "It's good to meet you."

"I'm honored, Ma'am," Zeke replied.

"Please call me Maddie," she said.

"Yes, Ma'am, I mean Maddie," Zeke said.

* * *

Taos made good time, he retraced his path back to Colorado. On one level, he felt that the trip was a waste of time, on another, it had been fruitful. He should have known that Ida would not have changed her mind about him. However, it was wonderful to see his family, and he realized that the ranch was doomed, and something had to be done to save his parents' and Sage's future. He had an idea, but he didn't know if the Colonel would go for it. He was pretty sure that Maddie would.

He had to get back to Maddie. He had been gone too long. Taos knew that it was only a matter of time before Doniphan McCarty made a move for Maddie's ranch. He felt helpless on the trail, and pushed Grant and the mule, hoping to cut a day or two off the trip.

* * *

"Maddie, do yu mind if I take a ride up ta yur High Meadow? McCarty's gonna want a report, an' he'll know if I ain't been up theah," Zeke said.

"Of course," Maddie replied. "Let's go."

Maddie spurred her horse, and Zeke followed.

They rode up the trail in silence. Zeke followed Maddie, and took in the scenery.

Maddie stopped when she arrived at the lip of the High Meadow. The view always took her breath away.

Zeke stopped next to her and whistled as he took in the scene.

"This sure is a beautiful place," Zeke said, finally. "I ken sure understand why McCarty wants it."

"It stays lush and green with plenty of water all summer, and anyone tryin' to rustle my cattle has to drive them down within eyesight of my ranch house," Maddie said.

"Ken we ride out?" Zeke asked.

"Of course," Maddie replied, and spurred her horse.

Zeke hurried to catch up, and rode in wonder at the beauty of the place. He rode through the herd of cattle, noting that the cattle had the double lightning brand.

"This meadow could sure hold a lot more cattle, Maddie," Zeke said.

"I made the mistake of trusting your boss," Maddie replied.

"Oh? What happened?" Zeke asked.

Maddie filled Zeke in on the branding fiasco.

When Maddie had finished relating the story, Zeke said, "Wal, seems they's no depths thet McCarty's ain't willin' ta sink to."

"I won't argue with that," Maddie laughed. She became serious. "Can I ask you a favor?"

"Sure, ma'am," Zeke replied.

"If McCarty asks, and I'm sure he will, tell him that you saw Taos," Maddie said.

"I will. But yu gotta give me a description. McCarty's gonna want ta know if I seen the right guy.

"Well, he has the bluest blue eyes that I've ever seen, and. . . ."

"Hold on, Maddie, yu gotta describe him like a man would, not his lover," Zeke interrupted.

Maddie flushed. "He ain't my lover!"

"But yu love him?" Zeke asked.

Maddie was taken aback. "Well, yes, I suppose I do, Zeke," she answered.

"Wal, he must be a good man, cause I can tell thet yur nobody's fool," Zeke said.

Maddie flushed again. "Thanks, Zeke. I'll try the description again. Taos is tall, nearly six feet, I guess. Like I said, he has blue eyes. He also has sandy hair. He's slim, but well-built. He carries twin Colts, slung low, like a gunfighter. He wears a black sombrero, and black chaps, and he rides a big bay stallion."

"That's better," Zeke laughed. "I ken take thet ta' McCarty."

"Thanks Zeke," Maddie said. "Hey, are you hungry?"

"I'm allus hungry, Maddie," Zeke replied, with a smile.

"Well, let's ride back to the ranch, and I'll fix you somethin' to eat before you head out.

* * *

It was late afternoon when Zeke arrived back at the McCarty ranch. Having met Maddie, his resolve to help pull down Doniphan McCarty was set. McCarty was doing all the things that he had accused Maddie of. Keeping a poker face was going to be the hardest part for Zeke, while he looked for evidence against McCarty.

Zeke's instructions were to report directly to Doniphan upon his return, so he rode to the ranch house rather than the barn. He'd have to take care of his horse afterwards.

He dismounted and tied his horse to the rail, and stepped up onto the porch. He knocked on the door, and after a minute, a young Mexican woman opened the door.

"Hola Señor Zeke," the young maid said.

"Hola Rosa," Zeke said. "Ken I see Mistah McCarty?"

"Yes, of course, Señor. Come in."

"Jus call me Zeke, ma'am," Zeke said as he took off his Stetson.

"Ci, Zeke," Rosa said, as her cheeks reddened.

Zeke followed the petite, attractive woman into the house.

When inside, Rosa said, "You wait here, I go get Señor McCarty."

Zeke looked around the entryway as Rosa fetched her boss. He was amazed at the opulence. He hadn't seen anything like this place before in all his travels.

He was looking at a silver and turquoise piece when McCarty entered, followed by Rance.

"You like that?" McCarty asked.

"It sure is sumpin'," Zeke replied.

"Well, work hard, an' have a little luck, an' you can own somethin' like it," McCarty said. "You have a report for me?"

"Sure, Boss," Zeke answered. "I rode up to the High Meadow like yu asked. I was lookin' at the herd fer an hour or so, when some hombre with a black sombrero and black chaps, ridin' a big bay horse rode up inta the caldera. Lucky fer me, he didn't see me, an' I was able to sneak out behind a line a' trees."

"Taos! Damn it!," Doniphan exclaimed while pounding his fist into his hand.

"Did yu see any of our cattle?" Rance asked.

"Nary a one," Zeke replied.

"Alright. Go take care of yur horse and grab somethin' ta' eat," Doniphan said.

"Thanks, Boss," Zeke replied.

* * *

After Zeke left, Doniphan poured himself a whiskey and another for Rance.

"Let's go out onta the porch. No ears out theah," Doniphan said as he handed Rance a glass.

Rance opened the door for his father.

They stepped out onto the porch and sat down.

"Thet fuckin' Taos. He's a goddamned thorn in my side," Doniphan said before taking a swig of his whiskey.

Rance took a gulp from his glass. "What's next?"

"If Taos is as fast as yu say he is, ain't none of our cowboys gonna match him," Doniphan said.

"I ain't neva seen nobody faster," Rance said.

Doniphan took another gulp from his glass. "An' if he hooks up with Nolan an' his deputy, thet's three good guns," he said.

We sure can't match thet," Rance said. "None of our cowboys is good gunmen, 'cept Zeke, mebe, but he's new, an' I don't think we can trust him yet."

Doniphan finished his whiskey. "We need a gun."

"A'int gonna argue with thet," Rance said.

"Follow me," Doniphan said, and stepped back into the house. He handed his glass to Rosa and said, "Fill it up."

"Ci, Señor McCarty," Rosa said.

Rance gulped the rest of his whiskey before following his father inside. He handed his glass to Rosa also, and said, "I'll have another."

"Ci Señor Rance."

As Rance followed Doniphan into the office, Rosa refilled the whiskeys. She carried them to the office and handed Doniphan his glass first. When she handed Rance his, he put his hand over Rosa's for a moment, and leered at her. With some effort, she was able to get her hand free.

"Thanks, honey," Rance said, as Rosa scurried out of the room.

Doniphan had ignored his son's lewd actions, and took 'out a sheet of paper, and a fountain pen. He dipped the pen into the inkwell and wrote a note on the paper. When it had dried, he folded it and handed it to Rance. "In the mornin', I want yu to ride inta' Telluride an' give this to the Telegraph Officer."

"What's this aboot, Pa?" Rance asked.

"We need a gun. Yu said it yerself," Doniphan said. "I know such a man in Leadville. He goes by the name a' Sutton."

"Oh, I heard a' him. He's got near thirty notches on his guns," Rance replied. "But we can't jus' hire him ta' murder Taos."

"Are yu thet stupid? We'll put Taos in a position where he has to draw, an' when he does, Sutton'll gun him down," Doniphan said.

* * *

Rance put the paper in his pocket and stormed out of the office. Once again, his father had belittled him. It was like a sport to his father, Rance thought. He swallowed his whiskey in a couple of gulps, and went to the bar. Rosa was not there to serve him, so he filled his glass again, and drank it down. He filled it again.

Rance felt the effects of the whiskey. He teetered his way around the house, and found Rosa folding laundry. He ogled her while he sipped at his whiskey.

Rosa was busy at her work, and didn't notice Rance standing there. She was singing a Mexican folk song called Palomita:

"Palomita vamos a mi tierra,

Y seremos felices los dos,

Gozaremos lo que un alma encierra

Y estaremos en gracia de Dios

¿Por que quiero de ti separarme?

Tengo otros amores, tengo otros consuelos.

Palomita, vamos a mi tierra

Y seremos felices los dos"

Translation:

Little dove, let's go to my land

And we will both be happy,

We will enjoy what a soul contains

And we will be in God's grace

Why do I want to separate from you?

I have other loves, I have other consolations.

Little dove, let's go to my land

And we will both be happy.

Rance finished his whiskey, and put the glass down. He walked up behind Rosa as she worked and grabbed her from behind. As he grabbed her breast with one hand, he covered her mouth with the other.

"Now don't say a word," Rance whispered into her ear as she struggled to get away.

Rosa could smell the whiskey on Rance's breath as she struggled to get free. His hold on her only got tighter with her struggles. She felt his hand explore her breasts, and was sickened.

Is this how I am going to lose my virginity? By the fumblings of some drunken bully? She thought.

Rosa knew she had to make a move quickly. Rance was much too strong for her to fight for long. She had to think quickly. As he mauled her, he began kissing her neck.

Rosa panicked and did the only thing that she could do. She kicked his knee as hard as she could.

Rance's grip loosened for just a moment, and Rosa broke free. Her dress ripped as she spun out of his clutches, and she slapped Rance as hard as she could. Then ran out of the room, and then ran out the back door.

"Son of a bitch!" Rance seethed.

* * *

Rosa ran away from the ranch house. She had to get away. She knew that she could not stay there with the embarrassment of what had happened, and Rance would take advantage of a similar situation. She had to get out, but how? Her money and clothes were in the ranch house, but she didn't dare go back in.

Rosa ran toward the stables. She'd take a horse and head south. She'd figure something out, but she had to get away.

As she ran by the bunkhouse, Zeke stepped out.

"Whoa, Rosa! What gives?" Zeke said as she flew by.

Rosa kept running.

Alarmed, Zeke followed her to the stables.

As Zeke entered the stables, he saw Rosa saddling a horse. He ran to her.

"What is it, Rosa?" he asked. Then, he saw her torn dress. "What happened?"

Rosa continued saddling the horse, tears streaming down her face.

Zeke moved between Rosa and the horse.

"Rosa, what happened?"

"Oh, Zeke!" she cried and wrapped her arms around him. "I can't tell you."

"Sure you ken. What happened?"

"I don't want you mixed up in my problems," Rosa cried.

"I can't stand heah an' let yu cry like this with a torn dress, an' do nothin' aboot it, Rosa," Zeke exclaimed.

Rosa looked down at her dress. The tear exposed a good amount of her breast. Suddenly self conscious, Rosa grabbed the torn cloth and covered herself up.

"It was that Señor Rance. He was drunk. He sneak up behind me, an' he done theese!" Rosa pulled at her torn dress. "Then he kees me. I kicked him, slapped his face an' ran out here."

"Somebitch!" Zeke exclaimed. "Yu finish saddlin' this hoss, an' saddle mine. I'll be back."

"Oh, Zeke, don' do nothin' crazy," Rosa begged at Zeke's back.

* * *

Zeke stormed through the back door of the ranch house. He knew right where he'd find Rance: at the bar, and he was right.

Rance was three sheets to the wind when Zeke found him.

Rance looked up to see a fist hit his face. The punch broke his nose, and he bled profusely. The next hit him in the ear, and knocked him out. Zeke kicked him in the stomach as he hit the floor.

Doniphan, who had entered the room as Zeke knocked Rance out, drew his pistol.

At the sound of the hammer being cocked, Zeke spun on a dime, and drew his own gun and shot the pistol out of Doniphan's hand. He shoved Doniphan against the wall as he passed by him.

Doniphan looked at his bloody hand. "You'll pay for this, Johnson," he yelled.

* * *

Zeke's eyes were wild when he entered the stables.

"Señor Zeke, what happened? I hear a gunshot," Rosa said.

"We gotta vamoose, Rosa," Zeke said. "McCarty will be after us afore long."

Zeke led the horses out of the stable and helped Rosa mount her horse before he mounted his.

"Let's go!" Zeke emplored as he spurred his horse and slapped Rosa's.

36

Chapter 36

Z eke and Rosa rode hard until they were off McCarty land.

"Where we going?" Rosa asked, mostly to the wind.

"I figger we head to Thunder Valley. Maddie Ferguson, if I judge her right, will take us in fer at least the night," Zeke shouted back.

The sun had long since gone down, so the couple picked their way along the San Miguel to Thunder Valley Ranch.

"Zeke, are you sure that Señora Maddie will accept us?"

"Rosa, once Maddie finds out what happened, she'll welcome yu with open arms," Zeke laughed.

"What about you?" Rosa asked.

"Oh, Rosa, don' worry aboot me. I'll figger somethin' out," Zeke replied.

"Tell me what happened," Rosa said.

"Wal, it happened pretty quick, Rosa, but when I found Rance in the bar, I broke his nose, then knocked him out. Doniphan came inta the room, and pulled on me. I heared the click of his hammer, so I spun around, drew iron and blew his gun outa his hand," Zeke said.

Rosa's eyes glowed, and teared. "Nobody has ever don' nothin' like dat for me. Thank you, Zeke."

Zeke's cheeks flushed. "Wal, Rance sure had it comin', Rosa, an' Doniphan got what he deserved too," he answered.

"How much more we gotta go?" Rosa asked.

"Aboot an hour, I reckon," Zeke replied.

"Señor Zeke, I must tell you. I have never had a man treat me so kindly. Not even my father," Rosa said.

Zeke's cheeks flushed again. "Wal, if nothin' else, my folks taught me to respect women," he said.

"That is much," Rosa said.

They rode in silence until Zeke spotted Maddie's ranch house looming in the darkness.

"We're almost theah, Rosa. I ken see the house up yonder," Zeek said.

"Good thing, I getting cold, tired and sore," Rosa said.

They crossed the stream that emptied the High Meadow, and worked their way up the trail to the ranch house without event.

"We's heah," Zeke whispered as he dismounted. He helped Rosa dismount, then tied the horses to the porch railing.

* * *

Maddie had always been a light sleeper, but after Cam and Tad were murdered, she became moreso. With the McCarty's out to steal her ranch, it was a matter of survival. She felt safe while Taos was at the ranch, but, since he left, she had become hypervigilant.

Maddie's evening had gone as usual. She had cooked and eaten her dinner, taken a shower, and as usual, took out her binoculars, and scanned the area before sundown. All was well.

She had gone to bed at her usual time, and struggled to fall asleep. That was as usual too. Eventually, Maddie was able to doze off.

After a few hours of fitful sleep, Maddie woke to the sound of hooves. Suddenly alert, she got dressed, buckled up her gun belt, and grabbed her shotgun. She lit a small lamp, which produced just enough light for her to see. Then, she waited and listened.

* * *

Doniphan bandaged his wounded hand. Zeke's bullet passed through the meaty part between his index finger and thumb. He was in a lot of pain, but lucky. If the bullet had gone through any other part of his hand, bones would have been smashed.

Rance had come to and was nursing his broken nose. Still drunk, he vomited.

Doniphan walked back into the barroom. He saw Rance on his hands and knees over a pile of vomit.

"You gonna tell me what the hell happened heah?"

"Zeke attacked me," Rance replied.

"Did he get yu drunk, too?" Doniphan demanded.

"No, Pa," Rance replied.

"Zeke seems like a pretty gentle guy. Yu mind tellin' me why I walked in heah to find him kickin' the bejesus outa yu?"

Rance struggled to get up. His shirt was an ungodly mix of blood and vomit.

"I'll get Rosa to clean this up," Doniphan said.

"She ain't heah," Rance mumbled.

"What did yu say?" Doniphan demanded.

"I said, Rosa ain't heah," Rance replied.

"Why ain't she?" Doniphan demanded, visibly angered.

"I was drunk an' got fresh with her, ripped her dress. She took off," Rance confessed.

"An' thet's when Zeke came in an' kicked yur sorry ass?"

"Yup."

"An' I got my hand near blowed off comin' to yur defense, you piece of shit.

Yu clean up this mess, an' yu better be in the saddle at sunup to deliver thet message," Doniphan said, then kicked Rance in the groin, which triggered another round of vomiting.

* * *

Maddie listened intently. She heard what she thought was cowboy boots on the porch. There was another sound, too. It was lighter, not boots at all. She could not make out the sound.

With the shotgun leveled at the front door, Maddie called out, "Who's out theah?"

She heard a voice through the door.

"Maddie, it's Zeke Johnson, an' I need yur help," the voice said.

"How do I know it is you, Zeke?" Maddie asked, her shotgun still pointed at the front door.

"Okay, t'other day, when yu showed me the High Meadow, yu asked me to do yu a favor. It was aboot Taos. Do yu remember?" Zeke said.

Maddie unlatched the front door, but kept the shotgun trained on it.

"It's open. Come in slowly," she said.

Zeke slowly opened the door and stepped in, followed by Rosa.

When Maddie recognized Zeke, she lowered the shotgun.

"Thanks fer lettin' us in. This is Rosa," Zeke said.

"Hello. Rosa," Maddie said, to the young, Mexican Woman.

"I am so honored to meet you, Señora Maddie," Rosa replied.

"Zeke, you mind fillin' me in?" Maddie asked.

Zeke's face reddened with rage as he recounted what Rance had done, and how he and Rosa ended up at Maddie's doorstep.

"Well, I can't imagine either one of you goin' back to the McCarty's anytime soon," Maddie said.

"But I'll have ta bring the hoss thet Rosa rode back," Zeke said.

"We can take care of that in the mornin'. Zeke, why don't you take care of the horses while I find somethin' for Rosa to wear," Maddie said.

After Zeke left, Maddie said, "Rosa, follow me."

Rosa followed Maddie into her bedroom.

"You are a lot shorter than me, but we'll find somethin' that'll fit," Maddie said. At five foot five inches, Maddie towered over the petite Rosa.

"Thank you, Señora," Rosa said.

Maddie searched through her dressers and found a nightgown that was short on her, so she thought that it would fit Rosa.

"Here, try this, darlin'," Maddie said as she passed the garment to Rosa.

Rosa took off the torn dress, revealing scratches across her breast.

"Oh, my poor dear!" Maddie exclaimed when she saw the wounds. "Let me clean that up for you."

Maddie left the bedroom and hurried to the kitchen where she got a bowl, filled it with water, and grabbed a piece of cloth. She returned to the bedroom, dipped the cloth in the water, and dabbed the scratches on Rosa's breast.

"Rance McCarty is an animal," Maddie said when she had finished cleaning the scrapes.

"Oh, Señora Maddie, I was so scared that he would take my virginity, Rosa said as tears streamed down her cheeks.

Maddie wiped Rosa's cheeks, and hugged her tightly. "You are a strong woman, Rosa. You'll get through this. Let's get you changed. In the morning, I can sew this dress for you, and hem a pair of pants to fit."

"You are so kind, Señora," Rosa replied.

"Let's get you into this nightgown, so you can get some sleep," Maddie said.

Rosa finished stripping and put on the nightgown. It was a bit big around her shoulders, but fit otherwise. Maddie handed Rosa a washcloth and a towel, and motioned to follow her.

Maddie led the way to the bathroom, and poured hot water into the sink.

"You get washed up while I check on Zeke," Maddie said.

"Gracias, Señora Maddie," Rosa replied as Maddie left the bathroom.

* * *

Zeke entered the front door as Maddie left the bathroom.

"How's she doin', Maddie?" he asked.

"She's pretty shook up. I cleaned up her wounds, and found her a nightgown. She's washin' up now. I'm gonna have her sleep with me, an' you can use the spare bedroom," Maddie said.

"Thank you, Maddie. I'm glad we could come heah," Zeke said.

"You're a good man, Zeke," Maddie said. "First thing in the mornin', you can deliver the horse to the McCarty's."

"Yeah, I don' want ta be accused a' bein' no hoss theif," Zeke said.

Rosa stepped out of the bathroom.

"Hey, Rosa. How're yu doin'?" Zeke asked.

"I much better Señor Zeke, thanks to you and Señora Maddie," she replied.

Rosa walked over to Zeke, grabbed his arms, stood on her toes, and kissed him on the cheek.

Zeke's face reddened immediately. "Wal, Miss Rosa, thet is sweet a' yu."

"Gracias, Señor Zeke. I don' know what that Rance McCarty would do to me," Rosa replied.

Maddie smiled at the young couple. Even after all these years on the ranch, her sense of romance had not left.

Seeing Zeke's shy awkwardness, Maddie stepped in, "Okay you two, lets get some shut eye. We have a lot to do tomorrow."

"Yes, Ma'am," Zeke replied. "I'll jus go warsh up."

Maddie walked over to Tad's, now Taos' room, and said, "You can sleep in here, Zeke."

"Thanks, Maddie," Zeke replied.

"Come, Rosa, let's get some sleep," Maddie said.

* * *

Rance dragged himself out of bed. His head ached from the whiskey, and his broken nose was swollen. He looked in his mirror and discovered that he looked like a racoon. His face was swollen, and he had two black eyes. He drank a quart of water in hopes of fighting off the cotton mouth.

"Thet somebitch Zeke is gonna get the business end a' my Colt, if I evah see him agin'," Rance said to his reflection.

Rance washed up and got dressed. Next, he made himself a breakfast of eggs and bread, before saddling up.

He checked that he had his father's message with him before riding out toward Telluride.

* * *

Maddie had woken up first. She washed and got dressed before putting on a pot of coffee. Next, she got the fire going, and started frying bacon.

Zeke was next to get up. He got dressed, and stepped out to the kitchen.

"Thet sure smells good, Maddie," he said.

"Coffee will be ready in just a few minutes, Zeke," Maddie replied.

"Is Rosa up?" he asked.

"Not yet, and I say we let her sleep as long as she needs," Maddie replied.

"I agree," Zeke said before going into the bathroom.

Maddie continued frying the bacon while Zeke washed up. The coffee began boiling.

"Coffee's ready," Maddie said when Zeke stepped out of the bathroom.

Zeke poured the hot liquid into two of the three mugs, and handed one to Maddie.

"Thanks," Maddie said as she took the mug of hot coffee from Zeke.

"After breakfast, I'll take thet hoss back ta McCarty's place," Zeke said.

Maddie was finished with the bacon. "How many eggs do you want?" she asked.

"Jus three, Maddie. I ain't all thet hungry this mornin'," Zeke replied.

"Three it is," Maddie said as she cracked eggs into the cast iron skillet.

Zeke sliced bread from a loaf that Maddie had baked.

Maddie filled the dishes and handed one to Zeke, who had just set the table.

"Thanks, Maddie," Zeke said as he took the dish and sat down.

"You're most welcome, Zeke," she replied.

They began their meal in silence.

Maddie stopped eating to take a drink of her coffee. "Have you thought about what happens next?" Maddie asked after swallowing.

Zeke put down his utensils and thought for a moment. "Wal, I have ta report ta Sheriff Nolan afore I do anythin'," Zeke replied.

"After that?" Madddie asked.

"I'm a cowboy, Maddie. I'll jus foller the tumble weeds an' see where I end up," Zeke replied.

"Have you ever thought about settling down?" Maddie enquired.

"I almost did once," Zeke answered. "But it didn't work out. That's how I ended up heah in Colorado."

"What about Rosa?" Maddie asked.

"Rosa? I hardly knowed her," Zeke said.

"She sure is smitten with you, Zeke," Maddie said.

Zeke reddened. "I best finish my breakfast an' get thet hoss over ta the McCarty's."

"I'm sorry, Zeke. I didn't mean to push you," Maddie said. "We can talk when you get back," Maddie said.

"It's alright, Maddie," Zeke said as he finished his breakfast. "This sure was good. I thank yu."

"I'll take care of the dishes. I'll see you when you get back," Maddie said.

"Okay," Zeke said, and stepped out of the house.

Maddie picked up the dishes and brought them to the sink. *Will Zeke even come back? He's got nothin' here to hold him. Hell, he doesn't even have to check in with Jim Nolan. He could just ride off.* Maddie thought.

* * *

Zeke rode out with Rosa's horse in tow. His thoughts returned to his conversation with Maddie. What should he do next? Was she right about Rosa? He hadn't thought about her in that way. Sure, she was very attractive, with sparkling black eyes and raven hair, but he really didn't know her.

"The thought a' settlin' down sure sounds nice," Zeke said to the open air. "Do I even dare dream thet? I got nothin' to offer. I ain't even got a job no more. The sheriff sure don't need me neither."

Zeke crossed the stream that drained the High Meadow in good time, and rode another hour to the ford across the San Miguel. From there, it was only a couple more hours to the McCarty Ranch. He'd keep his six shooter loose in his holster just in case he saw Rance. He didn't think that any of the cowboys would hassle him, and Doniphan wouldn't be shooting anyone anytime soon.

* * *

Maddie had just finished washing the dishes when Rosa came out of the bedroom.

"Good morning," Rosa said.

"Well, look at you," Maddie replied. "How are you feelin' darlin'?"

"I'm sore. It could be from fighting Rance McCarty or, it could be from riding here," Rosa said.

"It could be a little of both," Maddie said. "How about some coffee?"

"Yes, please, Señora," Rosa replied.

"Have a seat," Maddie said as she poured two mugs of coffee.

Maddie put the mugs down on the table and sat down across from Rosa.

"Thank you, Señora Maddie," Rosa said.

"Please, just call me Maddie."

"Ci, Maddie," Rosa replied.

"You hungry?" Maddie asked.

"Ci," Rosa said.

"I got bacon cooked. How about a couple of fried eggs?" Maddie asked.

"That ees perfect, Maddie," Rosa said. "I used to doing all the cooking and cleaning. Thank ju for everything."

Maddie got up and put the skillet on the stove. "You are welcome, my dear."

"Where is Señor Zeke?" Rosa asked.

Maddie cracked two eggs onto the skillet. "He's takin' your horse to the McCarty's ranch. He should be back this afternoon sometime. After breakfast, I'll get you somethin' to wear, and we can do the chores."

"I do the dishes," Rosa replied.

"Okay, honey," Maddie said as she put the eggs on Rosa's plate.

Maddie placed the dish in front of Rosa. "I'll look for some work clothes for you while you eat."

"Gracias, Maddie," Rosa said.

37

Chapter 37

Doniphan McCarty woke up ornery. His wounded hand was throbbing, and he was embarrassed, once again, by his ne'er do well son. His housekeeper was gone, so he had to make his own coffee and breakfast.

"Sonofabitch!" Doniphan exclaimed, when he walked into the kitchen. "I gotta make my own fuckin' coffee."

He struggled to get the stove lit, then, once lit, he started the coffee.

While the coffee was heating, Doniphan went out to the bunkhouse. The morning banter ended when McCarty entered.

"Listen up," McCarty said. "I want yu all to search for Zeke. He rode outa heah last night with one of my hosses an' my housekeeper. I want him back alive so I ken hang him. But, if yu gotta kill him ta bring him in, thet's okay."

"We know what Rance did, Boss," Jake Carson, the most experienced cowboy under McCarty's employ, said.

"It don't matter what Rance did. If yu wanna keep yur jobs, yu'll go find

Zeke," Doniphan demanded.

"What aboot Rosa?" another cowboy asked.

"I don't care aboot her. I can find another Mexican bitch anywhere," Doniphan said, then walked out of the bunkhouse.

* * *

I ain't bringin' Zeke in ta be hanged, and I ain't shootin' him neither," Bob Jackson said. "Rance got what's comin' ta him."

The other cowboys agreed.

"Look, we gotta make it look like we tried. Let's saddle up, ride out, and follow Zeke's trail. He's got aboot ten hours on us anyway. They ain't much chance thet we'll catch up with him an' Rosa as it is. We'll put on a show for McCarty, at least," Jake Carson argued.

The cowboys agreed, and went to the stables to saddle their horses.

After saddling up, the impromptu posse rode out, and quickly found Zeke's and Rosa's tracks.

* * *

Zeke saw riders on the horizon. They approached from the direction of McCarty's ranch. He knew that if he left the extra horse where he was and made a run for it, the posse would catch up with him, and see him as a coward. It was time to cowboy up. He'd continue riding toward the posse, and take the consequences. If nothing else, he'd die brave.

Zeke and the posse rode within pistol shot.

"Zeke, stop right theah," Jake Carson shouted.

Zeke stopped. "Howdy, Jake," Zeke replied.

"Halloo, Jake," Zeke said. "I got McCarty's hoss heah. I'm bringin' it back."

"I see thet," Jake replied. "McCarty wants us ta bring yu back so he ken hang yu."

"Yeah, thet ain't happenin'," Zeke replied.

"I'm gonna ride up ta yu, Zeke. I got my hands up," Jake said.

"Okay, Jake," Zeke replied.

Jake rode up to Zeke with his hands in the air. When he was within arm's reach, Jake reached out his right hand. Zeek took Jake's hand.

"Look, Zeke, ain't none of us is gonna take yu back ta McCarty. Yu did the right thin' last night. We's all agreed on thet," Jake said.

"Okay, Jake, so how do this play oot?" Zeke asked.

"We all ride over to the San Miguel, an you cross. We take the hoss an' ride back ta the ranch. We tell McCarty thet we lost yur trail, but found the hoss at the bank of the river," Jake answered.

"Thanks, Jake. I guess this is it, then," Zeke said.

They shook hands again, and Zeke turned and rode to the San Miguel, followed by the posse.

* * *

Maddie chose a flannel shirt and pair of britches that were a little small on her and brought them out to the kitchen where Rosa was washing the dishes.

"Rosa, let me hold these up to you," Maddie said.

Rosa stood away from the sink so that Maddie could hold the pants up to her hip. Maddie marked the pants at Rosa's ankle.

"Gracias Maddie," Rosa said.

"Hey, I'll be happy for the help today," Maddie replied as she sat down to start hemming the britches to fit Rosa's short stature.

After she finished the dishes, Rosa sat down at the kitchen table with Maddie.

"I can do that, Maddie," Rosa said.

"I'm sure that you can, Rosa, but I'm happy to do it for you," Maddie replied.

"Gracias, Maddie. You are too kind," Rosa said.

"Have you thought about what's next?" Maddie asked.

"I theenk I need to go back to Mexico," Rosa said.

"What about Zeke?" Maddie asked, ever the matchmaker.

"Zeke is a good man, and a handsome man. He's my hero, but what he want with me, a little Mexican girl?"

"You are very beautiful, Rosa. You have good skills. What man wouldn't want you?" Maddie asked.

"You are too kind," Rosa said. "But where am I to find work?"

"I have some friends in Telluride. I can ask them if they can find work for you in town, if you want. You can stay here until you find something," Maddie said.

Rosa got up and hugged Maddie. "Oh, Gracias Maddie!" Rosa exclaimed.

"You are so welcome, Rosa," Maddie said. "Here, I'm finished. Go try them on," Maddie said as she handed the britches to Rosa.

Rosa took the britches and the flannel shirt, and went into the bedroom to change, while Maddie picked up her sewing kit, then put the cleaned dishes in the cupboard.

Rosa came out of the bedroom dressed in the flannel shirt and britches. They were big on her, but Maddie had done a fair job at making the clothing fit.

"It'll do," Maddie said. "Let's go get some work done!"

* * *

Zeke was glad that he didn't have to ride all the way to the McCarty's ranch. The cowboys had much more freedom on the range. It would have been tougher on them to disobey McCarty at the ranch.

He re-traced his tracks from the morning and the night before. His thoughts drifted back to Rosa. *She sure is a looker*, he thought. *She's also very sweet. She's allus been kind ta me. Mebbe, I ken find work around heah, an' we ken make a go of it. Thet is, if she don' go back ta Mexico.*

Zeke reached the stream that drained the High Meadow, and knew that it wouldn't be much longer until he reached Maddie's ranch. He looked forward to seeing Rosa.

* * *

It had been a hard ride for Rance. His nose was swollen, his head ached, and his guts were sore from the kicks. He had quickly gone through the water in his canteen to help fight the cotton mouth. It was a relief when he reached the San Miguel, and he put his face in the water and drank directly from the river before filling his canteen. His horse drank from the river, also. Rance let his horse graze for a few minutes before mounting him and heading back on the trail to Telluride.

* * *

Doniphan was nursing his sore hand when the posse rode back to the ranch. While the other cowboys rode to the stables, Jake rode up to the ranch house.

This ain't gonna be easy, Jake thought while he rode up to the ranch house.

"Yu find him? Doniphan said, when Jake dismounted and stepped up onto the porch.

"We found the hoss thet Rosa took," Jake replied. "It was staked up next ta the San Miguel. The tracks ended at the river. We rode a mile up an' down each bank. Nothin'."

"Seems suspicious ta' me," Doniphan said. "I know yu didn't want to ketch Rance."

"Boss, yu know thet I neva' disobeyed an order in all the years I worked for yu, all the way back to South Dakota," Jake pleaded.

"Look, I know thet Rance is a no good scoundrel, but he's my son. If I eva' see Zeke in these parts, I'll shoot him dead, myself."

"I understand thet, Boss," Jake said before re-mounting his horse.

* * *

Maddie and Rosa had a busy morning. Eggs were collected, chickens fed, pigs fed, goats milked, horses let out to graze, and all the animals were watered. Rosa proved to be a huge help. She was much stronger than her petite frame suggested, and she was tireless.

Maddie thought about what McCarty had lost when Rance abused her. *I bet he's sure vexed at Rance,* she thought.

When she and Rosa finished with the chores, Maddie said, "Let's get somethin' cool to drink.."

"I like that idea," Rosa replied with a laugh, the first one since her ordeal.

The two women went onto the porch and Maddie motioned for Rosa to take a seat before she went inside.

Rosa was comfortable in the shade, and took a minute to reflect upon the last day. It was so different here. Rosa felt respected. She was always treated as a lesser by the McCarty's and most of the cowboys. Only Jake and Zeke had been kind to her. Rance always leered at her when he saw her, and had gone too far last night. She shook with shame at the thought.

Maddie stepped out onto the porch with two glasses of iced tea, and handed one to Rosa.

"Gracias, Maddie," Rosa said as she took the glass.

"Cheers," Maddie said.

"Gracias," Rosa replied. "Maddie, I have to thank you for not only taking me in, somebody you had never met before, but for showing me respect. Only Zeke, and one other cowboy ever showed me respect. Mr. McCarty always called me hee's 'Mexican Bitch', and Rance was always a peeg."

"Rosa, everyone deserves to be respected. I'm sorry that you got treated that way by the McCarty's," Maddie said as she sat down.

"You is good people," Rosa said.

"Well, thank you, Rosa," Maddie replied.

"I always been treated like a servant, even by my family. I have three brothers, and I always serve them," Rosa said.

"It sure is tough on women in this world," Maddie admitted. "We need to look out for each other."

"Ci, Maddie," Rosa said.

Maddie took a sip of iced tea. She looked out on the prairie, and something caught her eye. She grabbed the binoculars and put them up to her eyes. She scanned out near the bank of the San Miguel where she thought she had seen something. Sure enough, she spied Zeke riding back to the ranch.

"What ees it, Maddie?" Rosa asked.

"Well, it's only Zeke heading back!" Maddie replied.

"I see?" Rosa asked, excited.

"Of course," Maddie replied, and handed the glasses to Rosa.

Rosa put the field glasses to her eyes and found Zeke where Maddie had pointed. "Ah, I see him!" she exclaimed.

"He'll be here in about half an hour," Maddie said.

"May I wash up?" Rosa asked.

"Of course," Maddie said. "Let me get the shower ready for you."

"Shower? I not know?" Rosa asked.

"Come in. I'll show you," Maddie said.

They went inside, and Maddie got water heating on the stove. When it had heated sufficiently, she pumped it up to the tank above the shower.

"Okay, now strip and I'll show you how it works," Maddie said.

Rosa stripped naked, and stood, embarrassed, while Maddie got the water running.

"Make it quick, there isn't a lot of water in the tank. I suggest wetting yourself down, turn off the water, scrub up, then rinse off. Soap is on the ledge, and I'll put a towel out for you," Maddie instructed.

"Gracias, Maddie," Rosa said.

Maddie put out a towel for Rosa, and left the bathroom while Rosa showered. She had washed Rosa's repaired dress and underclothes while Rosa was sleeping, and put them on the line to dry. She went outside to check them, and they were dry. That was one thing that Maddie enjoyed about the west. It took no time for her wash to dry in the arid climate, compared to the high humidity in Virginia.

Maddie brought the clean clothes in and laid them out on her bed for Rosa to put on.

Rosa was amazed at the shower. She followed Maddie's instructions, and found that she had plenty of hot water to rinse off. When the water ran out, she closed the valve and stepped out of the shower. She picked up the towel, dried off, and looked at herself in the mirror. The scrapes on her breast were healing, and the dark blue bruising had faded a little. She wrapped the towel around herself, and left the bathroom.

"Your dress is on my bed," Maddie said.

"Gracias, Maddie," Rosa replied.

Maddie had picked a rose from the garden while Rosa was showering and handed it to her.

"For your hair," Maddie said.

"So beautiful, Gracias," Rosa said as she took the rose.

Rosa went into the bathroom to get dressed.

* * *

Zeke rode up to the ranch house. Maddie was on the front porch sipping iced tea.

"Howdy, Miss Maddie," Zeke said as he dismounted.

"Hey, Zeke," Maddie said. "I saw you ridin' back a while ago. You're earlier than I expected," Maddie continued.

Zeke stepped up onto the porch. "Wal, McCarty sent a posse out ta ketch me, and I ran inta them," he said.

"What happened?" Maddie asked, intrigued.

"I sure got lucky. Jake, the Cowboss, said thet Rance deserved what he got, an' he weren't gonna take me in. McCarty wanted 'em ta bring me in so's he could hang me. Jake said he'd deal with McCarty," Zeke said.

"You sure did get lucky. Do you think McCarty will let it go?" Maddie asked.

"Jake has been with McCarty a long time. He don' wanna chance losin' Jake. If Jake walks, all the cowboys will foller," Zeke said.

Just then, the front door opened, and Rosa stepped onto the porch. Her raven hair glistened in the sun and contrasted beautifully with the red rose. Her dark eyes sparkled as they took Zeke in.

Zeke was stunned by her beauty. "Rosa, I'm speechless," he said.

"You like?" Rosa said as she did a twirl.

"You gonna pick your chin up off the floor?" Maddie asked.

Zeke took off his hat. "Miss Rosa, I guess I jus nevah noticed how beautiful yu was."

"Gracias, Señor Zeke," Rosa said shyly.

Maddie handed Zeke a glass of iced tea.

"Thank yu, Maddie. I sure am parched," Zeke said.

"While you and Rosa visit, I'm gonna get water heated for your shower. I'm sure you want to wash off the trail dust," Maddie said.

"I'd sure appreciate thet, Maddie," Zeke replied.

Zeke invited Rosa to sit, then he sat down.

"I'm glad that you are back safe, Zeke," Rosa said.

"Thank you, Rosa," Zeke replied.

"Tell me about your ordeal," Rosa said.

Zeke filled her in on the day's adventure, and emphasized how good Jake was to him considering McCarty's orders.

"That Jake, he good frien'. You and he are the only men who were nice to me," Rosa said.

"He sure is," Zeke agreed. "Jake sure saved my hide."

"What will you do now?" Rosa asked.

"Wal, I sure enough ain't goin' back ta McCarty," Zeke laughed. "I hope ta find a ranch ta work at around heah. This country suits me. I've also made friends with the sheriff. Mebbe he can help me find somethin'. How aboot yu?"

"Señora Maddie said that she weel help me find a job in Telluride," Rosa replied. "I don' want to go back to Mexico."

"That would be great, Rosa," Zeke said. "Mebbe if we both stay around heah, we can see each other from time to time."

"I Like that, Zeke," Rosa replied.

Zeke's cheeks flushed.

Maddie stepped out onto the porch. "Okay, Zeke. It's your turn to shower."

* * *

Rance rode into Telluride, and tried to ignore the looks that he got on account of his beat up face. He stopped at the Telegraph Office and dismounted. He tied his horse to the rail, and stepped inside.

Hall, The Telegraph Clerk was shocked at Rance's face, but knew him well enough to know that mentioning the bruising would be bad for his health.

"Hello, Mister McCarty. What can I do for you?" Hall asked.

Rance reached into his chest pocket and pulled out the note. "Send this," he said and passed the note to the clerk.

Hall looked it over. "That will be two dollars and fifteen cents," he said.

Rance reached into his pocket and counted out the money. "Gettin' ta be highway robbery," he complained.

"I don't control the prices, Mister McCarty," Hall said.

"Jus get on with it," Rance said.

Hall sat down and sent out the message, then wrote up the receipt. He got back up and walked over to the counter and handed it to Rance. "Have a good day, sir," he said.

Rance nodded and left the telegraph office.

38

Chapter 38

Sutton was playing cards when a runner from the Telegraph Office entered the saloon, stopped, spied him, and ran to him.

The boy held out the telegram and nervously, said, "Mmmessage for you, Mmmmisterr Sssutton."

Sutton laughed as he took the message. "Relax, sonny, I ain't gonna shoot the messenger!"

He reached into his pocket, pulled out a silver dollar and handed it to the boy.

"Thank yu, sir," the boy said, and took off with a dash.

Sutton took a moment to read the telegram. When he finished, he said, "Sorry, boys, but I sure gotta run."

"But we ain't finished this hand," one of the gamblers said.

"Jus' leave my money in the kitty, an' keep playin'," Sutton said before he stood up.

Sutton's reputation with his side arms prevented any further argument, as the twin Colts slung low on his hips were there for all to see.

* * *

During the Civil War, Sutton had ridden with "Bloody Bill" Anderson, who had led a splinter group of Quantrill's Raiders. It had been said of Sutton that he was a born killer. His parents and sister were killed by a band of Jayhawkers, so, with nothing to lose, he signed up with the guerrillas. After "Bloody Bill" was killed in 1864, Sutton, still in his teens, moved west. Unlike the James brothers, who became outlaws, Sutton straddled the line. He became known as a hired gun, who would enforce the law for the highest bidder. The story was that Sutton had killed over thirty men, and now, Doniphan McCarty had hired him to kill one more.

* * *

Sutton rode to the Leadville Train Station and bought a ticket for him and his horse to Ouray, Colorado, which was just a short way from Telluride. The train was scheduled to leave in the morning. He would pack his gear tonight.

Leadville was roaring in the 1880s. The Matchless Mine itself pumped out $80,000 a month worth of silver. The area was first settled by white people in 1860 when gold was discovered. Most of the placer gold was gone by 1866, and Leadville became a ghost town. The few who did stay discovered in 1877, that the black sand that clogged up their sluice boxes contained fifteen ounces of silver per ton. A new boom began, and Leadville became the second largest city in Colorado, and featured visitors such as Oscar Wilde, Houdini, and Buffalo Bill.

In the 1880s, Leadville sported some 10 dry goods stores, 4 churches, 4 banks, 31 restaurants, 120 saloons, 3 daily newspapers, 19 beer halls, 70 law firms to abate claim jumpers, 35 houses of prostitution, and 118 gambling houses. At the time silver was discovered in Oro Gulch, Leadville had three separate red light districts. Men outnumbered women about five to one, and many women ended up as prostitutes. The city had a true wild west atmosphere. With so much money around, there were bound to be disputes. With little law around, men like Sutton were in high demand.

Sutton had tired of Leadville, however, and was glad to get the summons to southwest Colorado. He knew of Doniphan McCarty's reputation. He was a mean and tough son of a bitch, but his money was good. Sutton didn't care about the right and the wrong of a situation. That wasn't his business.

* * *

Sutton rode to his hotel, went to his room and collected clothes and brought them to the laundry to be picked up later. Then, he brought his horse to the livery next to the hotel, then went back to the hotel desk and arranged for a bath.

Sutton went up to his room to wait for the hot water.

After his bath, Sutton dressed, buckled up his ubiquitous gun belt, and put on his Stetson.

He left his room and went downstairs to the hotel restaurant.

As usual, the room quieted when Sutton entered. Besides his reputation, he made an imposing figure at well over six feet, about two hundred thirty pounds, cat-green eyes, and jett black hair with a little gray at the temples. The gun belt, and twin Colts only added to the mystique.

Sutton sat down at his usual table. It was situated in a corner where he could watch the door, survey the room, and no one could approach him from the back. No one ever took the table until after Sutton had eaten and left. A young upstart did once, and it didn't end well.

Sutton's usual waitress, Annabelle, approached. Annabell was in her early twenties. She had blonde hair and blue eyes, with a body that would wake the dead. She had come, all alone, to Leadville as the silver boom began, and, somehow, managed to stay out of the red light trade.

"Good evening, Mistah Sutton," Annabele said, as she put a glass of whiskey on his table.

"Thank you, Annabelle," Sutton replied.

"You want the usual, Mistah Sutton?" Annabelle asked.

"I'm heading outta town for a bit, Annabelle, I'll try somethin' differ'nt tonight. What do yu suggest?'

"The beef stew is very good, Mistah Sutton," Annabelle replied.

"I'll try that, then," Sutton said.

"Coming right up," Annabelle replied, with a smile.

Sutton watched the young waitress walk away. He admired her beauty, and the way her hips swayed as she walked.

Sutton took a sip from his drink and surveyed the room. It was filled with the usual smattering of business men, a few miners, couples who were traveling through, and some sightseers. The Hotel didn't allow prostitutes and saloon girls, and discouraged miners from entering the restaurant. One man stuck out to Sutton as not fitting in. Sutton's life depended on him reading people, and being ready for anything. He noticed the man taking a sideward glance in his direction. People always looked at him. Sutton was aware of that, but this was different. It gave Sutton an uneasy feeling. He knew to be prepared.

A short time later, Annabelle returned with Sutton's stew, and a small loaf of fresh baked bread and butter.

"Here you go, Mistah Sutton," Annabelle said as she placed the food on his table.

"Thanks, darlin'," he replied, which made her blush.

"I'll check on yu in a bit," she said, face still flushed.

Annabelle turned and went to another table to take an order, while Sutton ate his dinner.

Sutton continued to survey the room while he ate. He noticed the man get up from his chair and casually walk in his direction. Just to be safe, Sutton unholstered the Colt revolver on his left side, while continuing to eat with his right hand.

The man, who looked to be in his early twenties, not as tall as Sutton, and who had black hair and dark eyes, approached. He wore his guns slung low-a gunfighter, Sutton noticed.

"You Sutton?" the stranger demanded.

Sutton put down his spoon. "Who's askin'?" Sutton replied.

"My name's Mercer, Hank Mercer," the man replied.

"Do I know yu?" Sutton enquired.

"Yu killed my daddy," Mercer replied.

"Well then, I sure don' wanna have ta kill yu too," Sutton said. "Why don' you have a drink on me, then go home, sonny."

"I'll have a drink ovah yur dead body," Mercer said as he reached for his pistol.

Sutton fired and a bullet ripped through Mercer's heart. The young man was dead before he hit the floor.

Sutton threw money on his table, then walked past Mercer's corpse and the spreading pool of blood, and out of the dining room.

* * *

The next morning, Sutton had washed, got dressed and packed clothes before going downstairs for breakfast.

He walked to his table and noticed the blood stain on the floor in front of it. Sutton sat down and Annabelle was there in a minute with a mug of coffee.

"I'm sorry aboot leavin' yu a mess last night, Annabelle," Sutton said.

"I understand, Mistah Sutton. As I see it, that man didn't leave you any choice," Annabelle said.

"I appreciate thet, Annabelle," Sutton said.

"Can I take your order?"

"Sure. I'll have three eggs, bacon, and sourdough bread," Sutton said.

"I'll get that goin' for you," Annabelle said.

* * *

After breakfast, Sutton gathered his things and brought them to the lobby before going to the livery to get his horse. He tied up his horse and stepped inside to gather his gear from the lobby.

Annabelle was waiting for him. "How long are you gonna be gone?" she asked Sutton.

"Oh, a couple weeks or so, I guess. Why yu ask?" Sutton replied.

"I have a bad feelin', Mistah. Sutton," Annabelle replied.

Sutton put his hand under her chin. "Nothin' to worry aboot, Annabelle. It's just some desperate cowboy who's given a rancher a hard time," he said.

* * *

Sutton rode to the train station, showed his ticket, loaded his horse, and then took his seat.

He looked around the railroad car. It was starting to fill. Sutton noticed a couple families, some businessmen, and even a few cowboys in his car. He scanned everyone and no one gave him pause.

He settled in, ready for a long day on the rails.

Sutton's mind kept running back to his conversation with Annabelle. He didn't believe in premonitions, but she was very sure in her intuition.

* * *

Maddie had offered to go into Telluride to help Rosa and Zeke with employment opportunities. After an early, but hearty breakfast, Zeke saddled the horses while Maddie and Rosa packed lunches.

The sun was just coming up when they rode out for Telluride. The day was full of hope. The three rode along with Zeke telling stories of his adventures across the west and of the various ranches where he worked. Rosa talked of Mexico, and how she left to get away from her abusive father. Maddie shared the story of her childhood in Virginia, her marriage, trek west, and the murder of her husband and son at, what she assumed was, the hands of McCarty's hired guns.

"I sure is sorry," Zeke said, when Maddie had finished her story.

"It ees so sad," Rosa commented.

"Thank you," Maddie replied. "Now you understand my struggles with McCarty. He'll stop at nothin' to get my ranch."

The three rode into the woods, where it was noticeably cooler as the valley narrowed along the river. They stopped for a rest. They dismounted and let the horses drink.

"Oh thees feel much better," Rosa said, as she rubbed her sore rear end.

Zeke let out a laugh. "You need to spend more time in the saddle," he joked.

"Not if I don' have too," Rosa laughed, still nursing her bum.

While Zeke and Rosa were flirting, Maddie unpacked some jerky and other snacks.

After the break, they gathered the horses. Zeke helped Rosa onto her horse before he mounted his. Once Maddie mounted hers, they continued down the trail.

* * *

Taos made much better time on his return trip. Avoiding towns and not having to hunt or fish for food, along with staying out of jail, shortened his trip by days. He made it to Telluride in the late evening, and spent the night there. He had wanted to take a proper bath, get a haircut and a shave before seeing Maddie.

* * *

Taos got an early start in the morning. He stepped into Marissa's Cantina, and was greeted by the proprietor.

"Señor Taos, I no see ju for very long time," Marissa said.

"I been out to New Mexico on an errand, jus gettin' back," Taos replied.

"I glad ju are safe and sound, Señor. Ju want some breakfast?" Marissa said as she poured coffee for Taos.

"I sure would, Marissa. How about a half a dozen eggs, steak, and sourdough toast?"

"Ju got it, Señor Taos," Marissa said, then turned toward the kitchen.

After Marissa left, Taos thought about his plans for the day. He wanted to stop to see Bill Haney, who was always a good source of information. He also planned on checking in with Sheriff Nolan to get information about the McCarty's.

Marissa returned with Taos' breakfast. "Here ju go Señor Taos," she said as she placed Taos' plate and a glass of water, on the table. "Ju need anythin' else?"

"I'm all set, thanks," Taos replied.

"Okay, I check in with ju in a bit," Marissa said.

* * *

After breakfast, Taos rode to the stockyard to find Bill Haney. When he reached the office, Taos dismounted and tied up Grant at the hitching post. He knocked on the door before heading in.

"Mornin' Bill," Taos drawled as he stepped inside.

Bill Haney looked up from his paperwork. His eyes lit up when he recognized Taos, then, he stood up and walked around his desk to greet Taos with a handshake. "Good to see yu," Bill said as Taos took his hand.

"Just gettin' back from New Mexico?" Bill asked.

"Yup, got inta town last night, an' jus had some chow at Marissa's. I sure thank yu for vouchin' fer me while I was holed up in Durango" Taos replied.

"Glad to do it. Thet Marissa sure is sweet. If I had any courage, I'd ask her out," Bill lamented.

"Yu should. She ain't attached, is she?" Taos asked.

"Nope," Bill replied.

"Then do it," Taos laughed.

"I just might, at thet," Bill said.

"Anythin' interestin' goin' on?" Taos asked.

"It's been pretty quiet lately, but, now thet I think of it, I heered thet Rance McCarty rode inta town t'other day, an' he was beat up pretty bad.. He went inta the Telegraph Office, then rode outa town," Bill said.

"Thet sure is interestin'," Taos said. "I wonder what thet's all aboot."

"I dunno, but it can't be good," Bill said.

"I'd sure like ta buy a drink fer the feller that gave Rance McCarty that whoopin',￼" Taos laughed. He turned serious. "I wonder what his message was about, though."

"Why don't yu check with the Telegraph Office?" Bill suggested.

"I jus may do thet. I wanna talk with Jim Nolan too, before I head ta Thunder Valley," Taos replied.

* * *

Taos rode back into town and stopped at the Telegraph Office, which had just opened.

After dismounting, he tied Grant to the hitching post and stepped inside. Hall, the clerk, looked up when Taos walked in.

"Good mornin' can I help you?" Hall said.

"I sure hope so," Taos said, playing dumb. "My boss's son sent a telegraph t'other day, an' he may have had it sent ta the wrong person. It was Rance McCarty," Taos drawled.

"This is highly unusual, but I guess it won't hurt to let you know. I can't give you the contents, though," he replied.

"My boss, Doniphan McCarty would sure be obliged," Taos lied.

"Give me just a moment, while I look it up," the clerk said.

"I thank yu," Taos said.

Taos fidgeted around the office, then looked out the windows at the street, while the clerk looked through his records.

"Ah, here it is," said the clerk. "Let me see, it was sent to a Mister Sutton in Leadville."

"That's the right one. I sure thank yu. Rance was in a bad way when he rode in t'other day, an' his pa was afeared that he may have gotten the name wrong."

"I wasn't gonna say anything, but, yes, Rance was a mess. He looked hung over and was all beat up. Somebody gave him a thorough thrashing," Hall said.

"Yup, he weren't doin' so great. Thet's fer sure. I sure am obliged, an' I'll be sure ta tell Mister McCarty what a big help yu have been," Taos said.

"Thank you, sir," Hall said as Taos exited.

* * *

Taos untied and mounted Grant. He rode toward the Sheriff's Office. He thought about the name, Sutton. It sounded familiar, but he couldn't place it. He'd ask Jim Nolan.

When he reached the Sheriff's Office, Taos dismounted, tied Grant to the hitching post, and entered the office

"Wal looky-loo," Jim Nolan said, when Taos entered. "Ain't yu a sight fer sore eyes."

Nolan got up from his desk and extended his hand to Taos.

Taos shook Nolan's hand. "It sure was a long stretch on the trail, an' I'm glad ta be back. How's Maddie doin'?'

"Have a seat," Nolan said as he sat down at his desk.

Taos followed the suggestion.

"Wal, Maddie seems ta be doin' okay. I've been headin' out ta the ranch a couple times a week. I also met a young cowboy, Zeke Johnson, from Wyomin', I think. He was ridin' fer McCarty, but I convinced him ta be a spy, an' put him on the payroll," Nolan answered.

"Sounds good. Thank yu fer keepin' an eye on her," Taos said.

"How'd it go in New Mexico?" Nolan asked.

"Wal, I'm back fer good. I'll leave it at thet," Taos replied.

"Whatever yur feelin's, I'm glad thet yur back," Nolan said.

"Have yu heared of a man named Sutton?" Taos asked.

Nolan's jaw tightened, and his cheeks reddened. "Uh, yeah, sure. Why do yu ask?"

Bill Haney told me that Rance McCarty had ridden inta town a few days ago. He was all beat up. Bill said thet he went inta the Telegraph Office, then rode right outa town. I talked the clerk inta tellin' me who the telegram was sent to, an' he said a man named Sutton in Leadville," Taos said.

Nolan slammed his fist on his desk. "By thunder!" Nolan exclaimed. "This sure is bad news."

"Yu mind fillin' me in?" Taos asked.

This man Sutton is a ruthless killer. He rode with Bloody Bill Anderson durin' the war. All born killers, them. Since he moved west, he's been a hired gun hand. He allus gets the poor sonofabitch to pull on him first. Then, he guns him down," Nolan said.

"If I had ta guess, I'd say McCarty wants him ta come gunnin' fer me," Taos said.

"I have ta agree with yu," Nolan said.

"Anythin' else yu know aboot this man, Sutton?" Taos asked.

"He's fast. Fast as lightnin', I heared tell thet he's killed somewhere's ovah thirty men," Nolan replied.

"I guess I better be on the lookout," Taos said.

39

Chapter 39

Taos was glad that he had stopped to talk to Nolan. This Sutton was going to be a problem. He wasn't some young upstart trying to make a name for himself. He had done that, and lasted many years at his game. Of course, Sutton, according to Nolan, had killed mostly cowboys and drifters. He hadn't met many men who were quick on the draw. That may be one advantage for Taos. He knew, though, that Sutton would try to get under his skin, and make him draw. He'd be ready. If it meant dying, he'd be dying for Maddie, and that was a worthy cause.

Taos rode out of town along the San Miguel. He was happy to be near Maddie. Couldn't wait to see her. He missed those green eyes, her laugh, her hair, and just being close to her.

The sound of the boulder strewn river was music to Taos' ears, and the water cooled the air around the trail. It made for a pleasant ride.

Taos rode quietly, enjoying the scenery for about an hour. Then, he heard voices up ahead in the distance. He stopped to hear them better. He could make out two women's voices, and one man's. It was too far to recognize any of them. He waited.

* * *

Maddie, Zeke and Rosa were enjoying the ride up the San Miguel. It was a fun respite from the tension of the past few days, and Maddie enjoyed watching Zeke and Rosa flirt.

Maddie was ahead of the couple, and enjoying listening to them when she saw a horseman in the trail about fifty yards ahead. She stopped abruptly.

Zeke rode up next to her. "What is it, Maddie?" he asked.

"A rider up ahead," she replied.

"Let's move ahead slowly," he advised. "Rosa, yu stay heah."

Maddie took her shotgun out of its sheath, and Zeke loosened his six gun in its holster.

Zeke and Maddie rode up on the trail, while Rosa stayed back as instructed. The rider was in a shadow, so it was hard to make him out. After about ten yards, Maddie could see that the horse was a big bay, and the rider was wearing a black sombrero.

"Oh my God!" Maddie exclaimed, and spurred her horse ahead.

Zeke spurred his horse also, in hopes of keeping up.

* * *

Taos watched the riders move ahead. One woman stayed behind, however. After about covering a quarter of the way, the woman shouted something, and the two riders in the front galloped toward him. Taos drew his twin Colts. Then, the woman's hat blew off prevailing a long mane of honey colored hair.

"Maddie!" Taos exclaimed, as he holstered his irons. He spurred Grant ahead.

They covered the forty yards in seconds, and when Maddie reached Taos, she jumped off her horse and into his lap.

"Oh, Taos, she exclaimed and smothered him with kisses.

Taos wrapped her in his muscular arms. "I sure missed yu, Maddie," he drawled.

* * *

Sutton's three hour ride south to Poncha Springs was uneventful. The tracks in the west were a lot rougher than in the east because of the haste in which they were constructed. In the east, steam trains averaged between forty and fifty miles per hour, while in the west, by contrast, trains typically made twenty miles per hour. Rattling down the tracks for three hours was enough to tire most people out, and Sutton was happy for the layover in Poncha Springs.

The area around Poncha Springs was used as a winter camping ground by the Ute People. The first white visitors to the area were part of a Spanish expedition in 1779. After that French trappers and fur traders moved into the area. Both Zebulon Pike and Kit Carson have been credited for discovering the area's hot springs. In 1855, Colonel Fauntelroy and the 1st Cavalry marched over Poncha Pass and engaged a party of Utes. In 1860, Prospectors moved into the area, and the town began to grow in the 1870s, and had a year-round population of just over one hundred souls in the mid-1880s.

Sutton stepped off the train into a cloud of black smoke. The smoke began to clear as he walked further from the engine. He collected his horse, and rode to the livery.

After making arrangements for his horse, Sutton carried his bag to the Poncha Springs Hotel. He stepped into the lobby, took a moment to scan the room, then walked up to the desk.

"Good afternoon, sir," the twenty-something girl with blue eyes, auburn hair, and a face full of freckles, said in a lilting Irish brogue.

"Howdy, ma'am," Sutton said, as he tipped his hat.

"Would ye like to reserve a room?" she asked.

"Yes'm," Sutton said.

"And how many nights is it, then?" she said.

"It'll be just the one," he replied.

"Sure, right then. Just fill out this form and the price is three dollars, and that includes breakfast," she said. "If you want a bath, that's another fifty cents."

Sutton filled out the form, then took out four dollars. "I'll take a bath as soon as it's ready. Yu ken keep the change."

"Oh thank ye, Mister, ah," she looked at the form, "Sutton."

At the mention of Sutton's name, a man who had been loitering in the lobby, suddenly turned and left the hotel. Sutton caught this out of the corner of his eye.

The girl handed him his door key. "It's room number fourteen. Up stairs and to the right. We'll send for ye as soon as your bath is drawn."

"Thanks, ma'am," Sutton said, and picked up his bag and climbed the stairs.

* * *

Maddie introduced Taos to Zeke and Rosa.

"Sheriff Nolan sure speaks highly of yu, Zeke," Taos said.

"Thanks, Taos," Zeke replied.

"We were headed into Telluride to talk to Sheriff Nolan and to Marissa about jobs for these two," Maddie said. "Do you want to join us?"

"I'd sure love ta, Maddie, but I been pushin' Grant an' this pack mule hard, and ridin' back ta Telluride, then out ta the ranch may be too much on him," Taos said. "How aboot I head to the ranch, keep an eye on things, an' get supper started?"

"Alright, my dear. After a month, a few more hours won't make much of a difference," Maddie said.

Taos took Maddie in his arms, and kissed her.

"I'm so glad that you're home," Maddie said.

* * *

Taos saddled up, and watched the trio ride toward Telluride, before turning Grant and the pack horse, and continuing up the trail.

He was glad to have met Maddie on the trail. His heart soared. Seeing Maddie made Taos realize that she was the right woman for him. He also felt her love, a love that he had never known before; a love that was true and deep. It was a love to cherish and nurture.

* * *

"Dat Taos, he sure ees good lookin'," Rosa said as they rode down the trail.

"I sure think so," Maddie laughed.

Maddie felt like she was floating down the trail. Seeing Taos after all this time was bliss. She could tell by the way that he held her and kissed her that Ida Parker was no longer an issue, and she couldn't be happier. She could now start planning her life moving forward- with Taos.

Before long, they entered Telluride, and decided to start at Marissa's Canteen first.

As they entered, Marissa greeted Maddie and her companions.

"Hola, Señora Maddie, how can I help ju?" Marissa said.

"Hi Marissa, I was wondering if you needed any help?" Maddie asked.

"Don' you have enough to do with the ranch, Señora?" Marissa asked.

"Oh, not for me!" Maddie laughed. "For my friend Rosa here."

"Hola, Señorita Marissa," Rosa said.

"Ees nice to meet ju, Señorita Rosa," Marissa replied. "Jes, I do need help. Do ju have experience?"

"Most recently, I was working for Señor McCarty as a cook and maid," Rosa replied.

Marissa frowned. "Why ju leave dere?"

Rosa blushed and looked down. "Hees son Rance assaulted me, Señorita Marissa."

"Dat no good scoundrel!" Marissa replied. "I tell ju what, I try ju out for a week. If ju do good, I'll hire ju. I have a room behind the cantina dat ju can stay in. We talk money if ju work out. Ju can start dis evening."

"Oh, gracias!" Rosa exclaimed. "I not make ju sorry!"

"Let me show ju the room," Marissa said.

Maddie and Zeke wished Rosa the best and thanked Marissa before exiting the cantina.

"That was easy," Maddie said to Zeke as they walked to their horses.

"Ah can't thank yu enough, Maddie," Zeke replied.

"Let's hope that we have as much luck with the Sheriff," Maddie said.

They mounted their horses and trailed Rosa's horse, and rode to the Sheriff's office.

* * *

Sutton got the word that his bath was ready. He took out a change of clothes, and headed downstairs to take his bath.

The young woman at the desk saw him come down the stairs and greeted him.

"Hello, Mister Sutton, let me show you the way," She said in her lilt.

"Thank yu, ah?"

"It's Molly, Mister Sutton," she replied.

"Okay, Molly," Sutton replied as he followed the young Irish girl down a hallway.

They walked to a door with the number three on it. "Here ye go," she said.

"Thank yu, Molly," Sutton said as he entered the room.

Molly nodded and walked back to the lobby.

Two men walked up to her desk.

"Which room is Sutton in," the first demanded.

"I'll no tell ye that," Molly replied.

The second man stepped behind the desk, threw his arm around her neck, pulled out a revolver and held it to her temple. "Wrong answer," said in a menacing voice.

Tears welled up Molly's eyes. "I'll not tell ye," she insisted.

The man cocked his pistol.

"Okay. Please don't shoot me. He's in room three, God forgive me," she cried.

"I'll hold her here. You go take care of Sutton, Frank," the man holding Molly said.

"It'll be my pleasure, Dalton," Frank replied.

Frank walked down the hallway until he came to room number three. He stopped, drew his revolver and slowly turned the knob. He eased his way through the doorway and looked into the room. Sutton was in the tub facing away from him wearing his Stetson. *This is gonna be too easy,* Frank thought as he raised his weapon. He emptied his gun into Sutton's head.

Suddenly, Frank heard a click behind him. Cold steel pushed into the back of his head.

"Yu done killed my hat," Sutton said. "Yur gonna have ta pay fer thet."

Sutton pulled the trigger and splattered Frank's brains all over the room.

Sutton took a moment to replace the shell, then left the bathroom and sneaked back down the hall. He spied the other man holding a gun to Molly's head.

He stepped quickly, but silently out into the lobby, and said, in a loud voice, "Hey anybody heah see Frank?"

Dalton spun in Sutton's direction, and let go of Molly while he pointed his revolver at Sutton. "You!" he yelled.

Sutton's Colts had already cleared leather, and he sent hot lead into Dalton's chest, which dropped him to the ground, dead.

Sutton ran behind the desk and found Molly on the floor, crying.

"I'm so sorry, I'm so sorry. God forgive me," Molly wept.

"Here, get up," Sutton said, as he gave Molly his hand.

Molly took his hand and stood up. Tears streamed down her cheeks.

"Yu alright. He din't hurt yu none, did he?"

"No, Mister Sutton," Molly said.

"Then stop cryin'," he said.

"But I told him where you were," Molly cried.

"He had a gun at yur head. Now, I gotta go out an' get me another hat. I'll be ready for a bath when I get back," Sutton said as he walked to the door.

* * *

Zeke opened and held the door for Maddie, as she stepped into the Sheriff's office.

Jim Nolan looked up from his work when the door opened.

"Well, ain't this a nice surprise!" he exclaimed. He watched as Zeke followed Maddie in. "Wal, I see yu two have met."

"Hi Jim," Maddie said. "Yes, we have become acquainted, and Zeke has filled me in on his deal with you. We have a problem, though."

"What's that?" Nolan said, as he stood up.

Maddie filled him in on the ordeal with Rance and Rosa, and Zeke's involvement.

When she had finished, Nolan took a minute to think. He rubbed his chin and looked out the window.

Presently, he turned and spoke, "Wal, ain't thet sumpin'! I heered aboot Rance showin' up in town all stove up. This explains it. Couldn't a' happened to a nicer guy," he laughed. Nolan became serious. "Zeke, yur outa work, an' yu can't spy on the McCarty's, so yur no use fer me. Thet's what yur thinkin'. Right?"

"Thet aboot sums it up," Zeke replied.

"Wal, how aboot I keep yu on as a deputy? Telluride is growin' an' I sure could use an extra hand. I got it approved by the city council already. Thet's why I was able ta offer yu the spying job in the first place," Nolan said.

"Thank yu, Sheriff. I'll jus have ta find a place ta stay," Zeke replied.

"They's a room up above the jail. If yu want, yu can stay there as long as yu want, or until yu find somethin' better," Nolan offered.

"I'll take it. Thanks," Zeke replied.

* * *

Zeke had insisted on escorting Maddie back to the ranch. Although she liked being independent, she was glad for the offer, and gladly accepted it. Before leaving town, Zeke made a quick stop to see Rosa to fill her in on his news.

"This has been the best day," Maddie said, as they rode out of town.

"It sure has been. All around," Zeke agreed. "I'm so glad thet Sheriff Nolan can keep me on. I like it heah. It's nice country. I don' want ta drift no more. It's time to put down roots."

"That wouldn't have anythin' to do with a little dark-haired señorita, would it?" Maddie laughed.

"Too true, Maddie, too true, if I must admit," Zeke chuckled.

* * *

Taos got to work when he arrived at the ranch. He first took care of Grant and the pack mule. Next, he checked on the livestock, and gathered root vegetables, and dried beef from the root cellar.

He soaked the beef in water while he chopped the vegetables. Next, He got a fire started in the stove. When the beef was hydrated, he drained it and browned it in a cast iron skillet. When the meat was done, he put it, onion, carrots, and celery into a pot and added water. While the water heated, he scrubbed and chopped potatoes.

Taos poured himself a glass of whiskey and walked out to the porch.

* * *

Sutton was eating his dinner when the local Marshall, Micah Hurlocker approached.

"You Sutton?" Hurlocker asked.

Sutton looked up from his steak. "Who's askin'," he replied.

I'm Marshall Micah Hurlocker, the law around heah," Hurlocker replied.

"Have a seat, Marshall, yur makin' me nervous," Sutton replied.

The Marshall sat down across from Sutton. "So?"

"I'm Sutton."

"I heared aboot yu," Hurlocker said. "In town jus' a few hours, an' I got two corpses."

"Thet was self defense, Marshall. Yu ken ask thet girl, Molly," Sutton replied.

"Oh, I did, an' I agree it was self defense, but I keep a quiet town here, Sutton. Yur kind stinks of death. It surrounds yu. I suggest yu move along," Hurlocker said.

"Wal, as it is, I'm leavin' on the train in the mornin', Marshall, so yur town can go back ta smellin' like pig shit. Now, if yur done, I'd like ta finish my supper before it gets cold."

* * *

Taos had just put the potatoes into the pot when he heard hooves outside. He sped to the door and opened it just enough to see through. Excitedly, he swung the door open as Maddie and Zeke rode up to the house.

"Howdy!" Taos exclaimed as he stepped off the porch to greet Maddie and Zeke.

Maddie jumped off her horse and into Taos' arms. He let her down gently, and they kissed.

Zeke cleared his throat loudly. "Uh, I guess thet I'll take care of the horses, while yu two get reacquainted."

"Thank you, Zeke," Maddie replied.

"Seems like a good kid," Taos said.

"Yes, and he and Rosa are so cute together," Maddie laughed.

Taos took her hand and stepped up onto the porch with her. "How'd it go in town?"

"It couldn't have gone better," Maddie replied. "Rosa got hired by Marissa, and Zeke has a deputy position in town. Plus, they also have places for them to stay."

"Whew, good fer them," Taos said.

"Yeah, and good for us. Zeke will be a good ally against McCarty, and Rosa will be another friendly face in town," Maddie said.

They walked inside.

"It sure smells great in here!" Maddie exclaimed.

"I got stew cookin'," Taos said.

"Thank you for doing that," Maddie said, and kissed him.

Just then, Zeke entered the ranch house. "Don' yu two evah stop?" he laughed.

"Hey, we haven't seen each other in over a month," Maddie said. "Wash up for dinner. Taos made beef stew."

"Good, I'm starvin'," Zeke replied.

* * *

After dinner was finished and the dishes and their showers were done, Taos and Maddie stepped out onto the porch; each with a glass of whiskey, while Zeke took his shower.

"It sure is nice to be back," Taos said after he sat down and had a sip of whiskey. "Listenin' ta the river is some peaceful, an' the mountain views is spectacular."

"It's home, our home, Taos," Maddie replied. I'm so glad that you came home. I feel safe when you are near.'

"I won't ever leave yu, Maddie," Taos replied.

"You make my heart full," Maddie said.

"I sure gotta tell yu sumpin'," Taos said.

A worried look came over Maddie's face. "What is it darlin'."

"I talked to Bill Haney this mornin' an' he said thet Rance McCarty come inta town t'other day an' went ta the Telegraph Office," Taos began.

"And?" Maddie asked.

"So, I went ovah theah an' got Hall, the clerk ta tell me who the telegraph was sent ta," Taos continued. "Anyhoo, he contacted a man named, Sutton."

"Who's this Sutton?" Maddie asked.

"After I left the Telegraph Office, I went ovah ta see Sheriff Nolan, an' asked him if he evah heared aboot this Sutton," Taos said.

"What did he say?" Maddie enquired.

"He said that he nevah met him, but he sure heared of him. Seems this

Sutton feller is a hired gun. He's killed somewheres ovah thirty men, mostly homesteaders an' ranchers. Accordin' ta Nolan, he ain't nevah killed a real gun, but he is fast. He eggs 'em on till they draw on him, then he kills 'em. Thet way its self defense," Taos explained.

"And he's comin' here?" Maddie asked.

"Yup."

40

Chapter 40

Sutton boarded the train west. The ride from Poncha Springs to Montrose, some one hundred and twenty-five miles, would take about six hours. The train would make a quick stop in Gunnison to take on water for steam, and then move on.

Montrose was incorporated in 1882 as the Denver and Rio Grande Railroad reached the area. Montrose became an important railway hub and shipping center when a branch railroad line stretched south toward the mineral rich San Juan Mountains..

As the train pulled out of the station, Sutton's thoughts turned to the previous day. It seemed that every town had someone with a desire to either make a name for himself or someone looking for revenge. He didn't know either of the men that he killed yesterday, but they sure knew him. *Was it allus gonna' be like this,* he thought to himself. The one talent he had was killing, but leaving a trail of dead bodies wherever he went was getting tedious.

* * *

After breakfast, Zeke saddled his horse and said his goodbyes. Then, he saddled up and rode out.

"He'll do well. He's a good kid," Taos said as they watched Zeke ride off.

"He sure is," Maddie agreed.

"I'm thinkin' we should take a ride up ta the High Meadow, an' check on the beeves," Taos suggested.

"I think that is a marvelous idea," Maddie agreed. "After the chores around here are done, I'll make up a lunch basket, and we can make a day of it."

"I like thet idee," Taos replied .

* * *

The train pulled into the Gunnison Station. Sutton was happy for the chance to get out and stretch his legs, and grab a bite to eat.

Gunnison had been frequented by fur traders and trappers in the early 1800s, but when fur prices plunged in the 1840s, there was no work for trappers. The town was named after John W. Gunnison, a US army officer who came through the area in 1853 on a mission to map out a transcontinental railroad. The railroad ended up coming through in 1880, which greatly helped the mining community, and provided support for the new cattle industry. Due to the dry climate, farmers discovered that they couldn't make a living at farming, but cattle would thrive in the area.

Sutton checked on his horse, then found a small cantina, and entered. He was met by a Mexican waitress.

"Hola, Señor," the petite young lady said. "Ju want some lunch?"

"Howdy, Ma'am. Yes, I don't have a lot of time, what can you get me quick?" Sutton responded.

"I can get ju a corned beef sandwich, Señor. It be ready in just a few minutes."

"I'll take thet, an' a beer," Sutton said, and found a seat where he could survey the room, and most importantly, watch the door.

The waitress returned with Sutton's beer.

"Here ju are Señor," she said as she placed the glass mug on his table. "I be right back wit' jur sandwich."

Sutton nodded, and said, "Ma'am."

He took a long, slow draught of his beer. He watched people as a habit, and he looked for anyone who seemed nervous or fidgety. He relaxed as he found none.

The waitress returned with Sutton's sandwich. She placed it on the table in front of him. "Enjoy," she said.

"Thanks," Sutton said.

Sutton ate his lunch without incident. When he had swallowed the last of his beer, Sutton reached into his pocket, grabbed some money, and put a couple dollars on the table, and walked out.

When he reached the depot, Sutton took a few minutes to check on his horse, then took his seat on the train.

Before long, Sutton heard the steam pressure building. The train whistle blew, and the engine chugged down the tracks. It picked up speed as it left Gunnison. In another three hours, he would arrive in Montrose.

* * *

Maddie put lunch together as Taos saddled the horses.

When Taos had finished, he walked Grant and Maddie's horse to the porch, tied them to the railing, then went inside.

"Hosses are ready," he said when he entered the house.

"I'm almost done here, Taos," Maddie replied.

Taos walked over to Maddie. His spurs jingled as he crossed the floor. He put an arm around her waist and pulled her close. Maddie looked up at him, wrapped her arms around his broad shoulders, and kissed him.

Taos enveloped Maddie in his arms. Their kisses became more passionate.

He felt Maddie's ample breasts against his chest as their mouths connected in deep kisses. He caressed her, enjoying each curve of her figure.

Maddie suddenly pulled away. "Whew! If we don't stop now, we're gonna end up doin' somethin'."

Taos took a step back. "I sure am sorry, Maddie. I guess I got a little carried away."

"Oh, Taos, don't be sorry. I enjoyed it every bit as much as you. I just want us to be proper," Maddie said.

"I understand," Taos replied. "We best finish packin' up the lunch."

Together, they got the lunch basket together and Taos carried it outside and tied it behind his saddle. Next, he helped Maddie up into her saddle. Then, he mounted Grant and they rode off.

* * *

Zeke made good time on his trip to Telluride. He was tempted to see Rosa, but rode to the Sheriff's office first.

He dismounted, tied his horse to the hitching post, and stepped inside.

Nolan and Slade were in deep conversation when Zeke entered the office.

Nolan looked at the door, and his eyes widened with recognition as a smile spread on his lips.

"Wal, speak a' the devil! Slade, this heah is Zeke, our new deputy," Nolan said. "Zeke, this heah is Slade."

The two young men shook hands and exchanged pleasantries.

"Zeke, we was jus aboot ta get sompin' ta eat. Yu wanna join us?"

"As long as we's goin' ta Marissa's," Zeke laughed.

"Ah think thet ken be arranged," Nolan laughed.

The three men stepped out onto the street and walked toward Marissa's Cantina.

Marissa greeted them at the door.

"Hola mi amigos," she said. "Follow me. I get ju a table."

Marissa turned and led the men to a corner table. The room was busy, and many of the patrons greeted Nolan, who was a very popular sheriff, on the way.

"Ju all want beer?" Marissa asked.

"Sure," Nolan said. "Thanks, Marissa."

Jur waitress weel be right wit'ju," Marissa said as she left to get the beers.

A few minutes later, Rosa returned with the beers and placed them on the table.

"Buenos días," Rosa said. "What can I get ju to eat?"

"How aboot three bowls of Marissa's chili an' a loaf of bread," Nolan said.

"I happy to get for ju," Rosa said, her eyes focussed on Zeke's.

"Howdy, Rosa," Zeke said.

Rosa blushed. "Hola, Zeke. Ees good to see ju." She turned and scurried away.

"So, thet's Rosa," Nolan said. "She sure is purty. I ken see why yu is smitten wit' her."

"Nolan told me aboot how yu saved her from Rance McCarty," Slade said. Thet was a good turn. Ain't no knowin' what he might've done."

"Speakin' of the McCarty's," Nolan said. "Taos found out thet Rance had a telegraph sent ta' a hired gunman by the name a' Sutton. I imagine Doniphan is gonna make a play ta get rid a' Taos."

"I heared a' thet man Sutton," Slade said. "He's one bad hombre."

"If McCarty gets ahold a' Maddie's ranch, he'll control the valley. He'll dictate the price a' beef in the area, an' take over the whole town," Nolan said.

Rosa returned with a tray. She placed the chilli bowls on the table, and then the bread loaf, a knife, and a slab of butter. "Enjoy jur meals, señors," she said, again, with eyes on Zeke.

"She sure has eyes fer yu," Nolan laughed, when Rosa had left.

Zeke blushed.

* * *

Maddie and Taos had a pleasant ride up to the High Meadow.

"Ah'll nevah get tired a' this view," Taos said as they entered the caldera.

They looked out at the lush mountain protected caldera. Feeding cattle dotted the landscape, and the grass was an emerald green. It was such a far cry from the hot, dry prairie. It was heaven on earth this time of year.

They dismounted and hobbled the horses. Next, Taos took the lunch basket off Grant, and found a level piece of ground, and put it down. He stood up and looked out upon the caldera, and Maddie joined him. He put his arm around her waist and pulled her close.

"I love yu, Maddie," he said. "We're gonna get thru this business wit' Sutton, an' then we got our whole lives ahead a' us."

"We'll see it through, Taos. I know we will," Maddie said.

"Yu hungry?" Taos asked.

"I'm starvin'," Maddie replied. "Let me unpack the basket."

"Thanks, Maddie," Taos said, as he looked out on the cattle.

"Come and get it!" Maddie yelled.

Taos walked over to where Maddie had laid out a blanket, dishes, and ham sandwiches.

"This sure looks good, Maddie. I thank yu," Taos said as he sat down on the blanket next to her.

"Thanks, Taos," Maddie said.

They began eating.

"This is sure good, Maddie," Taos said.

"I'm glad that you like it, my dear," Maddie said.

"They's somethin' that I'd like ta talk ta yu aboot," Taos said.

Maddie finished chewing and swallowed before answering. "What is it?" she asked.

"We haven't had a chance ta talk about my trip back ta New Mexico," he said.

"That's true," Maddie agreed. "We've been pretty busy, and haven't had much time for talkin' since you've been back'."

"I told yu aboot the miners ruinin' the river thet my folks depend on," Taos started.

"Yes, of course," Maddie replied as Taos took a bite of his sandwich.

Taos finished chewing and swallowed. "Wal. they're cattle is still birthin' a lot o' cripples, an they ain't no fish nor bugs in the river. It's dead. I ain't sure how long they ken go on afore they go bankrupt," Taos explained.

"I'm so sorry, Taos," Maddie said. "Do they have a plan?"

"Not yet. I dunno how long it'll take fer the river to clean up, if evah. They have put so much work inta buildin' up the ranch. It's a shame," Taos said. "I was thinkin' thet if I could find a ranch fer sale around heah, they could move out this way."

"I have an idea," Maddie said.

"Yu do?" Taos asked.

"Why don't they just come here?" We could run a lot more cattle than we are now. Your parents, your sister, and your cowboys can all move out here. We just have to build a house for your parents and Sage, and a bunk house for the cowboys," Maddie said.

"You'd do that?" Taos asked.

"Of course, Taos," Maddie replied. "But you gotta make an honest woman outa me," she laughed.

Taos reached into his pocket and took something out. "I found this on my travels," he said as he handed Maddie a diamond ring. "If'n you'll have it."

Maddie took the ring from Taos, and put it on. Tears streamed down her eyes. "Oh Taos! Yes, of course I'll take it!"

* * *

Sutton's train reached Montrose in the late afternoon. It had been a long day. He spent a total of seven hours rumbling down the rails, and he was tired and sore.

He stepped off the train with his bag and went to collect his horse. He rode to the livery, and made arrangements for his horse to be boarded.

Sutton checked into the hotel and made arrangements for a bath. He hoped that a soak in the hot water would help his aches. Sutton hated traveling by train, but it was so much faster than by horse. He was happy for the short hour and a half ride to Ouray in the morning.

After his bath, Sutton enquired at the front desk for a dinner recommendation. He left the hotel and found the restaurant, a steakhouse called Cattleman's, and entered.

Sutton was met by a young Mexican woman with black eyes, and long black hair tied in a ponytail.

"Hola Señor, My name is Dulce, and I am jur waitress dis evening," she said.

"I'd like a table in the back facin' the door," Sutton replied.

Dulce took notice of Sutton's guns and made a knowing nod. "Follow me, Señor," she said, as she headed deep into the dining room.

Sutton followed her, and scanned the room. The dining room consisted of the typical crowd: a mix of cowboys, miners, business men, and gamblers. At the hotel, the clerk had told him that Cattleman's was the least rowdy place in town, and it was generally quiet.

Dulce stopped at a corner table. "How is dis, Señor?"

"It's good, thanks," Sutton replied.

"I get ju somethin' to drink, Señor?" Dulce asked.

"I'll have a whiskey an' a beer," Sutton replied.

"I be right back, Señor," Dulce said as she placed a handwritten menu on the table.

Sutton picked up the menu and looked it over. The choices consisted of a lot of beef, chicken, pork, deer and elk. Sides were potatoes, rice, and beans.

Dulce returned with Sutton's drinks.

"Here ju go, Señor," Dulce said as she placed Sutton's drinks on the table. "Ju ready to order?"

"I'll have an elk steak, medium, fried potatoes, an' beans. Ma'am," Sutton replied.

"I put jur order in, Señor," Dulce said and left with the menu.

Sutton downed his whiskey and chased it with a swallow of beer.

He noticed a few rowdy cowboys a few tables away, and hoped that they weren't going to cause any trouble. He wasn't in the mood.

* * *

After lunch, Nolan and his two lawmen met in the office.

"We gotta plan for this Sutton comin. I figger thet he'll be heah in the next few days," Nolan said.

"We can't jus run him outa town," Slade said.

"No, but we ken let him know thet we knowed what he's up ta," Nolan said. "Zeke, when he does show up, I want yu ta ride out ta the Ferguson place, an let 'em know. Pack clothes, cause I want yu ta stay out theah."

"Yup, Boss," Zeke replied.

"Pack plenty ammo, and grab one a' the Winchesters."

* * *

Maddie and Taos had enjoyed a pleasant afternoon, and after lunch, took a ride amongst the cattle to check on their condition. Then, they packed up the basket and headed for the ranch house.

"I can't stop lookin' at this ring," Maddie said, as they rode down the trail.

"I'm glad yu like it, Maddie,"

"Like it? I love it, and I love you," Maddie said.

Taos blushed. "Yu knowed I sure luve yu," he replied.They continued their ride in silence.

When they arrived at the ranch and dismounted, Maddie said, "If you take care of the horses, I'll get started on dinner."

"Yu got it," Taos said.

* * *

The cowboys were drinking hard and getting louder while Sutton waited for his meal. He was not a patient man, and the cowboys were getting on his nerves.

Dulce returned with Sutton's dinner.

"Here ju are, Señor," Dulce said as she placed Sutton's dish on the table.

"Thanks, Dulce," Sutton said.

"Anoder beer an' Whiskey, Señor?" she asked.

"Just a beer," Sutton said.

"Right away, Senior," Dulce said.

Sutton dug into his meal. *This elk is magnificent,* Sutton thought, after taking his first bite. He tried to ignore the cowboys who were getting increasingly annoying. He tried the potatoes, and they were also wonderful. The beans had been grown locally, and very good. Sutton was enjoying his dinner when he heard a commotion. He looked in the direction of the noise and saw the cowboys hassling Dulce. She had a mug of beer in her hand, which Sutton assumed was meant for him. One of the cowboys grabbed her and pulled her onto his lap, and tried to kiss her. Dulce slapped him across his face.

This gurl's got spunk, Sutton thought, as he watched the scene.

The other two cowboys laughed, which angered the one who had grabbed Dulce. He slapped her back and grabbed the mug of beer that she had in her hand and drank it.

That was it! Sutton had enough! He stood up and stormed over to the table.

"You son's a bitches leave her alone!" Sutton demanded.

"It ain't any a yur business, old man," the cowboy who was holding onto Dulce said.

"It was my beer thet yu just drank. Thet makes it my business," Sutton growled.

"I'll buy yu another, if that'll make yu happy," the cowboy said, as his buddies watched uneasily.

"Fust, yu're gonna let Dulce go," Suttun said.

"An if I don'?" the Cowboy said.

"Yu really don' want ta find thet out," Sutton said, very quietly.

"Yu don' scare me much, old man," the cowboy replied.

"Wal, she's wastin' her time with a sheep humper like yu, anyway, Sutton said.

The cowboy shoved Dulce off his lap and reached for his gun. "Yu sonofa...
"

He never got a chance to finish his sentence as a bullet hit him between the eyes.

The other two cowboys kicked their chairs back and reached for their guns. A big mistake. They were both dead before their forty-fives cleared leather.

"Oh thank yu, Señor,'' Dulce said as the dust settled.

"Yu okay?" Sutton asked.

"Ci, Señor, thanks to ju," Dulce said.

Just then, Marshall Lem Gramby, the town lawman, entered the restaurant. He was in his mid-thirties, had dark eyes, dark hair, and olive skin, and was tall and barrel chested. All in all, he was an imposing figure.

"What's goin' on heah?" he demanded as he looked at the three bodies on the floor.

"Dees man saved my life, Señor Marshall," Dulce cried, still shaken.

"Anybody see anythin' differnt?" Gramby asked the room.

The room was silent.

Gramby turned to Sutton. "Tell me what happened," he ordered.

"This'n," he pointed at the first cowboy, "grabbed Dulce heah, an' pulled her inta his lap and he tried to kiss her. She pulled away an' slapped him across the face. He slapped her hard, and pulled the mug of beer outa her hand, it was my beer, by the way, an' he drank it. I got up an' told him ta leave the gurl alone. He threatened me, an' drew on me. Then t'other two drew on me. It didn't end well fer any a' them," Sutton said.

"I ken see thet."Gramby said, then turned to Dulce. "Is this how it happened?"

"Jes, Señor Gramby," Dulce replied.

Gramby looked around the room. "Is this how y'all seen it?" he enquired.

There was a general murmur of assent from the crowd.

Sutton looked at Dulce. "How 'bout thet beer I ordered?"

41

Chapter 41

Zeke was up early, and had a quick breakfast at Marissa's, so he could visit with Rosa. He was the only customer this early, so she was able to sit with him while he ate.

"This sure is good, Rosa," Zeke said.

"Dee chef is berry good here," she replied.

"I knowed it's only a day, but how'r yu likin' it heah?" He asked.

"Señorita Marissa is so nice! My room is small, but better den de McCarty's had me in," Rosa replied. "How about ju?"

"Sheriff Nolan is a good man. He's sendin' me ta Maddie's ranch fer a few days. Seems they's a man called Sutton, who's a hired gun, headin' our way. He was hired by McCarty ta get rid a' Taos," Zeke said.

"Dis sounds very scary, Zeke," Rosa said. "I don' like it, not one bit."

"Aw, I'll be alright," Zeke replied. "Nolan said ta' not let this Sutton feller get unda my skin. Thet's what he does. He eggs fellers on, an when they lose they's temper an' draws on him, he cuts 'em down."

"He sounds like one bad hombre, Zeke, please be careful, for me," Rosa said.

"Sure, Rosa," Zeke said.

"I luve ju, Zeke," Rosa said. "Please come back to me."

Zeke flushed red. "Aw shucks, Rosa. I sure feel the same way aboot you," he replied. "I'll be careful."

Zeke finished eating his breakfast. "I gotta go," he said, and put money on the table and stood up.

Rosa stood up with him, and walked Zeke to the door. She grabbed his arm. "Kiss me, Zeke," she said.

Zeke took Rosa in his arms, and leaned down and kissed her. She returned his kiss and wrapped her arms around him.

* * *

Sutton had slept well with Dulce in his arms. After the incident, he had a couple more beers, and Dulce had practically thrown herself at him. Who was he to say no to a young, attractive woman?"

Dulce opened her eyes, and looked at Sutton, who also had just woken up.

"Good morning," she said. She still felt a glow from their lovemaking.

"Mornin'," Sutton replied, and got out of bed and pulled on his britches.

"You want to go another round?" Dulce asked with a devilish sparkle in her eyes.

"I got a train ta' catch," Sutton said as he continued dressing.

"Where ju going?" she asked, she pouted.

"Ouray, then ridin' ta Telluride. I have a job to do neah theyah," Sutton replied.

"When ju coming back?" she asked.

"I ain't," he said.

"What about me?" Dulce asked as tears welled up in her eyes.

"What aboot you?" He asked.

"Ju saved my life, we made luve," she cried.

"The guy drank my beer," Sutton said cruelly.

"Ju sonofabithch!" Dulce screamed at him. "I hate Ju! I gave myself to ju, and dis how ju treat me?" She jumped out of bed and slapped him as hard as she could, which left a dark red mark on his cheek. He hit her with the back of his hand and knocked her back onto the bed.

"Get dressed an' get out. I got a train ta' catch."

* * *

Maggie and Taos had had a wonderful evening. After dinner, they sat out on the porch and enjoyed the evening light and each other's company. They talked about the future, and watched the sunset.

They were up early, as usual. After coffee, Taos did the morning chores while Maddie cooked breakfast.

When finished taking care of the livestock, Taos walked into the house.

"It sure do smell good in heah!" Taos exclaimed.

"Go wash up. Breakfast is almost finished," Maddie said.

Taos grabbed the kettle from the stove and filled a wash basin and walked into the bathroom to wash his hands.

Maddie finished cooking the bacon, and put it into the warming section of the cook stove, along with the biscuits that she had baked earlier, to keep warm. Next, she put the bacon skillet back on the stove to heat back up and grabbed the bowl of eggs. She cracked five into the pan, as Taos came out of the bathroom.

"Lookin' good, Maddie, an' breakfast ain't too bad neither," Taos said.

"Ain't you funny," Maddie said.

Taos set the table while Maddie fried the eggs. When the eggs were done, they sat down to eat.

"This sure is good, Maddie," Taos said.

"Thanks, I'm glad you like it," she replied.

* * *

Sutton loaded his horse on the train, and carried his bag to his car and stepped up onto it. He found a seat in the back where he could scan the car. There were a few cowboys and miners already seated.

It was an hour and a half ride to Ouray, then he had to ride his horse to Telluride. He'd stay the night in Telluride and get an early start to the McCarty's.

The ride to Ouray was uneventful. Ouray was a mining town that was incorporated on October 2, 1876, and was named after Ute Chief Ouray. It was originally founded by miners of silver and gold, and once boasted that the town had more horses and mules than people.

When the train screeched to a stop, Sutton stepped off with his bag and collected his horse. It was only seventeen miles to Telluride, but the trail was rough and climbed over 13,114 foot high Imogene Pass. He wasted no time getting going on what he expected would be a six hour ride.

* * *

Zeke enjoyed being out early in the morning. He was happy with his new job. Sheriff Nolan was a good man, and Deputy Slade McDonald seemed solid too. He was worried about his assignment, though. He had killed a few times in self defense, but none of the men that he had gunned down were real gunmen. Sutton was.

Riding alone, Zeke made good time, and was happy to see Maddie's ranch come into view. It wouldn't be long now. He hoped that Taos and Maddie would accept his assistance.

* * *

After breakfast, Taos started splitting wood, while Maddie did laundry. Taos had his shirt off while he worked, and she couldn't help but admire his physique as she hung clothes on the line to dry.

"You want some water?" she asked. "It's gettin' pretty hot out here."

Taos wiped his brow with his gloved hand. He looked at Maddie, and said, "I sure is gettin' parched. A drink a' water'll do me some good."

Maddie dipped water from the barrel with a ladle and brought it to Taos.

"Thank yu, Maddie," Taos said before drinking. He handed it back to her when he had finished.

"Want another?" she asked.

"Thet was just right, thanks," he replied. As he cooled off, his eyes scanned the prairie.

"Rider comin'," he said. He grabbed his shirt and put it on. Then picked up his Winchester.

"Go get yur scattergun," he said.

Maddie ran inside to get the shotgun, and also strapped on her gun belt.

Taos had grabbed the binoculars, but the rider was still too far off to make an identification.

"Can you tell who it is?" Maddie asked when she stepped outside.

"Not yet," Taos replied."But he's ridin' our way fer sure."

"Do you think it is Sutton?" Maddie asked. Her voice quivered when she spoke.

"Hard ta tell from this distance. I suppose I ken tell in a few more minutes," Taos replied.

"We'll be ready for him," Maddie said. She tried to be strong, but, in fact, was deathly scared.

"Let me take another look see," Taos said as he lifted the binoculars to his eyes. "Ah, false alarm!" he exclaimed. "It's Zeke, sure enough."

Maddie let out a sigh of relief. "I'm glad," she said.

They watched, arms around each other as Zeke approached the ranch.

"I sure wonder what he's up ta'," Taos said.

"Maybe he has news about Sutton," Maddie answered.

"Makes sense," Taos agreed.

A few minutes later, Zeke approached the ranch. He crossed the San Miguel and rode up to Taos and Maddie.

"Hey, y'all," Zeke yelled as he approached.

"What brings yu this way," Taos asked, as Zeke dismounted.

"Sheriff's orders," Zeke said. "Sutton is expected anytime now, an' he wants me heah.

"I'm so glad that you're here. This Sutton character seems pretty scary," Maddie said.

"I sure agree, an' so does the Sheriff. Thet's why he sent me ovah," Zeke said.

"I think we'll need help, 'cause the McCarty's'll probably come along. Havin' an extra hand'll sure be helpful. Mebbe havin' thet star on yur chest 'll act as a deterrent," Taos said.

"Hey, how about some lunch?" Maddie asked.

"I'll nevah say no to yur cookin'," Zeke said. Let me take care a' my hoss fust."

"Let me give yu a hand," Taos said to Zeke.

"Come in and wash up, when you are done," Maddie said.

* * *

Taos walked with Zeke and the horse to the stable, where Zeke took off the saddle, and put it on a rack.

Taos took the saddle blanket, and hung it up to dry. "Yu know any more aboot this Sutton feller?" he asked.

Zeke began brushing the horse. "Jus what Nolan told me. He filled me in on how Sutton operates," he replied. "He expects thet Sutton'll be heah any time."

Taos had filled a water and grain bucket for Zeke's horse, and put them in a stall. Zeke walked his horse in.

"Wal, I sure do appreciate it thet yur heah. It makes Maddie feel better, too," Taos said. "Let's get washed up," Taos said.

* * *

Sutton had reached Imogene Pass in the early afternoon. His horse had labored to breathe in the high altitude conditions. The view of the San Juan Mountains was spectacular, but it was cold and windy up in the pass, and Sutton didn't stop to enjoy the scenery. The whipping winds made travel difficult, and he was happy to head down the southern side of the pass. When he found a protected spot, he dismounted and ate a sandwich. He also gave his horse some grain and water. There wasn't much up there, other than pikas and marmots.

After a short break, it was too cold to stay still for too long, Sutton mounted his horse and began the steep journey down to Telluride.

Sutton thought about the last few days. He had been hired to kill a man, but so far, he had killed a half a dozen and he hadn't even reached Telluride. He wondered if he could get McCarty to pay him for those dead men, and laughed to himself.

The last three men brought his count up to forty-two, not counting the many men that he killed during the war. This man, Taos, would make number forty-three.

* * *

Maddie had made ham sandwiches for lunch on fresh baked bread, and she put out a pitcher of sun tea. After cleaning up, the men sat down at the table.

"This sure looks good, Maddie. Thank yu," Taos said as he grabbed a sandwich off of the platter.

Zeke grabbed a sandwich also, and took a bite. "This is real good, Maddie," he said when he had finished chewing.

"You are both welcome," Maddie replied before taking a sandwich for herself.

"We should come up with a plan fer Sutton's arrival," Taos said before taking a bite of his sandwich.

Maddie poured iced tea for everyone.

"Thanks," Zeke said.

"Thank you, Maddie," Taos said.

"Any idees?" Zeke asked.

"I think that Sutton'll want ta use Maddie agin' me," Taos said.

"I agree. From what Nolan said, he tries ta find a weakness or a wedge ta use agin' someone," Zeke replied.

"Maddie, I think it's best thet yu stay close ta' the ranch, or stay near one a' us," Taos suggested.

"Okay, Taos," Maddie replied.

"I jus don' want ta give him no opportunity," Taos said.

"I don' think yu should be left alone, Maddie. One of us should be near at hand all the time," Zeke said.

"I agree. There's no tellin' what Sutton or the McCarty's 'll do ta get me in a predicament. They knowed thet if they get ta yu, they ken get ta me," Taos said. "An' keep yurself armed at all times," he warned.

"You two are startin' to scare me," Maddie said.

"Sometimes, it pays ta be scared," Zeke said.

* * *

Sutton reached Telluride by late afternoon. He found a boarding house to stay in near Popcorn Alley, Telluride's well known sporting district..

The woman at the boarding house had suggested Marissa's Cantina on Colorado Avenue as a good place to grab a bite to eat. Sutton got his horse settled, then walked the few blocks to Marissa's. It was good to be on his feet and walk after the rough ride over Imogene Pass from Ouray.

Sutton stepped into the cantina, and was met by Marissa.

"Good evening, Señor," Marissa said. "Ju here for dinner?"

"Yup," Sutton answered as he scanned the room, something that Marissa did not miss. Nor did she miss the twin Colts that were slung low. This man was a gunfighter.

"Ju can pick whatever table ju want, Señor, and I be right over. Ju want something to drink?"

"I'll have a beer," Sutton replied.

"Very good," Marissa said before going to fetch the beer.

Sutton looked around the room and spotted an empty table in the far corner from where he could watch the door. He walked over to the table and sat down.

Marissa walked over with Sutton's beer and a menu. "Here ju are, Señor. Please take a look at the menu and I be back in a minute to take jur order," she said.

Sutton picked up his beer and took a sip, then perused the menu.

Marissa went back to the kitchen and found Rosa, who was doing prep work for the upcoming dinner service.

"Rosa, I need ju to do something for me," Marissa said hurriedly.

"What is it?"

"I think that that man, Sutton, is here. Go out the back door and go to the Sheriff's office and tell Sheriff Nolan to come here pronto," Marissa said.

"Ci, I go now," Rosa said before she took off her apron and scurried out the back door of the cantina. She hurried the few blocks to the lawman's office on what is now Galena Avenue.

"Señor, Nolan," Rosa exclaimed as she burst through the door.

"Whoah, Rosa, what is it?" the lawman asked.

"Dat Señor Sutton, Marissa tell me to come. Ju come quick," she spat out.

"Hold yer horses, Rosa. Slow down, and tell me what's goin' on," Nolan replied.

Rosa took a deep breath. "I sorry, Señor Nolan. Marissa send me to get ju. She think dat Señor Sutton is in de cantina. She say come quick," Rosa said.

"I understand now, Rosa. Thank you. I'll ride right over. Yu take yur time goin' back. Understand?"

"Jes, Señor Nolan," Rosa replied.

* * *

Sutton was eating his dinner which consisted of a T-bone steak, mashed potatoes, and string beans, when Nolan entered. Marissa met him at the door.

"Hola, Señor Nolan. I thank ju for coming here," Marissa said.

"I'm glad thet yu let me know. Good work," Nolan replied. "Where is the sonofabitch?"

"He's in the back corner, Señor Nolan," Marissa said.

"Yup, I sees 'im," Nolan said. "Ken yu get me a beer? I want ta make it look casual."

"Jes, Señor Nolan," Marissa replied and left to pour the sheriff a beer.

Nolan stepped over to the counter while Marissa poured his beer.

Marissa finished pouring the beer and put it on the counter for Nolan.

"Thanks, Marissa," Nolan said.

He picked up the beer and sauntered across the room to where Sutton was eating.

"Howdy," Nolan said. "Mind if I sit down?"

Sutton looked up at Nolan and said, "I guess that star on yur chest says thet yu ken sit anywhere yu please."

"Wal thanks for the invitation, Mistah Sutton, is it?"

"Yu have me at a disadvantage," Sutton answered.

"I'm Jim Nolan. Sheriff Jim Nolan," he replied.

"It's a pleasure," Sutton replied.

"Yur reputation proceeds yu, Mistah Sutton," Nolan said.

"I suppose it is good to be known," Sutton replied.

"Depends on what yur known fer," Nolan said.

"No, they's nothin' worse than bein' forgotten," Sutton countered.

"I knowed why yu is heah," Nolan said.

Sutton's eyebrows raised. "Oh?"

"Yu was hired by Doniphan McCarty ta kill a good friend a' mine," Nolan said.

"This ain't personal fer me, Sheriff," Sutton said.

"Wal, it is fer me. I'll be watchin' yu, Sutton. I want yu ta know thet," Nolan warned.

"Yu knowed I nevah draw fust, I don't break the law," Sutton said.

"Eggin' on poor sodbusters till they pull a pistol outta their pants, ain't exactly givin a feller an even break. One a' these days, yur gonna pick on the wrong man, an' then it'll be yur cold corpse in a pine box," Nolan said.

42

Chapter 42

Sutton was up early and had breakfast in a little cafe. He didn't want to return to Marissa's Cantina. He had found out that it was a popular haunt of the lawmen, and he didn't relish another meeting with the sheriff. Not yet, anyway.

He rode out of town along the San Miguel, as directed by the telegram. The trek was coming to an end, and Sutton hoped that he could get the job over with, and head home. He had saved a good deal of money over the years, and increasingly thought of hanging up his guns. Maybe this would be his last job.

* * *

Nolan woke up early and got dressed.

"Are you sure you have ta go?" Didi said.

"Oh, Didi, we went all thru this last night," Nolan replied.

"Yeah, and I ain't any less afraid this mornin'," Didi pleaded.

"I got my newest deputy out theah. I think he's a good man, but he's young, an' I don' know how he'll act in a fight. It's also my duty ta be theah. I'm the sheriff. If I only act like a sheriff when ain't nothin' happenin' what kind of sheriff would I be?" he argued.

"I understand all that," Didi cried. "I know I'm bein' selfish, but to me, yur my husband, not the sheriff..'

Nolan took Didi in his arms and kissed her. "I luve yu, Didi. I allus will. "Ill be back in a couple a' days."

"I love you too, Jim. Just come back to me. Okay?"

"Okay."

* * *

It was late morning when Maddie noticed a rider on the horizon. She called for Taos and Zeke.

"What is it, Maddie?" Taos asked when he arrived at her side.

"Rider," she replied. "Look yonder." She pointed to a rider who was in the direction of Telluride.

"Zeke," Taos yelled. "Let's get ready. They's a rider comin'."

Zeke checked his guns and strode up to Taos and Maddie. "Yup, I see 'im."

"Maddie, yu should get inside, and lock the doors, and close the shutters. Make sure thet yur guns are ready, Taos said. Then, he grabbed the binoculars from the porch and put them up to his eyes. "Still cain't tell," he said.

* * *

Nolan had been in numerous gunfights over the years. He was pretty quick on the draw, but he hadn't been in a real gunfight for a while. This could be a real test. He wanted to be brave in front of Didi, but he wasn't all that confident in his quick draw anymore.

He was happy when Thunder Valley Ranch came into view. Every time he rode to the ranch, he could see what Cam and Maddie saw when they first staked their claim. It had so much potential, and if Cam and their son, Tad, hadn't been murdered, it would have been very successful by now. Taos was a godsend to Maddie, and he could see the improvements in a very short time. That could all be destroyed by the McCarty's and their hired gun, Sutton.

* * *

Taos looked through the field glasses every few minutes. Zeke was fidgety. Finally, Taos was able to make an identification.

"Good news, it's Nolan," he said.

Zeke let out a sigh of relief. "I'll go get Maddie."

When Maddie had joined them, Taos said, "They must be some news fer him to ride all the way out heah."

"I agree," Maddie said.

The trio watched as Nolan approached.

Taos was the first to greet him. "Halloo, Nolan," he yelled as the sheriff rode up.

"Halloo, the ranch," Nolan replied as he dismounted.

Taos put out his hand to Nolan. "Good to see yu Sheriff, but I guess they's sump'n' wrong."

"Sutton rode inta' Telluride last night, an' out agin' this mornin'," Nolan replied.

"He'll head ta the McCarty's today, an' I expect he'll make his presence known tomorrow," Taos said.

"Thet's what I figgered, and wanted ta give yu a heads up," Nolan said.

"Thank you, Jim," Maddie said. "Taos and I are lucky to have such good people on our side."

"Them McCarty's are bad sess," Zeke said. "Havin' rode with their cowboys fer a bit, I hope thet they will back off when they see me. None of 'em care fer Doniphan or Rance."

"Then, why do they stay," Maggie asked.

"They pay better than anyplace else," Zeke replied.

"An' they expect a lot more than ridin' hosses an' babysittin' beeves, I bet," Nolan said.

"I can vouch for that," Maddie added.

* * *

Sutton arrived at the McCarty Ranch in the mid afternoon. He was tired, parched, hungry, and in a bad humor. The directions led him to believe that it was a much shorter ride than it turned out to be.

He rode through the gate and up to the ranch house.

Doniphan was on the porch. "Sutton?" he asked, as the killer rode up.

"That'd be me. Sure is a hell of a long ride out heah," he said. "You Doniphan McCarty?"

"Aye. My son is inside. Let me get him. Yu go ta the stables, an' one a my cowboys'll take care of yur hoss," Doniphan said.

"Thanks," Sutton said. He rode over to the stables, where a young cowboy met him.

"Nice spread," Sutton said.

"It's pretty good territory, an' Mr. McCarty pays well. I got no complaints," the cowboy replied.

After dismounting, Sutton walked the fifty yards back to the ranch house. Doniphan and another man, whom he assumed was his son Rance, were waiting for him on the porch.

Doniphan offered his still bandaged hand when Sutton stepped up on the porch. Sutton shook Doniphan's hand, and then Rance's.

Sutton sized up Rance, who's face still had a lot in common with a raccoon, and instantly knew why he had been hired. Rance was a worthless low life. His eyes were dull, and Sutton assumed that Rance was as dull as his eyes.

"Yu must be parched, how aboot a whiskey?" Doniphan asked.

"I sure could use one," Sutton replied.

"Rance, go get a bottle of the best," Doniphan said.

"Yes, Pa," Rance answered, and stepped inside the house.

"How was the trip?" Doniphan asked.

"I hate those god damned trains," Sutton answered. "Sure they's fast, but they rattle yur bones somethin' awful," Sutton replied.

Rance returned with three glasses and a bottle of Kentucky Bourbon whiskey.

"You broke out the good stuff," Sutton remarked. "All's I've had is thet rotgut, they serve in them small towns."

Rance opened the bottle, and poured a couple fingers in each glass, then passed one to Doniphan and Sutton.

"To success," Doniphan said, before sipping from his glass.

"To success," Sutton and Rance echoed.

They sat down, and Sutton spoke, "Tell me aboot thet Taos feller."

"We don't know too much aboot him," Doniphan replied. "All a' sudden, he showed up an' was workin' fer Maddie Ferguson at the Thunder Valley. We had her on the ropes, an' I think she was aboot to sell her ranch ta me. Then he shows up, an' there's no deal."

"He's got wild eyes, an' he's fast as lightnin' on the draw. He carries two guns, slung low," Rance added.

Doniphan poured another round for each of them.

"He ken be hot headed," Rance said.

"Wal, thet sure ken be helpful ta me," Sutton said. "If I ken heat him up enough ta draw on me, we'll be all set.

"When do yu want ta get started?" Doniphan asked.

"I think we should pay this man, Taos, a visit in the mornin'," Sutton replied.

"Alright, then," Doniphan said. "Rance, go tell the boys that we'll be ridin' out after breakfast, an' they should be well armed."

* * *

It was evening, and the air had cooled considerably. Taos, Maddie, Nolan, and Zeke sat on the porch and watched the colors of the sky change with each minute.

"It sure is beautiful heah," Taos said. "Look at the way the colors of the sky is reflected on the San Juans."

"I'm glad that you love it here," Maddie replied.

"Hey, I jus noticed. What's thet ring on yur finger?" Nolan asked.

Maddie blushed. "You're some lawman, it took you all this time to notice it?" she laughed.

"Wal, yu knowed men ain't good at noticin' thet kind of stuff," Nolan squirmed.

"Men!" Maddie laughed. "Well, you asked, so I'll tell ya'. Taos asked me to marry him!"

"Wal, congratulations!" Nolan said.

"That is great!" Zeke echoed.

"Have yu set a date yet?" Nolan asked.

"Not yet. We want to wait until this business with Sutton is over," Maddie replied.

"I suppose thet makes sense," Nolan replied.'

"We also have to let Taos' family know," Maddie said.

"I sure hope thet yu can make it happen before the snow flies," Nolan said.

"Me too," Maddie replied.

"We should get ta bed early," Taos said. Tomorrow's gonna be a big day."

43

Chapter 43

Taos was up before anyone else. He enjoyed the early morning. The birds sang softly, and the sun's glow was just coming over the San Juans. He did the morning chores around the ranch in an attempt to keep himself busy. He didn't want to focus on what he expected would happen. He gathered eggs last and brought the basket inside, where the others had awakened and were having coffee. He could feel a pall over the room.

"Good mornin'," Maddie said, timidly, when Taos entered with the eggs. She took the basket and placed it on the counter, then wrapped her arms around him and they kissed.

"Hmmm, good mornin'," Taos said, after their kiss.

"A mug a' Arbuckles?" Nolan asked.

"Sure," Taos replied.

Nolan poured coffee into a mug and handed it to Taos.

"Thanks," Taos said.

Nolan nodded.

In the meantime, Maddie had sliced and started frying bacon.

Zeke poured himself a second cup of coffee. 'Anybody else want any?" he asked.

He had no takers.

Taos took a sip of his coffee. "That bacon is startin' ta smell good." He was trying to make conversation. He could feel an uneasiness in the room, and hoped to break it. "Okay, y'all, we knowed thet we got a day ahead a' us. It could get ugly, but we gotta keep loose. Bad attitudes make fer bad results.'

"Yur right," Nolan agreed.

"Taos, it's so hard. You came back to me, and we've got plans. We've got our future planned out, and now this. . . this, killer comes into town with one goal in mind; to shoot you dead!. How do you expect me to feel?" Maddie cried.

Taos took Maddie in her arms. "Oh, Maddie. It'll be alright. I'll be alright. We'll be alright." he said.

"How can you be so sure?" she said, between sobs.

Taos brushed her hair out of her eyes, then caressed her face. "Oh, darlin'," he said. "I been thru this before. I've dealt with men like Sutton. I knowed what makes 'em tick, an' I can use thet again' him. He don' hold all the cards heah. Trust me, Maddie."

Maddie buried her head in Taos' chest, and sobbed.

* * *

Doniphan woke up in a great mood. He was finally seeing his plans come to fruition. Sutton would kill Taos, and anybody else that got in his way. Doniphan could then force that Ferguson woman to sell at a price that he dictated. Once he got that ranch, he could control cattle prices all over the territory. Ferguson never made anything of that ranch. In Doniphan's mind, she deserved to lose it. Never mind that Doniphan had ordered Cam and Tad Ferguson's murders.

After getting dressed, Doniphan walked into the kitchen where his new housekeeper was cooking breakfast. To replace Rosa, he chose a plump, middle-aged woman named Betsy, who had come to the west with her husband after the war. They had been homesteaders, but her husband died when he was thrown from his horse. Since then, she had worked in restaurants and saloons. Doniphan had found her at a saloon in Telluride and offered her twice what she was making. She threw off her apron and followed him out to the ranch. She was a hard worker and a good cook. She wasn't much to look at, which pleased Doniphan, but rankled Rance.

"Good mornin', Mister McCarty, Betsy said, pleasantly. "How are you today?"

"It's gonna be a good day, Betsy, I ken feel it. Watcha got cookin'?"

"I got biscuits an' gravy, an' fried eggs, Boss," she said.

"Rance and Sutton should be heah in a few minutes, an' then we'll eat," he said as he poured himself a mug of coffee.

"Yes, Boss," she replied.

Doniphan took his mug and walked outside. He had removed the bandage from his hand. It wasn't completely healed, but he believed that he could draw and fire his pistol. The sun was just up and spreading an orange glow over the prairie. "This is all mine," he said out loud. "Today is the beginning of the end for Maddie Ferguson."

He walked back inside where Sutton and Rance were now up and drinking coffee.

"Mornin'," he said, when he saw the two others. "You ready fer breakfast," he asked Sutton.

"I could eat," Sutton replied.

"Betsy, yu want ta get them eggs cookin'?" Doniphan said.

"Yu got it, Boss," Betsy replied before cracking eggs into a large cast iron skillet.

"Rance, while the eggs are cookin', go make sure thet the men is gettin' ready," Doniphan said.

"Yes, Pa," he said, and stepped outside.

Doniphan and Sutton sat down at the table.

Betsy delivered their plates, and put Rance's together.

The two men ate in silence until Rance came in and sat down.

Betsy brought his plate to him.

"They gettin' ready?" Doniphan asked.

"I had ta light a fire under 'em, but they'll be ready when we are," Rance replied.

* * *

After breakfast, Taos and Maddie walked, hand in hand, down to the San Miguel. There was a bench that Cam had built by the shore, and they sat down.

"Maddie, everythin's gonna be alright," Taos said.

"How do you know that?" Maddie cried.

"Yu gotta believe in me, Maddie. Afore I showed up heah, I spent a yeah in the saddle, an I met up with a lotta hot hands with a gun. I survived, an' I'll survive this. I know how these men think an' act. Sutton thinks he's comin' heah with the upper hand, an' thet's where I got him," Taos said.

"I do have faith in you, Taos. But I'm scared," Maddie said.

"Maddie, it's okay ta be scared. But yu got ta trust me, an' yu gotta be strong," Taos replied.

* * *

After breakfast, Doniphan gathered his cowboys outside the stables.

"Men, this heah is Mistah Sutton, he's gonna help us with a problem, namely, thet man called Taos, who's been a thorn in our side since he showed up this past spring," Doniphan said. "We's gonna take care a' thet today, with Sutton's help. Yu knowed thet I've offered Misses Ferguson a fair price fer her ranch, an' she's refused me. She can't make a go of it, even with this Taos feller. If'n she was smart, she would see thet she can't make it. We's gonna help her figger thet out today, with Mistah Sutton's help."

"This sure sounds like bad sess, Boss," Jake said. "I ain't sure thet I want ta go along."

"What we do today, Jake is fer the future of the ranch, an' yur future, all a' yur futures, I already pay better'n any outfit in the state. When I get Misses Ferguson ta sell, an we can expand the herd, yur salaries 'll go up."

"Yur askin' us ta do a lot more'n cowboyin' today, Mistah McCarty," one of the cowboys said.

"Alright, I'll pay every man who rides with me today an extra ten dollars fer the day. If yu don' ride with me, I'll pay yu what I owe yu, an' yu can pack your shit an' leave," Doniphan said.

They all agreed to ride with Doniphan. That brought the total to fifteen men, including Sutton, Doniphan, and Rance.

"Alright, let's mount up, an' ride," Doniphan said.

* * *

Taos and Maddie walked back to the ranch house, where Nolan and Zeke were waiting. They stepped up on the porch, and Maddie said, "Anybody want another coffee?"

"I'd sure like one," Nolan said. Both Zeke and Taos nodded in the affirmative.

"Okay, I'll get a pot started," Maddie said. She had to keep herself busy. If she let herself be idle, the thoughts and fears would be right back in her head. She filled the pot with water, poured in coarsely ground Arbuckle coffee, and put it on the stove to boil.

While Maddie made the coffee, the men strategized.

"When they come, I want ta stand in the middle. Nolan, yu stand ta my left. I'm right handed, an' even though I shoot with both hands, my left side ain't as good. Zeke, since yu is less experienced, stay on my right," Taos said.

"Thet makes sense," Nolan agreed.

"I don' know how many of 'em they'll be. Zeke, yu got any idee?" Taos asked.

"It could be as many as a fifteen if evabody comes. Thet includes Sutton,

Doniphan, an' Rance," Zeke replied.

"Alright, I'll take care a' Sutton. I'm hopin' if I ken put him down, t'others 'll back down. But they's no tellin' fer sure."

"It's a pretty tough crew," Zeke said.

"Yup, an' they've done some pretty rough stuff," Nolan said.

"I only rode with 'em a short time, but mebbe, that 'll keep a couple of em from joinin' in," Zeke said, hopefully.

"Yeah, but we can't count on thet," Taos said.

Maddie stepped out onto the porch with the coffee pot and four mugs. The men stopped talking.

"Why so quiet?" Maddie asked as she put the coffee pot and mugs down on a table.

"We's just anticipatin' the coffee, Maddie darlin'," Nolan said.

"I ain't buyin' what you're sellin'," Maddie replied.

"Maddie, ta be honest, we was strategizin'," Taos said.

Maddie poured the coffees and handed them out. "And, where do I fit in?" she asked.

Taos passed out the coffees, and handed one to Maddie last. "Maddie, I want yu to stay in the house, an' be ready ta shoot," Taos said.

"I don't want to hide in the house while y'all risk your lives for my ranch," Maddie said.

"Maddie, it ain't like thet," Taos said. "If yur out heah when they come, it'll give Sutton ammunition agin' me. When the shootin' starts, yu be ready ta shoot. Them McCarty's is gonna do whatevah they can ta get this ranch."

"Okay, Maddie said. "Let's have our coffee while it's still hot."

"I'll second thet," Nolan said, and took a drink from his mug.

* * *

Taos scouted the prairie with binoculars for the umpteenth time. He scanned the area where he expected McCarty and his men to ride from.

"I see a cloud a' dust," Taos reported. "Make sure yur guns is loaded an' ready ta go. Yu too Maddie.'

They all checked their guns and ammunition.

"Remember what I said. Let me deal with Sutton. Nolan an' Zeke, watch the sides. Maddie. If we call, yu come out with thet scatter gun blazin'," Taos said.

Maddie stepped up to Taos and put her arms around him. "Please be careful, my love," she implored.

Taos took Maddie in his arms and kissed her. "Bein' careful will get me dead. I gotta be reckless an' aggressive, if'n I wanna live,'" Taos replied.

"Oh, Taos, please don't talk that way. It scares me," Maddie replied.

He kissed her again. "Now go inside," Taos ordered.

Maddie stepped in the house and slammed the door.

"She sure is madder'n a hornet," Nolan said.

"Good, thet'll keep her from bein' scared," Taos replied.

The riders were now in view, and Taos counted fifteen. "Looks like we's outgunned five ta one. Let's hope our irons bark louder than theirs," he laughed.

The three men stepped off of the porch. Nolan stepped about twenty feet to the left of Taos, and Zeke, the same distance to the right, and waited for the riders to approach.

The McCarty's, Sutton, and their men filed across the bridge spanning the San Miguel.

When they had lined up with Sutton in the middle, flanked by Rance on his right side and Doniphan on his left, Zeke called out to Jake. "Jake, is yu gonna be a part a' this?"

Jake looked at Zeke, then at Doniphan and Sutton. "I see yur wearin' a badge, Zeke," Jake said.

"Yup, Zeke replied. Yu wanna come ovah ta the right side?"

Jake thought for a moment. "I don' wanna be part in no murder, Boss," he said to Doniphan.

"Go ahead. Join yur friends, but yu'll regret it," Doniphan said as he and the others dismounted.

Jake spurred his horse forward and Doniphan drew on him and shot him in the back. Jake dropped off of his horse. He was dead before he hit the ground.

Taos saw his opportunity. While the others were watching Jake, he charged forward, lifted his pistols, and shot Sutton in the forehead with his right hand, and Rance, in the heart, with his left hand.

Guns erupted on both sides, and men jumped for cover. Doniphan spun around and pointed his pistol at Taos and pulled the trigger.

Taos, hit in the side, spun to the ground.

Nolan and Zeke poured lead at the cowboys to keep Taos covered. Nolan dropped two, and Zeke plugged another.

Taos, his shirt soaked with blood, scooted behind the water trough, and shot at Doniphan, and hit him in his right thigh.

"Yu sonofabitch," Doniphan screamed, as he emptied his revolver at the trough and Taos. He grabbed his second pistol, but was too slow. Taos had lifted himself up and fired. A bullet ripped through Doniphan's left shoulder. Taos stood up and charged at Doniphan.

The cowboys and Zeke and Nolan had all taken cover, and were firing to keep each other pinned down. That left Taos and Doniphan alone.

Taos reached Doniphan just as he fired. The bullet grazed Taos' head, but did no real damage. Taos lifted both his guns, and put two slugs in Doniphan's chest. Doniphan fell backwards, and Taos stood over him. Doniphan pleaded for mercy, but Taos had none of it. He raised his Colt and fired one last shot into Doniphan's face.

"That's it!" one of the cowboys yelled. "Ain't no sense fer us ta' fight for dead men."

"Drop yur guns an' step out," Nolan ordered. The cowboys complied.

When the gunfire stopped, Maddie ran out of the house. She arrived on the scene just in time to see Taos drop to the ground.

Maddie screamed and ran to Taos. He was face down, but she could see the blood stains on his shirt. She knelt down and rolled him over, and discovered that his face was covered with blood.

"Oh Taos," Maddie cried. She felt for a pulse, and felt a faint one. "Don't you die on me!" she shouted at him. "Get some water and rags!" she ordered, and Nolan sprinted to the house, while the others circled around the couple.

Nolan returned with a pot of water and a pile of rags.

"Thanks, Jim," Maddie said, as tears streamed down her cheeks. She dipped a rag into the water and wiped Taos' face clean. She discovered the wound just above his right ear, cleaned it, and bandaged it.

"Jim, help me get his shirt off," Maddie asked.

Nolan knelt down on the other side of Taos from Maddie, took out a knife, and started cutting the shirt. There was a lot of blood. Finally, working together, they were able to remove the shirt, which revealed a gaping wound in Taos' right side.

Maddie flushed it with water to make for a better view. Nolan inspected the wound.

"Looks like the bullet hit a rib, cracked it, an' bounced off'n it," Nolan reported. "He's sure one lucky hombre."

"He don't look too lucky to me," Maddie snapped. "He's lost a lot of blood. Help me get him inside where I can clean him off and stitch him up."

Nolan, Zeke, and a couple of McCarty's cowboys helped carry Taos into the ranch house, where Maddie directed them to put him on the kitchen table.

"Zeek, go get more bandages out of that cupboard over yonder," Maddie said, as she pointed to the cupboard in question.

"Yes'm," he replied and fetched the bandages.

Nolan filled a pot of water, and put it on the stove to heat up, while Maddie wiped the wound clean. "Somebody grab thet whiskey jug on the counter."

One of the cowboys ran over, grabbed it, and brought it to the table.

"Thanks," Maddie said.

Nolan brought the pot of hot water to the table. Maddie washed her hands, then flushed the wound with alcohol, then water.

"It's a good thin' thet he's out cold," Nolan said. "I cain't imagine thet this'd be fun ifn' he was awake."

"It ain't much fun this way, either," Maddie snapped back.

Maddie packed the wound with bandages, and then, with Nolan's help bandaged up Taos' torso. Next, she took the initial bandage off of Taos' head, and washed the wound and put on a fresh bandage.

"Can y'all carry him to his bed?" Maddie asked.

The men picked him up and carried him to the bed in what had been Tad's room.

* * *

While Maddie sat with Taos, the men buried the dead. McCarty's men were lost as what to do next.

"Boys, why don' yu go back ta the ranch an' keep it goin' until I have time ta talk ta the judge, an' get this all figgered out," Nolan said.

The eight cowboys left saddled up.

"No hard feelin's," Nolan said. "Y'all was doin' what yer boss told yu. I'll be by in a few days."

The cowboys tipped their hats and rode across the bridge and headed west.

Nolan and Zeke walked back inside and checked in with Maddie.

"How's he doin'?" Nolan asked.

"He's alive. His pulse isn't any stronger, but it's there. His breathing is shallow," Maddie replied.

"Zeke, I'd like yu to ride inta town, pronto, an' fetch the doctor," Nolan said.

"There's a doctor in town?" Maddie asked, surprised.

"Yup, Telluride is growin' up. His name is Doc Hauser, an he's been heah aboot a month."

Maddie grabbed some beef jerky from a crock, and handed it to Zeke. "You'll need something to eat," she said.

"Thanks, Maddie," Zeke said.

"Thank you," she replied, and gave him a hug, and a kiss on the cheek. "Now, go get that doctor!"

"Sure," Zeke said and ran out the door.

"Maddie, why don' yu take a break. I'll sit with Taos fer a bit," Nolan said.

"Thanks, Jim," she replied. "I just want to clean myself up, and change into something that isn't covered with blood. Then, I'll be back."

* * *

Maddie and Nolan took turns keeping watch over Taos. Nolan cooked dinner, while Maddie stayed with Taos. After dinner, Maddie went back to watch Taos.

"Jim, why don't you get some sleep. You can use my bed. I'll wake you if anything changes," Maddie said.

"Yu sure?" he asked.

"Yes. I can't thank you enough for all that you have done for me.

Maddie sat with Taos deep into the night, and eventually fell asleep in her chair.

She had been in a deep slumber for a couple of hours, when something woke her from her sleep. The day's first light filtered through the curtains.

"What's a man gotta do ta get a cup a' coffee around heah?" Taos said.

The End

44

Chapter 44

E njoy a preview of the next Ben Adams Western Novel: Comes a Rustler

45

Chapter 45

"What's a man gotta do ta get a cup a' coffee around heah?" Taos said.

Maddie was now wide awake. "Oh, Taos, you are awake!" she cried.

"I sure am sore," Taos replied. He tried to sit up, but searing pain in his side stopped that effort.

"Here, let me help you," Maddie said. She put her arm under Taos' shoulder, careful not to disturb the bandage that covered the wound on his side.

Taos let out a groan as Maddie helped scoot him up into a sitting position. Then, she stuffed a pillow behind his back for support.

"I was so scared. You've been out since yesterday afternoon," Maddie said. "How are you feelin'?" she asked.

"My head sure aches, an' my side feels like I got hit with a sledgehammer," Taos replied.

"Well, you got a pretty bad crease on the side of your head. A half an inch over, and you'd be dead," Maddie said.

"I guess thet I'm one lucky hombre," Taos drawled.

"Can I get you anything?" Maddie asked.

"I sure would like some water. My mouth is as dry as a bowl a' sand," he said.

"I'll be right back, my love," Maddie said. She kissed his forehead as she stood up.

While Maddie fetched a class of water, Taos tried to recollect the happenings of the day before. His head was foggy, and the more he tried to think, the greater the pain in his head.

Maddie returned with Taos' water, and handed it to him. "Just sip it, darlin'," she said.

Taos was tempted to gulp it, but followed Maddie's instructions.

"I can't remember what happened," Taos shared.

"I missed most of it, because I was inside, but when the shootin' stopped, I ran outside, an' saw you collapse," Maddie shared. "Oh, Taos, it was dreadful!"

"I sure am sorry to scare yu like thet, Maddie," Taos said.

"Jim Nolan stayed the night. How about I put a pot of coffee on, and he can fill you in while I make breakfast?" Maddie said.

"Sounds like a good idee," Taos said.

Maddie got up and stepped out of the bedroom.

When she stepped into the kitchen, she saw that Sheriff Jim Nolan was already up and making coffee.

Good Mornin', Jim," Maddie said,

"Haloo, Maddie darlin'," he replied. "How's the patient doin' this mornin'?"

"He's awake, but in a lot of pain. Says he can't remember much of what happened yesterday. Thanks for gettin' the coffee started, by the way," Maddie said.

"Wal, he did get a good crease in the side a' his head. Mebbe thet has somethin' to do with it," Nolan replied.

"I told him that you would fill him in once the coffee was boiled," Maddie said.

"Sure I will," Nolan said.

* * *

"Mornin' Taos," Nolan said, as he passed the cowboy a mug of coffee.

"Howdy, Jim. an' thanks fer the mug a' Arbuckles," Taos said.

Nolan sat down beside the bed. "Maddie said thet yu don' remember much of yestiday's events," Nolan said.

"Last thin I remember was Doniphan McCarty shootin' thet man, Jake, in the back," Taos replied.

"Wal, it sure took off from theah!" Nolan exclaimed. "When Jake hit the ground, we was all frozen in shock, except yu. Yu went inta action. Yu pulled both yur irons, shot thet gunman, Sutton in the face with one hand, an' gave Rance McCarty a plug in the chest with t'other. Next, we all opened fire. It was bedlam. Doniphan winged yu in the side. Then, yu charged him an' hit him in the chest. He sent one at yur punkin', then you shot him in the face. Next, I seen yu collapse. Afta' thet, McCarty's men surrendered. Thet was aboot it."

"Whooee, I sure don' remember much a thet," Taos replied.

Maddie entered with a chair. "Breakfast is almost ready," she said. "We can eat in here."

* * *

"Taos, as soon as I get breakfast cleaned up, I'm gonna clean your wounds," Maddie said. "Zeke rode into town yesterday to fetch Doc Hauser, but I don't expect them to be back here until mid-afternoon."

"Maddie, I don' mind doin' the dishes, ifn it'll help," Nolan said.

"Thanks, Jim," Maddie said.

Maddie and Nolan carried the dishes into the kitchen. Maddie had a couple of pots on the stove to keep warm for washing the dishes and cleaning Taos' wounds. Nolan filled the sink with the dirty dishes and poured hot water over them while Maddie prepared washcloths and bandages.

"Heah, let me carry thet for yu," Nolan said, as Maddie picked up a pot of hot water.

"Thanks, Jim, Maddie said, and put the pot back down.

Nolan picked up the pot and carried it into Taos' room, followed by Maddie, with washcloths and bandages,

Nolan put the pot down on the bedside table.

"Thanks, Jim," Maddie said.

"My pleasure," Nolan said.

"You ready?" Maddie asked Taos, as she sat down next to the bed.

"I guess. I know thet I sure couldn't ask fer a purtier nurse," Taos replied

"Well, I see that I've got to start with the wound on your head," Maddie laughed.

"My head might be hurt, but my eyes is still workin'," Taos said.

Maddie ignored the comment and took the bandage off of Taos' head, and inspected the wound. She cleaned it, and patted it dry.

"How's it lookin'?" Taos asked.

"I don't see any infection. I think that it'll heal just fine," Maddie said.

"Thet's good. Thanks," Taos said.

"Let me help you sit up, so I can look at your side," Maddie said.

Together, they were able to get Taos moved up so Maddie could work on his wound. She took off the old bandage, and noticed pus on it. She also smelled infection. "Looks like it got infected. Let me clean it up," Maddie said. As she cleaned the wound, she noticed that it felt hot to the touch. "I'm gonna get some whiskey, and dab it on the wound," Maddie said.

* * *

Nolan had just finished up with the breakfast dishes when Maddie came out of Taos' room with a basket full of dirty bandages.

How's it lookin'?" Nolan asked.

His head wound looks good. The wound on his side is infected, though," Maddie said as she put the dirty cloths in the stove to burn.

"Good thin' thet Doc Hauser is comin'," Nolan said.

"I'm doing my best, but I'm no doctor," Maddie replied. Then poured whiskey into a cup. "I'm gonna try cleaning it with some whiskey."

She took the cup of whiskey back into Taos' room, and sat back down in the chair. Taos had dozed off again. Maddie gave him a little nudge to wake him up.

"You were sleepin', my dear," Maddie said.

"I'm sorry, Maddie," Taos said. "I sure am tired."

"It's your body going through the healing process," Maddie replied. "This is gonna' sting a little." Maddie said, as she dipped a cloth into the cup of whiskey. Next, she dapped the wound on Taos' side. "Let's hope that this works," Maddie said.

"Whoo Wee, thet sure does sting," Taos laughed.

When she finished cleaning the wound, Maddie dabbed it dry and bandaged it. "All done," Maddie said. "Why don't you try and get some sleep? I'll check back in with you a little later," Maddie said, and kissed Taos' forehead.

* * *

A few hours later, Taos was woken from his slumber by the clatter of hooves. As he gained consciousness, he noticed that his headache had subsided, but the wound at his side ached badly.

Presently, he heard voices and a commotion in the house. His head was still somewhat foggy, but he recognized the voice of Maddie, and Nolan. There was another voice that he didn't know.

Maddie walked into Taos' room followed by a bespectacled man who was small of stature and balding, and carried a black leather bag.

"Taos, this is Doc Hauser," Maddie said.

"Haloo, Doc. thanks fer comin' out heah ta look at this ol' cowpuncher," Taos said. "Please forgive me fer not gettin' up."

Doc Hauser looked Taos over. "How are you feeling?" he asked.

"Fair ta midlin', I guess, Doc," Taos replied.

"Let me take a look," Hauser said. He took the bandage off of Taos' head and inspected the wound. "Well, Misses Ferguson, you have done an excellent job on this wound," Hauser said.

"My father is a doctor back in Virginia," she said.

"Well, you must have been a good study at his knee," Hauser replied. He replaced the bandage on Taos' head. "Change the bandage each day until it is completely scabbed over. Then it is best left open to the air," Doc Hauser instructed.

"Will do," Maddie replied.

"Alright, let's take a look at the other wound," Hauser said.

Maddie helped the doctor sit Taos up, and held him while Hauser unwrapped the bandage.

Doc Houser examined the wound.

"This one is infected, but not too bad, yet," Doc Hauser said. "Misses Ferguson, please bring me some hot water.

"Yes, Doc, and, please call me Maddie," she replied.

"Alright, Maddie," he replied.

Maddie left to get a pot of hot water while Doc Hauser talked to Taos.

Doc Hauser looked over his spectacles at Taos. "Maddie said that you don't remember much of yesterday's, ah, conflict. Do you remember anything else from the day?"

"I remember the mornin' an' McCarty an' his men ridin' up, but it's pretty foggy after thet," Taos replied.

"My guess is that you have a concussion. You will have to take it slow for the next couple of weeks, and if you get a headache, take a break," Doc Hauser said.

"Okay Doc," Taos replied.

Maddie returned with the water.

"Maddie, I was just telling Taos that I believe that he has a concussion. It is a mild brain injury. I warned him that he needs to be careful and not overdo it. If his head starts to ache, he needs to take a break from his work.

Also, he should stay out of the bright sun for a week or so. If it bothers him, he needs to get inside, or in the shade," Doc Hauser said.

"I got it, Doc," Maddie said.

"Do you have any whiskey in the house?" Doc Hauser asked.

"Yes," Maddie said.

"Can you get me some, and a couple glasses?"

"Sure, Doc," Maddie replied and left to get the whiskey.

Doc Hauser cleaned the wound on Taos' side.

Maddie returned with the whiskey and glasses. "Here you are, Doc," she said.

"Thanks, Maddie," he replied as he took the jug and glasses. He poured the first glass and handed it to Taos. "You want to drink this down, son," he said.

Taos gulped down the whiskey and handed the cup back to the doctor, who refilled it and handed it back. Have another, you're gonna need it," doc Hauser said.

"Thanks, I think, Doc," Taos said and gulped the whiskey down. He handed the cup back to Doc Hauser.

The doctor put the cup down on the side table. Alright, we need to get you on your side, so I can work on that wound.

Maddie stepped over and helped Doc Hauser get Taos on his side. Next, the doctor poured out a glass of whiskey, then took a few instruments out of his bag and soaked them in the cup.

"This is going to hurt, young man," Doc Hauser said. "If you need more whiskey, let me know."

"I got quite a bit on board already," Taos said.

"I'm going to be poking and prodding in the wound," Doc Hauser said.

"Do yur worst, sawbones," Taos said.

Doc Hauser took a forceps and probe out of the alcohol and began his work. "I can see where the bullet hit your rib. It's splintered, and I can see some lead. I'll have to take care of that if you are going to heal properly," Hauser said.

Taos grimaced as Hauser worked on his rib. Maddie took his hand, and he squeezed hard. Hauser took out a few shards of bone, and pieces of lead that were lodged among the shards.

"Okay, I'm going to dig around your ribs and look for pieces of bone and lead. You might want another shot of whiskey," Doc Hauser said.

"Good idee, Doc," Taos replied.

Maddie poured another cup of whiskey and helped Taos drink it.

"Okay, Doc. I'm ready," Taos said.

Doc Hauser got back to work.

Maddie took hold of Taos' hand again. He grimaced, and sweat appeared on his brow. Maddie wiped Taos' face with her handkerchief.

"All done," Doc Hauser announced. "I'm going to put some iodine in the wound, then bandage you up."

"Thanks, Doc," Taos said.

* * *

After patching Taos up, Doc Hauser walked outside with Maddie.

"I left you some iodine. You should clean his wound, treat it with iodine, and change his dressing every day. If the infection gets worse, let me know. I expect that you will see improvement in a week, and if all goes well, he should be pretty well healed in two weeks," Doc Hauser said.

"Thank you so much, Doc," Maddie said. "Do you want to stay for lunch?"

"I should get back to town," Hauser replied.

"How about I make sandwiches for you, Jim and Zeke to take with you?" Maddie offered.

"I would appreciate that," Doc Hauser said.

"Thet sounds good, Zeke said.

"Maddie, do yu want me to stay?" Nolan offered.

"Thanks, Jim, but you need to go back to your wife. I'm sure that she misses you. We'll be fine here," Maddie said.

46

Chapter 46

About the Author

John Kenealy is a Special Education teacher who minored in American History in college. He got hooked on Western Novels at an early age, when introduced to Zane Gray's writing by his father. John has traveled extensively throughout the American west.

Made in the USA
Columbia, SC
15 April 2023

15420087R00170